Shadow of Time

Jen Minkman

© 2012 by Jen Minkman

Cover design by Clarissa Yeo

This book is copyright. Apart from fair dealing for the purpose of private study, research, criticism or review, as permitted under the Copyright Act, no part may be reproduced by any process without the prior permission of the author. You are welcome to share this book with friends who might like to read it too, however.

In beauty may I walk;
All day long may I walk;
Through the returning seasons may I walk.

Beautifully will I possess again
Beautifully birds
Beautifully butterflies...

On the trail marked with pollen may I walk;
With grasshoppers about my feet may I walk;
With dew around my feet may I walk.

With beauty before me may I walk
With beauty behind me may I walk
With beauty above me may I walk
With beauty all around me,
may I walk.

In old age, wandering on a trail of beauty, lively;
In old age, wandering on a trail of beauty, living again...
It is finished in beauty.

(Traditional Navajo prayer)

One

"Come on, car. Just a few more miles."

Hannah Darson sighed so hard she blew strands of dark-blonde hair from her face that had slipped out of her ponytail. Tightly gripping the steering wheel of the old, gray Datsun, she tried to relax her tense shoulders. Not to mention the rest of her body. She was exhausted from being on the road since early morning, driving from Las Cruces to her mother's log cabin close to Lake Powell. Even more importantly, she was anxious, because she was practically out of fuel. And out of options – she hadn't passed any gas stations for a while.

Hannah shot a nervous glance at the fuel gauge on her dashboard. It had been in the red for some time now. The route through Navajo Nation hadn't exactly taken her through densely populated areas.

When the road curved to the left, Hannah suddenly spotted a small gas station next to the exit to Glen Canyon Dam. Hallelujah! Danger of getting stranded without fuel averted.

"Whoohoo!" she shouted at the top of her voice, gunning her Datsun to the entrance of the station. Nothing would rain on her parade now. Summer had started, her first year of teaching was over, and she was going to spend July and August here, in Arizona. Ben, her younger brother, was already waiting for her at the log cabin in St. Mary's Port. She'd missed the place. The last time she'd stayed in their cozy little cabin was four years ago.

Endless days on the beach and sipping drinks in the shade of umbrellas lined up on the deck of the local restaurant were awaiting her. Plus, there'd be countless trips to the Navajo reservation. She and Ben even had childhood friends there.

Humming happily to herself, Hannah parked her car next to gas pump number two. "It's raining *men*!" she sang-shouted, blaring along to the song on her car stereo.

The guy standing next to pump number three was just done getting gas for his motorbike. He looked sideways and his mouth curled up in a smile. The Datsun's roof was down, so he'd caught her shouting her lungs out.

Hannah bit her lip. Damn. Her neighbor turned out to be a total hottie. She shot him a look that lasted a tad too long, then blushed, rummaging through her bag to find her money and pretend she'd already forgotten about him. As if.

Furtively, she looked him over again as he strolled off to pay, helmet in one hand and sunglasses on. Yup, this was typically her – scaring off the local hunk by being a total idiot. She rolled her eyes at herself.

The motorcycle driver was clearly from the Navajo reservation. His red-brown skin was dark and offset by the white of his sleeveless shirt. He had a small hair braid on one side, a turquoise bead and a red feather decorating the bottom. That feather had to be the symbol for one of the local clans of the Navajo – or Diné, as they called themselves. Her once-best-friend on the reservation, Emily Begay, also belonged to the Feather

Clan. Emily should be about twenty-one by now, just like Ben. Hopefully she'd run into Em this summer.

Just to make sure, Hannah completely filled up her Datsun so she wouldn't be short on fuel anytime soon. When she was done, she went into the building and got in line for the pay desk.

There. The Navajo guy had just paid for his gas. He stuffed the receipt into the pocket of his jeans and sauntered to the exit, passing the shelves with chewing gum and candy bars. And then, out of nowhere, he looked her right in the eye.

"Hi." His voice was deep and beautiful and just as impressive as his looks. He stared at her through his tinted sunglasses, a hint of a smile on his face, like he was amused by some private joke.

Hannah looked up at him dumbfounded. *Wow*. He wasn't blanking her. He was still talking to her. So maybe she should talk back.

"Um – hey," she stammered feebly and stared at him all owl-faced. For a moment, it seemed he wanted to say something more, but he didn't. He just gave her another sunny smile before leaving the building. Navajo Hunk started his motorbike and put his helmet on before tearing off at break-neck speed.

Hannah groaned inwardly. Way to go with her conversational skills. She quickly paid for the fuel and got back in her car to drive the last few miles to St. Mary's Port.

It'd be nice to cook a big meal together with Ben. Or maybe they should go to the local restaurant. Ben wasn't famous for his culinary talents, and the last thing she needed now was slaving away in the kitchen herself. Hannah fumbled around in her bag to find her phone. One missed call, from her brother. She phoned him back.

"Heya sis!" Ben picked up on the second ring. "Where the heck *are* you?"

"I'll be there in ten. Where the heck are *you*?"

"On the beach. Where else? I'll come home and help you unpack."

"Okay, cool. See you soon!" She clicked off.

When Hannah turned into the driveway next to the log cabin, Ben was sitting on the stairs leading up to the porch, smoking a cigarette. His dark-blonde hair had already turned a lighter shade in the sunlight. He was wearing a big, showy pair of sunglasses to shield eyes just as bright-green as hers.

"You're here!" he boomed enthusiastically, jumping up and giving her a bear hug.

"Hi bro. How've you been?"

"Incredibly hot. I've been on the beach a lot." Ben dragged Hannah's suitcase up the stairs, while she carried two heavy bags with food and toiletries. She put the food in the kitchen and walked to the door of her old bedroom.

Opening the door, she fell silent for a moment. Everything was just as she remembered it. The big, comfortable bed in the corner, the sturdy table against the wall, the flowery curtains in front of the window looking out on the lake – it was like no time had passed at all.

"I've already made your bed," Ben pointed out, coming in after her and putting the suitcase down.

"Thank you so much. That really helps. My back hurts from all the driving."

"Let's go out for dinner tonight, then. We don't need to cook. There's a nice new place at the beach with grilled fish on the menu. We could try that."

"Sounds great!" Hannah went out to get the rest of her stuff from the car. In the meantime, Ben grabbed two beer cans from the fridge. He and Hannah toasted when they sat down on the porch.

"To a long and carefree summer," Hannah said.

Ben grinned. "Sure thing. St. Mary's Port has missed you."

"How's Emily, by the way? I was thinking about her at the gas station. There was a Navajo guy walking around there from the same clan." She felt herself blush and quickly took a swig of beer from her can.

"She's fine! She was asking about you."

"Does she still live in Naabi'aani?"

Ben nodded. "Yeah, she just finished her studies. She's a certified naturopath now. Her practice is on the rez, in Naabi'aani, but she also works at the homeopathic pharmacy in town."

"Wow! Good for her. And what about Josh - have you seen him yet?"

"Sure. We meet every summer. He still lives there with his parents. He just finished high school."

Hannah smiled, staring out over the lake spreading out at the bottom of the hill like an unfathomable, giant mirror. It was great this place hadn't changed in her absence. Everything was still as beautiful as she remembered, and their old friends were still around too.

Hannah glanced down at her watch. "When does the pharmacy close? Do you think I'll have time to say hello to Em?"

"She's not working today." Ben dug up his cell phone. "But she will be tomorrow. She asked me to tell you to call her. I have her number here."

"I'll send her a text. Once Emily starts talking, there's no way to stop her."

After Hannah tapped out a text message to her old friend, she and Ben leisurely strolled to the beach and sat down at a table on the deck of 'The Winking Shrimp'.

Hannah let her gaze wander over the calm water of Lake Powell, where people were swimming, riding paddleboats or walking along the shoreline. She took in the red rocks of Antelope Island across the water, their almost luminescent shapes like ancient castles in the setting sun. The nameless small island just off the coast looked like a dark, blood-red stain on the water.

"We have new neighbors, by the way," Ben told her. "The cabin to our right was bought by a couple with two daughters our age. Ivy and Amber."

"Oh, really? That's great! Let's organize a barbecue and invite them sometime."

"Good idea. I took the old barbecue from the shed yesterday and cleaned it. I was in one of those moods again."

"A *cleaning* mood? What do you mean, 'again'?"

Ben smirked. "As friendly as ever. Come on, pick something from the menu. Anything at all."

Hannah smiled. "Are you buying?"

Ben opened his mouth to say something, then fell silent. His eyes widened. "Oh," he mumbled, patting his pockets. "Oh, *damn*."

"Yeah, right. Drop the act."

"Look, I'm really sorry. I think I left my wallet in my car."

She laughed. "No worries. I'm used to your chaotic lifestyle by now."

"What do you mean, chaotic? I'm getting better at planning my life all the time. Don't tell me you didn't notice I brought my textbooks."

"I saw a pile of something in the living room, yes."

"Well, that pile means I'm gonna catch up on stuff from last year," Ben said, a self-satisfied look on his face.

"Good for you. Any resits straight after summer?"

Ben didn't reply. He was staring at the water. "Hey, I think Josh is on the beach." He got up from his chair. "Hold on, I'll tell him we're sitting over here." He walked off the deck toward the water. Hannah tried to see where he was going, but the beach was still quite crowded and soon she'd lost sight of him.

After some minutes, she turned in her chair to see whether Ben was coming back yet. His glass of beer had been on the table for a while, and her brother hated lukewarm beer – with a passion. She spotted him down by the jetty with the small rowing boats, enthusiastically waving his arms and telling a tall guy next to him some elaborate story.

Hannah swallowed hard and squinted against the sunlight. That guy next to Ben – but that couldn't be. She couldn't believe her eyes. That was the Navajo guy. The guy who'd laughed at her poor attempt at singing. The guy who'd playfully said hello and given her this intense look while she gaped at him like a dumbstruck idiot. So Ben knew him?

Her heart skipped a beat when she suddenly realized why the local native hunk was walking next to her brother.

That was Josh.

Two

This couldn't be happening.

How could she have missed that it was Josh? Then again, he'd changed in four years' time. Nobody aged seventeen should even be allowed to look that grown-up. Ben's younger, scrawny Navajo side-kick was most definitely a thing of the past.

All of a sudden, Hannah was painfully aware of the creases in her T-shirt, her poor excuse for a hairdo and the bags under her eyes. On top of that, there was sheer panic. Panic because all those trivial things apparently acutely mattered to her so much. She had to get a grip. He was seventeen and she was twenty-three. She was miles above all this.

Hannah forced herself to let out her breath, releasing her death grip on the table at the same time. Still turned around in her seat, she shouted to Ben: "Your beer is getting warm! Hurry up." Then her eyes darted to Josh, who was now coming up to the table.

"Oh – hey," she managed to say in a surprised tone of voice. Again, the same line. Sure, why not? Since it had worked so well the first time around.

"Hi." He sank down on the chair next to her. "Again."

"So... I already met you this afternoon." Hannah tried to give him a casual smile, quickly reaching out to shake Josh's hand. He grabbed hers and she felt the water on his skin. He'd just been swimming in the lake. Drops of water still clung to his broad shoulders, and his hair was wet at the tips.

"Yep." His grin suddenly made him look cheeky and young, but incredibly irresistible. "I must say, it was a touching reunion."

Hannah laughed nervously. "So, you recognized me?"

"Of course. But I guess you didn't see it was me."

Hannah bit her lip. "No."

"I see," he said softly. "Is that why you blushed when I said hi?"

Hannah froze, praying to the heavens she wouldn't blush yet again. "Um, yes. I was a bit surprised, I guess." She slowly pulled her hand from his, quickly grabbing her glass to busy herself.

"So you already ran into each other today?" Ben asked with a smile, apparently unaware of the tension between them. "Small world, right?" He gulped down some beer and pulled a face. "Yuck. It's too warm."

"Order a new one," Josh suggested. "And while you're at it, order me an apple juice."

"Fine with me. I forgot my wallet. Hannah's buying tonight."

"Am I?" Hannah raised her eyebrows. "You think I'll be more generous now that Josh is sitting with us?"

"I'm counting on it," Ben replied with a smug face. "Josh, what would you like to eat?"

"I could do with some grilled trout."

Hannah nodded. "Great, that's what we were having anyway. I'll go tell them to put some extra trout on the grill."

"I can go," Ben offered.

"Nah, I'll go. I have to go to the restroom anyway."

Plus she didn't want to be stuck on her own with Josh all of a sudden. She got up and made her way through the crowd seated at the small wooden tables on the deck. After going into the restaurant and changing their order with the first waiter she spotted, she went to the ladies' room to give herself a good talking-to in the mirror over the sinks.

"Hannah Darson," she told herself sternly, while trying to untangle her messy hair. "You're going to act normally around Josh. You've known him since he was shitting his diapers. You taught him how to color inside the lines. You helped him build sandcastles on the beach. This will end *right here*."

She closed her eyes, remembering how Josh had stepped onto the deck and approached their table – his swimming trunks just a little bit too low-slung on his hips, his shoulders just a little bit too broad for a seventeen-year-old, the muscles in his arms just a little bit too taut to take her eyes off them, and the look in his eyes just a bit too wise for his age.

No. This would not be so easy.

ॐॐॐ

When Hannah came back, Ben was just lighting a cigarette.

"Nasty habit," Josh remarked.

"Isn't tobacco a holy plant in your culture?" Ben threw back, taking a drag.

Josh grinned. "Still." He eyed Hannah as she sat down again.

"Don't ask me to back you up," she said. "I only quit myself a few months ago."

"You were a smoker? I don't remember that."

"Just for a short while. During my last year with

Greg, when I started working. Mainly stress-related, I guess."

"Oh," Josh said, staring into his glass of apple juice. He was silent for a moment. "So... you guys broke up?"

"Yeah, about eight months ago."

"And now? Are you dating someone else?"

Discussing her love life with him was the strangest sensation. Last time she'd seen Josh, he'd just been a young boy. Hannah cleared her throat and quickly shook her head. "No, actually. I'm fine on my own. You know, a bit of me-time. I need freedom."

In the silence that followed, she cringed. In hindsight, that hadn't come out the way she wanted. In fact, she positively sounded like she wasn't interested in dating for the next ten years. All she needed was a T-shirt saying 'Don't Ask Me Out'.

"You know, you've always needed freedom," Josh suddenly said warmly. "You're like a butterfly. Beautiful, fragile, and hard to catch."

Hannah blinked. What the hell was she supposed to say to that?

Fortunately, Ben saved her from another awkward silence. "Are you exploring your Navajo background again, Josh? White Americans don't believe in totem animals, FYI."

The conversation continued, mainly between Ben and Josh. Hannah decided to play wallflower for the rest of the evening, so she wouldn't blurt out more stupid remarks or blush again when Josh teased her.

"I'll pick you up in my car tomorrow," Josh told Ben after their trout dinner. "We should go fishing. Grilling your own fish is so much better."

"You have your own car?" Hannah asked in surprise, temporarily forgetting she wanted to stay out of the conversation.

"Yeah, a Mustang. My family gave it to me when I passed driver's ed."

"How about that motorcycle? Don't tell me you own a vehicle fleet on the rez."

"No. I borrow the bike from my cousin sometimes."

"You have a license for the bike, too?"

Josh shrugged. "No one's ever pulled me over," he replied placidly. "Don't tell on me." He gave her a conspiratorial smile, and her heart skipped a beat. Why did he have the power to do this to her?

"Are you planning on passing the test at some point, though?" she quickly went on.

"Yeah, when I turn eighteen and get some extra money." Josh leaned into her. "It's my birthday soon, so maybe that will ease your mind."

"That's right!" Ben exclaimed. "Beginning of August, right? Are you going to have a party?"

"Of course he will," Hannah said. "He's going to be a real man!" Hopefully, Josh hadn't caught her scooting away as he leaned into her like that. She thought he was man enough *now* to make her heartbeat go through the roof when he came so close.

Josh laughed. "Actually, I already am. In our tribe, the initiation ritual where a boy turns into a man takes place on the boy's fourteenth birthday. We all take a vision quest."

Ben whistled. "Wow, you grew up early."

"You're right." Josh grew silent, staring into the distance. He suddenly seemed lost in thought.

Hannah observed Ben in surprise. How strange Josh had been through an important ritual without telling Ben about it. Judging from the confused look in Ben's eyes, this was the first time he heard about Josh's vision quest.

"Well, I still think you should throw a party," she said, breaking the uneasy silence.

Josh blinked and nodded slowly, coming back to reality. "Yeah, I will. Consider yourselves invited."

The waitress showed up to clear the table and put down three dessert menus. Ben quickly picked out what he wanted, and took Hannah by the hand when the jazz band in the corner started playing 'I 've Got You Under My Skin'.

"Come on, let's dance," he suggested, pulling her from her seat.

Hannah followed her brother to the edge of the deck, where they stepped onto the sand. Within minutes, more dancing couples had joined them on the beach.

"I'm so glad I'm going to be here all summer," Hannah sighed, beaming at Ben. "My first year of teaching was kind of stressful. I needed this. It's just like old times."

Ben smiled. "That's why I said you should spend your vacation in St. Mary's Port. It's the best place to relax and let go of things. I knew you'd enjoy a nostalgic summer."

The song had come to an end. With a start, Hannah saw Josh coming toward them from the corner of her eye. Her heart sped up to a hum. Was he going to ask her to –

Josh casually tapped Ben on the shoulder. "Can I have the next dance?"

"Sure." Ben shrugged, letting go of his sister. Hannah felt her heart in her throat when Josh lightly put one hand on her back and used the other to grab her hand.

"Do I have your permission too?" Josh asked with a smile as Ben walked back to the table.

"Y- yes." She was momentarily lost for words.

"Wow, you sound eager," he said dryly.

Hannah laughed nervously, realizing she sounded

just like the giggling freshman girls she'd taught this year. Maybe she should have been more understanding toward them – she wasn't doing a whole lot better at the moment.

"Uhm..." Hannah started out, fumbling indecisively. "I don't really know what to do." Because obviously, she'd been wasting her money taking dancing lessons for two years. She couldn't come up with anything. *Anything*. Except pressing her body against him and hoping it would look like some sort of dance.

Josh smiled. "Come here." He pulled her even closer. Hannah felt his body against hers, his hand on her lower back.

"Put your chin on my shoulder," he mumbled into her ear.

"But – I won't be able to see where we're going." Immediately, she realized just how stupid that sounded. Like Josh would abduct her while dancing on the beach, with her brother in plain sight.

She heard him chuckle. "I'll give you a live report. Okay?"

Hannah gave up and put her head on his shoulder. She stared at the tables on the deck, the beach stretching out behind them, and the blood-red evening sky. If only the beauty of the surroundings would calm her, but it didn't. The warmth coming off Josh's body and his arms around her completely confused her. Although Josh had promised her a live report, he didn't speak at all during their dance together. He turned her around in a circular dance that had no name, but she didn't care. It felt perfect.

Did Josh even have the slightest idea of the effect he had on her? She would have loved to glance up and see the look in his eyes, but she didn't dare. Hannah's gaze wandered over his shoulders, where small grains of sand were stuck to his skin, catching the light from the setting sun. They reminded her of stardust, and of the starry skies she'd always looked up at when she was a little girl, lying in the grass, finding the constellations.

Her eye fell on a birthmark under Josh's collarbone. It was shaped like an animal. Strange – she couldn't remember seeing it before.

"Did you always have that mark?" she wondered softly, absently touching his skin with her index finger. Josh stopped breathing, and she looked up. He was staring at her hand, and then briefly at her. His gaze drifted to the sand below their feet.

"No," he replied after a long, awkward silence. "Last time you saw me I didn't have it yet. I got it – after that."

"Oh." Well, that was weird. After all, they were called 'birthmarks' because people were born with them. "It's shaped like an animal," she pointed out, suddenly realizing her hand was still on his chest. She quickly let it slide down.

"A bear," he said crisply. He avoided her eyes and scanned the deck behind them. "Let's go eat our ice creams."

Hannah frowned. Something in his attitude had clearly changed after she mentioned his birthmark. "Look, I'm sorry if I was prying."

He looked down at her, a sudden touch of tenderness in his eyes. "You're not prying," he said softly. Then he pressed his lips to her hand – the hand he was still holding – in a quick, soft kiss. He stepped back and headed toward the table. Hannah let her hand fall to her side, exhaling slowly.

With a sour face, she rubbed her forehead. Yep, Ben was absolutely right. St. Mary's Port was definitely the *best* place to relax and let go of things.

Three

That night, Hannah strolled back home in silence, Ben walking next to her. She would have liked to share with him how the evening with Josh had confused her, but perhaps she wasn't ready for Ben to know yet. Still, it felt weird not to say anything to him. She always talked to Ben about everything that was on her mind, and he was the same with her.

Absently, she looked up to see some people sitting on the porch of the neighboring house, their faces illuminated by the large candle on the table they were sitting at.

"Let's go and say hi," Ben said, following her gaze. He waved at the new neighbors and pulled Hannah along to their front porch.

Hannah was quickly introduced to the Greene family – Ivy and Amber, two red-haired sisters, and their parents Paul and Sarah. She and Ben sat down on one of the porch benches to tell the neighbors some stories about their previous summers in St. Mary's Port.

As Ben told Paul where the best fishing spots were, Hannah's gaze wandered to the book Amber had in her lap. "Herbal Remedies," she read from the cover. "You reading that for fun or for school?"

Amber shrugged. "I'm going to study naturopathy after the summer, but I haven't started yet. So I guess that means it's for fun."

Hannah chuckled. Yup, she and Amber would get along well. "Well, if you like picking herbs and wild plants, you should help me and Ben sometime. We're going to do a barbecue with some friends from the reservation soon. We used to do those at the lake every summer. Ben and Josh would catch fresh fish, and Emily and I would pick berries. Like real hunter-gatherers."

"We'd love to join you! Dad taught us how to fish," Ivy offered. "With us on your team, you'll never go hungry."

Hannah groaned. "What? Nobody wants to help me pick berries?"

Ben chuckled, a large grin taking up his whole face. "Oh, don't worry. Josh will help you out. I bet you can't wait to go off into the woods with him."

Hannah opened and closed her mouth again, trying to suppress the blush creeping up her face. "Ben," she hissed indignantly, shooting him a withering look.

"What?" He shrugged vaguely, turning away from her to light a cigarette.

After talking to the neighbours for a few more minutes, they decided to go home, wishing the Greenes a good night.

As they trudged back to their own cabin in awkward silence, Hannah bit her lip. Shouldn't she say something? Finally, Ben cleared his throat, sitting down on the porch steps. "Uhm – sorry I offended you before. You know."

"What do you mean?" Hannah replied softly.

"About the woods." Ben glanced sideways. "About Josh. I didn't want to tick you off. You just seemed to have, like, a really great time with him tonight."

Hannah shifted. She couldn't really deny Ben's joke had made her uncomfortable – he'd seen her go red.

"You didn't tick me off," she finally said, because Ben kept staring at her, his face a big question mark.

"Then what?"

Hannah sighed. She brushed an imaginary speck of dust from her skirt. "I felt caught."

"So you like Josh." It wasn't a question, but a statement. Hannah looked sideways, suddenly so nervous she wished she could take a drag of Ben's cigarette. He followed her gaze and held out his cigarette. "Want to share?"

"No, thanks. I shouldn't start smoking again."

Ben shrugged. "So – do you?" he asked.

"I don't know," Hannah muttered, staring at a dark stain in the wooden floor of the porch, suddenly thinking of Josh's birthmark. "I mean – I've known him since forever."

"Seems like a good starting point." Ben put an arm around her shoulders.

Hannah snatched the cigarette from Ben's fingers. "Just one drag," she grumbled, displeased with herself and her bad habits.

Ben gave her a warm smile. "I'm sorry, sis. I'll stop goading you, okay?"

Together, they finished the last bit of the cigarette and then went into the cabin for a good, long night's sleep.

ಾಾಾ

The next morning, Hannah was woken up by bright sunlight streaming in through the window, shining directly in her face. Oh crap – she hadn't closed the curtains yesterday. Groaning, she turned her back to the window.

Still a bit groggy, Hannah heard Ben talking on the

phone in the kitchen. "No, she's still asleep. I'll say hello to her when she wakes up. How's Paris?"

That must be Katie on the phone. Her brother's girlfriend was touring Europe by train during her summer break. Paris was the third city on her list.

"You want more coffee?" a familiar voice suddenly addressed Ben.

Oh. Josh was here, too. A slight smile tugged at her lips as she sat up in bed.

Hannah listened absent-mindedly to one end of the conversation between Ben and Katie on the phone, not quite ready to step outside just yet. She was eager to talk to Josh, but the thought of having him around all morning actually made her nervous.

Oh, geez. She was really *into* Josh. She couldn't deny it.

Hannah sat up straight, staring at herself in the mirror on the wall above her bed. She'd been in a steady relationship for years. It had been a while since she'd fallen in love. Was it even real? After all, what did she really know about this new, seventeen-year-old Josh? The thirteen-year-old boy from four summers ago seemed like a different person.

She got dressed slowly, trying to get the creases out of her red linen dress. She put on a pair of black flip-flops and quickly dragged a comb through her hair before stepping out of the room. After all, there was no reason to show herself sporting a disastrous hairdo yet again.

"Good morning," she hollered upon entering the kitchen. Ben and Josh looked up from their breakfast plates with wide grins. "Enjoy," she went on with a glance at the pile of pancakes on the table.

"Did you sleep well?" Ben asked.

"Like a log."

"Would you like some pancakes too?" Josh asked, nodding at the pile.

"In a minute. First I'll grab some O.J., and then I'll have a shower."

"Why did you get dressed if you still need to take a shower?" Ben asked with a grin. "Were you wearing silly pajamas unfit for public display?"

"Didn't have any on. I forgot to pack them," Hannah said without thinking. She could feel her cheeks flush and quickly turned around to pour herself some juice from the carton on the counter. "I'll buy a pair of PJs in the village later on. And while I'm at it, can I get you guys anything?"

Ben chuckled. "How about getting us some more fishing rods?"

Hannah glared at him. "Sure, I'll get the neighbors new fishing rods so I'll be my own berry-picking team for the barbecue."

Josh looked up. "What barbecue?"

"Why don't you tell him about our barbecue plans while I hit the shower?" Hannah quickly stalked out of the kitchen before Ben could crack any more jokes about berry-picking and teaming up with Josh in the woods.

When she got back to the kitchen freshly showered and made-up, the breakfast table was empty. That was a bit disappointing – Ben and Josh had already left without saying goodbye. Hannah sat down to make herself a small stack of pancakes with butter and syrup, humming along to the radio. Still whistling, she walked to the fridge to get some more orange juice, pouring herself a large glass. When she closed the fridge door, Josh was suddenly back in the kitchen, standing right next to her.

"Oh, hi," she said, a bit taken aback. "I thought the two of you had already left."

"We're leaving in a minute." He smiled at her.

Hannah shuffled past him and sat down at the table again, gulping down a large swig of juice and cutting off a piece of her pancake.

When she looked up. Josh was leaning against the kitchen counter, resting his hands on either side, staring back at her. She swallowed hard. Wasn't this silence awkward? Maybe she should make conversation.

"You want some?" she asked, pointing at the pancakes in front of her. "I can't finish them all by myself."

He shook his head. "No, thanks. I'm full."

Hannah put the fork in her mouth and slowly chewed a bit of pancake.

"So, what do you think?" Josh asked, a small smile dancing on his lips.

"Uhm – tasty," she mumbled with her mouth full. Puzzled, she looked back at him, and then it clicked. "Oh! Did *you* make them?"

"Yep. Used special flour from the rez. Don't look so baffled, I have many talents you have yet to discover." He sported a cocky grin, and Hannah blinked, literally forcing the blood away from her face. He was doing it on purpose, she could feel it.

"So it would seem." She laughed nervously. "Well, at least they taste a lot better than Ben's baking blunders."

"Hey, that sounds like a cool name for a bakery. Can't you just picture it as a store sign - 'Ben's Baking Blunders'?" He made a stately gesture.

Hannah burst out giggling, nearly choking on her pancake. Josh quickly walked over to her and carefully patted her back. "You okay? I'm sorry I'm so hilarious."

"You're too modest." Hannah coughed, catching her breath again before she looked up at him, suddenly registering that his hand was still on her back. It made her insides turn to goo.

Right at that moment, Ben entered the kitchen. "I found the air beds," he told Josh, his gaze wandering from Josh's hand to Hannah's flustered face. Why did she feel like he'd caught her doing something naughty?

Josh let his hand fall from her back, taking a step toward Ben. "Good, let's go then," he said, suddenly in a hurry. He joined Ben and they clattered out of the kitchen.

"See you tonight," Ben shouted over his shoulder. "I'm cooking for us. You can invite Emily too!"

"Yeah, I will." She didn't dare ask who exactly he meant by 'us'.

༄༄༄

At noon, Hannah threw her cell phone, keys, and purse into her handbag and left the cabin. It didn't take long to find Grassroots, the vegetarian restaurant in the village center. Her gaze drifted to a Navajo girl sitting at a small table outside.

"Uhm... Emily?" she ventured.

The girl looked up from the magazine she'd been reading, a wide smile appearing on her face. "Hannah!" she exclaimed enthusiastically, getting to her feet. "You're back!"

"Em!" Hannah hugged her old friend tightly. "It's great to see you again. You look good."

"Well, I *should* look good. I just had four weeks of vacation, so I'm well-rested. But I'm also really enjoying my new job now. I finished my studies in Tuba City two months ago, and I still had four weeks off before starting my job at the practice. I went camping by the lake near Navajo Mountain with my sister, and after that Yazzie and Josh helped me build my own *hoghan* in

Naabi'aani. I don't live with my parents anymore."

It turned out nothing had changed in the past four years – Em still talked at two hundred miles an hour.

They went inside, chatting excitedly, and chose a table near the window. Emily ordered the day's special for the two of them before pouring Hannah a glass of water from the jug on the table.

"Hey, Josh wears an exact feather like that in his hair," Hannah commented when Emily's feathered hair bands caught her eye.

"That's right. His father's clan is my mother's clan. Feather People." Emily shrugged. "Well, I don't mind Josh copied my style. It looks good on him, don't you think?"

"Yeah, it does." Hannah blushed. Of course, anything would look good on him. If Josh decided to wear a bucket on his head she'd still think it looked sexy. Quickly, she gulped down some water and stared intently at the menu. "Oh, by the way, Ben invited you to dinner tonight. He's going to cook for us."

Emily's face twisted. "*Ben* is going to cook?"

"He's going to try. No problem, we'll help him. Besides, we still have some leftover pancakes from breakfast. Josh made them, with special flour from the rez."

Yup, she was definitely babbling. About Josh - while she was supposed to ask Em about herself, not harp on about her latest Navajo obsession. She was a bad friend.

"I bet Josh is going to have a good time at Diné College," Emily said. "I really liked the campus."

"So Josh is also going to Tuba City? He did tell us he was going to college after the summer, but he didn't say where."

"Yeah, it's about time he went to a reservation school. He was sort of rebellious during his senior year at Page High School."

"Oh, really? How so?"

"The usual. Kicking against standard American culture, disobeying rules going against his traditional upbringing, refusing to use his last name on tests because the Diné don't even originally use the binomial system. Oh, and when Josh and his band played this 'anti-U.S.' song by Blackfire – that's a Diné band – he managed to offend the entire teaching staff. Blackfire's lyrics aren't exactly subtle."

Hannah smiled. "You sound like you kind of enjoyed their rebellion."

Emily grinned. "Oh, come on. Every generation needs rebels. Leave that to the Rezboyz."

"The Rezboyz? Sounds cool. What does Josh play in the band?"

"The guitar. Amazingly well, by the way. I can't believe he picked it up so fast. He sounded like a pro."

Great. Emily was unwittingly fueling her feelings for Josh even more by showering praise on his musical skills. This was driving her nuts. It was time to discuss a different subject. "By the way, we're going to have a barbecue on Friday," Hannah said. "We invited our new neighbors too."

"Sounds like fun. Count me in."

"Which days of the week are you off? I'd love to drop by Naabi'aani so I can admire your hoghan."

"Come by on Saturday. I'm not working, plus there's a dance and a rodeo. Remember Hosteen, our old neighbor? His family's organizing it."

After lunch, Emily went back for her afternoon shift in the pharmacy, leaving Hannah to do some shopping on her own. She made her way to St Mary's small main street for her second mission of the day – buying PJs she deemed fit for public display.

Four

"We're *back*!" Ben's voice boomed like a foghorn when he entered the kitchen, just as Hannah emerged from the shower. She'd spent the rest of the afternoon sunbathing on the beach.

"I'll get dressed!" Hannah shouted back through the door with a chuckle. Quickly, she slipped into a black summer dress and ran a comb through her wet hair.

"What's for dinner tonight?" she asked casually, stepping into the kitchen. Her gaze landed on Josh, who had his back turned to her.

Ben was rummaging through the fridge. "No idea," he mumbled.

"Sounds promising," she deadpanned.

Josh let out a chuckle, turning around to face her. "Well, at least we still have those pancakes."

"Did you invite Emily?" Ben asked.

"Yeah, she'll be here around seven, once she gets off work. Oh, she said she'd bring dessert."

"Great. That's one thing less to worry about, then." Ben closed the fridge. "I'll take the car and drive to the store." He got the keys from the kitchen table and stomped off toward the door.

"Wait up," Hannah mumbled, following Ben without

thinking. Maybe she should come with him. The thought of staying behind with only Josh for company made her a little bit nervous.

"You need anything?" Ben gave her a puzzled look.

She hesitated, suddenly feeling like an idiot for practically running away from the log cabin. "Yeah, why don't you buy me some oranges. See you soon."

Grudgingly, Hannah walked back in. "You want anything to drink?" she asked Josh.

"Sure. Some bottled water, if you have it."

Hannah sat down at the table, pouring him some water. When she met his gaze, she caught Josh eyeing her with a half-smile.

"What are you humming?" he asked softly.

Hannah felt her cheeks go warm. "I was humming?"

He chuckled. "Yeah, you were. Didn't you notice?"

"No. Maybe it's because I'm working on a song."

"Really? You should play something tonight. You brought your guitar, right?"

She shook her head. "I haven't finished composing it yet," she said shyly, suddenly remembering how Emily had praised his guitar talents. She probably couldn't hold a candle to him.

"No worries. Let me know when you're done."

Hannah nodded, shifting on her chair self-consciously. Why couldn't she have a relaxed conversation with Josh anymore? "So what have you guys been up to today?" she quickly asked.

"Oh, we drove to Antelope Point Marina. We tried out Ben's new fishing rods, but we didn't catch anything. Too crowded, I guess."

"So Ben bought new rods? Well, I hope you'll catch more on Friday. If not, it's going to be an embarrassing party. We invited three more people for the barbecue."

"I'm sure they'll take the bait here at St. Mary's

Port."

"Hungry fish." Hannah got up. "Speaking of which – I'm kind of hungry myself. How about some olives and crackers before we start cooking?"

She grabbed a container of potato salad, a jar of olives, and some garlic butter from the fridge, shoving everything into Josh's hands before dashing to the kitchen cupboard to get some crackers.

Josh put the snacks on the table, one arm carelessly slung over the back of his chair. His long hair moved in the breeze coming from the fan in the corner. A gleam was dancing in his dark eyes as he watched her. Did he sense how awkward she felt?

"You want white or whole-wheat crackers?" she managed to choke out, holding up two different packs.

"I don't care," Josh replied. "Whatever you're having."

Hannah picked whole-wheat and sat down to spread some garlic butter on them. "Damn, that butter is rock-hard," she muttered. As she tried to smoothen it out with her knife, she accidentally broke the cracker in two.

Josh snickered. "Here. Have some salad." He pushed the container of potato salad toward her.

"You play the guitar too, right?" she quickly asked, to avoid another silence. "What kind of music do you guys play?"

"The Rezboyz mainly play cover songs by Diné bands."

"That's what Emily told me. Rebellious Blackfire stuff, huh?"

He shot her a lopsided smile. "You and Em were gossiping about me?"

"No, we weren't." Hannah blushed. "We only said nice things about you, I swear."

"Thanks. You're a true friend."

"You're welcome." Hannah rolled her eyes. "Besides, I wouldn't know what nasty things to say about you."

"Oh, I bet Em told you I was nearly pulled off stage by angry teachers during the school talent show."

"Yup. She said the Rezboyz were provoking the audience."

He laughed. "The lyrics are kind of, uhm, politically incorrect."

"You write your own songs, too?"

"Yes, but my songs are much more mellow."

"So, you're going to play some of your songs tonight?"

Josh tilted his head. "Only if you promise me you'll play me some of yours at the barbecue on Friday."

Hannah bit her lip. "Fine."

He smiled. "Come on. You know you can sing. I was truly impressed with your performance at the gas station."

She moaned. "Shut up, or I'll never have the courage to sing again."

"But I'm serious!" Josh gave her a crooked grin. "You sounded so passionate, yet so aggressive."

"Shut. *Up.*" She tried to sound stern, but failed. With a wide grin, she grabbed a piece of the broken cracker from her plate and threw it against Josh's shoulder. He stared at his shoulder, remaining silent for a few seconds.

"Food fight!" he suddenly hollered, unexpectedly throwing an olive from his plate against her forehead.

"You're on!" Hannah grabbed the bottle of water from the table and splashed some in Josh's face. Sputtering, he got up, ran around the table and filched the bottle from her. The next thing she felt was a stream of water running down her back. Jumping up from her chair, she went after him. "Give it to me!" she laughed, grabbing the bottleneck, covering his hand. He put out his other hand and in turn covered her hand with his.

"No," he said defiantly, holding her gaze.

Hannah fell silent. She looked up at Josh, feeling the warmth of his hands on hers. Gingerly, she grabbed the bottom of the bottle and half-heartedly tried to twist it from his hands. "Let go," she mumbled.

He took a step forward. "No," he repeated, more softly. He leaned into her, his dark eyes fastening on her face. Hannah's heart started to beat wildly. Suddenly, she knew for absolutely sure he was going to pull her and the bottle against his chest. He was going to kiss her. Swallowing hard, she took a step back in confusion. Maybe this was getting too close, too fast.

"Josh..." she started, suddenly lost for words.

The silence stretched.

"I'm sorry," he finally mumbled, letting go of the bottle.

Oh great. Somehow, she'd managed to make it sound like she was telling him off. Josh probably wouldn't come close to her in the next two decades. She had to fix this.

But sadly, she didn't get the chance. The front door swung open. "Hey! I'm here!" Emily hollered enthusiastically.

Grumbling inwardly, Hannah put the bottle back on the table, desperately seeking Josh's eyes, but he'd turned away from her to make his way to the living room. "I'm going to get your guitar, okay?" he muttered, disappearing through the door.

Hannah shot her friend a bashful look. "Hi, Em."

Emily's eyes drifted over the puddles on the floor and the crumbs on the table. "Okay, what happened here?"

"Accident." Hannah practically ran over to the sink to get a rag. "I'll clean it up." She started scrubbing the table and only stopped her maniacal cleaning attack when she noticed Emily was watching her from a corner of the kitchen with amusement in her eyes. Emily cleared her throat. "Let me rephrase that," she said with a chuckle. "What *happened* here?"

"Nothing."

"Yeah, sure. I was just imagining all that awkwardness when I came in a minute ago."

"Yeah, you were. There's nothing wrong."

Emily looked sideways to the living room door and raised her eyebrows. "O-kayy," she drew out. "Whatever you say. Where do you want me to put the dessert?" She pointed at the plastic bag on the kitchen table.

"What is it?"

"Apple pie."

"Sounds good," Josh said, walking into the kitchen. He was carrying Hannah's guitar in one hand. "Do you mind?" he asked, holding it up.

"No, of course not," Hannah assured him. "I've been told you play well."

Emily smiled. "Like Mark Knopfler." She padded toward the fridge. "Shall I put it in here?"

Hannah looked nonplussed. "What... the guitar?"

"No, you idiot, the apple pie. Not the sharpest tool today, are you?"

"Here comes today's chef," Ben announced at that instant, appearing in the doorway with two bulging grocery bags in his hands. He put the bags on the floor to hug Emily. "Hi Em! Are you going to join Hannah and be my second kitchen assistant?"

"That might be wise," Emily grinned.

"I'll go sit outside on the porch and play something." Josh held up the guitar. "The kitchen is too small for four people anyway."

"Lazy rezzy," Ben tsked.

Josh gave him an innocent smile. "Arrogant paleface," he replied placidly.

Hannah grabbed the bag of tomatoes to cut. The kitchen window was slightly ajar, and she could hear Josh plucking the strings and humming a tune. Emily was right – he sounded wonderful. His voice was deep and melodic. She hoped he'd play some more music after dinner. If he did, she'd stick to her end of the deal and play something on Friday. Which meant she had to try and come up with awesome lyrics to accompany that melody she'd been working on within the next two days. No pressure.

Just then, Emily poked her. "Drifting off?" she giggled, looking at the tomato on Hannah's cutting board. She'd chopped it in at least thirty pieces.

"Yeah, I guess. I'm a bit tired."

"So, what was up with Josh? He seemed a bit out of sorts when I came in."

"Oh, nothing. We were having a water fight and I got annoyed with him. He didn't want to help me clean up." Brilliant. She sounded like a fifty-year-old schoolmarm. Maybe she should just shut up and stick to chopping vegetables for a while.

༒༒༒

"This spaghetti is fantastic," Emily commented, once they were all sitting on the porch having dinner. Ben looked proud of himself.

"Yeah, great tomato sauce," Josh agreed. "Maybe you can make some more of this stuff when you come to the rodeo on the rez this Saturday." It was tradition to bring some food for the family organizing the event.

Hannah finished her last bit of Coke and got up to get some more. No one seemed to pay attention to her, but when she got to the kitchen, Ben turned out to have followed her.

"What's suddenly going on between you and Josh?" he asked flat-out, his eyes searching her face.

She shifted uncomfortably. "Uhm, what do you mean?"

Ben shook his head with a smile. "Don't give me that line. Something definitely happened when I was gone. Josh is acting weird. He keeps sneaking glances at you. You know – the same way you struggle not to stare at *him*. Did you guys kiss or something?"

A flush raced under Hannah's skin. "Uhm, no," she stammered. "For a moment, I thought he … so I pulled away… so, he must think I…" Her voice trailed off.

"You want me to tell Josh you like him?" Ben somehow always managed to decipher her incoherent rants. "Man to man?"

"No, Ben. Please. Just keep out of it, will you? I just have to think it over, okay?"

Her brother smiled. "Okay. Whatever. Relax. I'll sit back and wait while you think things over for the next two months."

Hannah pulled a face. "You know me too well."

They went back outside and sat down at the table. Emily and Josh were just talking about traveling.

"I made a trip to the four holy mountains last spring," Josh said.

"On foot?" Hannah asked incredulously. She knew the Navajo legend of the mountains bordering Diné territory on four sides, as defined by their ancestors. Today's Navajo Nation was within the imaginary lines formed by connecting the holy mountains on the map.

"I went by car," Josh replied. "Walking it was a bit

too much for me."

"Wow! I'm surprised you left the rebellious motorcycle at home."

"Well, it was sort of a pilgrimage for me. I didn't think it was appropriate to break the law. I left our village at dawn and visited the mountain in the west first."

"Why there?" Hannah inquired. "Shouldn't you start in the east? Where the sun comes up?" Okay, she sounded like Miss Smarty-Pants, but she didn't mind airing her knowledge to impress Josh a bit.

"I had my reasons. I wanted to evoke the powers of our ancestors, feel the spirits of the past, and go back in time."

Hannah blinked and couldn't help staring at him. What he said was beautiful. Josh was the most unusual seventeen-year-old guy she had ever met.

"The Diné all have a strong bond with the past, huh?" Ben said. "It really fascinates me. You always have a story for every occasion, and everything is connected. Balanced. What's the word for it again?"

"*Hózhó,*" Hannah supplied. "Right?"

Josh nodded. "You know what, this is the right moment to sing my song for you guys. It's about balance and beauty." He got Hannah's guitar from behind his chair.

"What's it called?" Ben asked.

" 'In Beauty May I Walk'. It's a translation of a famous Diné prayer."

"Wow, you put that to music?" Emily smiled. "Let's hear it!"

Josh started to play. Hannah leaned forward in her chair and cupped her chin in her hands, her elbows leaning on the table. She stared at him. The melody he was playing and the words he was singing were so beautiful and so fragile that she hardly dared to breathe. She didn't want to make any unnecessary sound. He sang about returning seasons, birds and butterflies, and the dew at his feet on the trail of life.

Ben was the first to break the silence when the song was over. "Wow, Josh, that was great. You're really talented. I feel honored you wanted to sing this for us."

Josh looked up shyly. "I'm glad you liked it."

"I bet Sani is going to be on your case for changing the words of the prayer, though," Emily said with a wink.

"He changed something?" Ben said.

"Yeah, in the second verse. The original doesn't feature butterflies."

"That's right." Josh carefully put the guitar against the porch railing. "I liked the lyrics better that way." His gaze drifted to Hannah, who fell silent, remembering how Josh had compared *her* to a butterfly yesterday evening. But he couldn't possibly have changed the lyrics of his traditional song with her in mind. That was absurd.

"Shall I clear the table?" she offered, so no one would stare at the slight blush creeping up her face. "Let's make room for the coffee and apple pie." She started to clear away the plates, and was happy Emily got up to help her.

"Who's Sani?" Hannah asked curiously as she and Em were rinsing the plates in the kitchen sink.

"You never met him?"

"Not that I'm aware of, no."

"Well, I'm not surprised. He is our traditional medicine man, our *hataalii*." Em's voice dropped a notch. "Sani used to stay out of our clan affairs. That's why you probably never noticed him when you hung out with us in Naabi'aani when we were teenagers. But lately, he's been minding our business a lot more, ever since..." She hesitated. "Ever since Josh grew closer to him. Josh is also part of the Feather Clan. It's been four years since things started to change, and it has to do with the special position Josh seems to have within the tribe, according to the *hataalii*."

Hannah's curiosity piqued. "So – what kind of position is that?" Apparently, Josh had gone through more than just one metamorphosis in the years of her absence.

"No one knows exactly. It all started when Josh came back from his vision quest. It's common for a teenager to consult the elderly people in the village after returning from a quest, so nobody batted an eyelid when he went to Sani for advice. But people did raise eyebrows when it turned out he *only* wanted to talk to Sani, and refused to even speak to his grandparents about what he saw."

"And now what?"

"Now? He's just part of the community in Naabi'aani. But at the same time, it feels like he's standing on the sidelines. Sani talks about him as if we should treat him with more respect than you'd expect for a seventeen-year-old guy from a normal clan. To tell you the truth, I'm a bit puzzled Josh still hangs out with Ben like nothing changed."

Hannah stared out of the kitchen window, absent-mindedly piling the plates in the sink. She didn't know what to say.

Emily sighed. "Look, it's not like Josh doesn't belong anymore. He's still part of us, of our clans, but he's just ... different. Sometimes it's like Sani interferes in his life too much and doesn't allow him to be a teenager anymore."

"But I don't see any awkwardness between you and Josh. You seem to be relaxed around him."

"That's because I'm not on the rez now. I feel free here, and Josh is more relaxed outside of Naabi'aani too, though he does tense up occasionally."

True – Josh had suddenly been miles away when she asked him about his birthmark last night. What had that been about?

Emily coughed. "I can't help but notice that Josh is different around you, though. Not as relaxed as with Ben. He *looks* at you. So intently."

"You noticed, huh?"

Emily smiled faintly. "Well, I'm not blind, thank you very much." She gave her friend a mischievous smile, then put a hand on Hannah's shoulder. "Be careful, okay? I know what Josh can be like. One moment he's letting people in, the next he's pushing them away. I just don't want you to get hurt."

At that moment, Ben walked into the kitchen and girl time was over. They helped Ben cut the pie and pour coffee and tea for the four of them. When they came back outside with the drinks and trays of food, Josh was sitting on the porch steps, gazing into the distance, as if his mind had wandered to a place where he could feel the spirits of the past.

five

When Hannah woke up the next morning, the house was strangely quiet. As she stepped into the kitchen, her gaze drifted to the driveway. Ben's car was gone, so he was probably visiting Josh in Naabi'aani today. Well, so much the better. She could do with a day of peace and quiet, without having to worry about other people. Especially after yesterday and all the awkwardness with Josh.

At eleven o'clock, she got into her car and drove away with a backpack full of food and drinks, enough to last her all day. On a sudden whim, she decided to drive to Page. The small town had a library she wanted to visit, although she couldn't remember where exactly it was situated. The last time she'd borrowed a book there was when she'd been fifteen.

After parking the car, Hannah strolled to Church Row, a street with tiny shops, restaurants and a lot of old church buildings. A second-hand music store immediately caught her eye. Several crates of vinyl were on display underneath the awning outside.

Wow, that shade looked really inviting. The heat outside was already scorching, so Hannah thankfully slipped under the canopy and rifled through the crate of records right next to the entrance. She loved vinyl. One of her most prized possessions back home was a turntable.

Her eyes drifted to the shop window. Inside, there was even more music for sale. She should check out the CD selection next.

Suddenly, her breath hitched. A familiar-looking someone was bent over the A-to-C section. It was Josh.

He looked up, as if he'd felt the weight of her stare, and Hannah quickly ducked her head again. She didn't want him to think she was spying on him. Inconspicuously, she glanced up through her eyelashes. Josh was still looking at her, standing in the back of the store, without waving at her or making any move to attract her attention. Hannah couldn't see whether Ben was also there, but he couldn't be far. Josh and Ben had planned to spend the day together, after all.

Why was Josh staring at her like this? Why didn't he come outside and say hi? Hannah swallowed and wiped the sweat off her forehead. She felt strange. Grabbing the crate of records, she tried to keep her balance. A buzzing sound filled her head and she felt dizzier by the minute.

And all of a sudden, she knew that this had happened before, having the strongest, strangest sense of *déjà vu* ever. It was like she'd felt this a long time ago. This feeling of longing for Josh, and at the same time, this total sense of separation from him. A sharp, stabbing pain in her heart because all he did was observe her, unwilling to move, unable to reach out and touch her.

What was happening to her? Staggering backwards, she fumbled in her bag to find a bottle of water. Maybe the heat outside was becoming too much for her. She couldn't shake the absurd feeling that Josh was somehow pushing her away.

Well, she wouldn't be the one to break the spell by walking into the store and saying hello. If he didn't want to talk to her, fine. That was his choice.

Still feeling slightly dazed, Hannah turned around and took several deep breaths, her vision becoming clear again. It was time to stick to her original plan and visit the library. The building would be air-conditioned, so she could cool down and get herself together.

She grabbed her backpack and hurried to the street corner where she'd spotted a town map in the bus stop. Without looking back at the store, she made her way to South Lake Powell Boulevard and climbed the broad stone steps leading up to the library. Once inside, she plunked down on the nearest couch she saw and opened her bag.

To her own surprise, she pulled out her notebook and a pen instead of her water bottle. That feeling of *déjà vu* had given her a sudden flash of inspiration. Frantically scribbling, she jotted down a set of lyrics for her song. No way would she have the guts to sing it to Josh, like, *ever*, but at least she'd managed to get the confusing emotions out of her system for now.

Hannah put away the notebook before getting up and wandering through the library, slowly making her way to the section on religion and spirituality. After a bit of browsing, she picked four books about Navajo religion and vision quests. Flopping down on a couch next to the Mythology shelves, she put the pile of books on her lap and got out her notebook once more.

"A young man coming back from a vision quest sometimes carries material objects or otherwise symbolical marks handed down to him by his spiritual guide," she mumbled to herself, scanning the page for more information. Josh had seen or experienced something during his vision quest that he didn't want to discuss with anyone except Sani. Could that bear-shaped birthmark have something to do with it? She was almost certain he'd gotten it after his quest. He hadn't had it last time she'd seen him, and he'd looked so absent-minded when she'd asked him. So faraway.

Hannah jolted when her cell phone started to vibrate in her bag. It was a message from Ben. "sis! r u in page 2?? i just saw ur car :)"

She stared at the text. Ben's message made it painfully clear that Josh hadn't told Ben she'd been outside the music store. So he obviously didn't want to talk to her. Heck, he hadn't even tried to run after her or call her.

She dropped the phone in her lap, feeling miserable. Okay, Josh had every right to think she wasn't interested in him after the 'kitchen incident'. But he didn't have the right to ignore her like he was doing now. Why was he acting like that?

"You know what? Screw this," she mumbled, switching off her phone. No meeting up with Ben when Josh was tagging along. Things were complicated enough as they were. Besides, she had a perfectly good reason to switch off her phone – she was in the library.

A voice interrupted her train of thought. "Excuse me. You still reading that?"

Hannah looked up and saw a brown-haired guy standing next to the couch, pointing at the book about Navajo religion lying on top of her bag. He looked about her age.

"I'm sort of done with it," she replied. "Why? You want to borrow it?"

The guy grimaced. "You could say that. I've been searching the library for that book for hours."

"Oh, I'm so sorry! I just took it from the shelf to flip

through it."

"Yeah, thought so. According to the computer system, no one borrowed it, so I knew it still had to be on the premises. My most recent genius idea was to look for people reading books *inside* the library."

"What do you need it for?"

"I'm writing part of my dissertation about the Navajo culture." The guy extended his hand. "My name's Nick, by the way."

"I'm Hannah." She shook his hand. "Well, in that case you've come to the right place. Page isn't far from the reservation."

Nick flopped down on the couch despondently. "You make it sound so easy. The truth is, I don't know anybody in Navajo Nation, and most Navajos aren't exactly eager to talk to a paleface asking them all kinds of questions about their culture and customs. So books are my best friends at the moment."

"Maybe I can help you out. My best friend actually lives on the rez. And my brother's best friend is also Navajo. I could ask them to talk to you."

Nick's face lit up like a light bulb. "Really? Do you live in Page? Can you introduce me to them?"

"I don't live here. Me and Ben are staying in my mom's log cabin in St. Mary's Port for the summer. Why don't you drop by on Saturday? We were planning to go to the rez for a rodeo anyway."

Nick looked so excited she half-expected a 'you're-my-savior' hug from him. "That would be awesome! I'm staying with my uncle in Page, but I can borrow his car and drive to St Mary's. No problem."

Someone next to them distinctly cleared his throat. Hannah looked sideways and caught a dismayed librarian glaring at them. They were clearly talking too loud. "Let's go outside. I think our enthusiasm is bothering people."

Nick followed her stare. "Good idea. I want to borrow this one." He grabbed the book about Navajo religion and followed Hannah to the library desk. A few minutes later, they were outside, walking toward a bench in the shade.

"So why did you decide to write about the Diné?" Hannah inquired.

"Well, I'm a history student, but I took a few extra courses in sociology. I started to read a lot of background information about the birth of our nation, and about the way the European colonists dealt with the original inhabitants of this country." He waved the book in his hand. "And I was wondering if it's possible to explain why the Native American culture couldn't withstand white domination by looking at it from a sociologist's point of view. My uncle lives close to the reservation, so I picked the Navajo history as a case study."

"Oh, I'm sure Emily and Josh can help you with that. Especially Josh. He knows a lot about his own history, but don't expect an objective story."

"Sounds good. Where and when do we meet up on Saturday?"

Hannah looked around. "Why don't we talk some more and grab lunch somewhere? I brought my own lunch, but those peanut butter sandwiches can wait."

They got up and walked to the main street to find a place to eat. While Hannah was leafing through the library book about Navajo religion, Nick scrolled through the playlist on Hannah's iPod. She was happy she'd met him. She felt completely comfortable around him.

"You want another drink?" she asked Nick, who was staring past her.

"You know what? There's a Navajo guy standing across the street keeping his eagle eye on us."

Hannah felt her heart skip a beat. Oh help. She knew what was would come next.

"Hey, Hannah!" Ben's voice called out. She turned around and sure enough, her brother and Josh were coming toward them. "I phoned you and texted you," Ben continued when he got to their table. "Don't you have your cell on you?" He took the seat next to Hannah.

"I do. I just switched it off, I was in the library."

"We saw your car up the road," Josh said. "Have you been in Page for long?" He sat down next to Nick.

This was crazy. So he was still pretending he hadn't seen her at the music store. "Since this morning. You?"

"Yeah, us too."

"Let me introduce myself." Nick shook Josh's hand. "Nick Hartnett. I met Hannah in the library. I'm working on my final thesis about Navajo culture." He launched into a full-fledged saga about his dissertation, telling Josh everything about the research he'd done so far, all the while bombarding him with questions. Josh immediately got caught up in Nick's stories and didn't as much as glance at her anymore.

Okay, that was *it*. She'd had enough. First he completely blanked her at the record store and now he gave her the cold shoulder again. Distant much?

Ben flagged down the waiter to order some food as well. He poked Hannah. "We should invite Nick for our barbecue tomorrow. So Josh and he can talk some more."

Hannah shrugged. "Yeah, whatever." For the moment, she didn't feel like being a part of *any* activity involving Josh anymore. He could go on running hot and cold without her getting in the way of his mood swings, for all she cared.

※ ※ ※

After lunch, Nick decided to go back to the library and look up some more things for his dissertation.

"What are you guys up to?" Hannah asked Ben and Josh, once they'd paid and walked away from the restaurant.

"We're going to drop by the visitor's center to get a program for Movies in the Park," Ben replied. "You know, the open-air movie theater. You coming?"

"Nah. I'm going to skip town and go to a quiet spot for a while. Sit and watch nature run its course."

Josh looked up. "By yourself?" he asked, sounding intrigued.

Like *he* cared. He'd left her standing by herself this morning too.

"Yes, by myself. I can't open up to my environment with other people around. Call it meditation or whatever."

"Beware, Crazy Hermit on the loose," Ben teased.

Hannah punched him. "Sticks and stones..." she replied. "Yada, yada. See you guys later."

"But – what time are you going to be home tonight?" Ben sounded a bit worried all of a sudden.

"No idea. I'm not going to keep an eye on my watch the whole time. That's not really my idea of a relaxing, peaceful afternoon."

"Do come back before nightfall." Josh unexpectedly put his hand on her shoulder.

"Oh. Okay," she stammered. So he did care about her after all. "Will do."

She waved at the two guys and turned around. As she started the car and drove off, she could still feel on her skin where Josh had touched her.

☙ ☙ ☙

Twenty minutes later, Hannah had found herself a nice, quiet spot on Lake Powell Beach. She breathed deeply in and out, letting the beauty and tranquility of her surroundings sink in. The longer she sat at the lakeside, the more she became aware of how much she could hear all around her. Nature rustled and moved without pause. A soft wind tousled her hair, a small bird sat tweeting on a branch, the leaves of the trees whispered in the breeze. She spotted a beautiful, dark-blue beetle crawling past her feet, making its way toward the rock next to her.

So this is what young Navajo men learned to listen for during their vision quests. They'd go off into the wilderness for days without food or water, learning how to be in sync with nature. They'd find edible plants, learn to listen for subterranean springs, train themselves to hear animals coming from miles away.

Maybe that was why Josh seemed so mature – he was so much closer to nature than anyone she knew, and he seemed so much more human for it. He was so different from her other friends.

Hannah closed her eyes and leaned her head against the rock behind her. She'd planned to spend some alone time, but now that she *was* alone, she couldn't stop mulling over things that niggled at her mind. Plus, her backside felt sore from sitting in the sand, and the little flies buzzing in and out of the shrubs had all apparently decided to crawl into her ears. No vision quest for her today, then.

Grumpily, she snatched her backpack from the rock behind her and pulled out her book. If she couldn't sit still and enjoy the view, she could at least try and read a few chapters. Hannah threw a soggy sandwich in the sand next to her to lure away the flies. Any bug in its right mind would prefer peanut butter to her earwax.

Fortunately, it didn't take long for her to get into the story. By the time she finally looked up again, the sun was already setting. She'd better go home.

Quickly, she packed up and climbed the hill separating the shoreline from the gravel road running alongside the lake.

Once back at her car, she opened the trunk to get a cardigan, her eyes drifting to the gas tank hatch. It was ajar. That was weird. How could it be open? And *why*?

Hannah slammed the trunk shut and put on her cardie, bending over to take a closer look at the hatch to see if it was broken.

Nope. Nothing wrong. She'd pop down to a garage tomorrow and have it checked out just to be sure.

Hannah closed the hatch, got in and turned the key. A cold sweat broke out when she suddenly noticed the fuel gauge on the dashboard.

It was below the red line. The engine didn't sound too good, either.

"What the hell?" Hannah banged her fists on the steering wheel, cut the ignition and got out again. She stamped to the side of the car and took another look at the gas tank hatch. Her eyes drifted to the gravel road beneath it.

There were footprints there. And was that spilled liquid? Shaking her head in disbelief, she crouched down and picked up some dirt. It smelled like gas. Oh, this could *not* be happening! Someone had stolen her fuel. If she ever got her hands on the asshole who'd done this...

Cursing under her breath, she sat down behind the wheel again. What was she supposed to do now? There was no gas station around here. The closest one was the station where she'd bumped into Josh, and she was never going to make it there on the few drops of fuel left in the tank.

With a desperate groan, she got out her phone and called Ben. He had to pick up. If he didn't hear his phone, she had no idea what to do.

Fortunately, Ben answered on the third ring. "Hey, Han! Where you at?"

"You're *not* going to believe this. I got myself stranded somewhere along Lake Powell. Some idiot drained my tank. They stole my fuel. I can't go anywhere."

Ben was silent for a moment. "We'll meet you there," he said. "Where are you exactly?"

"Close to that tiny beach where we used to go for picnics with mom."

"We'll be there in twenty. We'll pick up a jerry can of gas on the way."

"Wait, Ben. Don't – don't hang up yet. Can you keep talking to me?" A shiver ran through Hannah. The sun had nearly set, it was getting pitch-dark, and she had no idea what kind of people were around. Apparently, not every passer-by was someone she would want to run into. Least of all her gas thief.

"Sis? I'm driving. I'll give the phone to Josh."

Hannah swallowed. "Hey," she heard Josh on the other end of the line. "You okay there?" He sounded worried.

"Not really. I'm out of fuel. Someone stole my gas, and now I'm stranded here all by myself, and it's getting dark. I don't know what to do."

"First of all, get into the car and lock the doors. And stay on the phone until Ben and I get there."

Hannah did what Josh told her.

"Did you at least have a nice afternoon?" he went on.

"Yeah, I was sitting by the lake to enjoy the view. I read for a while too."

"Good. We picked up a ton of brochures at the visitor's center, and we made tacos for dinner. I bet they'll still taste nice when we get home."

Hannah's lips curled up in a smile. "Sounds good. I wish I were home right now."

"I bet. Well, it won't take long. Ben is driving like a maniac."

In the background, Ben let out a cackling laugh, and Hannah grinned. "Are you sure you still feel safe yourself with him behind the wheel?" she said.

"Of course. I drive like that, too."

"Oh, how nice of you to tell me. I'll never get into a car that you're driving, then."

"Too bad. I just planned all kinds of nice trips for us with that pile of brochures as my guiding light. Don't you want to join me?"

She blushed. His stand-offish attitude was clearly gone again. "By the way," she changed the subject, "I was wondering this afternoon about that school you said you wanted to found on the rez. How will you set that up?"

Josh started telling her about his plans to found a native secondary school in the vicinity of Naabi'aani, and Hannah shared a few 'teacher-fresh-out-of-college' stories with him.

"Sounds like teaching isn't that easy," Josh concluded after listening to one of Hannah's anecdotes about the freshman group that had given her nightmares.

"Oh, you'll do fine. You seem sort of strict."

"Of course I am. Pupils will tremble as I enter the classroom."

Hannah rolled her eyes. "Yeah, that sounds very

pedagogical."

"Oh, we're at the gas station, by the way."

"Hmmm. Ben *really* drives like a maniac."

"Yeah, he'll only be a minute, there's no one here. Everything will be fine. Don't worry, okay?"

Her gaze drifted to the road ahead of her. Oh, crap. In the darkness, she could see three guys were approaching her car. They looked drunk. One of them was carrying a half-empty case of beer, and the other two were shouting at each other in unsteady voices.

"Shoot." She couldn't help whispering into the phone. "Josh. There's a bunch of drunks walking in my direction. They've seen my car." One of the guys was pointing at her Datsun right at that moment. "Oh, damn."

"Are your doors still locked?"

"Yes," she quivered.

"So just ignore them. They can't bother you when they can't get in."

"I suppose." Despite his words, her heart was beating in her throat.

In the meantime, one of the guys had stopped next to her window. He bent over to look at her through the glass. "You okay in there?" he asked.

"Yeah, I'm fine." Hannah swallowed hard. "My car broke down, but help is on the way."

"Would you like a drink?" the second one asked, holding up a beer bottle.

"No, thanks."

"Can't we sit in your car for a while?" the guy next to her asked in a velvety voice. The third one plonked down on the hood of the Datsun, staring at her through the windshield without saying a word. The look in his eyes was downright creepy.

"I don't think that's a good idea." Her voice was

getting shaky. "I don't know you guys, and I'm all alone. No offense."

Her eyes were darting from one guy to the other. The way they moved was odd. It was like their bodies responded to one another, reminding her of a documentary she'd recently watched about packs of wolves and their group behavior. Goosebumps spread all over her arms.

"Come on, don't be a party-pooper." The guy on the other side of her door tried the handle and discovered the car was locked. He violently pulled the handle again, a few times. The sound echoed in Hannah's ears like it was coming from far away.

Oh my God, she had to do something before this got out of hand. Say something. Scare them off.

"Keep your dirty paws off my car," she barked, as snippy as she could manage. "I just told you to stay out of my car. Are you deaf?" She fixed the guy with an angry stare. He wasn't even that much older than the pupils she taught. She could do this outside the classroom, too. Make clear where her boundaries were.

The guy on the car hood crawled closer and tapped a finger on the glass, leering at her. "Maybe you're blind," he replied. "There's three of us and only one of you. You really think we can't force you out of that old car if we want to?"

A cold shiver ran down her spine. Her right hand reached for the glove compartment, finding the unloaded gun she kept there for emergencies. "Just in case," her mother had said when Hannah first got her driver's license. She wasn't a big fan of firearms, but right now she silently thanked her mom.

"Fine." She pointed the gun at the guy on the hood. "Go force the door open. Let's see how far you'll get after that."

They stared at her wide-eyed. The guy in front of her slid off the car hood. "Come on, let's go. That chick is nuts, " he muttered, kicking against the front tire and glowering at her. "Have a nice life."

Hannah followed the guys with her eyes until they disappeared into the dusk. She let out a shaky breath. Her heart was hammering like crazy.

"Hannah?" A tinny voice piped up from the passenger's seat. "You still there?"

She grabbed her cell phone. "Yeah, I'm still here," she replied softly.

"If I *ever* get my hands on those bastards." His voice trembled. "Are they gone?"

"Yeah."

"We're almost there, sis," she heard Ben shouting in the background. "Hold on just a little longer."

Hannah put the gun down. The grip had turned all sweaty in her hand. "Gotta go. My battery is almost dead."

"All right."

"And Josh?" She sighed. "Thanks for your help."

She hung up just before the battery died, sagging back in her seat. After five minutes, the headlights of Ben's car appeared in her rearview mirror. Hannah unlocked the door and staggered outside. Ben parked next to the Datsun after which he and Josh got out. Ben got to her first, hugging her tightly.

"Hey," he whispered in her hair. "This is quite a night, huh?"

Now that she was safe, Hannah started to shiver uncontrollably. She could feel Josh rubbing her back to calm her down. For a while, the three of them were just standing there. Ben was the first to pull away from their group hug to get the jerry can. "Let's feed your car, okay?"

Hannah turned around to face Josh. "Thanks for your pep-talk on the phone. I really don't know what I would have done without my helpline."

Josh smiled. "I'm sure you would have been just as brave." He noticed the way she rubbed her hands over each other, and silently took them in his. "You cold?"

"Yeah. Stress, I guess." Her hands warmed up against his palms. Hannah looked at Ben, catching the glance her brother shot at her hands safely tucked away in Josh's. She sighed. "God, I'm *exhausted*."

"You should sit down." Josh pulled her toward the Datsun's passenger seat.

"But – I have to drive."

Josh shook his head. "No, I'm driving. You're too shaken." He helped her into the seat, but didn't let go of her hands straight away. "I'll drive safely," he added with a grin. "Trust me."

"I trust you." Hannah closed her eyes.

"Are you done filling her up?" Josh asked Ben.

"Yep, all clear. You driving Hannah's car?"

Ben shut his car door and started up the engine. Josh sat down next to her, turning the key in the ignition. She closed her eyes again when they drove off, feeling her entire body relax.

"Just rest," he said. "You'll have to wake up for tacos when we get home, though."

"Hmmm." She dozed off, thinking about the way she'd felt when he held her hands. Josh was six years her junior, but somehow, she felt inexplicably safe with him. She wasn't sure she wanted to feel that way about him, though. The age difference wasn't bugging her that much, but his mood swings were. Plus the fact that Emily had warned her about Josh pushing people away.

Hannah fell into a deep sleep. She didn't notice the car pulling into the driveway. She didn't wake up as

Josh lifted her and carried her inside, and Ben tucked her in.

That was the night she dreamed about the burning village for the first time.

Six

Clouds of smoke billowed above the primitive hoghans of the small settlement. Hannah panted. She was on the run from a group of Mexican-looking soldiers. Even though she'd never seen soldiers dressed like them in her life, she instinctively knew they were from Mexico, and they didn't mean well.

"Run!" she cried out to the people she met on her way through the village. In front of her, she saw burning hoghans and Navajo people trying to put out the fire with buckets of water. Hannah knew she was looking for someone. Someone who meant a lot to her. She bumped into fleeing villagers and tripped over her own feet, scraping her knees when she fell down. Frantically, she tried to stay out of sight of the Mexicans on the village square by hiding underneath some thorny bushes.

And then, her eyes focused on a figure running across the square. He came closer and spotted her, but he averted his eyes so he wouldn't alert the soldiers to her presence. Hannah stared up in utter confusion. That man who was trying to protect her was the man she'd been looking for. And it was *Josh*.

He looked older, about thirty years old, but it was definitely him. He was wearing traditional clothes and carrying a bow, which he presently raised to draw the string and release an arrow at the approaching soldiers.

Behind him, a hoghan collapsed under its own weight, spitting up flames and smoke toward the sky. Hannah coughed, her eyes beginning to tear.

And then, she jolted awake, startled by the sound of her phone. Someone must have charged it. Hannah opened her eyes and wildly flailed her left arm to grab it from the bedside table.

"Hey, Nick," she answered in a groggy voice after glancing at the display. "How's life?"

"Wonderful. You don't sound very alive yourself, though."

"You woke me up," Hannah groaned. "Sorry. I was supposed to text you yesterday, but I forgot."

"What time are we meeting up?"

"Josh and Emily will be here around five. So if you want to talk to them about your thesis..."

"Great! I'll be there. What's the name of your street?"

"It doesn't have one. Once you get to St. Mary's Port, just follow the signs saying 'Log Cabin Park' and you'll end up here."

"Okay, see you later then. Sorry I woke you up."

"No problem. Bye."

Hannah threw her phone back on the bedside table and stretched her arms and legs, staring at the ceiling. That dream. It had been so bizarre, and yet so life-like. She could still smell the burning wood and hear the villagers scream. She'd never dreamed in Spanish before. She'd been able to understand those soldiers, even though they'd had a strange accent. In a flash, she remembered the Josh from her dream. Older, with a more worn and muscular body and an alert attitude that made him look like a born warrior. And yet, his eyes had been the same when he looked at her. So intense and gentle.

Hannah shivered despite the heat. Dreaming about Josh wasn't that strange – after all, she'd been thinking about him a lot lately – but dreaming like this was. It had felt like a blast from the past.

"Hey," Ben called out from the other side of the door. "You awake?"

"No, I was on the phone in my sleep."

Ben opened the door with a cheeky grin. "Snarky as ever. So, how are you feeling, Sleeping Beauty?"

Hannah yawned. "I slept well. Sorry for skipping dinner." She conveniently forgot to mention her strange dream. She was *so* not about to fess up to Ben and say she'd dreamed about his best friend playing her protector in some pre-Civil War setting. He'd probably think she was losing it. If she ever had it, to start with. She groaned and got out of bed.

"How about some tacos for breakfast, then?" Ben pointed at the plate on the kitchen table. "I saved two vegetarian ones for you."

"Wonderful." Hannah smiled at her brother and sat down at the table.

"Ivy said they'd be here at four," Ben said. "What about Nick? What did he say when you called him in your sleep?"

"Oh, he'll be here at five. Let's go out and get groceries before they show up. We don't have enough stuff to feed all of our guests."

"Amber and Ivy promised to bring drinks for everybody. Josh is bringing some burgers, and I said we'd get ice cream and stuff to make salad. We'll pick berries some other time."

"Sounds like a plan." Hannah sank her teeth into one of the tacos and finished it in a heartbeat. She was really hungry.

After she scarfed down her breakfast, they got into Ben's old Chevy convertible with the top open. While Ben started the engine, Hannah hit the side of the car stereo, which made it sputter to life after a few seconds. It was set to a radio channel playing lazy country music.

"Good. You still know how my radio works." Ben chuckled. He was notorious for never throwing anything out until it crumbled to dust in his hands. His car stereo was so old it needed special treatment.

As Johnny Cash crooned through the speakers, Hannah sank into the car seat, absently looking out at the reddish-brown desert and the deep-blue sky above. It was going to be a hot day. Already, shimmering heat was radiating off the asphalted road in front of them.

A cold shiver suddenly ran down her spine as Hannah remembered last night's events. She couldn't believe she'd threatened people with a gun, even if it had been an unloaded one.

"You okay, sis?" Ben interrupted her thoughts. "You're so quiet."

"Still thinking about last night. It bothers me that I scared those guys off by pulling a weapon."

Ben gave her a bug-eyed stare. "*What?* I didn't even know you had a gun!"

"I told them I wasn't interested in their company, but one of them flat-out told me they'd force the doors open if I didn't unlock the car myself."

Anger flared up in Ben's eyes. "What a bunch of assholes."

"Yeah, that's when I suddenly remembered the unloaded gun in my glove compartment. Mom gave it to me so I could defend myself if something ever happened to me. I guess I was supposed to buy bullets for it, but I never did."

Ben shook his head, his mouth set in a firm line. "You know what? I think we should go down to the police station. You have to file a report. Who knows, those creeps could be stalking and harassing other girls, too."

Hannah fell silent for a moment, then nodded. "Let's. I'd rather forget about the whole ordeal as soon as possible, but I don't want those guys bothering other women."

Once in Page, Ben parked the car on the square in front of the police station. He followed Hannah inside. "Where can we report a case of harassment?" Ben asked the middle-aged police officer who greeted them when they entered the station.

"Please follow me." The man walked them to one of the interrogation rooms and sat down at the desk himself, pulling the computer keyboard toward him. "My name is Graham Curry. I'll draw up the report for you."

Hannah started telling her story. She slowly drank the coffee another police officer brought for her and described the guys who'd threatened and harassed her in detail.

"Is it okay if I go to the supermarket?" Ben whispered, while officer Curry was busy typing the report. "I'll see you outside when you're done, okay?"

Hannah nodded, quickly finishing her description for the police officer. She mentioned Josh in her story as well, since he'd heard the guys' voices over the phone. He was the closest thing she had to a witness. When she got out of the police station and made her way to the Chevy, she briefly wondered if Josh had a cell phone or a landline at home. Officer Curry had asked her for contact details, but she only knew Josh's last name was Benally and that he lived in Naabi'aani.

"Does Josh have a cell?" she inquired, when Ben returned with the groceries and they both sat down in the car.

Ben shook his head. "No. Why? You want to call him?"

"Nah," Hannah said, too hastily.

Ben looked at her sideways, shooting her a cheeky grin. "Of course you do."

She blushed. "Stop teasing me. I was just wondering because that cop wanted to have Josh's number. I mentioned him in the report."

"No. Josh doesn't have a phone. He doesn't see the point. Naabi'aani doesn't have coverage half of the time anyway, so I can see why. His uncle and aunt have a landline, so if they need to speak to him, they can call him there."

"I don't think they'll need to." Hannah absently picked at the hem of her dress. She'd actually love to talk to Josh for a while, but she'd see him tonight, and she would wait for that moment to find out whether he'd be his friendly self – or his distant self.

That afternoon, Hannah lounged around on the beach by herself as Ben stayed in the cabin and devoted himself to cramming for some resits after his vacation. Unfortunately, she'd forgotten to apply sunscreen to the backs of her knees, so by the time she got up from her towel to go home, she couldn't even stand up straight because her skin stretched too much, causing a stinging pain. Just her luck.

When Hannah finally arrived at the cabin and limped up the porch steps in agony, Ben raised his eyebrows. "What the heck happened to you? Someone stole your wheelchair on the beach?"

Hannah glowered at him. "*Not* funny. My knee-pits

are sunburned. I can barely walk." She smiled at the two neighbor girls sitting next to Ben on the bench. "Hi there."

"You should put some herbs on them," Amber suggested. "Mixed with yogurt."

Ivy laughed. "Listen to the witch. A potion for every ailment."

Amber poked her. "Keep mocking me and I'll turn you into a toad."

Ben got up. "Okay girls, let's go down to the lake and catch some fish."

"Not me," Hannah protested. "I'm a cripple, and by the way, Nick will be here at five. I'll stay here and be the welcome committee."

"Sure. Go pamper yourself. There's some after-sun lotion in the bathroom."

After Ben's car had driven off the sandy track toward Lake Powell, Hannah got up, took a shower and applied some lotion on her burning legs. Just as she stumbled into the kitchen, she heard a car engine outside. Sounded like Nick was already here. Hannah got her guitar from the living room and went outside to greet her new friend.

Instead, she found herself face to face with Josh, who just stepped out of his car parked next to the log cabin.

"Oh. Hi." She swallowed, watching him lift two heavy bags from the back seat. "You're – early."

"Hey, don't sound so surprised." Josh walked up the steps. "I know punctuality is not my strong suit, being Indian and all, but really. There's no need to rub it in." He grinned at her, disappearing into the kitchen to put the hamburgers in the fridge.

Hannah let out the breath she'd been holding. This was awkward with a capital A. It hadn't occurred to her that Josh could get here first. Now she'd be alone with him until Nick and Emily got here, and she felt nervous at the prospect. Which was stupid. This was the perfect opportunity to discuss that almost-kiss where she'd accidentally, well, *rejected* him.

Or maybe she should just shut up about it. Josh was just a regular, seventeen-year-old guy learning the ropes and flirting with her before moving on to an actual potential girlfriend his own age.

"So, how are you feeling?" he asked.

She turned around and unwittingly smiled when he gently put his hand on her shoulder. "Better. Ben made me go to the police and file a report, by the way."

"I can imagine."

"Oh, I mentioned your name in the report. You're the only one who heard those guys talk."

"Sure. If I can help or testify against them, let me know. I hope they'll get arrested."

"Me too. They only took off because I held them at gunpoint."

Josh frowned. "You have a weapon?"

Hannah nodded gingerly. "Unloaded, though."

"So that's why they suddenly decided to leave you alone," he said grimly.

"I really don't like guns." Hannah stared at her hands, somehow feeling like Josh was judging her.

"Hey. I know. It wasn't your fault."

She looked up, and for a split second she saw his face as it had been in her dream last night – older, wiser, and completely focused on her. She stared into his dark eyes and heard people shouting in Spanish, smelling the burning fire of her nightmare.

"Would you like something to drink?" she broke the silence.

Josh blinked, shaking his head as if he'd been lost in thought as well. "Yeah, sure. I'll just have a Coke." He smiled at her and grabbed a can from the table.

Hannah plopped down on the porch cross-legged and watched Josh taking a long drink, sitting down on the steps, his back against the railing. She absent-mindedly plucked the top string of the guitar she'd put in her lap, tuning it up a bit. When she looked up again, she caught Josh staring at her hand as it touched the strings. His gaze wandered upward and he looked into her eyes. Hannah bit her lip. The only thing she heard was the wind in the trees and her own frantic heartbeat.

She broke eye contact and looked down at her hands. And suddenly, she was playing her own song. She *wanted* to play this song for him alone.

The only thing Hannah focused on was controlling her breath and getting rid of the ball of cotton in her throat. When she finally started singing, she somehow remembered every word of the lyrics she had written down only yesterday.

Look at me
Look for me
Oh, embrace me
Hold me strong.

I have wandered the ages
I have roamed the earth
I have crossed space and time
for your song.

I have waited
I am waiting
I will wait for you;

One and thousand summers long.

When the last chord faded, Hannah looked up,

meeting Josh's eyes. He was staring at her so intensely that her brain flatlined.

Josh put down his drink, shifted onto his knees and leaned over to her, putting one hand on hers – the hand that had plucked the strings – and using his other hand to push away a stray lock of hair from her face. Then he pressed his lips to her cheek. It felt so warm, so familiar, and yet so brand new.

When Josh moved away from her, he finally broke the silence. "That was the most beautiful song I've ever heard," he said earnestly.

A shaky breath escaped her lips. "Thank you," she whispered with a blush.

He smiled faintly. "Don't thank me. I should thank *you* for singing to me."

Hannah looked down at the neck of her guitar. Her heart was dancing in her chest. She'd sung her new song for Josh alone! If only he knew she'd written the lyrics with him in mind.

Josh scrambled to his feet, gazing at the road. "Is that Nick?" He tilted his head to an old, green Jeep coming around the corner.

Hannah put away her guitar and got up too. "Yeah, that's him," she said, when she saw a brown-haired guy wearing aviator sunglasses sitting behind the wheel.

"Do me a favor," Josh said in a serious tone. "Please stop being insecure about your music. You really don't need to be."

"O-okay," she stuttered, a bit overwhelmed.

"Good." He put his hand on her arm for a moment before walking down the steps and getting his car keys out to move the Mustang and make room for Nick's Jeep.

As the two guys sat down at the table to go through Nick's notes, Hannah installed herself on the porch steps with a book. She didn't read a single word, though – all she did was listening to the warm timbre of Josh's voice, telling Nick about the history of his people. The kiss he'd pressed to her cheek played over and over in her mind. By the time Emily showed up at the log cabin, Hannah was glad to be able to take a walk and get things off her chest.

"Hey Em," she said, putting her book down. "Where's your car?"

"At home. My dad gave me a ride this morning. I can drive back with Josh later." She waved at him and then eyed Nick. "Who's that?"

"Come on, let's go for a walk." Hannah steered her friend away from the cabin before she'd strike up an entire conversation with Nick. There'd be plenty of time to do that later, and right now, she just wanted to get away for a while.

Emily chuckled and followed her obediently. "Sure. Are we going to talk about, uhm, *someone*? Is that why you're herding me out of here?"

They strolled down the sandy path toward the beach. Hannah stayed quiet.

"So. You look sort of – dreamy," Emily ventured after a minute.

"Hmm?"

Her friend chuckled. "Don't play innocent. You really like Josh, don't you?"

Hannah gave up. "Yeah. I do." She smiled faintly. "I just played my new song for Josh. Alone."

"Wow! What did he think?"

"He said he'd never heard a more a beautiful song. And that means a lot, coming from someone that talented."

Emily smiled. "I'm happy to hear he's so sweet to you. It's obvious he feels close to you."

"I wouldn't mind feeling him even closer."

"Ooh, Slutsville."

Hannah giggled. "Shut *up*."

They walked past the deck of The Winking Shrimp. Hannah's gaze wandered to the jetty where Josh had been next to Ben a few days ago, nearly giving her a heart attack with his sudden re-appearance after their meeting at the gas station. Last time here, she'd been a high-school student, and Josh had still been a kid. On the reservation, he'd always called her *sha'di* – the Navajo word for older sister. Josh called Ben *shik'is*, his brother and friend. In Diné culture, it was common to avoid using people's names in their presence out of respect. Family members were addressed by their title, because those relations were important. Even the name 'Josh' was a nickname based on his real Navajo war name. It was a name devised to be used by whites. Josh had once told Ben and her his real name, though, but she'd forgotten it along the way.

"What's Josh's real name again?" Hannah wondered aloud.

"*Shash*," Emily replied. "It means 'bear' in our language."

Hannah blinked. "You mean the animal?"

So his name referred to the strange birthmark on his chest? That was just freaky. Of course, if it had actually *been* a birthmark, it wouldn't be so strange – his grandparents could have given him the name because of his mark, but that wasn't possible. Something inexplicable must have happened during his quest. But what could it be?

The two girls sat down at the waterside. Hannah gazed at the beach, where a group of guys were sitting around a bonfire, roasting marshmallows. Even though the three boys didn't look like the drunk teenagers of last night, they reminded her of them. Somehow, their presence *felt* the same. She shivered.

Emily followed her stare. "What's up? You look spaced out."

"I was harassed by some guys last night," Hannah said softly.

"What, really? Those guys over there?"

"No. I just ... they sort of reminded me of the situation." She quickly told Emily what had happened. She didn't want to dwell on it for too long. Thinking about it cast a shadow over her good mood.

"Good idea to file a report," Emily said. "I hope they get arrested. You're lucky nothing happened to you."

Nothing had happened, but somehow she now felt irrationally scared of people who had nothing to do with her assailants. Maybe that fear had made her dream such strange things last night. It was as good an explanation as any.

ce ce ce

When the two girls got back to the house, Nick was hammering away on Ben's laptop while Josh was stirring up the coals on the barbecue.

"Enjoy your walk?" Josh asked when Hannah came over to him.

"I did. Enjoy Nick's interview?" She looked at Nick, who was now typing and chatting to Emily at the same time. "I see he's still processing data?"

"He borrowed Ben's laptop so he could take notes faster." Josh wiped the sweat off his forehead. Hannah laughed when he smeared a stain of soot across his eyebrow.

"What?" he asked, a faint smile around his lips.

"You on the war path?" she teased, laughing even

more when she saw the bemused look in his eyes.

"You talk in riddles," he said with a grin.

"You have a war stripe on your brow." Hannah reached out and rubbed the black stain, trying to get it off his skin.

Josh moved closer. "Where?" he said, reaching for his forehead. His fingers touched hers, and he looked at her from up close.

"Yes – there," she stammered.

"Is it gone?" he mumbled.

"Yes."

"Do I still look like an idiot?" He stared down at her with a twinkle in his eyes.

"No." Hannah wondered when exactly her entire vocabulary had turned monosyllabic. She stared at him in the silence stretching between them.

"Josh, could you come over here for a minute?" Emily called out. She was still helping Nick with his notes.

"Yep." Abruptly, Josh whipped around and walked up the steps. Hannah listlessly prodded the barbecue coals with a pair of tongs, trying to breathe evenly. He was driving her absolutely *insane*. This whole situation was.

As she put on the first burgers, Hannah scanned the sky for stars. Dusk was setting in. In the east, a pale crescent moon rose in the cloudless firmament.

"I bet we'll see a lot of stars tonight," she said hopefully to Josh, who just put some bottles of sauce on the table next to the barbecue.

"You like star-gazing, right?"

Hannah nodded. "As a child, I could find all the constellations in the night sky. I knew all their names, too."

"Me too. The Diné don't have the same

constellations, though. You want me to teach you a few?"

"Sure!" For all she cared, Josh could teach her how to add and subtract. As long as he wasn't distant or cold toward her. So far, the day had been wonderful in that respect, though.

At six o'clock, Ben and the neighbors proudly carried a bucket full of fish to the barbecue.

"I'll gut those in a minute," Josh offered when Ivy and Amber handed him the catch of the day. They all shook hands and introduced themselves.

"Hi, I'm Emily Begay. Hannah told me you are going to study natural medicine," Emily said to Amber. "I just finished my studies, actually!"

Within minutes, Amber and Emily were engaged in deep conversation about medicinal herbs used by the Diné on the reservation. Nick put away Ben's laptop and helped getting the food ready.

By the time it was really getting dark, everybody sat on the lawn in front of the cabin enjoying the grilled trout. Meanwhile, Ben was playing some golden oldies on Hannah's guitar.

"What kind of food should we bring along to the rodeo tomorrow?" Nick inquired when they were all sitting around the campfire after dinner.

"Everything but alcohol," Josh said.

"Is that a taboo in your culture?" Ivy asked.

Josh nodded. "It is officially forbidden in Navajo Nation. On the rez, they call it *tó tsi'naa'iiáhí* – the water that drives the mind crazy. I stay away from it as much as possible," he said pointedly.

"You have bad experiences with alcohol?" Amber asked, picking up on his tone.

Josh hesitated. "I've seen a close relative slowly going to ruin because of the stuff," he finally said in a taut voice.

Hannah frowned. Who was Josh talking about? She knew all members of his immediate family, and they definitely weren't alcoholics.

Ben gave his friend an equally confused look. "Who are you talking about?"

The circle of friends around the fire fell silent, and in that silence, Josh shrugged noncommittally. "Never mind," he mumbled, a guarded expression on his face. "You don't know him."

Ben decided to drop the matter. He looked away and started to tell Nick about last year's rodeo in Naabi'aani, clearly trying to ignore Josh's strange remark.

When the heat of the fire became too much for her, Hannah leaned backwards on her elbows to cool off. Josh leaned backwards beside her and eyed her questioningly. "Tired?"

"A bit." She felt languid from staying close to the fire for so long, staring into his eyes from up close, the two of them breaking the circle around the flames.

"Too tired for star-gazing?" he continued.

"I'm never too tired for that."

Josh looked up. "We can't see anything from here."

Hannah paused. "No," she admitted.

"Come on," he whispered, climbing to his feet.

Hannah's heart started to thump in her chest. She scrambled up too, wincing slightly. The backs of her knees still stung like hell. Taking a few hesitant steps, she stumbled after Josh to the side of the cabin.

"You okay?" he asked.

After the bright firelight, her eyes had to get used to the dark of the summer night. Hannah could only make out the outline of Josh's head and shoulders.

"Yeah," she replied. "I just like walking like a chimp. It's so charming."

He chuckled and craned his neck to stare up at the sky. She followed his gaze.

"You know, when I was little I used to watch the skies and look for the place where the angels lived," she said softly. "I really thought God was somewhere among the stars."

"And now?"

She paused. "You mean, why I watch the skies now?"

"No. Where you think God is." For some reason, the question didn't sound weird or pompous, coming from him. He just sounded interested.

"Well – I think God is everywhere. But people don't open up to His presence on a daily basis. They close off."

Josh didn't say anything. He just slipped an arm around her shoulders and stood a bit closer.

"You think?" he asked. "Is that what you do, too? Close off?"

She shook her head. "No, I don't. But I guess most white people walk the earth as if it's hostile territory. They have this urge to control and subdue nature. So, they take God out of the equation, out of this world, far above it. And your people place God in everything. That's why the earth is their home. I think." She blew out a breath. End of philosophical rant. Had she lost him now?

"You're right. We deeply respect the earth, and we're a part of her." Josh turned his face toward her. "You see the differences between our cultures so clearly," he said softly. Somehow, he sounded wise beyond his years, and for a split second, it felt as if he was addressing her as her senior. In a flash, Hannah saw his face, older than she'd ever seen it in reality – the face from her dream last night. She couldn't get the image out of her head.

"Uhm, you said you'd point out some of the Navajo constellations to me," she said, when he stared up at the sky and remained silent.

Josh tilted his head to the Big Dipper. "Náhookos Bika'ii. The protective father-figure of our night sky." He made a quarter turn and indicated Cassiopeia. "And that's the mother of the stars, Náhookos Bi'áadii."

Hannah took it all in. It was a shame she couldn't tell Josh anything about the mythology behind the constellations she knew, even though she knew all the names by heart. There were no fathers or mothers in her firmament.

"You're close with your parents?" she suddenly blurted out, not really knowing where the question came from.

Josh hesitated for a second. "I guess."

"Doesn't sound like you really feel it," Hannah observed.

"I love my parents. I just don't talk to them a lot anymore."

"Well, how many seventeen-year-old guys do?"

"With us, they do."

"But you don't?" His sudden honesty and frankness opened up new avenues. She didn't want to pass up this chance to ask Josh some personal questions.

"No. I don't." The silence between them stretched out. Hannah held her breath. Even the world around them seemed to stop breathing for a moment. Everything was quiet.

"I just – clammed up," he whispered, barely audible.

Hannah wished she could see his face. His voice sounded so lonely and so melancholic that she instinctively put her hand on his shoulder. "You – you shouldn't," she stammered.

"I can't help it. I can't help myself."

"Can *I* help you, then?" Hannah asked quietly.

He put his hand on hers, pressing a soft kiss on the back of her hand as he lifted it from her shoulder. "I don't know," he said.

Hannah stared at him, even though she couldn't see his eyes in the dark. She wanted to do something, reach out, say kind words that would make him feel supported, but she could feel the wall between them almost like a physical object.

"Hey! Hannah!" Nick suddenly called out from the campfire. "Where are you? We're going to play Truth or Dare!"

She bellowed: "No, thanks. Ben knows me *way* too well for that. I'm not going to go there." Besides, who knew what would happen if she stayed here with Josh a little longer?

Josh snickered beside her. "On the other hand, *we* know Ben very well, too," he pointed out. "Let's go join them."

So nothing would happen. The moment was over. His sudden openness disappeared beneath the waves again, and she'd bet half a month's salary it wouldn't resurface any time soon. She was going to *kill* Nick for interrupting their conversation.

"Come on," Josh mumbled, letting his arm slide off her shoulders before lightly grabbing her hand as they walked back to the group.

They were holding *hands.* Hannah's heartbeat picked up, and she had a smile plastered on her face when she sat down near the fire. Okay, maybe she wasn't going to kill Nick after all. This was pretty perfect.

Seven

The next morning, Hannah awoke completely drenched in sweat. Echoes of voices screaming in a foreign language still resounded in her head. Slowly opening her eyes, she breathed deeply in and out. A feeling of dread had settled in the pit of her stomach, and it wouldn't go away.

She'd had another nightmare. Hannah couldn't remember much, but she did know that the old village had been the setting again. There'd been violent attacks by soldiers, but there'd also been people around her that she trusted – people who protected her. And the older version of Josh had been among them.

This time, the end of her dream had been different. She'd met Josh somewhere on a rock plateau near a precipice overlooking a canyon. He had spoken Diné Bizaad, the Navajo language. The strange thing was, she'd been able to understand him in her dream, but couldn't remember what he told her now that she was awake.

She did remember that she'd been upset by his words – she had run away from him because her heart told her she had to. The image still haunting her now was Josh's older face, full of pain and sadness, and the way he'd looked at her when she turned around to face him one last time.

Groaning, Hannah got out of bed and dragged herself to the kitchen. It was less stuffy than her bedroom, but it was still hot. She needed to freshen up. After popping two slices of bread into the toaster, she took a quick shower and got dressed in light summer clothes.

A soft wind caressed her face when Hannah stepped onto the porch. She looked to the left and saw Ben's car was gone. Chewing her toast, she walked back inside and got her wallet from the kitchen table, blinking in surprise when her eyes fell on the clock above the stove. It was almost twelve o'clock. No wonder Ben was gone – he'd probably given up on her crawling out of bed today.

Hannah closed the door behind her and strolled down to the tiny supermarket in St. Mary's Port to buy some canned goods that she and Ben could bring to the rez as a gift. It was tradition to bring the family organizing the rodeo something that could be used for cooking, like corn flour, mutton, dried beans or pumpkin.

Once inside Safeway, Hannah first made her way to the aisle with flour and baking products. This wasn't her lucky day – the Blue Bird flour was nowhere to be found. She couldn't get away with buying another brand. The fry bread just wouldn't taste the same.

A bit lost in thought, she picked up a bag of different flour from the top shelf when she suddenly heard two voices coming from the next shopping aisle. They sounded familiar.

Hannah strained her ears and stopped breathing. Her hands began to shake. She'd swear the people talking in the next aisle were the guys who'd harassed her on Thursday night. Their voices sounded just the same.

Slowly, she shuffled forward, cautiously sticking her head around the corner like a spy. There they were. Two men in plaid flannel shirts. They were about thirty years old and both were carrying a case of beer. Hannah shuffled into the aisle, listening intently to the two men. Okay, this was freaky. They sounded exactly like her bullies, but they were definitely not the same guys. With a frown, she passed the two men on her way to the pay desk. Was she beginning to imagine things?

When Hannah got to the queue, she almost tripped over a display full of Blue Bird flour sacks and a garish-colored sign screaming 'Buy 2 Get 1 Free!!' at her.

With a smile, she bent over to pick up two sacks, accidentally bumping into someone behind her when she stepped back.

"Hey, Hannah!" It was Amber. She looked down at the flour sacks. "Oh – Blue Bird flour. I was going to get that, too."

Hannah smiled. "No problem. Let's both get one. It's on sale anyway." She tossed one of the sacks into Amber's basket. Obviously, Amber had asked Emily what kind of food to take to the rez today. Yesterday, Emily and Amber had been chatting to each other all night and they'd even swapped phone numbers, because they had an instant click. More than just a click, actually – Hannah was sure she'd seen some sparks fly between them.

It was enough cause to make her a bit jealous, actually. At least Amber had managed to get Emily's phone number. Heck, she'd practically sat on Em's lap yesterday evening. Josh didn't even have his own land line, let alone a cell phone. Of course, *she* had to fall head over heels for a guy with Amish ideals. And on top of all that, she was having weird dreams about him.

"You okay?" Amber asked. "You're looking sort of stressed."

"Yeah, I'm all right," Hannah said, trying to forget

her dark thoughts. "I was just thinking of a dream I had last night."

"Oh? What about?" Amber put the two sacks of flour on the conveyor belt.

"It's kind of difficult to explain. It was like watching a few movie scenes, but not chronologically. Josh appeared in my dream, too, and somehow I really hurt him, but I don't know how or why."

"You dream about him a lot?" Amber asked. "Sorry for being curious. It's just that – I see…" Her voice trailed off.

"What?" Hannah urged her on.

Amber looked around uncomfortably. "Shall we go outside first?"

"Sure." Hannah quickly paid for the groceries. She was dying to know what Amber had to tell her.

On their way out they passed the two men with beer bottles. They were leaning against the wall on either side of the door, standing in the shade. Hannah glanced sideways, and a feeling of being observed by the two crept up on her as she and Amber moved away from the supermarket. Swallowing down the lump in her throat, she increased her pace. Why couldn't she shake the feeling that she knew those guys? It was ridiculous. Their voices sounded similar to those of her attackers, but that's where every similarity ended – they were twice as old, for crying out loud. She was starting to get paranoid. If she kept feeling this stalked, maybe she should go back to the police station and ask for victim service.

Quickly, they made their way to the square in front of the Grassroots café, sitting down on a bench in the shade. "So," Hannah turned to Amber. "What did you want to tell me?"

Amber shrugged. "I can see auras sometimes." She

furtively gauged her neighbor's reaction.

"Okay." Hannah smiled at her encouragingly.

Amber bit her lip. "When I see Josh's aura – and yours – well, they react to each other. That in itself isn't strange. I mean, they're energy fields, but..." She looked at her hands sitting in her lap. "I have never seen two auras so *attuned* to each other. Okay, I saw it once with an elderly couple from Pensacola, in a local elderly home during my summer job. They were both eighty years old, they'd been married for sixty years, and they were still in love with each other. It was wonderful to look at. So pure and intense."

Hannah felt her heart speed up. "Well, I've known him for a long time. He's always been Ben's best friend. We sort of grew up together."

Amber shook her head. "No, that's not it. Your souls look *entwined*."

Hannah stared at her dumbstruck, making Amber shift uneasily. "Sorry. I probably sound like a lunatic."

"No. No, you don't. There's definitely a connection between us, but I don't understand why it's so strong all of a sudden. Or why it turned into something else." She blushed.

"Did you tell Ben about your dreams?"

"Not really. I did tell him how I feel about Josh. But he doesn't know I've been having weird dreams about Josh, too."

"What about that evening at the lake when you were harassed? Doesn't that still give you nightmares?"

"Yeah, that doesn't help either. I still have the feeling…" Hannah paused.

"What?" Amber prompted her.

"Okay. This is going to sound bizarre, but I have the feeling I'm being watched. That somebody is after me." Hannah cleared her throat nervously. "I know it sounds like textbook paranoia, but I can't help it."

"Well, you don't strike me as a nutjob, so maybe something is going on for real. Just keep your friends close by. We'll protect you if someone's really after you."

Suddenly, Hannah had an idea. "Could you do something for me?" She got up and took a few steps up the road. "I want to go back to Safeway for a minute."

The two girls walked back to the supermarket, carrying the sacks of flour in their arms. Hannah looked around and spotted the men she'd overheard talking in the store. They were still near the supermarket, hanging around in the shade by the side of the road. A third man about the same age had joined them. Hannah observed the men, going cold all over when the newcomer abruptly whipped around and fixed her with his stare. The other two turned their heads at exactly the same moment. Three pairs of eyes observed her and Amber. Time slowed down. The sun dimmed as all sounds around her were muffled. Hannah's heart pounded frantically.

With difficulty, she tore her eyes away from the men, making the world turn again. "Amber," she hissed. "Can you look at those guys' auras?"

"I'll try," Amber replied, without asking why. She peered intently at the trio across the street. Hannah didn't follow her gaze. The way the three men had just eyed her gave her the absolute chills. They were probably wondering why Amber was looking at them so intently, but right now, she couldn't care less. She simply *had* to know if something was off about them, and maybe her neighbor could see if there was.

Amber grabbed her arm. "They're walking away," she inadvertently whispered.

Hannah watched the three men moving away from

the supermarket, their movements unnaturally synchronous. They turned the corner without looking back. Once they'd disappeared from view, she let out a huge sigh of relief.

"Well?" she asked tensely.

Amber's eyebrows knitted together. "Nothing," she replied, looking a bit stupefied.

Hannah raised her eyebrows. "What do you mean?"

"I couldn't see an aura around any of them."

Hannah blinked. "So…"

"So, I may have suddenly lost my abilities, but I don't think so. I don't always see a full-fledged aura with colors and shapes, but I always see *something*. A sort of glow, a life-force, a certain charisma."

"But not with them?" Hannah still looked at Amber, nonplussed.

"No." Amber hesitated and turned pale. "I have this feeling…"

"Yes?"

"It felt like I was looking at people who weren't actually here. As if they were mirror images. Or people who are dead. They don't have auras either."

Hannah gulped. Her instinct hadn't betrayed her. There *really* was something off about those men. But what on earth was she supposed to do with this information? She'd have a hard time explaining to the police she was being stalked by guys who weren't really there.

She turned to Amber. "Can you please keep this to yourself? I don't think people would understand." She could vividly imagine Ben's face if she told him a demented story like this.

"Actually, I don't really understand it myself," Amber replied with a vacant stare. She chewed her lip. "But if anyone did, it'd be Emily. She talks a lot about mystical experiences with her patients. You could ask her what she thinks this is."

"You've really been chatting about tons of stuff with Em, huh?" Hannah suddenly said with a wink.

"Yeah." Amber turned red. "I had a good time last night."

"So, just chatting, huh?"

Amber blushed even more. "Uhm, yeah. So far."

She'd been right about the sparks flying, then. Good for Em!

"What about you and Josh, then?" Amber inquired.

"Oh." Hannah couldn't help smiling. "We just chatted. And watched the stars."

"So far," Amber added playfully.

"Yeah." Hannah grinned. "So far."

When she got back to the cabin, Ben was just finishing up the batch of pasta he'd promised to cook for their rodeo-day-out.

"Look, I got us tickets for Movies in the Park next week," he proudly announced, pointing at an envelope lying on the table. "Everybody's tagging along."

"Cool." Hannah let out a sigh as she sat down at the table to have a look. Ben's lighthearted chatter about the movies they were going to screen almost made it possible to forget about the bizarre encounter she'd had this morning. Sitting there, with the bright sunlight streaming in through the windows, it suddenly seemed ridiculous she'd felt threatened and freaked out by a bunch of lumberjack guys carrying beer cases, auras or no auras. And yet, she couldn't get it out of her head. Those guys – they'd given her this look of recognition. *That's* why she'd felt so uncomfortable under their gaze. Even though it was impossible, these men knew her somehow. Was she going nuts?

"You want to tag along to the beach?" Ben interrupted her train of thoughts. "I'm going for a quick swim before Nick shows up here for the rodeo."

"No, I just want to stay in," she said listlessly. "Play a bit of guitar."

"Sure thing." He gave her a hesitant smile. "You okay?"

"Yeah. I just…" Should she tell Ben about those weird guys in the village square? It would just freak him out. "I didn't sleep too well."

"Okay." He shrugged. "Is that why you slept in?"

"Yeah." It was as good an explanation as any.

"By the way, me and Josh are going on a hike to Rainbow Bridge after the weekend. Nick is tagging along. He's going to make sure he keeps Wednesday, Thursday and Friday free in his schedule so he can come with us to the rez."

"That… that long?" Her heart sank. That meant she'd all by herself in the cabin for days.

Ben cocked his head and put a hand on her shoulder. "Hey, no worries. I bet Emily can stay with you for a few days if you still feel uneasy. You know, after your run-in with those creeps."

Hannah looked up at Ben, touched by the fact that he knew something was bothering her. He just didn't know the whole story.

"Yeah, I might do that." This whole unreasonable anxiety thing was utterly frustrating. Normally speaking, she loved some alone time. Stupid aura-less woodchoppers.

Once Ben had left the cabin with a beach bag slung over his shoulder, Hannah went into Ben's bedroom to get his laptop. She wasn't planning on playing the guitar at all. Ben probably wouldn't approve of her using his horribly expensive roaming internet USB modem – or understand why she wanted to do a Google search for 'people without auras' – so she'd decided to not even ask.

She opened the laptop and waited for Windows to start up and the internet to connect. Then, she Googled the topic and browsed through the meager list of search results. No real hits except a website maintained by an aura reader who claimed that people without an electromagnetic field had crossed over to the other side – or were about to pass away.

Hannah shivered. Maybe Amber had made a mistake after all. Perhaps she hadn't been receptive to the men's auras. There was simply no other explanation. Unless they really *were* dead.

After putting Ben's laptop back on his night table, Hannah settled herself against the porch railing and tried to concentrate on her book. When Nick parked his Jeep next to the cabin at three o'clock on the dot, she'd managed to forget about the events of this morning, if only for the time being.

Nick walked up the porch steps. "Hey Han, look at what I brought!" He held up a notebook. "So I can scribble down some notes this afternoon."

"Whoa, someone's going to be a busy-bee."

"Yeah, or a brainiac, more like." After putting the notebook down on the table, Nick pulled two packs of ground coffee from his bag. "And I bought this. Does coffee make a good gift?"

Hannah nodded. As she poured Nick a glass of soda, he rambled on. "You know, it's really awesome I met you in Page. Without you and your friends, I'd be stuck at a dead end with this whole dissertation thing. But now I'm feeling so inspired. Josh told me so many things about Diné history and traditions. It's downright freaky he knows that much. I mean, does he ever sleep?" He opened his notebook. "I love the Diné way of life. That principle of always being in balance with the forces of nature and supernatural powers? It's fantastic."

Hannah smiled. "Yeah, they call it *hózhó*. It means beauty, harmony and balance all in one."

Suddenly, Nick looked past her at the road. "Look, there's a dog standing there." He frowned. "Actually, it looks more like a wolf or something."

Hannah turned around and blinked in surprise. Was that a coyote standing by the side of the road? It couldn't be. Of course, they were native to Arizona, but they rarely ventured out to populated areas. The animal stood among the shrubs across the road – immobile, menacing, fixing her with a predatory stare.

Her heart skipped a beat when two other coyote-like dogs emerged from the bushes and lined up on either side of the first one. The animals remained still, keeping the same posture while watching her. Six yellow-brown eyes observed her with unsettling intensity.

Uncertainly, Hannah took a step back, the hairs on her neck prickling. Three guys. Three men. And now, three dogs. What the *hell* was going on? If Nick hadn't been here, she'd have thought she was imagining things, but the animals really were there, across the road, pinning her with their stares.

"Hannah? You okay?" Nick gave her a worried look, shaking her by the shoulder. Only now, she realized there must be sheer panic in her wide-open eyes. "Are you afraid of dogs?"

She blinked rapidly. "No," she managed to choke out. "I just…"

Before she could say anything else, the nearby grumble of a car engine grew into a roar. A large pick-up truck appeared around the corner, trundling past the cabin in clouds of dust. When Hannah looked at the bushes on the other side of the road again, the three coyotes had vanished.

She shook her head. "I just don't like coyotes very much," she finished feebly.

"Well, they're gone now. Shall I get you a drink?"

Hannah nodded listlessly, following Nick inside to get some water. She rubbed her forehead and breathed deeply in and out. Okay, so it was sort of weird that she'd seen three coyotes near the cabin, but she shouldn't link up events that had nothing to do with each other. She had to stop riling herself up like this.

When Ben and the neighbors all returned from the beach, she'd managed to calm down again. Eager to make a good impression on the rez, Hannah went to her bedroom and changed into a new pair of jeans and a black halter top. Rummaging around in her beauty case to find a nice piece of jewelry, she pulled out a necklace with turquoise beads. She remembered making it by hand, together with Josh, sitting in his aunt's hoghan on a rainy day when he'd been nine years old. She'd always kept the necklace because she loved the color so much. Thinking back to that afternoon, she wondered if Josh still remembered they'd made this necklace together.

When she stepped outside, Amber was already in the back seat of Nick's jeep with her sack of flour and a six-pack of soda cans in her lap.

"Hey." Hannah plunked down next to Amber. "How was the beach?"

"Fantastic. How are you? Were you able to unwind a bit?"

"Yeah, sure." She didn't feel like mentioning the coyote-dogs-whatever that had shown up at the log cabin.

Ben and Ivy got in, Nick started the Jeep and it didn't take them long to get to Lakeshore Drive, driving in the direction of Page. "Where to next?" Nick inquired once they'd passed the Page welcome sign.

"Keep going south." Ben pointed at a few road signs. "If you follow Navajo Route 20 you'll end up in Naabi'aani."

They passed the intersection at Big Lake Trading Post were Nick stopped to get some gas. Everyone in the Jeep was in good spirits. Nick switched on the radio and tuned in to a Native American-sounding channel with panpipe music, so Hannah thought up a song to teach the newcomers some important Navajo words. By the time the first hoghans of Naabi'aani came into view, Nick and the neighbor girls knew that *ahe'hee* meant 'thank you', *ya'at'eeh* was 'welcome' and *ayor anosh'ni* 'I love you'.

"Park it here." Hannah indicated a free spot at the side of the road. They'd walk the last bit to Emily's parents' house because the road was blocked by a multitude of cars and RVs further up ahead.

Once everyone had gotten out, Hannah and Ben led the way toward the Begay family hoghan, elbowing their way through the crowd on the village square.

"What's that smell?" Nick sniffed, looking around. "Makes me hungry."

"Traditional frybread," Hannah replied. "And it's a traditional calorie bomb, too."

Nick grinned. "No problem. I have a lightning-speed metabolism. I never gain weight."

"I hate you," Hannah sing-songed.

"Honey, I love you too. Or should I say: *ayor anosh'ni*?"

Hannah let Ben, Nick and the girls go ahead of her as the crowd closed in around them. She trailed behind Nick, making her way through the mass of people, passing a family with three small children clinging to their mother's bright red skirt, begging their father for candy. Hannah gave them a friendly smile when she passed by. The kids on the reservation always reminded her of cheerful, tiny Inuit – the same slanty eyes, the same tanned skin and the same thick, black hair. Sometimes their entire appearance changed when they got older, Josh being a case in point. Come to think of it, where could he be? Hannah looked around and tried to spot him among the people in the crowd.

Her heart started to hammer in her chest when she saw him on the other side of the field used to host the dance festivities.

He wasn't alone. He was standing next to a drop-dead gorgeous woman with long, black hair – a broad smile on his lips and his hand tightly holding hers.

Eight

Ouch.

She never knew she could be this jealous. Hannah desperately tried to calm herself. Josh was allowed to stand hand in hand with a girl. It didn't have to mean anything. Right?

In the meantime, Josh had spotted her too. He started to cross the makeshift dance floor, still holding the girl's hand. Hannah's jaw clenched as she tried to ignore the sinking feeling in the pit of her stomach.

Josh stopped in front of her and looked down with a broad smile. "Welcome! *Ya'at'eeh*. You just got here?"

"Yeah." She made a halfhearted attempt at smiling back. "We were on our way to Emily."

He nodded, his eyes scanning her face curiously. "You all right? You look a bit pale."

Oh, she *couldn't* be better. Suffering from nightmares, chased by aura-less lumberjacks, and stalked by coyotes. And meanwhile, he'd managed to hook up with Miss Navajo Nation.

"Of course I'm all right," she snapped irritably. "Why wouldn't I be?"

Josh almost imperceptibly raised an eyebrow. "Never mind. By the way, have you met my cousin yet?"

His cousin? She blinked owlishly. "No, uhm, I don't think so."

"This is Linibah." Josh pointed at the pretty girl next to him. "She's visiting from Chinle with her husband and kids."

Hannah smiled widely, hoping the relief wasn't too apparent on her face. "Oh! it's very nice to meet you." She shook hands with Josh's cousin. "I'm Hannah."

Ben appeared next to her. "Are you coming or what?" he asked. "Or do you want to drag that sack of flour around all day long?"

Both guys snickered, and Hannah sheepishly joined in.

Josh smiled at her. "Blue Bird flour? That's very thoughtful of you." His eyes drifted to the turquoise necklace she was wearing, and his smile intensified. He didn't say anything about it, just gave her a happily surprised look. "So, let's go and say hi to Hosteen's family. Emily's already inside."

He led the way toward an octagonal hoghan. When their group entered, the father, mother and two sons of the Hosteen household stood up from the buck skin on the floor they'd been sitting on.

Hannah blinked her eyes when they suddenly bowed in reverence for Josh, who emerged from behind Hannah and started to speak to his clansmen. Everyone else in their group fell silent.

Now Hannah finally understood what Emily had tried to explain to her about the people of Naabi'aani – Josh's tribesmen were in inexplicable awe of the seventeen-year-old guy she'd known all her life. He was the focus of everyone's attention, and it felt natural. She could see the respect and admiration in their eyes when he talked to them in Diné Bizaad, their own language.

When Josh was done speaking, Ben came forward

with his container of pasta. Hannah shuffled after him to shake hands with the Hosteen family.

One by one, the presents were handed over. Afterwards Josh led them out of the hoghan to sit down in the grass on the left side of the house. People were sitting around cross-legged, chatting and eating the food that the Hosteens had prepared for the occasion.

"Don't you want anything to eat?" Hannah asked Josh, when he plonked down next to her only holding a can of Coke.

"No, I'm doing the opening ceremony for the rodeo. I'd rather do that on an empty stomach."

"Oh? What kind of performance?"

"Singing. And hand drumming."

"So you're going to sing a traditional song?"

Josh nodded. "I'm one of the two *hataalii* of Naabi'aani. Sani is the oldest medicine man of the village, and I am the youngest."

Hannah gaped at him. Emily had mentioned Josh being close to Sani, but she'd left out that he was a medicine man himself. "Where on earth do you get the time to become so good at everything you do?"

He looked back at her. "Well, time..." he started out, his voice trailing off. "Let's just say I'm a quick study."

A woman walking around with bowls of corn porridge on a tray tapped his shoulder. Josh declined, but nudged Hannah. "*Sha'di*? You want another bowl?"

Hannah gulped down a sudden lump, looking at Josh tongue-tied. Okay, that was clear. Crystal. Not *shilah* to address her as a female friend. He'd just called her *sha'di*, like before. His big sister. So nothing had changed after all. She swallowed back sudden tears.

Still in a daze, Hannah turned around when she heard Josh's mother call out to them from a distance. She was walking toward them, addressing her son. "*Shiyáázh?*"

Josh turned around and smiled up at her. "Hey, *shimá*. Is it time already?"

"Yes, they expect you in the tent."

"Good luck," Hannah mumbled as he got up and disappeared in the crowd to prepare for his ceremony. It was actually a relief he was gone. That way, she was able to catch her breath and try to convince herself it was no big deal that he didn't like her like that.

Nick sat down next to her. "Man, I *love* this place! The people here are so different than what I'm used to. They're so friendly and unassuming." He put away his notebook and pulled a camera from his bag. "I'm planning on filming Josh's performance. You think he'll mind?"

"No, he won't," she replied flatly.

Absently, Hannah looked around, suddenly spotting a tall, lanky Navajo guy waving at her. He started walking toward the group of visitors from St. Mary's Port. Confused, she poked Emily.

"You know who that is?" she hissed.

Emily looked up and followed her gaze. "That's Yazzie! Don't you recognize him?"

Hannah batted her eyelids in astonishment. Yazzie had always been a short and chubby guy before. Apparently, he'd finally had a growth spurt – she wouldn't have recognized Josh's cousin, who would take them to Rainbow Bridge on his boat tomorrow, if Emily hadn't clued her in. She scrambled to her feet. "Hey, Yaz!" she waved.

When Yazzie stood face to face with Hannah, he was at least four inches taller than her. "Hi, *biligaana*!" He embraced her in a warm hug. "You ready for the show?" He was wearing skinny dark-green jeans and a black t-shirt saying 'Rez Litter'.

Hannah couldn't help giggling. Yazzie had always

addressed her and Ben that way – *biligaana* meant 'paleface' in his own language.

Yazzie tilted his head to the field surrounded by a large crowd of spectators. "I saved some standing-room for you guys. Follow me!"

He elbowed his way through the multitude, everybody following him in single file. Just before they reached the fence bordering the rodeo ground, they hit an open spot, like Yazzie had promised them. Hannah looked aside and unexpectedly saw Josh's father standing there. She'd have thought he was with his son in the tent, helping him prepare. Or maybe not. That was probably Sani's job.

"*Ya'at'eeh.* Hello everybody," he said, shaking hands with all of them. He kissed Hannah on the cheek. "It's been a while. Good to see you again." He smiled widely, and the crow's feet around his eyes suddenly reminded her of Josh's older face in her dream.

A loud drumstroke interrupted their conversation. Everyone turned toward the field to watch the ceremony.

Josh entered the rodeo grounds, wearing an amazing Diné outfit. His upper body was clad in a long-sleeved velvet blouse. His hair was wrapped up in a headband and tied into an eight-shaped bun, and he was wearing pants in a warm, red-brown color. Dangling from a chain around his neck was a stunning round pendant with inlaid turquoise stones. He was carrying a large drum in one hand, and a long, thin wooden beater in the other.

The chatter died down, the crowd becoming silent. In that silence, Josh started to drum softly but intensely, singing at the same time. His voice rose above the beat of the drum. Hannah couldn't help but marvel at him as he performed the traditional song with such ease that it seemed he'd been a *hataalii* for years. His voice sounded different from when he'd sung his own song.

For a split second, it felt like a completely different person was standing there on the ceremonial field – as if Josh were someone else.

Another, older man entered the field to do a hoop dance, accompanied by Josh's singing. When the song was over and Josh and the hoop dancer trotted off the field, there was no applause, just a respectful silence. Slowly, the crowd started to murmur again, some of them dispersing to the bleachers lined up in a semi-circle around the rodeo grounds.

Nick turned off his camera and gave the thumbs-up to Hannah. "Got it! Available on DVD soon."

"What's going to happen now?" Hannah wanted to know, when a set of speakers on the other side of the field started to emit upbeat music.

"It's time for the *naa'ahóóhai*," Yazzie replied.

She raised an eyebrow.

"The rodeo," he translated enthusiastically, tilting his head at the field. "Oh, and there's dancing on the lawn across the road."

"That sounds like a safer option," Ivy remarked drily.

Yazzie grinned. "Okay. Dancing it is then."

As they all made their way to the other side of the road, Josh joined them out of nowhere, falling into step next to Hannah.

"Hey there," she said with a slight smile. "That was one hell of a performance."

"Thanks." He beamed at her and joined her at the side of the make-shift dance floor.

As the speakers lined up around the field started blaring out country music, Yaz grabbed Ivy's hand. "Come on, let's hit the dance floor!"

"Sure," Ivy laughed.

Emily shot a glance at Amber. Apparently deciding it

was time to pluck up some courage, she grabbed Amber's hand and smiled at her. Amber's cheeks filled with color. Without saying a word, she followed Emily into the crowd.

Nick looked around uncertainly. "So Josh, how about me asking a Navajo girl to dance? Is that even allowed?"

Josh snickered. "Yeah, sure. We don't *completely* hate palefaces, you know."

"That sounds promising," Ben commented with a grin.

"If you ask a girl to dance and she gives you some coins, she's declining," Josh explained. "If she accepts, it is custom to give her a few coins after the dance."

This prompted both Nick and Ben to take off and try their luck.

"I don't even have coins on me," Hannah complained, fumbling through her pockets.

Josh had a mischievous glint in his eyes. "Sounds like you're going to be busy."

Hannah grinned. "Not necessarily. I can't refuse the first guy asking me, but if he pays up enough for my impressive dancing skills, I can stave off suitors with those coins for the rest of the evening."

"You want to dance?" Josh suddenly said, a smile playing on his lips. He extended his hand to her, a laugh in his voice but his eyes serious.

Oh. She totally hadn't seen that coming. Hannah blushed, putting her hand in his. "Yes, of course," she stammered.

At that exact moment, Josh's dad appeared out of nowhere. "Hey, *shiye*." He put an arm around his son's shoulders. "I'm glad I found you. They need you."

"What for?"

His dad started to explain something to him in Diné Bizaad. Josh let go of her hand with a sorry expression on his face.

"I have to assist Sani with something that can't wait. I'll see you for dinner at my parents' place, okay?" he said.

"Oh. Okay," she replied flatly.

"Sorry," Josh added, and then he was gone, following his father to wherever Sani was hanging out. Hannah stared blindly at the field. Emily and Amber were dancing together like there was no tomorrow, and for just a moment, she felt more lonely than ever.

🙢🙢🙢

When the sun had almost set, Hannah walked with her friends to the street where Josh's family had their large, octagonal hoghan. They'd all been invited to dinner.

While the Navajo family was busy cooking on outdoor grills, Hannah's eyes wandered to the smaller, hexagonal hoghan to the right of the main building. Of course, it could only belong to one person. She couldn't contain her curiosity, so she left her friends sitting outside the sweatlodge and made her way to Josh's private hoghan.

Gingerly, she stepped inside. Her gaze quietly touched the walls, the two burning candles on the floor giving off a soft light, illuminating the medicine wheel on the far wall. In the middle of the house, there was the typical fireplace – the center of every hoghan. To her right, some cupboards lined the walls. Four bookshelves had been attached to the wall opposite the entrance. And in the far right corner, a mattress was on the floor covered with a hand-woven Navajo blanket. Next to it was an armchair that Josh apparently used as a makeshift guitar stand and clothes rack. An oval-shaped mirror was fixed to the wall above the chair.

On a peg above the bed, Hannah discovered the most beautiful dreamcatcher she had ever seen. It contained blood-red thread, turquoise beads, feathers and silver-colored yarn. Her breath caught in her throat as she bent over and took a closer look at the intricate piece of art. The power contained within this dreamcatcher was almost palpable. Had Josh made it himself? It had to be his. She could somehow feel it.

Hannah took a step backward and started to check out the content of the bookshelves. There were textbooks and boxes full of traditional jewelry, but also an impressive collection of novels and scientific journals. She picked up a book lying a bit apart from the others with the spine cracked open somewhere in the middle.

"*Edward T. Hall*," she mumbled softly, reading the title on the cover. "*An Autobiography.*"

"He lived and worked in Navajo Nation," Josh's voice suddenly sounded from the doorway. Hannah almost jumped out of her skin, whipping around and putting the book back like a child caught red-handed. Josh sauntered inside, smiling at her. "You can borrowing it if you want."

"But – you're reading it. Right?" Hannah objected. Crap. She had no idea how to save face. She'd just barged into his home without permission and she'd been going through his stuff.

"I've read it before." Josh shrugged and picked up the dog-eared book. He was silent for a moment. "I actually met the author."

"Oh, really? Where?"

"At one of his lectures. He was a speaker at a conference in Tuba City a few years ago. I talked to him after his lecture to discuss his work with him."

Hannah blinked and made a quick calculation. "So – how old were you then?"

Josh bit his lip, a guarded look in his eyes. The look she'd seen too many times already. "Fifteen," he mumbled.

"Wow." She eyed him incredulously. "Well, I'm impressed. I wish *my* fifteen-year-old students were interested in going to historical lectures."

"You can always try and inspire them." Josh smiled faintly. "Take them to a lecture some time."

"I doubt Edward Hall will come and speak in my neighborhood any time soon."

"No, he won't. He passed away this year."

For a split second, Hannah could swear tears were welling up in his eyes.

"Oh. Did you know him personally?" she asked, confused by his strong reaction.

She could see how Josh was grappling with finding an answer. "No," he finally said, but somehow, it didn't sound like it was the truth. Why would he lie about something trivial like this, though?

Josh put the book back and tilted his head to the dreamcatcher. "So what do you think?" he asked, quickly changing the subject.

"Amazing. I've never seen such a pretty dreamcatcher."

He smiled. "Maybe we can make one for you next week. I'll make sure I bring some stuff along."

Hannah slowly nodded. Admittedly, the intense dreams she had were freaking her out, but there was clearly something they were trying to tell her. If the dreamcatcher did what the legend said and proved to be effective, she'd never have nightmares again, but she also wouldn't discover new things.

"By the way, I'm sorry I broke into your hoghan. I didn't mean to snoop around." Of course, that was *exactly* what she'd meant to do, but she still felt the need to apologize.

Josh took her hands in his. "Don't be silly. You may always enter my home, *sha'di*." Hannah felt his palms warm against her fingers and tried to dismiss the cold feeling spreading through her heart when she heard him use the sister word again. He couldn't help seeing her like that. She had to get her act together.

"I like your hair like that," she said softly, looking at the bun. "I haven't seen you wearing it like this very often." Well, except in a dream.

"It's a *tsiyeel*, an eight-shaped hairbun for traditional occasions. Actually, I'm going to get rid of it now. It's sort of tight." He raised one hand to untie his headband, trying to untangle the bun with the other.

"Can you..." he started, and Hannah nodded shyly. She moved behind him and untied the headband for him. After that, she combed his thick, black hair with her fingers. It smelled a bit sweet. "You put anything in it?" she asked.

He reached for a pot of coconut cream on one of the shelves and handed it over to her. Hannah rubbed some of the grease onto her hands and applied it to Josh's long hair. Now and then, her palms touched the skin of his scalp, his shoulders and neck, and she felt her fingers tingle from that skin contact. Silently, she moved a little bit closer to run her fingers through the hair falling on either side of his face, wanting to brush it over his shoulders, when her one hand accidentally caressed his cheek.

She bit her lip and felt the blood rush to her face. Fortunately, Josh was facing away from her, so he couldn't see the expression on her face.

Then her gaze drifted across his shoulder to the mirror above the chair. Her own blushing face was staring back at her, and so was Josh.

Her heart skipped a beat when he turned around and looked down at her.

God, he was standing so close. If only she could pull him even closer and kiss him. Or make a casual or funny remark to get rid of the sickening tension in the air. Unfortunately, she couldn't do funny right now. It wasn't funny. It was painful, it was entirely her own fault, and Josh was no doubt wondering why she was gaping at him like this. Hannah looked down at the floor, completely flustered.

As if her guardian angel had decided to butt in and save her, someone whistled outside at that moment. After a few seconds, Yazzie stuck his head round the door. "Dinner's ready. Are you two coming?"

Josh faintly smiled at Hannah. "Well, you heard the man. Let's go, *sha'di*."

Hannah winced. Thank God she hadn't just made the blatant mistake of kissing someone who thought of her as an older sister and nothing more.

"Yeah, let's," she replied, slogging defeatedly out of the hoghan and following Josh and Yazzie to sit down for dinner.

ক্ক্ক্

It was late in the evening when the gang finally made their way back to St. Mary's Port. Hannah sat silently in the back of Nick's Jeep, contemplating the night sky stretching out above the mesas, the dark desert landscape gliding past her. She was happy the night was over. She was dead beat.

When Nick dropped her, Ben, and the neighbor girls off at the log cabins, Amber followed her. "Hey, wait up a second," she called out, her voice urgent.

Hannah stopped in her tracks, waiting for Amber to

continue.

"I asked Emily what she thought of aura-less people," Amber whispered. "I didn't tell her why I was interested, but she mentioned *chindi* – witches. According to Navajo religion, they aren't strictly human anymore, so that would explain the lack of aura."

Hannah stared at her neighbor, a shiver running down her spine. "Witches?" she whispered back. The day on the rez had calmed her down somewhat, but now her uneasy feeling about the three men in Safeway came back with double intensity. "Did she mention what to do about them?"

"No, she didn't. I didn't ask too many questions, though. Maybe you'd like to grill her on the subject yourself when you feel ready."

Hannah didn't respond. Quite frankly, she didn't feel ready for anything except lying down and sleeping a dreamless sleep for at least twenty-four hours. "Thanks, Amber. We'll discuss it later. I need some eye-shut first."

Hannah went inside, flinging herself down on the bed. She didn't even bother to take off her clothes. She longed for peace and quiet, harmony and balance, *hózhó*.

Unfortunately, her subconscious didn't take that wish into account. That night, once again, she dreamed about Josh trying to save her from the clutches of Mexican soldiers. Once more, she left him at the precipice overlooking the canyon, his hair flying in the wind and tears streaming down his face.

The only thing different this time were the three intimidating shadows waiting for her at the foot of the hill, staring at her with hollow, dead eyes as she ran away.

Nine

"Ben?"

Hannah peeked into the kitchen. No sign of her brother. But she could have sworn she'd heard a voice calling out her name. What had woken her up so suddenly?

Groggily, she stumbled back to bed, trying to rub the sleep from her eyes. She downed the entire glass of water standing on her bedside table. Maybe she'd been dreaming again. But what about?

For a minute, she couldn't recall a single thing, but as she got up and went over to her closet to get some clothes, it came back to her. The precipice. The sinister apparitions at the foot of the hill.

What in the world was going on with her? All the elements of her dream obviously had to do with things keeping her mind occupied in real life, but that didn't explain why her mind would make up such a bizarre storyline to cope with them. And why it was always the *same* storyline.

With a frustrated sigh, she slammed the closet door shut and walked back to her bed with a green tank top and a denim skirt in her hands. From the nightstand, she picked up the turquoise necklace she'd been wearing yesterday and sullenly put it back in her jewelry box. The necklace she'd worn yesterday. The necklace she'd made together with Josh, her *little brother*. Who happened to be her lover in her nightmares. Why was her life so terribly unfair?

Maybe a shower would cheer her up. She made her way to the bathroom and took a long, hot shower. After all, Ben was still asleep, so she could take her time.

After getting dressed, Hannah took a mug of coffee outside, walking down the steps to find a spot on the grass to enjoy the morning sun. She found herself right where she'd been star-gazing with Josh two days ago. It was getting warmer already, and the world was waking up. Birds twittered in the trees next to their cabin.

Hannah's eyes drifted across the garden and caught on something lying at the edge of the lawn. Something turquoise, partially covered by blades of grass. Curious, she scrambled up to take a closer look.

Her jaw dropped when she saw what it was. Her turquoise necklace. Hannah bent over to pick it up. Her body went cold with anxiety. But that was impossible – she knew for sure she'd put it back in the box in her room before she went out. Could someone have been in her room, going through her stuff, while she was taking a shower?

Her fist closed tightly around the necklace, the beads pressing into her palm. And then, her eye fell on something else – pawprints. In the sand bordering the lawn, there were clear animal footprints. It looked like a dog had walked around their cabin – or a coyote.

Hannah inhaled sharply before breaking down into tears. Sobbing desperately, she sagged down on the ground, tears running down her face. Seriously, what was *happening* to her? The weird dreams, the three guys harassing her, coming back to her in different forms – and now this.

"Han! What's wrong?" She looked up to see her brother running down the porch steps. He kneeled next to her and hugged her in a warm embrace

"Ben, I'm going nuts," she said desolately. There – now at least she'd said what *she* thought. That would take the edge off this conversation.

"You look frazzled. I don't know what's wrong, but you can tell me. Come on, spill."

"It's difficult to explain where it all started." Hannah thought back to the moment she'd been sitting in the car, surrounded by the drunks circling her Datsun like a pack of wolves. "Probably when those guys harassed me."

Her brother sighed. "Yeah, I suspected that was going to be a problem at some point."

"I also have dreams," she quickly went on, before she'd lose her courage.

"About those assholes?"

"No. About Josh." Hannah felt the heat creeping up in her face.

"Well, that's not so strange, right?" Ben smiled.

"Yes, it is. Hear me out. In my dreams, I live in this Navajo village, in the past, and Josh is there too. It feels like he's my lover in the dream. And every night, he tries to save me from Mexican soldiers attacking our village, and at the end of the dream, I break up with him on the edge of some canyon."

"And the dreams started after you were harassed?"

Hannah nodded. "Yeah. Straight after that."

"Maybe you just feel the need to be protected by Josh," Ben philosophized. "And you're dreaming about the past because you've heard him talk about Navajo history a lot lately."

"Hmm. You could be right." Hannah exhaled. Ben's

explanation was a better alternative than her own supernatural hocus-pocus.

"I think you should drop by the police station tomorrow and ask for victim services, though," Ben continued. "Maybe they don't think your case is serious enough, but it won't hurt to try."

She put her head on his shoulder. "Thank you."

As she hugged he brother, the beads of the necklace turned sweaty in her palm. Stubbornly, Hannah silenced the voice niggling at her mind that something didn't add up. She'd probably put the necklace in her skirt pocket instead of in the box, and then it must have fallen out. There was simply no other explanation.

"What time will Josh be here for our boat trip to Rainbow Bridge?" she asked, as Ben and she scrambled to their feet.

"He won't. He just called to tell me that he's expecting you guys at Wahweap Harbor at noon. That's where Yazzie keeps his boat."

"Okay, fine. I'll wait until Amber and Ivy wake up. I haven't seen any life signs at the Greenes' yet."

Ben grinned. "If they're still not up at eleven, we'll visit them, banging drums and shaking rattles."

Laughing, they walked back to the porch. Ben fixed some more coffee for the two of them. He sat down with a pile of textbooks, starting up his laptop to show Hannah the pictures Katie had sent him from Barcelona. Looking at Ben's girlfriend's photos allowed her to take her mind off things, at least for the moment.

Tomorrow, she'd drop by the police station. Ben was right – she could use all the help she could get.

ಹಿಹಿಹಿ

At ten to twelve, Hannah drove off with Ivy and Amber

in the back seat of her Datsun. Nick and Ben weren't tagging along today – they'd see Rainbow Bridge during their hike next week. The car raced down Lake Powell Drive, and it didn't take long before Wahweap Harbor appeared in the distance. Hannah parked her car alongside the road leading down to the small harbor. The girls walked down the asphalt path, meandering past jagged rocks, ending at the jetty where Yazzie's boat was anchored. It was twelve o'clock sharp.

"Wow, you girls are right on time!" Josh appeared on deck as they approached the boat. He was wearing old jeans with the legs cut off, worn flip-flops, and his hair was tied into a ponytail. Of course, in this heat, he wasn't wearing a shirt. Which was no reason to ogle his chest, Hannah reprimanded herself. So he was walking around shirtless. So what? He'd been walking around shirtless in summer his entire life. Nothing had changed, except her perception of him.

"H-hey," she said nervously, despite telling herself off. "How are you?"

Josh gave her such a heart-wrenchingly sunny smile that Hannah felt her heart skip a beat. Who exactly was she trying to fool with her 'he-is-just-your-brother' mantra?

"I'm fine!" He walked down the gangway to help Amber and Ivy climb on board. When Josh grabbed her hand to help her up, he caught her eye. "*Sha'di*. How are you?" he asked softly. Somehow, Josh had picked up on her stressed mood.

She gave him a pained smile back. "I'm okay. I talked to Ben today. He made me promise I'd drop by the police station again and ask for victim services. Ever since I was attacked, I keep – seeing things."

Josh froze. "What kind of things?" he asked, suddenly sounding apprehensive.

Hannah stared at her feet. "Nothing special."

"If someone scares you," Josh started out. "Or – something. Can you tell me?"

Hannah looked up curiously, surprised at how anxious he sounded. "Yeah, sure. I don't think there's anything to worry about. It's just in my mind."

"You promise?" he insisted.

"Yes, I promise." Hannah almost felt like crossing her fingers behind her back. Of course she didn't have the slightest intention of telling Josh about all the bizarre dreams she'd had about him lately. Talk about embarrassing.

She'd just jumped off the gangway onto the boat when Yazzie walked down the jetty and climbed on board too. "*Ya'at'eeh, biligaana,*" he called out cheerfully to the girls. "Hey, *shitsílí,*" he went on to greet his cousin.

"Hey back, *shinaaí,*" Josh replied. They always used the Navajo words for younger and older brother – or cousin; there was no real distinction between the two in Navajo – to address each other. Yazzie and Josh usually spoke a mixture of English and Diné Bizaad to each other. It had taught Hannah quite a few words in past summers. Heck, maybe she should start calling Josh *shitsílí* too – just to make it absolutely clear where they both stood.

Josh pushed off the boat as Yazzie fired up the engine, lightheartedly chatting to his cousin.

No reverence there. Apparently, Yazzie hadn't caught on when the whole all-bow-down-to-Josh thing had happened in Naabi'aani, because he treated his cousin no differently. Or maybe he just didn't give a hoot. Yazzie had never really cared about rules, written or unwritten.

"Rainbow Bridge, here we come!" he trumpeted,

standing at the ship's wheel. Today, he was wearing a black hat and a T-shirt with some punk band's logo on it. Actually, he reminded Hannah of some sort of Native pirate.

"All he needs is a parrot," Josh observed at that moment, following her stare.

She laughed. "Yeah, or an eye-patch."

"Yo-ho-ho, and a bottle of rum," Yazzie growled.

Hannah leaned her back against the railing and stared out over the water as Josh rummaged around in the minibar to get something to drink. Ivy sat down next to her and switched on her video camera. "I'm so happy we're going to visit the sandstone bridge," she said, her voice chipper in happy anticipation. "I promised my parents to tape the whole thing." She filmed the boat leaving Wahweap Marina, gliding past the brown and red rock formations along the shoreline. Soon, they were on their way to the jetties constructed near Rainbow Bridge.

The boat trip took about two hours, which the girls used to their advantage by sunbathing on deck. Thankfully, Josh had decided to put on a shirt, so Hannah didn't need to try and avoid looking at his divine body anymore. The walk from the docks to Rainbow Bridge took them another half hour.

Every turn in the road showed them new colors, different kinds of rocks and plants. Ivy had the time of her life with her dad's borrowed video camera, and Josh enjoyed himself pointing out all kinds of geological phenomena to them. After a while, they stopped talking altogether, but Hannah didn't mind – the silence and the intense heat on the path between the rocks made her feel kind of humble. When she finally caught sight of the sandstone bridge she still knew from a childhood visit long ago, she stopped dead in her tracks. Rainbow

Bridge was like a theatrical backdrop for a Native American movie, and breathed so much ancient mysticism and wisdom that she was glad there were no other day-trippers at the scene.

"Magnificent, huh?" Amber gasped beside her.

"Yeah, that's exactly the word I'd use here," Hannah agreed with a smile.

She started walking again and slipped into the shade of the bridge to take in the beautiful surroundings. It almost felt as if she'd been here before the world had discovered this place – a longer time ago than she could possibly remember.

Her musings were interrupted by the sound of howling, far away in the distance. She froze. Her heart was suddenly lumped in her throat. She didn't know much about wild animals, but that definitely sounded like a coyote. *Again*, a coyote.

In a sudden panic, she looked to Josh for council. That didn't help. To her amazement, he gave her an equally panicked look back, running toward her, then suddenly changing his mind and slowing down to a stop. He stood there, a few paces away from her, clearly debating with himself. It was a mystery where his indecision had come from, but Hannah didn't have the courage to take the few remaining steps separating them to grab his hand. He looked completely stumped. What the hell was wrong?

Meanwhile, Yazzie had noticed her anxiety. He rushed over to calm her down. "Hey, don't worry," he reassured her. "That was far away. They're wild animals, but they'll never attack humans if they're outnumbered. This is just one coyote."

"You think so?" she asked uncertainly.

"I know so. Just relax." He put his hand on her shoulder. "There's five of us, so we have nothing to fear."

Hannah glanced around. Yeah, maybe Yaz was right. Clearly, she was the only one with a problem. Ivy hadn't even looked up when the coyote howled, and Amber was busy snapping a few pictures of a rock pillar. She'd been the only one freaked out by the howling. She – and Josh.

"*Shitsilí?*" Yazzie shot Josh a worried look. "You all right, man?"

Josh gawked at his cousin as if frozen in time before his eyes darted to Hannah. He let out a shaky sigh. "Yeah, I'm okay," he replied in a distant voice. "No worries."

Before they even had the chance to ask Josh more questions, he turned around and stalked away, disappearing behind an overhang to the left side of Rainbow Bridge. Yazzie shrugged, stifling a curse when he followed Josh. "*T'ahálo!* Wait up! What's wrong?"

Hannah waited a few minutes for Yazzie to come back with Josh in tow. When that didn't happen, she absently made her way to the other side of Rainbow Bridge, sitting down with her back against the sandstone interior of the arch. Amber joined her.

"It's truly amazing, this place," Amber said with awe in her voice.

"Yeah, it's pretty awesome, isn't it?" Hannah smiled at Amber. "Glad you came along?"

The red-haired girl nodded. "Definitely. I'm just a bit disappointed that Em couldn't come."

Hannah winced a bit. She really couldn't stand listening to someone else's lovey-dovey stories right now. "You'll see her soon, I bet."

They sat in silence for a while until Amber decided to get up and walk around some more. Hannah was happy to stay put, resting her head against the stone surface and listening to her iPod. She didn't want to hear a single coyote howl anymore.

Scrolling through her playlist, Hannah settled on a mellow tune from her New Age collection and closed her eyes to relax, the sun warming her entire body. The bushes around her stirred in the wind, making a rustling sound fitting right in with the panpipe tune she was listening to. A fly landed on her forehead, and she brushed the insect away with her hand.

The next thing she felt was an icy gust of wind stinging her face.

With a gasp, Hannah opened her eyes. The entire landscape around her had changed into a winter wonderland, covered in snow. She was standing now, still next to Rainbow Bridge. Her feet were clad in boots made out of some kind of dark leather. Snowflakes clung to her cheeks, melting where they touched her skin, the bitter wind burning her lips. The rocks she leaned against were cold as ice. And to her left was the older version of Josh from her dreams, wearing a heavy, traditional cloak and roughly-woven, woolen pants. He was watching her anxiously.

And then, she heard coyote howls coming from behind her.

Turning around, Hannah saw three strange shadows standing there. They were watching her and Josh with murderous eyes, red-glowing in the scant light of the wintry, late afternoon.

Her heart turned cold as ice. One of the apparitions took a step forward and morphed into a coyote, jumping at her, its teeth flashing.

"God, no, *please!*"

Hannah woke herself up with a scream of pure fear, her hands balled into tight fists to ward off an attack that wouldn't come. Her eyes snapped open. That's when she noticed she was still sitting, her back against the warm sandstone of Rainbow Bridge. This was still the same summer afternoon. And Yazzie and Josh were beside her, the latter with a mortified look in his eyes.

Josh kneeled down and stroked her hair. "*Sha'di!* What's wrong?"

Hannah looked up at him. Strange. His eyes were red-rimmed, as if he'd been crying. This, somehow, caused her to start crying herself. She couldn't stop it. Shaking with sobs, Hannah climbed into his embrace, huddling against Josh.

"I had such a terrifying dream," she finally whispered.

"You were asleep?" he asked in surprise.

She hesitated. "Well, it was more like some kind of vision, actually."

"This is a sacred place," Yazzie pointed out, crouching down next to them. "Some Diné come here on vision quests. But it's not common for people to experience visions when they're not actively looking for them through meditation."

Josh frowned. He slowly let go of Hannah and shifted back. "What did you see?" His voice sounded tense, although he was clearly trying very hard to seem calm.

Hannah hesitated. What was she supposed to say? "I'd really rather not talk about it."

Josh's gaze didn't leave her face. She could tell he wanted to ask her more, but he didn't.

She bit her lip. Only a few hours ago, she'd promised to tell him if things were bothering or frightening her. But where to start? And how to phrase things and not sound crazy? She'd already vented this morning by voicing her irrational fears to Ben. That would have to be enough for now.

"I'll drop by real soon and make you a dreamcatcher, okay?" Josh then said quietly, giving her hand a reassuring squeeze. It took him a long time to let go of it, like he didn't want to leave her behind when he finally got up and walked away. He was clearly still rattled. By what, she had no idea.

Yazzie was still facing Hannah, regarding her thoughtfully. "Maybe you're highly sensitive to the spirits around you. Have you ever seen inexplicable things before?"

Hannah thought back to the past week. "Lately, yeah."

"You might have an unexplored talent for it," he said.

Hannah twisted her face in a wry smile. "That sounds awesome. Can I still swap it for something else? I'd rather learn how to fill in my tax return."

Yazzie snickered. "Good idea. In that case, you can come and help me at my hardware store if you want." He got to his feet and stuck out his hand to pull her up. "Come on, let's take a final stroll to the viewing point."

Ivy and Amber joined them, all of them climbing the rock rising up next to the sandstone bridge so they had a nice view of Rainbow Bridge and its surroundings from higher up. Slowly, Hannah calmed down, listening to the neighbors' cheerful banter. She had no idea where Josh was, but it was clear he needed some alone time. His antics were starting to puzzle her more and more.

At half past three, Yazzie suggested walking back to the docks. They descended from the viewpoint and made their way back to the path leading to the jetty.

"Where did Josh go?" Ivy wondered aloud.

"Oh, he went back early," Yazzie improvised. "He said the heat was bothering him, so he wanted to get something to drink."

Yazzie kept up a steady pace, and it wasn't long before Hannah was so hot she was longing for a drink herself. The water bottle in her bag was almost empty. When they rounded the last corner and saw Yazzie's boat in the distance, all four of them were exhausted. They found Josh sitting on the deck next to the wheel, staring out over the water. Hannah grabbed five bottles of water from the mini-bar, handing two to Josh and Yazzie.

Josh looked up. "*Ahe'hee.*" His eyes were distant. He got up and positioned himself behind the wheel. "I'll steer her out, *shinaaí*," he told his cousin.

Yazzie nodded, shooting a sideways glance at Hannah that was clearly loaded with 'maybe he and I should talk alone'. A good thing Yazzie took it upon himself to interrogate Josh about what happened at Rainbow Bridge, because she wouldn't even know where to start.

Hannah took the other three bottles to the bow, where Ivy and Amber had slumped down on the deck. They both looked worn-out but satisfied. Hannah didn't say much as the boat pulled out of the inlet and set sail back to Wahweap. A shadow had tainted this place, and it made her immensely sad. Rainbow Bridge was supposed to be a sacred place, but all it had brought her were horrible visions. Hopefully, Yazzie was wrong about her developing some sixth sense. She really didn't need that on top of everything else.

By the time she made her way back to the ship's wheel, Josh had fled below deck to play some music on an old guitar lying around.

"Hey, *biligaana*," Yazzie waved at her. "Can you get me another bottle of water? I'm starting to feel like a phoenix here. You guys should make sure the captain stays alive."

Hannah got another drink from the fridge and handed it to Yazzie. He sat down on the deck, holding the wheel in one hand, putting the bottle to his lips with the other.

"So. What's up between you and Josh?" he asked with the subtlety of a sledgehammer.

Hannah blushed. "What do you mean?" she replied awkwardly.

Yazzie shot her a look from underneath his black hat. "Oh, come on. I may look stupid, but I'm not blind."

Hannah let out a disgruntled sigh. "Nothing's up," she snapped sarcastically. "I'm just not sure how to behave around him anymore."

"Well, he seem to be having the same problem around you."

"So?" Why was Yazzie rubbing it in? Wasn't it embarrassing enough that she was crushing on his younger cousin, who kept calling her his big sister in front of everybody?

"So if he likes you and you like him, what's the problem?" Yazzie asked, quirking an eyebrow.

Hannah's mouth fell open. "Uhm, how about getting a hearing aid? Did you somehow miss the fact that he calls me *sha'di*?"

Yazzie gave her a blank stare, then started to laugh out loud. "No, he doesn't," he finally said.

"*No*? What do you mean, no?" Hannah demanded to know.

He leaned back, eyeing her pensively. "He used to call you *sha'di* when he was a kid, but he calls you *shan díín* now. It means sunbeam."

Hannah's stomach made a perfect revolution. Was this true – had Josh been calling her his sunshine for the past two days? An inane grin spread across her face. "Oh," she said stupidly.

Yazzie grinned back. "I mean, we as Diné can hear

the wordplay on the word for older sister, but Josh doesn't call you that anymore. He's turned it into something else."

Wow. She suddenly felt a lot lighter.

Yazzie winked at her. "I hope this was a useful one-on-one."

"Yeah," Hannah said breathlessly, deciding to kick Emily's butt the next time she saw her. Couldn't her best friend have told her Josh called her his ray of sunshine all the time?

When the boat got back to Wahweap Harbor, Ben was waiting for them at the docks. He hugged her tight when she stepped ashore. "Hey sis, how've you been today?"

"I'm fine. We had fun. So, did you miss me so much you decided to wait for me here?"

"Of course. I'm glad you guys are back again. I was beginning to feel like Gandalf, sitting around in a cabin all by myself with just piles of dusty books for company."

Hannah snickered. "I admire your endurance."

"Studying is good for me," Ben said fervently, as though he was trying to convince himself.

"As long as you don't take those books with you on our camping trip," Josh warned, walking up to them. "That would truly worry me."

Ben scoffed. "And me. You don't seriously think I'd slog around on the rez with twenty pounds of textbooks in a backpack? That would make me certifiable."

As Ben and Josh walked back to the harbor entrance, chatting about their planned hike, Hannah looked around to see where Ivy and Amber were. Maybe they could all grab dinner together. She wanted to stay close to Josh for a bit longer, now that Yazzie had given her the heads-up about her nickname. Life looked a lot rosier all of a sudden.

To her disappointment, Josh announced he was going straight home when they were all standing in the parking lot. He avoided her gaze when he said it. She couldn't understand what was up with him. Was he still upset about the howling coyote at Rainbow Bridge? That didn't make much sense. She had far *more* reason to be upset after that terrible vision.

"I'll see you soon." He gave her a quick hug. "Take care of yourself, okay?"

Hannah nodded, pressing her body against his a few more seconds than usual.

When Josh drove away, he left her in Wahweap with a myriad of unanswered questions.

Ten

The trip to Rainbow Bridge and her terrifying visions had prompted Hannah to take a sleeping pill that night. Whenever she took a soporific, she never dreamed.

She never really felt good after a pill-induced sleep, either. With a foggy, still half-sedated head, she stepped into the kitchen the next morning.

"Hey," Ben greeted her, just closing one of his textbooks. "I'm heading out to get some camping gear with Josh. Will you be all right?"

"Yeah, I'm going to grab lunch with Emily." Hannah hesitated. "Say hello to Josh, okay?" she added.

"Will do." Ben put his thumb up. "Have fun with Em. And drop by the police station when you have the time."

Hannah nodded, plodding to the fridge to get some juice. Just when she'd poured herself a glass, she heard her cell phone beep in her room. Still groggy, she walked back and read the text message. 'hi han! can u make it @ 2? nick will b there 2. xoxo em.'

She texted back, feeling a dull headache coming on. It seemed she was left with only two choices – having night terrors or feeling like a wreck all day. Maybe she should cut back on the sleeping pills next time. Half a dose would probably work as well.

Hannah sat down at the table outside, staring out over the lake. A glance at her phone told her it was already quarter to twelve. She actually still needed to drive to Page and contact the police again – after all, she'd promised Ben – but she'd changed her mind about the whole thing. Victim service was there for victims, and nothing had really happened to her. Police Officer Curry was a nice guy, but hopelessly unqualified to deal with strange visions, looming shadows, or dreams about coyotes and murderous Mexicans.

At quarter past one, Hannah packed up to go to Grassroots and meet Emily. She stepped inside and spotted her friend sitting at the same table as before.

"Hey Em! Nick's not here yet?" Hannah pulled out a chair and sat down.

"He's running late. He just texted me."

"Oh, no worries. In fact, we need some private time, my girl. I officially want to blame you for holding out on me. You're the worst BFF ever."

"Huh? Why?" Emily raised her eyebrows.

"Like, couldn't you have told me that Josh has been calling me 'sunbeam' for the past few days?!"

Emily gave her a baffled look. "Oh, I thought he'd tell you himself at some point. Or you'd ask him what it meant. Cute nickname, right?"

"Uh, *no*. I thought he was calling me his older sister."

"Why the hell would he? Isn't it glaringly obvious that he likes you?"

Hannah stopped short, her face flushing red. "You – you really think so?"

Emily sighed theatrically. "Yes. I really think so. And so do you. Come on, admit it. Even a blindfolded mole can see he's interested in you, you nutcase. I had no idea you'd misunderstood him or I would have told you, of course."

Hannah bit her lip. "Okay, I hope you're right. He was suddenly being so distant yesterday. Weird things have been going down at Rainbow Bridge."

"Oh?" Emily grabbed her hand. "Actually, I've been meaning to ask you. Last night Amber was grilling me about people without auras, and she went all secretive on me and told me I should ask you if I wanted to know more? So here I am, asking you, wanting to know more."

Hannah felt a grin spread across her face. "Hold on, Em. When, exactly, did you meet Amber?"

Emily suddenly turned a bit red herself. "Just, late last night," she mumbled evasively. "After work. I met her – we met at the beach."

Hannah sucked in a mock scandalized breath. "You *truly* are the worst BFF ever! You don't share things with me anymore, not even going on a private date with my neighbor girl."

Emily cleared her throat and shook her head. "Let's skip that for now, okay?" she deflected. "First, I want to know about the strange things you just mentioned."

Talk about changing the subject. Now she had to fess up to being stark-raving mad – there was no way around it. Hannah looked around furtively, letting out a sigh when the door swung open and Nick stepped into the café. "Let's wait till we're all properly sitting down," she stalled.

"My dissertation is well under way," Nick beamed, sitting down at their table. "It should be, too. I'm off on that trek through the rez with Ben and Josh. We'll take three days, they said. And how are *you* doing? Seriously, you look like a car hit you." He shot Hannah a questioning look.

She shrugged, staring at the palms of her hands as if the answer was written there. "I'm just so tired. I didn't sleep well. Yesterday, at Rainbow Bridge, I heard this coyote howl in the distance. Josh heard it too, and he looked at me in this – this *anxious* way, as if he was in a panic and wanted to protect me. But he didn't. He stayed away from me. Yazzie thought he was acting weird, too. After that incident, Josh kept his distance all afternoon."

"Coyotes?" Nick's eyebrows furrowed. "Didn't we see coyotes at your cabin too, before we went to the rodeo? Or were they just dogs?"

Hannah breathed in and out, trying to suppress her feelings of terror. In her mind, she relived the moment the shadow from her vision turned into a coyote. "I don't know," she blew out defeatedly. "I just don't know. Do you guys think I'm getting some kind of supernatural warning?"

Emily arched an eyebrow. "Why supernatural?"

"Well, I sort of zoned out at Rainbow Bridge. There's no other way to describe it. One moment I was relaxing in the sun, and the next I had a vision of a wintry landscape and three creepy, shadowy figures watching me. One of them shapeshifted. He morphed into a coyote."

"You were in a trance?" Nick asked in surprise.

"Something like that, yeah."

"It happens during vision quests as well," he said, leafing through his notebook. "Images of the past are experienced as if they're happening in the present," he read out loud from his notes.

Hannah swallowed. Slowly, it began to dawn on her. The dreams and the terrible vision seemed to come from the same time period – from the past. Josh had looked the same, as if he was about thirty years old. Could she actually be seeing things that had happened in the past?

"But – what have I ever done to see those images? I keep dreaming about things I've never seen before, but they seem so real, so I don't think my mind is fabricating them. What should I..."

Her words locked in her throat when the waitress put the quiche they'd ordered on the table. Great. She sounded like the village idiot, babbling about supernatural warnings and apparitions in the middle of a café.

Emily put a reassuring hand on Hannah's arm. "You know what? I need to be in Naabi'aani today and tomorrow morning, but I can come straight to your place tomorrow afternoon. I'll stay with you for a few nights when Ben is away. And we'll figure this out. We can make a list of everything you've seen and experienced and try to make sense of it. Don't think you're losing it – spirituality is a constant in our culture, so at least you blend right in with us Native Americans."

Nick put his arm around her shoulders. "And I'll try to sound Josh out about what happened at Rainbow Bridge during our hiking trip. Maybe he's overly sensitive to spiritual things, being a medicine man and all. I can tell you one thing, though – he likes you. I don't need crystal ball-gazing or Tarot to tell you that."

Hannah blushed. So Nick saw it, too. Was she the only one walking around with blinkers on? "Thanks, guys. You're the best friends ever."

In the meantime, a thunderstorm had erupted outside. After lunch, Hannah walked back in the summer rain, glad it was freshening up her foggy head. Her heart sped up as she neared the log cabin. Maybe Ben would be back, together with Josh.

Her face fell when she saw the empty driveway, but she forced herself not to feel disappointed. Whistling a tune, she made a shopping list and got into her Datsun to drive to the big supermarket in Page. Luckily, she found a parking spot close to the entrance.

Still humming to herself, Hannah pushed her cart through the aisles and decided to stock up on burgers from the frozen food section. Maybe Ben wanted to organize a barbecue again after getting back from their hike.

When she emerged from the store with two bulging bags in her shopping cart, the sky had cleared and it was bright and sunny. Next to her stall, another car was waiting, with the top down, its indicator lights blinking.

"You leaving?" the young guy behind the wheel asked. Next to him was another guy who looked exactly like him, and an older man who was clearly their dad was in the back seat. For some reason, they were all giving her the once-over.

Hannah nodded. "I am. I just need to put my groceries in the trunk."

The guy smiled. His eyes bored into hers, and Hannah blinked uncomfortably. Why was he staring at her like that? In fact, why were they *all* staring at her?

She whipped around and opened the trunk to put away her stuff. She could feel the guy in the driver's seat watching her. A tingling feeling between her shoulder blades told her that she was being observed. When Hannah furtively looked over her shoulder, she saw the guy's twin brother and dad were also still staring at her with the same piercing look. Six cold eyes were trained on her.

Her heart tapped anxiously against her ribs. Quickly stuffing the last pack of frozen burgers into one of the boxes in the trunk, she mumbled: "I'll be right back," before pushing the cart back to the store entrance with her best attempt at a stony face.

This was nuts. Why was she being so paranoid?

Those people had *scared* her. But why? There was nothing wrong. That family was just waiting for her to leave. They just wanted her to hurry up. Hannah wiped off her sweaty palms on her pants, cursing inwardly.

After putting the cart away, she deliberately strolled back at a leisurely pace to catch her breath. By the time she got back to the Datsun, the twins and their dad had disappeared. Probably moved on to greener pastures. She hadn't been quick enough for them. Well, so much the better. She was glad to be rid of the trio with their creepy, staring eyes. There'd been something deeply unsettling about them.

During the drive back, it started to lightly rain again. Halfway through, she had to put the roof back up. When Hannah parked the car on the driveway, Ben still wasn't back.

"I'll be home after dinner," a text message on her cell said. She'd left the thing on the kitchen table.

Determined not to feel empty and neglected, Hannah went out to get the groceries from the car and then sat down to a nice cup of tea, cupcakes and a documentary on National Geographic. It was the first time this vacation she'd turned on the TV – it was time for some mindless distraction.

~~~

Over the course of the evening, the sky cleared again. By the time it turned dark and Hannah went out to sit on the front porch with a pizza and a can of beer, some stars were already visible. In the west, she saw the planet Venus twinkling on the horizon. It brought back memories of stargazing with Josh. He'd told her about the constellations in the sky. He'd whispered to her that he had closed off from deep communication with his family. Funny how that story about the distance between him and his parents had brought her and Josh closer together in that moment.

Just after nine o'clock, Ben's Chevy finally appeared around the corner. He honked at Hannah sitting outside, waving cheerfully.

"I see you had dinner by yourself?" he asked with a tilt of his head toward the pizza leftovers on her plate.

"You haven't eaten yet?" Hannah said in surprise. "I thought you were still in Naabi'aani, having dinner with Josh."

Ben shook his head. "No, Josh had to leave for Tuba City in the afternoon to get some registration forms for college, and I'd promised him to drop by Yazzie's in Wahweap to arrange for a permit. You know, to hike on the rez. He can get us a discount. Josh wanted to have some sort of official consent from the tourist board, because he's taking both me and Nick for three days. We don't want to steal jobs from the official guides and not pay anyone anything."

"Well, you want me to make you a pizza?"

"That'd be awesome. I want to do some more cramming tonight, so I could use some fuel." He tilted his head at the pile of textbooks on the table.

"Wow. Who are you and what have you done with my brother?" Hannah chuckled.

Ben smiled sheepishly. "Yeah, Josh kind of inspired me. He is so dead serious about college, you know. We talked a lot about the education system in Navajo Nation. Josh wants to set up some sort of program to stimulate young people to get a proper education and be more prepared for the world out there. So they won't touch drugs, join a gang, or be hit by continuous unemployment. He says the country needs more schools. His latest idea is to found a college in Kayenta with some other people when he's older."

"Wow. He sure is passionate about this whole thing."

"Yeah, that seems like the right word for it." Ben dumped his shoulder bag on the floor and rummaged through it. "Oh, before I forget – Josh gave me this. He said it's for you."

Hannah smiled in surprise when her brother handed her a brown paper bag. "Really? What is it?"

"He said there's things in it to make a dreamcatcher. He's going to help you make one after we come back from the rez."

Hannah blushed. "Cool. Thank him for me when you see him tomorrow, okay?"

She curiously opened the bag. Inside, she found a ring of intertwined twigs, a brown leather cord, a reel of strong, thin yarn, feathers, silver thread and red beads. The whole collection already looked pretty now. Josh would undoubtedly turn this into an awesome dreamcatcher.

After changing into her pajamas and crawling into bed, Hannah indecisively eyed the strip of sleeping pills. That road would lead to another throbbing headache in the morning, for sure. Maybe she should give the night a try without medication.

After all, how bad could it possibly be?

༄༄༄

Pretty bad, it turned out.

That morning, she woke up screaming, sitting bolt upright in bed. Bewildered, Hannah stared up into Ben's anxious face. Her brother was sitting on the edge of the bed, his hands around her shoulders.

"What's the matter?" Her voice cracked in her throat. Her mouth was so dry she started to cough. Ben handed her the glass of water on her bedside table – the water she hadn't used last night to take her pill. She gulped it down eagerly.

"You were dreaming," he replied, wiping the sweat off her brow with one hand. Only now, Hannah felt how clammy her pajamas were, sticking to her back.

"Why are you here?" she asked, confused.

"You were screaming like crazy." Ben shook his head in disbelief. "I swear, it sounded like someone was murdering you. I half expected to find somebody in the room with you."

"Was I screaming for help?" Hannah whispered, throwing the blankets off. She was still feeling way too hot.

"No, you kept yelling 'Go away!' and you were crying." He rubbed his face and sighed, his gaze drifting to the pills on her bedside table. "Did you use those?"

"Not last evening."

Ben fell silent. "I'm really worried about you," he said at last, pulling Hannah into an embrace. "I heard you screaming a few nights ago, too, but it wasn't nearly as bad as it was now. It all started after you were stranded at the lakeside."

"I'm worried too," she said timidly. "It's like I'm losing my mind. I mean, really, what is the big deal? Some drunk lowlives threaten me and I chase them away with a gun that's not even loaded. Why should I still freak out about that?"

Ben sighed. "I wish you could just wake yourself up from a nightmare. I usually do that when I have a really nasty dream."

"Wake yourself up? How?"

He laughed. "Well, you can do it on one condition – you have to be aware you might be dreaming. If you want to check if that's the case, you just watch your own hands in the dream."

Hannah frowned. "Why?"

"Because you can never count the fingers of your own hand in a dream. The minute you try and you fail, you wake up."

"Wow." She shook her head. "Interesting. Unfortunately, I'm *never* aware I might be dreaming. I always think it's real."

He stroked her head. "And you don't remember what you dreamed about now?"

"Nope. Not a clue," she blew out.

Ben got up. "Look, I have to go. Nick's waiting for me. But I'll talk to you later. We'll be back here before going to the rez to meet up with Josh."

"Thanks, Ben," Hannah said quietly. "For everything."

"Emily is coming over, right? Just talk to her about it. Take those stupid sleeping pills, even if you don't like them. Drop by the police station – and once Josh makes you a dreamcatcher, you hang that next to your bed, okay?"

Hannah nodded, waving feebly at Ben as he walked out the door. God, her entire body was covered in sweat. She had to get out of bed and take a shower. That'd make her feel better.

When the hot jet of water hit her sticky back and she closed her eyes, Hannah suddenly remembered her nightmare.

She'd been standing on a hilltop in a storm. It had been near that familiar precipice, looking out over a canyon that looked a lot like Canyon de Chelly on the reservation. A long time ago, she'd visited the place with Ben and her mother, but she still knew what it looked like. In the dream, dark clouds had drifted across the sky, and those three sinister shadows had been right in front of her. They'd looked so terrifying that just the memory of seeing them made her gasp for breath again. Pure evil radiated from their faces.

In her nightmare, the three creatures had driven her back toward the edge of the precipice, their red eyes aglow and teeth bared. Her arms had crawled with insects, all of a sudden. She could feel them walking on her skin, under her hair, her feet.

That's where the dream had ended, because that's when Ben had woken her up. Hannah sucked in a breath and opened her eyes again. She sagged down to the floor of the shower cabin, puting her arms around her knees. Despite the hot water beating down on her, she was shivering.

This time, she wouldn't hold back when she talked to Emily. She'd describe every minute detail of her dreams and visions, and tell Em what fears were plaguing her during the day, constantly lingering at the edges of her mind. And she'd tell her friend about the strange things that had been happening.

Someone had really stolen her necklace and put it outside on the lawn. She'd bumped into three creepy auraless lumberjacks in the supermarket. Three coyotes had shown up at the cabin to ominously stare at her. And so help her, something had definitely been off about the three people waiting for her in the Safeway parking lot. She just *knew*.

Quickly, Hannah stepped out of the shower cabin and got dressed in a bikini top and a short skirt. Time to get out of here and leave the horrible memories of her nightmare behind for a while. Sitting on a sunny beach would cheer her up.

In the kitchen, she poured the last bit of coffee Ben had left in the pot. A cup of yogurt made for a nice, light breakfast. Hannah absently ate her yogurt and stared out the window. She should bring lots of sun cream, bottled water, her iPod, a book, and –

Her thoughts came to a screeching halt as she spotted a familiar motorcycle coming up the road to their house. Her heart rate went up a few notches.

It was Josh. What was *he* doing here? He wasn't even supposed to show up here today!

She swallowed hard, putting away her coffee cup and walking toward the front door before changing her mind and charging back to the kitchen table.

Maybe he wouldn't even come in. Maybe he would leave again when he saw Ben's car wasn't here. Maybe she should have put on some more clothes. A bikini-top-short-skirt combo was definitely not in her top ten list of suitable outfits to conduct awkward conversations in. She'd been nervous about seeing Josh again for days, and this so did *not* help.

At that moment, the door swung open.

"Hey," Josh said softly, stepping inside.

"Hi," she replied just as softly. She cleared her throat, edging toward the wall to get to the trash can and throw away the empty cup of yogurt she was still holding.

"Ben's not here," she went on, looking back at Josh. A flush raced up her cheeks when she saw his gaze briefly linger on her breasts before settling on her face again.

"Yeah. I, uh, saw that," he stammered. "His car's gone."

Hannah didn't miss the hint of insecurity in his voice, and suddenly it dawned on her. Josh was nervous about this conversation, too. Maybe not as nervous as she was – she didn't think it was humanly possible – but still.

"Yeah," she managed to croak out. "He went to

Page. To pick up Nick."

Josh nodded, taking a deep breath as he stepped toward her. "Hannah. I want to say I'm sorry."

In the silence stretching between them, she felt a stone grow in the pit of her stomach. "Sorry for what?" she finally said, her voice tight.

Josh ran a hand through his hair and let out a nervous laugh. "For being so weird around you. I can see it makes you nervous. But I can't help it." He looked down to the tip of his feet. "I just wish I could be normal around you. You know, like we used to be."

Her heart beat wildly in her chest. So Josh thought she wanted things to go back to normal. Well, who could blame him? She'd frozen or freaked out whenever he'd tried to turn this into something more than it had been before.

Hannah bit her lip. "I don't know how to hang out with you anymore either. And sometimes, I can feel you're so distant, you know, like you're hiding yourself?"

Oh, damn her babbling. She had to get to the point.

"It's just difficult to be around you for me, because I like you too much," she mumbled. There, she'd said it.

Josh looked up with wide eyes, taking another step toward her. And then, he gently caressed her cheek with soft fingers, touching the skin of her waist with his other hand, slowly running it up to her ribs. A shiver ran through her. As his brown eyes fastened on her, she was sure her heart had never beaten faster than this.

"Really?" he whispered, so full of longing it almost brought tears to her eyes. Josh bridged the small distance between them, pressing his body against hers.

Her heart skipped a beat. Then his lips kissed her mouth, soft and warm. She closed her eyes and pushed herself up toward him to meet his mouth and kiss him back. Hannah heard him gasp for breath, pressing his mouth to hers more urgently this time. She circled his waist with her arms and slid up one hand under his shirt to caress the warm skin of his back. He pressed her up against the wall, letting one hand slide up her body and briefly cup her breast before landing in her neck. She moaned almost imperceptibly. Josh caressed the sensitive spot behind her ear, running his fingers through her hair.

This was even better than she'd imagined. She'd never been kissed so cautiously, tenderly, tortuously slowly and sexily at the same time. This should never stop. Hannah softly pulled Josh even closer and kept welcoming his kisses. Somehow, this felt like they were lovers who'd been separated for years, trying to catch up on what they'd missed in mere moments. She kissed him and caressed him everywhere, keeping her eyes closed to let the moment last forever. Somehow, it felt like their bubble would burst once she looked at him again.

When Josh finally let go of her a little bit, he kept holding her, his face close to hers. Unwillingly, she opened her eyes and saw his up close.

"I could kiss you all day long," he whispered. He touched her cheek, his breath slowing down. "But I'm scared. Scared I'll have to talk when I stop kissing you." He closed his eyes. "Scared I'll have to explain to you why I'm so distant sometimes."

"Then don't," Hannah replied. "Don't stop. You don't have to talk if you don't want to."

Josh gave her such a sweet smile she felt butterflies flitting around in her stomach. He bent over and kissed her lightly on her cheeks, her forehead, her closed eyelids.

"I've never felt this connected to anyone, you know that?" she whispered breathlessly into his ear.

His arm slid around her waist. "I haven't felt like this for a very long time," he confessed in a husky voice, and for some reason, it didn't sound strange. It felt like Josh had waited all these years for her to come back to the reservation.

He gazed into her eyes. *"Ayor anosh'ni,"* he mumbled, almost inaudibly.

Hannah closed her eyes and savored his words. He had always loved her, but now it was different. Now it was so much more.

And then, a wave of dizziness crashed over her out of nowhere, like someone had smacked her on the head. In a flash, she saw Josh's older face – the face from her dreams. The Josh who tried to save her night after night, whispering that he loved her in Diné Bizaad.

With a start, she opened her eyes. The vision had been so life-like. She stared at Josh, shivering when he stared back at her with the same amount of shock in his eyes. He stepped backwards, letting go of her hands.

"Josh," she stammered, confused. "What's the matter?"

He bit his lip, a look of muted sadness in his eyes. "Nothing." He stroked the back of her hand, sighing deeply. "Give me time."

"Okay," Hannah agreed, even though his sudden mood change confused her. No matter how strangely he behaved, he was worth having patience for.

Suddenly, the approached sound of Ben's Chevy disrupted their embrace. Hannah shot a glance out the window.

"Ben's back," she said.

"Yeah." Josh cleared his throat. "I didn't come to see *him.*"

She blushed. "Oh."

He smiled and turned a bit red himself, slowly letting

go of her.

"So, you want to sneak out before he comes in?" Hannah giggled nervously.

Josh chuckled in response. "Nah, that's okay. I'll stay."

When Ben and Nick entered the kitchen, Hannah was sitting at the dinner table and Josh was leaning against the counter, sipping from the cup of coffee she'd left there.

"Hey!" Ben arched his eyebrows. "What are you doing here?"

"We were meeting up here, right?" Josh asked, trying his best to sound clueless.

"Uhm, *no*. We were supposed to meet up in Naabi'aani. Which seems the logical course of action. To me, at least."

"Aren't we picking up stuff at Yazzie's?"

"Nick and I offered to do that." Ben grinned. "Idiot."

"Oh, well," Josh shrugged. "I'll join you guys then, since I'm here anyway."

"Are we leaving now?" Nick asked.

"Yazzie won't have our gear ready before eleven," Ben said with a glance at the clock. "Let's have a drink and run through the list to see if we have everything." He turned to Hannah. "You going to the beach?"

"Yeah, in a minute. I want to make some sandwiches before I leave."

She got up and walked to the counter, reaching out for the jar of peanut butter behind Josh. Her arm touched his, and a pleasant tingling sensation shot through her body. She looked sideways. Josh returned her private stare, smiling slightly. Blushing, she looked away again. He really had the power to set her on fire – too bad he was leaving for that hike today.

When Hannah stepped outside and passed Ben on the

porch, he stopped her. "What was that look you shared with Josh in the kitchen?" he inquired, eyeing her with a playful smile.

"What look?" she said innocently.

Ben tilted his head. "How long had he been here when I came back?"

"Long enough," Hannah replied with flushed cheeks. She couldn't help grinning when Ben took her hand and squeezed it.

"Great," he beamed. "I'm happy for you. Not to mention off the hook. This means I don't have to pull off a full-blown 'hit-on-my-sister-you-slowpoke' propaganda program anymore."

Hannah burst out laughing. "You were gonna do that? How sweet."

"Of course, sis." He eyed her seriously. "Feel better, okay? Promise me you'll talk to Em and the police."

"Yeah, will do." She was looking forward to meeting Emily – she'd have something to tell her besides sinister stalking stories.

After Josh, Ben and Nick had left for Wahweap at a quarter to eleven, Hannah locked up the cabin and walked down to the beach, humming a tune to herself. Her problems hadn't disappeared completely, but this morning had definitely cheered her up – a lot.

Eleven

That afternoon, the Greenes' car pulled around the bend just as Hannah returned from the beach. Paul honked and waved at her as he parked. A few seconds later, the entire family spilled out of the car, looking sun-tanned and upbeat. Except Ivy, Hannah noticed as she veered off to say hi to her neighbors. The eldest girl looked sick.

"How was Monument Valley?" Hannah inquired.

"Amazing," Ivy replied. "But way too hot for me. I have a splitting headache. Amber thinks I've got heatstroke."

"Will you join us for dinner tonight, Hannah?" Sarah said warmly. "Amber invited Emily too, so it'd be sad if you were sitting all by yourself one door down."

In the meantime, Ivy staggered inside to lie down. Paul and Sarah got back in the car to get some groceries in Page, and Amber walked with Hannah to the other cabin so they could chat without keeping Ivy awake.

Amber's eye was caught by Yazzie's motorcycle on the drive. "Hey, who left the bike here?"

"Josh did." Hannah couldn't help blushing a bit. "He was here this morning."

Amber's eyes widened. "Wait a minute. Why the flustered look?"

"Well. He came here to talk. To me."

"Uh-huh," Amber pushed. "So?"

"So, he wanted to apologize for being so weird around me lately."

"And? Did he succeed?"

"Yeah, he did. I couldn't be angry anymore when he kissed me."

Amber's face split into a grin so wide it almost didn't fit on her face. "Oh my God! That's *awesome*, I'm so excited for you!"

"I know, right? I'm so happy. But, I'm also still confused. All those weird dreams I'm having about him – and I know he shuts people out, but I don't know why."

"Well, you have all summer to figure him out. I wouldn't worry about it."

"His behavior is not what worries me most. It's my nightmares."

"They've become worse?"

Hannah fell silent. The last time she'd told Amber about her dreams, she'd only seen Josh and the primitive village under attack. In the meantime, the terrifying vision of the snowy landscape and the shapeshifters at Rainbow Bridge had come into the equation. Amber didn't know about those things yet – only Emily and Nick had heard that story.

"I can't even sleep without taking pills anymore," she mumbled. "At least when I take a sleeping pill, I sleep so deeply I don't dream. Or at least, I don't remember it. Without them, I have such horrible nightmares that I shout bloody murder in my sleep. Ben woke me this morning because I was screaming and crying."

Amber shot her a perplexed look. "No way. So what do you dream about?"

Hannah shivered despite the heat. "I can't really explain. There's always an onmipresent feeling of danger. Soldiers are attacking the village, murdering people. But my last few nightmares featured these sinister apparitions looking like shadows. There's always three of them. They stare at me, or ... " She took a deep breath. "Or they change into some kind of monsters."

Amber shook her head. "I'm sorry, but that doesn't sound like a normal response to being harassed by a bunch of drunks. It's almost like – like you're bewitched or something. You saw something scary when you went to Rainbow Bridge with us too, right? Some kind of vision? Emily mentioned witches when I talked to her about people without auras. Plus, some years ago I read a lot of stuff about voodoo and witchcraft where people cast a spell on you or jinx you. Something like that might be happening to you."

"What else did Emily say?"

"I don't remember exactly. She'll be here any minute. Maybe we should wait for her."

Hannah suddenly smiled, giving Amber a cheeky look. "Yeah, I heard you invited Emily for dinner. So what's the deal between you two?"

Amber's face turned as red as her hair. "We have this thing," she said shyly.

Grinning widely, Hannah got up to get a bottle of soda from the kitchen. She was just pouring drinks for Amber and herself when she heard Emily's old Beetle outside, coming up the road and screeching to a stop next to the cabin with a cracking exhaust pipe.

"Hi!" she called out cheerfully, stepping onto the porch. She hugged Hannah, quickly kissed Amber on the lips, then sat down. "How's your day been, girls?"

"Good. I just got back from Monument Valley. It

was fantastic," Amber said.

"And yours?" Emily turned to Hannah.

"Can't complain. I kissed Josh."

"Really?!" Emily's voice shot up two octaves. "When?"

Hannah spun the story of how Josh had visited her in the cabin that morning. Emily smiled, but a hint of doubt still lingered on her face. That was no surprise – after all, her friend had warned her about Josh's inexplicable mood swings, and in all fairness, she was right.

"So let's talk about your dreams and visions." Emily dug up a notepad and pencil from her bag. "When did they start?"

"I was harassed by the lake on Thursday night. Ben and Josh picked me up because I ran out of fuel. That night, I had my first nightmare."

"What did you dream about?"

"About a traditional village." Hannah closed her eyes to recall the images. "A Navajo village. With primitive hoghans, the kind with dried-up clay on the outside. People were wearing old-fashioned clothes, and the village was attacked by Mexicans."

"How do you know they were Mexicans?"

"Did they wear sombreros?" Amber inquired.

Hannah couldn't help stifling a nervous laugh. "Not the big ones. They wore some kind of smaller hats, uniforms, and they spoke Spanish. In my dream, they clearly sounded Mexican. After that first nightmare, I dreamed about the attack several more times, and it's always the same people burning down the village."

"So, what are they doing exactly?" Emily continued.

"Like I said, the village is burning. I think they set it on fire. In my dream, I'm running from the soldiers, looking for someone who I know can protect me."

"And that person is...?" Emily scribbled down a few

notes and then looked up at Hannah expectantly.

"Josh," Hannah confessed with red cheeks. "But he looks different. Older. He's also wearing traditional clothes, and his hair is up in a bun like last Saturday at the rodeo. He seems about thirty years old."

"Is he your lover in that part of the dream?" Emily asked.

Hannah hesitated. She suddenly realized something new. "No. No, he isn't. I can feel he's really important to me, but he is not my husband. Not anymore." She fell silent. That was an interesting discovery.

Emily pondered over the things she'd written down. "So, does he save you in the end?"

"I have no idea. I'm hiding from those Mexicans, and Josh sees me, but he looks away on purpose so he won't alert the Mexicans to my presence. After that, I make a sort of leap in time, and the next thing I see is the hilltop where I leave him."

"Tell me more." Emily picked up her pencil again.

"We are near a precipice looking out over Canyon de Chelly – I think. He tells me a story in Diné Bizaad, looking solemn. I get up and walk away from him, because I feel an overwhelming urge to be free. It feels like – like breaking up."

Amber and Emily stared at her nonplussed. "That's quite a saga," Emily mumbled. "And that eerie feeling? Was it there the first time you had a strange dream?"

Hannah shook her head. "No, not like that. The third time I was having the same dream, there were three shadows waiting for me at the foot of that hill where I'm leaving Josh behind. The same three apparitions I saw in the vision at Rainbow Bridge."

Emily nodded slowly. "You said one of them turned into an animal?"

"A coyote. And those sinister apparitions haven't left

since. They keep invading my dreams. Last night, I dreamed I was looking out over Canyon de Chelly, facing the wind. The three creatures were approaching me, their faces distorted, looking like coyotes with bared fangs. Then, all of a sudden, there were bugs crawling all over my body. In the dream, it felt like I was about to jump into the abyss and commit suicide so I could finally have peace."

Talking about her nightmares was useful for linking up dream events, but it also made her relive all the terror she'd felt. Hannah shuddered.

Amber tapped her shoulder. "You think those aura-less men have something to do with your dreams?" she asked gingerly.

Hannah nodded defeatedly. "Yeah. It's like my dreams blend in with reality. Those three entities are after me in *real* life. Not just in my dreams."

Emily put her hand on Amber's arm. "You saw something strange? Is that why you wanted to know about people without auras?"

"When I ran into Hannah in the supermarket on Saturday, I told her I can see auras. In turn, she told me about her weird dreams and her feelings of paranoia."

"I bumped into these three men in Safeway who creeped me out big time," Hannah explained. "I just didn't know why. I mean, two of them were talking in the aisle next to me and they had the exact same voices as the drunk guys who harassed me, but they looked nothing like them. Still, I couldn't shake the feeling something didn't quite add up."

"So Hannah asked me to walk back to Safeway with her and have a look at those men," Amber added.

"And you saw something weird," Emily concluded.

"You bet I did. Those three had *no* auras. Nothing, nada, zip."

Emily fell silent for a long time, mindlessly doodling underneath her notes. When the silence became too oppressive for her, Hannah cleared her throat. "So, your thoughts?"

"Have you felt threatened by other people besides those men at the supermarket lately?" Emily asked without looking up. Her voice was so serious it scared Hannah.

"Well – not people. Coyotes. Three of them, near the cabin on Saturday, just before we went to the rez," she mumbled. And then she remembered the twins and their dad at the parking lot, waiting for her to leave, staring her down like they were about to murder her. She swallowed. "Actually, I have. Groups of three. I just thought it was in my mind. I thought I was going nuts."

"If I'm right about this, that's exactly what they want you to believe." Emily grabbed her hand. "Please listen to me. You're not crazy."

Hannah nodded curtly. "Okay. So what the heck is going on?"

"I think you've become the target of something I don't even want to say out loud," Emily whispered.

The hairs on Hannah's arms prickled. Emily had such a grim look on her face she almost felt like running, just so she wouldn't have to listen to whatever came next.

"*Yenaldlooshi,*" Emily spoke, almost inaudibly. "Skinwalkers."

They were all completely silent for a moment.

"What's that?" Amber whispered.

"They're witches or warlocks – *chindi*. They never work alone, but in threes. The Diné don't speak their name aloud, because it invokes them or attracts misfortune. Skinwalkers use black magic to change into coyotes so they can harass and terrorize people. If powerful enough, they can also change into other beings or copy other people's appearances. Often, they will use their mental power to drive you insane. They influence your thoughts to make you believe you're crazy, or to make you harm or kill yourself. It's the nastiest form of *ánt'iihnii* – witchcraft."

Hannah couldn't help giving Emily a completely stumped look. Despite the heat, she suddenly felt cold as ice. Things like these didn't exist. Right? At least, not in *her* world. On the other hand – Emily's story was beyond bizarre, but at least it accounted for what she felt. So she wasn't crazy – she was cursed. Under a spell. Chased by supernatural beings.

"I know it sounds impossible," Emily went on, an insecure quiver in her voice.

Hannah swallowed. "No. I believe you. I really do. But you know, stuff like this doesn't happen in my life. I have such a different background from yours – no yarns about magic and mystery told by ancestors. My mother never even bothered to pretend Santa existed."

"Do you think the dreams are all caused by some sort of curse?" Amber wanted to know.

"I'm sure of it," Emily replied. "You started having the dreams when you first met the three warlocks. Skinwalkers can use their powers to read people's minds, to break into their thoughts."

Hannah shivered, thinking back to the moment she'd heard a coyote howl near Rainbow Bridge. Maybe Josh had felt something was wrong with her. Was that why he'd looked so scared?

"So, those drunk guys – and the men at Safeway – and those coyotes near my house – they're all the same three people?"

She remembered the way her attackers had moved. How much their behavior had reminded her of a pack of wolves. Actually, she knew the answer to her own question. Her gut feeling hadn't betrayed her, but she couldn't quite grasp the truth.

"It's just too unreal," she whispered, as Emily nodded. "I know it's true, I know you're right, but my brain can't process it."

"Why are they after Hannah?" Amber blurted out, sounding rebellious. "What has she ever done to those monsters?"

"Usually, they choose their victims out of revenge, or they've been bribed to target someone."

Hannah collapsed back into her chair. She had absolutely no clue why anyone would want to put a spell on her, least of all a Navajo. "Have you heard about this happening before? A *biligaana* cursed by skinwalkers?"

"Can't say I have. People are still terrified of them on the rez, especially in backwater villages. There's tons of stories about people being harassed by *yenaldlooshi*, and they happened quite recently. But you don't hear a lot about this kind of thing outside Navajo Nation."

"Can I stop it?" Hannah's hands balled into fists. "How do I fight them?"

"If you know who the skinwalker is, you can call out his real name when he attacks you in his coyote form. That will kill him."

"How is she supposed to do that?" Amber threw in. "They keep shape-shifting!"

"I never said it was easy."

Hannah refused to give up. "Okay. What else?"

"Not much. The only other way to stop them is to shoot them with bullets dipped in white ash. That will incapacitate them for a while or even kill them sometimes. But you don't need to be that radical. Their influence can be weakened by using certain herbal extracts."

Emily rummaged around in her bag and pulled out a traditional medicine bundle. It was a small bag made of deer leather, with frills at the bottom decorated with little blue and red beads. "I brought this for you. The beads have a symbolic value. The stitching on the front depicts a sandpainting used in the Evil Way Ceremony, to ban evil spirits. The pouch contains corn pollen, cedar ash and dried juniper berries. That should be enough to protect you for a while."

"You suspected this was going on?" Hannah asked, her eyebrows arched. "Or do you carry things like that around all the time?"

"Well, I heard you mentioning shadows turning into coyotes during our lunch together, and that made me think. I talked to Sani and I asked him for help. He gave me advice on what to do if the problem turned out to be related to skinwalkers."

So Emily had visited the village *hataalii*. The man who had such a big influence on Josh – the only person who knew what had happened during his vision quest. Sani, who burdened Josh too much with rituals and traditions of all kinds. She didn't want to be helped by him – in fact, all she wanted was to separate Josh from his old *hataalii* sidekick and teach him how to communicate a little bit more with the world around him – but her options were limited. At this juncture, she could use all the help she could get.

"Thank you so much." Hannah put the bag on the table. When she touched it, a wonderful, tingling feeling spread through her body, so it was obvious the pouch was having a positive effect. Maybe she could put it on a cord and wear it around her neck, underneath her shirt. At any rate, she'd put it by her bed tonight, for lack of a dreamcatcher.

Emily got up. "Who wants coffee?"

Amber and Hannah raised their hands in silent unison.

While Emily was banging away at making them drinks in the kitchen, Amber leaned into Hannah. "You know – those dreams you're having about Josh? I can't shake the feeling they're trying to tell you something, but these skinwalker creeps break into your dreams and turn them into nightmares. I mean, why would a bunch of witches want to make you dream about a guy you're in love with?"

"Beats me. I thought Josh was a recurring theme because I think about him a lot."

Amber frowned. "But then why would it be set in the past?"

"Care to share your theory?"

Amber fidgeted with her red hair. "Well, I think you've experienced all the things you're seeing for real."

Hannah blinked. "Huh?" she said unintelligently.

Amber hesitated. "Maybe you know him from a past life. Something like that. It would explain the entwined aura thing."

"I have to catch a breather." Hannah rubbed her face. "One minute I have this run-off-the-mill simple little life, and the next thing I know, I'm caught up in some bizarre folklore tale featuring witches and reincarnation."

She got up when she heard her cell phone buzzing in the kitchen, darting inside to read the text message she'd received.

"hey sis! u OK down there? it's nice & hot on the rez. josh = walking around w/ a wide smile plastered to his face all day long. it's starting to get on my nerves ;) "

She bit back a laugh, quickly texting back she was fine. Ben never failed to cheer her up. She suddenly missed him terribly, already regretting the fact she couldn't tell him Em's story about the skinwalkers. Ben was so down-to-earth he couldn't even board a plane. If she sprung these myths about witches and black magic on him, he'd cart her off to the nearest loony bin. Still, she looked forward to seeing him again on Friday. Plus, the fact Josh seemed to be in the best of moods ever since he kissed her was touching.

When Emily and Amber went back to the neighboring cabin to check on Ivy, Hannah made her way to the living room and dug up the leather cord from the dreamcatcher stuff Josh had given to her. He surely wouldn't miss a small piece of string from the heap of accessories.

With careful fingers, she tied the cord around the top of the medicine bundle, putting it around her neck and underneath her clothes. It was amazing how powerful the thing was – she felt strong, and so completely different compared to this morning, even if she now knew that evil witches were after her. Their spell had made her feel anxious, suppressing her natural instinct to fight. But now she was ready for battle. Sani's remedy was doing its job perfectly.

Twelve

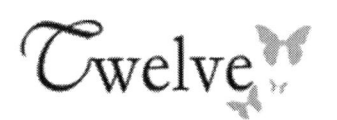

That night, there were no dreams. At least no dreams Hannah could remember. She woke up without the usual headache – as a precaution, she'd just taken a homeopathic sedative Emily had given her – and stretched her legs and arms. The kitchen door slammed shut in the next room, so Emily had probably just left for work.

"Hannah?" she suddenly heard Amber's voice through the door. "You awake yet?"

"Yeah, only just." She got up and stepped into the kitchen, where she found Amber sitting at the table.

"Did you have a good night's sleep?" the neighbor girl asked.

"Yup. Smooth sailing. No nightmares." She grinned at Amber. "So, you girls made any plans to meet up later?"

"We're just going to hang out tonight," Amber replied, clearly trying to assume a carefully neutral tone. " I'll be staying here for the next couple days. My parents are taking Ivy to Window Rock, but I don't mind lounging around here."

"Let me get this straight. You're skipping a trip to Window Rock so you can bum around with us? You are so in love," Hannah established dryly.

Amber couldn't help giggling. "Okay, guilty as charged. There's just something about Navajo people, you know?"

"So, what do your parents think of Em?"

"Oh, they love her. I can tell."

"You told them that you two are an item?"

"Don't have to. They're not blind." Amber got up from the breakfast table. "By the way, I have to go. I promised I'd spend some time with them before they're off to Window Rock at noon. See you tonight, okay?"

"Say hi to your family from me," Hannah called after her.

As soon as she'd scarfed down her breakfast, Hannah went into Ben's bedroom to drag out his laptop and USB modem again. This was going to be expensive, but fortunately, Ben would only see the bills after he got home. She just had to know more about the history of Navajo Nation, now that she was slowly starting to believe she'd dreamed about real past events.

After doing a Google search on 'Navajo History' she clicked on a few links that looked interesting. "The Long Walk," she mumbled to herself, scrolling through a page filled with details about the cruel transportation of Navajo natives to a reservation in the east of the country, at which they were forced to walk for days without pause. It had happened just after the Civil War. Before that, Mexicans had still been active in Navajo territory. Hannah pulled the laptop closer when her eyes fell on a description of Mexicans stealing people to turn them into slaves – entire villages had been ransacked, women and children abducted to serve in the mines. The website featured some scans of black-and-white photographs of soldiers wearing uniforms that looked strikingly familiar. Her heart started thumping even louder when she saw some old pictures of Navajo villages built just after the Navajo people's release from the reservation in the east. The houses looked exactly the same as in her dreams. Octagonal, low constructions with dark clay on the outside.

Oh my God. So now she knew. It wasn't just her imagination, and those skinwalkers were probably not making her dream about the past either. If this was true – if she really knew Josh from a past lifetime – shouldn't she tell him?

She cringed. Not the most brilliant of ideas right now. They'd just shared a few kisses together – hardly the right moment to claim they'd already shared an entire life together. Josh would probably think she was a sucker for predestination and get out while he still could.

Still, she couldn't let things rest. Even though Amber and Emily tried to distract her by taking her out that afternoon and keeping quiet about the skinwalker curse, she couldn't stop thinking about her – now absent – dreams about the past.

On Friday morning, she finally decided to go back to the Page library and bury herself in history books. If that didn't help, she could ask Nick for help. After all, he'd been reading up on Navajo history a lot.

"You're all set for a day trip to remember?" Emily asked dryly, when Hannah clomped out of her bedroom with a shoulder bag crammed full of notebooks, pens and a big bottle of water.

"Yeah, I'm off to the library. I want to read up on Navajo history, now that my dreams about the past have stopped."

"Ah. Because of the reincarnation hypothesis," Emily nodded. They'd talked about it last night, Amber playing the part of talk show host, making her case for her past-life theory.

"Well, yeah. I really want to find out whether all those images I've been seeing are real memories. Maybe not the most exciting trip ever, but hey."

"Why don't you just take Ben's laptop to Grassroots?" Amber asked. "They have free WiFi there. Seems a lot easier than perusing books in the library."

"Are you kidding? Ben's laptop is carbon-dated. There's no WiFi adapter on that thing," Hannah complained. "He hasn't bought new stuff in *years*. He'd rather wait till things disintegrate before he replaces anything."

Emily suppressed a giggle. "Poor you. Well then, the library it is."

The three girls cleaned up the kitchen. Emily and Amber went on a trip to Water Hole Canyon, while Hannah drove off to Page Library to plow her way through piles of books, seated on the very same couch where she'd met Nick the week before. Her cell phone was switched off. She'd called her mother in Alaska – who was staying with their aunt for the summer – for a quick chat, but now it was time to leave the modern world behind for a while.

The hours flew by. Hannah completely lost herself in the nineteenth-century history of the reservation and the Diné people. She was so focused on her books that she forgot to have lunch altogether. When she finally switched on her phone again and read a text from Ben saying they were on their way back, she felt weak with hunger. The good thing was that she had ten pages of notes. All the info she'd gathered in the library made her head spin. The more she'd learned about Diné history, the more she'd gotten convinced she really was seeing images from the past in her dreams. The descriptions of the tumultuous time period between 1800 and 1840 on Navajo soil exactly matched her dream experience –

she'd lived an unsafe, troublesome and dangerous life.

On her way back to the Datsun, Hannah's stomach no longer twisted with hunger pangs, but with nerves. She'd see Josh again, and last time they spoke he'd said he needed time. How would he react to her after three days of separation?

Heart in throat, she drove back to the log cabins and bit her lip when she saw the empty driveway. Okay, so they weren't back yet. No problem – she was in dire need of a fresh shower and some serious lunch anyway.

After showering, Hannah settled on the porch steps with a book. Her heart sped up to a hum when at three o'clock sharp, she could hear the Chevy's engine rumbling in the distance.

Josh parked the car on the drive and turned down the volume on the radio to shut up Ben, who was singing along.

"Hey, sis!" Ben bounded out of the car and up the porch steps. His nose was sunburned, and his blonde hair had gotten even lighter in the past few days. "You still alive?"

"Barely. I was bored to death without having you guys around, obviously."

As Ben hugged her tight, Hannah was acutely aware of Josh turning off the engine, locking the car door and approaching the steps leading up to the porch. When her brother let go of her and popped open one of the beer cans on the table, Josh sidled up to her. A blush crept up her face as she gazed into his dark brown eyes.

"Hey, *shan díín*," he said softly, a gentle smile on his face.

"H-hey," she stammered. "How – how have you been?"

Just great. The desire pulsing through her veins was turning her into a monosyllabic, stuttering idiot again.

Hannah wished she could fling herself into Josh's arms and get a hug from him, too. A long and intense one. But Ben was sitting right here – it'd be downright embarrassing to have Ben bear witness to a prolonged 'My Best Buddy is Groping My Sister' show. Or the other way around. So far, Josh wasn't making a move.

"We had a good time," Josh said. "The weather was great, no flash floods, and we visited all the sites I wanted to show to Nick. Mission 'Promote the Rez' accomplished."

Ben and Josh went on to tell Hannah about their hike on the reservation. Hannah told Ben a convenient lie about dropping by the police station. She also told her brother she hadn't suffered from nightmares any more after he left on Wednesday, but of course she couldn't tell him why.

"Good to hear." Ben patted her on the shoulder, giving her a warm smile.

Hannah flinched. Damn, she felt awful, having to keep things from him. She wished she could tell him about the skinwalker curse, but there was no point freaking him out or being put into a straitjacket before the barbecue had even started.

"Wonderful." Josh chimed in. "But I'm still going to help you make a dreamcatcher. I haven't forgotten."

It was strange to see him again. Strange, because somehow it felt as though Wednesday morning had never happened. Josh sat across from her, a little ways away from her, and he didn't try to hold her hand or scoot closer. He'd said he needed time – and she was willing to give him what he asked for – but still. She felt a bit betrayed by the polite distance he was keeping. Now it *really* felt like she was his big sister. She was actually happy she could flee to the kitchen and prepare the burgers and salad when Josh and Ben got up to fire up the barbecue.

Hannah set the microwave to defrost the burgers, then rummaged through the fridge to pull out the ingredients for a niçoise salad. Cutting the onions was a horrible job – she always cried her eyes out, no matter how sharp the knife or how quickly she turned on the tap. With a grunt, Hannah tried to rub the tears from her cheeks with the back of one hand.

"Hannah?" a voice piped up behind her.

She saw Josh stepping into the kitchen through a blur of tears. He moved up next to her, putting an arm around her shoulders. "Are you crying?" he asked gingerly.

Her heart melted into a puddle when she heard the worry in his voice.

"Yes. It's that onion." She pointed an accusing finger at the cutting board.

Josh started to laugh. "Don't tell me. What did that onion do to you?" he asked, all fired-up. "Did it call you names? Hit you? Don't be afraid, I'll protect you."

Hannah bit back an inane giggle. "Nutcase," she blurted out, rubbing the tears from her eyes.

"Crybaby," he teased.

Hannah bit her lip. His teasing called for a smart comeback, but the look in his brown eyes suddenly made her forget all her vocabulary. Silently, Josh pulled her closer, using one thumb to wipe the tears from her cheeks. "There," he said. His fingers brushed her upper lip, where a single tear had landed. Hannah stared at him speechlessly, her breath hitching in her throat. Josh pushed her up against the kitchen counter and looked at her longingly.

"I really missed you," he whispered.

Hannah's heart almost exploded with love. "I missed you too," she mumbled.

Josh lowered his head and lightly kissed her brow.

Her heart stopped when his hands slid down to her hips and he kissed her again, on her mouth this time, hungrily. She closed her eyes and pressed her lips against his mouth with a soft groan, suddenly wanting him so much it ached.

Before Josh could deepen the kiss, Ben stomped into the kitchen. "Where are those burgers? Oh, here they are," he muttered, yanking the microwave open.

"Sorry," Josh said, turning around. Hannah turned beet red.

"No problem," Ben replied with a smirk. "Don't mind me. I'm not here."

"Come on, I'll help you grill the burgers," Josh offered. He let go of Hannah, but not before planting a feather kiss on her mouth, grinning boyishly. She stared at him as he walked away from her, her eyes roving over his muscular arms and broad shoulders. Completely dazzled, she went back to cutting the onions and mixing the salad. Wow. She suddenly felt a *lot* better.

When she came outside with a bowl of salad, Ben asked her to keep an eye on the burgers as he and Josh unpacked the camping gear. Barbecue tongs in hand, Hannah's mind drifted as she stared at the beautiful red mountains on the other side of Lake Powell. Maybe she should go camping on the rez as well. Emily could join her, or Ben – or Josh. She wouldn't mind pitching a tent with him and get all close and personal inside it. She smiled dazedly, still not entirely able to believe her luck. For once, she was experiencing a pleasant vision.

The smell of scorched veggie burgers brought her back to reality, though.

"Hey, what's burning?" Ben shouted, pulling at the ground sheet balled up inside the Chevy's trunk.

"Oh, shoot." Groaning, she tried to save her veggie burgers by flipping them again. Oh well – the other side didn't look so bad.

Josh stormed out of the log cabin holding another pair of tongs to help her out. "Firefighter to the rescue," he chuckled. "Food hasn't been your best friend tonight so far, huh? First that onion and now the burgers."

Hannah rolled her eyes. "Honestly, I think it's me. Don't blame the food."

"Good thing I'm always around when you're in trouble."

Hannah snorted. "Oh yeah? Maybe it's you. *You're* trouble."

Josh fell silent and stared at her, the smile fading from his lips. Gingerly, he took a step back.

Okay. Clearly, she'd said something wrong. But what? "I was just fooling around. Sorry."

Josh let out a shaky breath and nodded. "Yeah. I know."

"Sorry," she clumsily repeated.

"It's okay," he said curtly, turning around to help Ben fold the ground sheet.

Hannah sighed. If only she could find out which buttons to push and which ones to leave alone, or discover what his touchy-feely subjects were. Because she sure as hell wasn't going to stay away from him. The attraction between them was so strong she felt it in every fiber of her body. Even now, when he was standing at a good twenty paces away from her, she could sense his presence, his aura reaching out to her.

Sure, being with Josh would be challenging. But it would be even more difficult to not be with him.

༄༄༄

"Man, that trek through the rez made me hungry." Ben burped, gulping down his last swig of beer. "Let me do the dishes and leave you two turtledoves outside." He got up and piled up the plates to take them to the kitchen.

Josh grinned. "Thanks, *shik'is*. It's dreamcatcher time."

Hannah got up and fetched the paper bag from the living room. Hopefully, Josh wouldn't notice she'd already cut off a piece from the leather strap to make a necklace for her medicine bundle. It was astonishing how much the magical item influenced her peace of mind. She could feel the leather press against her ribcage, just right of her heart. It made calmness spread throughout her body. All fear was gone. In fact, she was even slightly curious what would happen if she ever ran into the skinwalkers again.

Josh was pensively staring into the flame of the lantern on the table when she returned. Josh looked up and pulled her down next to him, so close she could feel the warmth of his skin, making Hannah blush lightly. "Hi," she mumbled. "Here's the stuff we need."

He pulled the ring made of twigs from the bag. Hannah watched Josh wind the strap around the first bit of the ring, moving his long, slender fingers slowly on purpose so she could see how he did it. "Now you try." He handed her the dreamcatcher hoop. His fingers touched hers for just a split second, but it made her shiver pleasantly. Carefully, she tried to imitate Josh and wind the strap around the twigs as tight as she could.

"Like this?" she asked quietly, looking aside.

"Yeah – like that," he replied in a husky voice. "*Jó nizhóní*. You're doing great."

It felt inexplicably comfortable when he talked to her in Diné Bizaad. Somehow, it reminded her of her dreams of him, talking to her in his own language. Could she risk telling him something about her visions?

Josh picked up the white thread, then took both her hands and showed her the best way to attach it to the ring and start the weaving pattern. As he was watching her weave, he suddenly brought up dreams himself.

"The Diné believe the night sky is filled with thoughts, good and bad ones," he softly told her. "They can enter a person's dreams. The dreamcatcher catches those thoughts, giving you the good ones only."

Hannah finished the first round of stitches, starting the second round with Josh's instructions.

"When the entire inner part of the ring is filled with the woven thread, you leave a small hole in the middle. That's the gateway for the good dreams to enter your mind. The bad dreams get stuck in the web and dissipate in the first light of day."

Hannah looked up to see if Ben was still busy in the kitchen, but the light above the counter was out. The window looking out over the porch was dark. In the flickering light of the candle flame, Hannah saw her own face reflected in the glass, Josh's face right next to her. He watched her with an almost imperceptible smile. The soft light gave them both a halo, and for a moment, Hannah could almost understand what kind of aura Amber perceived whenever she observed the two of them together.

Josh's smile grew cheeky as he turned toward her and pressed a light kiss to her cheek, so soft it felt like a butterfly landing on her skin.

"Stop weaving for a minute," he whispered close to her face, taking the ring from her hands and picking up the silver wire from the table. "I'm going to weave in some silver. And turquoise."

"There's no turquoise bead in the bag," Hannah pointed out.

Josh laughed warmly. "I know. You'll get mine."

Hannah's eyes widened as she saw his hands fumbling for the small braid in his hair. He held it up in front of her. "Why don't you take it out," he said. It was the turquoise bead he always wore in his hair, together with the small red feather symbolizing his father's clan.

"But," she stammered. "But that's your – thingie. You always wear that."

"That's right," he nodded solemnly. "It is my thingie. And now I'm giving it to you." The corners of his mouth tipped up in a smile.

"Well – okay," Hannah gingerly accepted. She carefully took the bead out of his hair, putting the red feather with the other feathers from the paper bag. Mouth agape, she watched Josh weave the bead and the silver wire into a tiny shape in the upper left corner of the dreamcatcher, on top of the work she'd already done. He tied a knot, wove the white thread a bit further and then gave the ring back to Hannah.

"Wow! It looks like a little butterfly," she mumbled, staring at the pattern he'd made.

"No, seriously? What a coincidence," he snickered.

"Oh, shut *up*." She pushed him playfully, unsure what attitude to adopt. This meant a lot to her. Josh had given away the bead symbolizing his clan to decorate her dreamcatcher.

He didn't reply, but leaned into her and kissed her slowly and softly on the mouth. They were both completely silent for a moment. No sound was heard, apart from the radio in the kitchen playing a mournful piano tune. Josh put his hand on her knee, sending a tingling sensation up her thigh. He came closer still, his hair tickling her cheek, his other hand stroking her neck. If only she wasn't holding that stupid dreamcatcher. All she wanted now was to fling her arms around his neck, press herself up against him and kiss him like there was no tomorrow. But if she dropped the dreamcatcher and started groping Josh instead, she'd probably ruin his work.

Dazedly, she opened her eyes when Josh let go of her and ended the kiss. He rubbed his cheek against hers.

"You shouldn't lose the thread," he whispered, his breath faster than usual. His eyes wandered to the dreamcatcher in Hannah's hands.

"When you kiss me, I always lose the thread." She smiled shyly.

Josh smiled back, his cheeks turning a lovely shade of pink. He gently caressed her upper arm and stared at his own tanned hand on her light skin. "When I start touching you, all I want is to hold you forever. But that feeling also scares me." He looked up with uncertainty in his eyes, his voice wavering. "I haven't opened up to anyone like this, not for a very long time."

Puzzled, Hannah blinked her eyes. What was he talking about? He hadn't been a bachelor for *that* long. She took hold of his hand, looking into his dark, melancholy eyes.

"I'd like to, though. You can't imagine how much," he continued softly.

Hannah nodded. "You need time. That's okay." Actually, it was sort of weird, but she could see Josh meant every word he said. He was battling some demons in his head, that much was clear.

At that moment, Ben stepped out of the log cabin. "Hey, that's one cool dreamcatcher! You made that all by yourself?"

"Not the bead and the butterfly. But the rest, yes."

"Good to know. If you ever get tired of teaching high-school French to pimply teenagers, you should start your own New Age store selling those things."

Hannah chuckled. Silently, she worked on, finishing

the weaving and helping Josh fix the three large feathers to the bottom of the ring. He stuck his tiny red feather under the large bead in the middle, and finally used the last bit of leather strap to make a loop at the top so she could hang the dreamcatcher on a peg in the wall. "Here you go," he said, dangling it on her outstretched index finger and pressing a kiss on the palm of her hand.

"I can't thank you enough." Hannah was completely enthralled by the wonderful piece of Diné art she'd made almost entirely by herself.

"You don't know that." Josh got a mischievous dimple in his cheek. "Why don't you give it a try?"

Ben chuckled. "He's challenging you, sis. What are you going to do about it?"

Blushing, Hannah threw her arms around Josh and snuggled up against him.

"Thanks," she mumbled against his neck, kissing him just below his jawline. His arms pulled her closer, and she was where she belonged.

꽃꽃꽃

Later that night Amber, Ivy, and Emily joined them for drinks. Ivy told them stories about her visit to Window Rock earlier that day. "Our parents also want to visit Canyon de Chelly. That's going to be a two-day trip at least."

Amber nudged Emily. "You want to join us? I bet my parents wouldn't mind."

"Yeah, sure! I'm sure I can fit it in."

Hannah sat up when she heard the name of the canyon from her dreams. She'd been there years ago, when she was fifteen. Actually, she was dying to visit the place again. "Sounds cool. Can Ben and I come, too?"

"Of course you can. The more, the merrier."

"What about you?" Hannah asked Josh. Would she be able to remember anything important if she visited the canyon with him? Not the happiest memories, probably. If Amber's theory was correct, she'd decided to break up with him in a previous life near that canyon.

"No, I don't think I'll have time. I still have to drop by Tuba City to take care of college stuff."

"Are you looking forward to going to college after summer?" Ivy asked.

Josh nodded enthusiastically. Hannah listened to him talking about his plans to get a degree and start a school in Kayenta. He wanted to make sure more young people would rediscover their roots and say no to gangs and drug abuse.

"Are drugs such a problem on the rez?" Amber asked, sounding a bit shocked.

"Yeah, especially meth," Josh said grimly. "Methamphetamine. Cheap as dirt and just as widespread. One of my cousins from Chinle got addicted to the stuff a few years back. She's cured now, but she was still psychotic for a full year after quitting meth."

"How did she manage to stay off drugs?"

"I helped her."

"Really? I didn't know," Ben piped up in a surprised voice.

Everyone was silent, looking at Josh expectantly. "Yeah, I organized a two-day ceremony for her," he mumbled. "A *hataalii* eradicates the evil from someone's body by using sandpaintings, sacred chanting, and a prayer circle of friends praying for the patient."

"Did Sani help you?" Emily inquired.

"Yes, although he didn't join me when I went to Chinle. He instructed me how to go about things, and he made me a *jish* to use during the ritual. That's a *hataalii* medicine bundle," he explained to the others.

The conversation buzzed on for a while, but Hannah couldn't focus anymore. She'd shared a look of surprise with Ben when Josh told them about the ritual he'd done for his cousin. The fact Ben had never even heard the story before, was telling enough – once again, it was clear there were big parts of his life Josh didn't want to share with anyone except Sani. It all came back to the old man in Naabi'aani who obviously had such a big influence on Josh. She'd only seen him from a distance, that day at the rodeo, but she hadn't forgotten that Sani had ruined her chance to dance with Josh that day because he'd suddenly needed his assistance. Of course, it was ridiculous to be jealous of some old medicine dude, but still – that old medicine dude knew more about Josh than she did.

"I'm going home," Josh announced when it turned dark. The moon graced the night sky, almost full.

"You want to take the tent and the ground sheet with you?" Ben asked.

"Uhm – on my motorcycle? You're full of good ideas."

Ben laughed. "Oh yeah, I forgot."

"I'll take them with me in the Mustang. I'm dropping by tomorrow."

"I bet you will. Can't stay away from my sister, can you?"

Josh thumped Ben on the back with a huge grin, said goodbye to the others and then slid his hand into Hannah's. She got up and followed him down the steps, beaming with a sort of pride because everybody saw them holding hands.

They sauntered toward the motorbike, and Hannah leaned against the rear wheel. "Look, the moon is almost full," she said, looking up.

Josh followed her gaze and smiled. His arms circled her waist and he pulled her against his body, stroking her back, trailing his fingers down along her spine. Her heart raced as Josh gently rubbed his nose against hers.

"That moon is beautiful, but you ... " He watched her from up close, his eyes riveted on her face. "You're even more radiant. You make the sunlight stick to your skin, caress your face, play with your hair, kiss your mouth." His fingers acted out what his voice was telling her, and when his mouth landed on hers, Hannah groaned softly. Her heart was beating so fast she was sure it would spin out of control. Josh made her feel beautiful like never before. Only he could pull off telling her stuff like that without sounding sappy.

Josh let out a sigh, then let go with a look of regret on his face. He gave her a last peck on the lips and started up his motorbike.

Hannah watched the red taillights recede in the distance when he drove away. For a split second, they reminded her of the glowing, red eyes of skinwalkers. It made her shiver. In that moment, the full moon looked ominous, associated as of old with people magically transforming into animals.

No, she had to stop thinking dark thoughts. The nightmares had stopped bothering her, now that she was wearing the medicine bundle. The dreams and the curse were bound to stop altogether the minute she went back to Las Cruces at the end of summer break. She didn't care anymore what had brought on the curse – she just wanted to be happy and enjoy the love running through her veins like liquid sunlight.

Thirteen

"I'm happy things worked out between you and Josh," Nick said. They were sitting in his uncle's garden enjoying a late breakfast and a pot of tea. "You should have seen him during our trek. Whenever Ben or I mentioned your name, his face lit up like a light bulb."

Hannah smiled, sitting back in her chair as she finished her cup of tea.

"So, any more strange visions?" Nick then asked curiously. "You strike me as a lot calmer than last week. Is it because of Josh and his good influence on you?"

Hannah instinctively reached for her medicine pouch. It was tied around her waist, hidden under her pants. It was a hot day today and she was only wearing a tank top, so she couldn't hide the *jish* anywhere else. She hadn't really talked to Nick since last week. Funny how her anxious feelings seemed more like a bad dream to her now.

"They don't bother me anymore," she quickly replied. "Ever since Josh helped me make a dreamcatcher, they're gone."

The dreamcatcher had been above her bed since Friday night. She hadn't seen the skinwalkers in her dreams anymore, nor had she experienced any more flashes from the past – unfortunately. By now, she was dying to know what was true of Amber's theory about past-life experiences. She'd spent a lot of time together with Ben and Josh in the past few days, and she'd caught herself staring at Josh trying to recall his older face from her dream. Would he really look like that when he grew older? It wasn't entirely implausible.

"Great!" Nick said. "Go, old traditions. Dreamcatchers should be standard fare for therapists and psychologists."

Hannah smiled and got up. "I'm going to hang out at the lakeside. Want to join me?"

Nick shook his head and pointed at the piles of notes and books gathered on the table with a grimace. "It's not a question of wanting. Duty calls."

"I'll catch you later then." She hugged him as they said goodbye at the front door. "If you have any questions, you know where to find the Diné experts."

Whistling to herself, Hannah got into the Datsun and drove down to the lake. She decided to sit at the exact same patch of beach she'd sat before. It was a scary idea to go back to the place where she had her first encounter with the skinwalkers, but that was exactly why she wanted to do it. Facing her fears was the best way to overcome them.

Hannah parked her car and grabbed her bag from the passenger's seat, clutching the pile of magazines she'd bought in Page this morning in her other hand. After climbing the hill that separated the lakeside from the road, she made her way to the same rock that had been her picnic spot last week.

Contrary to last time, there were other tourists on the beach. She could make out a family with a picnic cooler and a brightly-colored beach umbrella in the distance. Hannah let out a relieved sigh. Facing her fears was all very well and good, but the presence of other people definitely made her feel safer.

She'd just finished reading the first article in her New Scientist magazine when a blue, plastic ball came out of nowhere and flopped down onto the sand in front of her feet. Looking up, Hannah saw a girl of about eight years old running toward her from the other side of the beach. Smiling, she picked up the ball and waited for the little girl to reach her. Two other girls, slightly younger, were running after their sister. At least she assumed they were sisters, because the three girls looked very much alike.

Hannah cast a glance aside to the family with the picnic cooler – two boys were playing beachball with their dad. They sure had a lot of kids.

The oldest girl now stopped in front of her. "Hello, miss," she said politely. "I'm sorry we almost hit you. Can we have our ball back?"

Hannah held it up to her. "Of course you ... " she started out, and then stopped breathing as the hair on her arms stood straight up. She stared at the child in front of her incredulously. The girl had a strange eye color – yellow-brown. Her sisters, appearing on either side of her, gazed back at her with the same disconcertingly wolfish eyes.

What was happening? Who *were* these kids?

The girl aged about six standing on the left giggled, and her sisters did the same, their eyes all watching Hannah's face with unsettling intensity, staring straight past her outstretched hand holding the ball.

A cold hand closed around her heart. They were *not* children. She could sense it – she could tell, from every move they made, from the mocking smile present on each of their faces.

"Thank you," the oldest girl in the middle said, her

hand touching Hannah's fingers as she took the ball from her. Hannah closed her eyes, breaking into a sweat. The light touch sent a horrible shiver through her body. That kid better stay away from her. If the girl *dared* touch her again...

She balled one hand into a fist, then stopped, her heart lodged in her throat. What the hell was she about to do?

"Come on, let's go," one of the younger girls said, turning around. She darted away, laughing at the top of her voice, and her sisters followed suit. Their laughter sounded challenging, ominous, provoking, as they ran in the direction of the family with the picnic cooler.

Hannah's stomach churned as she got up, her legs trembling. She wasn't going to stick around to find out whether those girls belonged to the Happy Beach Parasol family or not. She had to get off this beach, right *now*.

With shaking hands, she stuffed the magazines into her bag and ran up the hill to get to her car. Still shivering, she crawled behind the wheel and slammed the door shut with an angry thud, blindly staring at her hands clasped together in her lap.

Something had been wrong with the three girls. The looks they'd given her, the way they'd talked to her and mockingly laughed at her – it couldn't be a coincidence. Or could it? Oh my God. She'd almost hit one of them. Used violence to scare away kids. Little girls. What would the parents have done if they'd seen that? If those people with the umbrella had even *been* their mom and dad.

Defeatedly, Hannah rested her head on the steering wheel and started to cry. When would this nightmare end? Emily's medicine bag may not be enough after all. Or maybe she was just really going nuts, seeing things and being spooked for no reason.

☙ ☙ ☙

When Hannah got home, she found the log cabin empty. No one was there for a bit of mindless chit-chat to take her mind off things. Hannah read Ben's sticky note on the fridge, telling her he'd decided to drive to Page for some shopping.

Fortunately, she'd meet up with Josh today. He was picking her up this afternoon to visit Antelope Canyon.

The sound of his Ford Mustang surprised her as she was busy making toast with jam in the kitchen. A wide smile appeared on her face. He was early. Apparently, he couldn't wait to see her either.

With butterflies flitting around in her stomach, Hannah walked out the door to welcome him. Josh was just strolling up the lawn in dark blue jeans and a slim-fit brown shirt, wearing the same sunglasses he'd worn on the day they had bumped into each other at the gas station. He had a black Stetson on his head and brown cowboy boots on his feet. He looked absolutely stunning. She hoped she wasn't drooling by the time he walked up the steps to the porch to lock her in a warm embrace. Hannah put her head on his shoulder. This was just what she needed after that strange morning on the beach.

"Hey, honey," she whispered.

"Hi, *she'at'eed*." He called her his girlfriend in his own language now. It still made her blush.

Josh smiled when he caught her red cheeks, running his hands lightly down her back, caressing the exposed skin just above her tailbone. Hannah snaked her arms around his waist and snuggled up against him. His fingers were warm on her skin, his lips even warmer on her mouth when he kissed her. She responded and kissed him back eagerly, feeling all warm inside when he carefully touched her cheek, almost seeming afraid to disturb the crackling tension between them. She kissed him, and kissed him, and had lost all track of time when Josh finally released her and took a step back. His eyes were close, love and desire evident in his dark irises.

"I feel so safe when I'm with you," she whispered.

"When I'm with you, I forget everything around me," he spoke softly. "It's like time stands still, and I can step out of its shadow."

Hannah fell silent, lost for words. The way Josh opened up to her touched her heart in so many ways, even though his remarks were cryptic at best. "I'm uh – going to change into something more suitable, okay?" she stuttered, trying to regain her composure. "So I won't burn alive during our trip."

Josh blew out a breath. "You do that," he replied, his eyes sweeping over her bare shoulders and plunging neckline. "Make sure you cover your shoulders or you'll look like a lobster."

Hannah quickly disappeared into her bedroom and pulled a generic white T-shirt from her closet. It would reflect the sunlight and it was big enough to hide her medicine pouch under when she wore it around her neck. She preferred feeling it close to her heart. Maybe that's why she'd gotten scared again at the beach – the medicine bundle hadn't been at its usual spot between her breasts. And the last thing she needed this afternoon was being plagued by irrational fears or visions when she would venture out with Josh alone for the first time. Just the two of them.

Her stomach clenched. She hadn't been truly alone with him since their first kiss. All the time, she'd hung around with him and Ben. Or him, Ben and everyone else. The thought of going out with just *him* actually made her sort of nervous. Which was stupid – Antelope Canyon wasn't exactly deserted at this time of day. They'd probably trip over tourists wherever they went.

Josh took her hand when she stepped outside. "So, shall we?" he mumbled.

She nodded and swallowed down the lump in her throat.

Hannah tried to relax in the Mustang's passenger seat, turning her face to the bright skies above. It looked like it was going to be a fantastic day with lots of sun. Which was good, because Antelope Canyon would look stunning with the bright sunlight slanting into the famous, narrow slot canyon, lighting up its red sandstone walls. A river used to run through it, gradually paving a way into the rocks until it had turned into the canyon it was today, but the water had dried up a long time ago. The Diné saw Antelope Canyon as a sacred place, although much of its sanctity had disappeared with the advent of hordes of tourists eager to see the natural wonder.

"I bet it'll be busy today," Hannah said.

Josh sighed. "Yeah. I still don't get why my people decided to open the canyon for everyone to see. We kept the location a secret for years."

"The root of all evil?" she ventured.

He twisted his face. "Yeah. Money makes the world go round, right?"

She chuckled. "Speaking of which, don't I need to pay you? You know, for being my tour guide today?"

"I'll think about it." Josh gave her a mischievous wink.

Hannah bit back a nervous giggle. She couldn't help letting her imagination get the better of her. By the time Josh parked the Mustang on the sands close to the slot canyon, she wished the droves of tourists would magically disappear from the famous gorge so she could stroll – or fool – around with Josh without any inquisitive eyes around.

"We'll have to walk the last bit," he said, sticking a reservation permit in the left corner of his windshield and stuffing the tickets he'd bought in LeChee in his back pocket.

"Is someone going to check those tickets?" Hannah thought aloud.

Josh sniggered, slinging an arm around her shoulder. "Hey, don't be a cheapskate! We're not going to sneak our way in. It's bad enough we're not hiring a professional, official guide for this visit."

"Oh, I think you're professional enough. And I'm not just saying that because I'm in love with you."

"No?" Josh arched an eyebrow. They had reached the entrance of the canyon.

"No, I'm not. You just know your stuff. A lot of stuff, in fact." Hannah stepped forward, but was stopped by Josh's arm blocking her way.

"Aren't we forgetting something?" he mumbled into her ear. He pulled her against him, making her heart speed up.

"Oh, uhm, yeah," she stuttered with a blush. "I have to pay the professional guide."

"What do you think he'd want from you?" Josh said with a mock-pondering look on his face, challenging her with a hint of a smile.

She bit her lip. "Tough question."

He grinned boyishly before leaning into her, pushing her back against the rocky walls. The stones had heated up in the hot sun, scalding her skin. "Ouch!" she giggled. "It's burning me."

Josh laughed out loud, pulling her into the canyon by

her arm. Inside, the rocks were shrouded in shadows. Once again, he slowly pressed her up against the wall, making her shoulders rest against the cold stone.

"That better?" he whispered, his mouth turned up in a teasing smile. Hannah looked up at him, and was struck by the tenderness in his eyes. He didn't just see her blushing cheeks or her soft lips – he saw *her*.

When he gently kissed her, a shaky breath escaped her lips and she closed her eyes. His hands roamed her upper body, running down her spine tantalizingly slowly. He opened her mouth with his tongue. Cautiously, but deliberately, and with such obvious desire that it made her knees turn to jelly. She wound her arms around his neck and moved in closer, when she suddenly heard the echoing voice of a real professional guide bouncing off the canyon walls. In the background, she heard the murmuring whispers of a group of tourists.

With a flushed face that undoubtedly made her look like a radiant tomato, Hannah scooted away from Josh. Darting a look over her shoulder, she saw their performance had garnered a few stares of criticism from the elderly people in the group.

Josh let go of her and followed her gaze. "Don't worry," he said, kissing her lightly on the tip of her nose. "They're just jealous they can't make out with *their* guide."

Hannah chuckled nervously. "So, has payment been sufficiently settled, then?"

"You bet." Josh grabbed her hand. "Now that Mr. Benally has received his paycheck, he will show you the nicest spots of the canyon."

She grinned foolishly, trailing behind him as they entered Antelope Canyon. Even though she'd been here quite a few times, the place never failed to impress her. The different shades of red and yellow in the rock walls were magnificent. She took one picture after another with the camera she'd brought along, asking the next couple they encountered to take a picture of her and Josh, standing hand in hand close to a spot where the sunlight hit the canyon floor directly. In the picture, their faces were flooded with light from the glow of the sunbeam's reflection in the sand.

The entire walk through the canyon took them about twenty minutes including photo stops. When they were at the end, Josh suggested they visit Lower Antelope Canyon as well. "There'll be fewer people there," he said. "All the photographers will be coming to the Upper section because of the light. Lower will be practically deserted right now."

They turned around and ambled along the same way they came. The next big group of tourists would only get here around three o'clock, according to Josh, so they had the canyon all to themselves on their way back. Sunbeams entered the canyon at regular intervals, illuminating the clouds of dust swirling around in the air, the sand scuffed up by the footsteps of people who had passed here not long ago. The fine dust transformed into mysterious shapes in the air – delicate, white apparitions looking like spirits twirling in the sunlight. Hannah stopped in her tracks to watch the phenomenon. "Look at that," she whispered in awe. "It's like an angel is dancing in the light."

Josh hugged her from behind, looking at the dust devils in silence. "This is why the Diné think this place is sacred," he quietly said after a minute. "You can connect with the spirit world – by passing into the veil."

Hannah turned around in the circle of his arms and looked up at him curiously. "The veil? That sounds fascinating."

"It's the other side – the deeper level of existence

that the white people call the Otherworld, Heaven, the hereafter, the faerie world. All of that wrapped into one. The veil is everywhere around us. It is a link with the past, a way to talk with our ancestors. A world between worlds that you can enter in deep meditation to see what has already happened and what will happen. It is the world we visit when we go on a vision quest."

"Did you see things from the Otherworld as well when you did yours?"

Josh nodded, getting the absent look in his eyes Hannah had come to know so well by now. "Yes," he replied. "Many things."

"So have you seen things from the future as well?" Hannah rushed on. She didn't want to lose Josh, his mind wandering to a place where she couldn't follow.

"You see what happens, but you make your own future. You get wise counsel, and those words of wisdom should be enough."

"What were they? Your wise words?"

Josh stared into the distance, past the sunbeams and the dancing spirits in the air. For a second, Hannah thought she'd scared him off, before he turned his face toward her again. The light in his eyes was gentle and unafraid. He no longer wanted to shut her out. "I was told to make peace, and to find it for myself."

Hannah stared at him in awe. "That's beautiful," she whispered.

He bent down and kissed her with incredible tenderness. "Yes. Yes, it is."

Holding hands, they strolled back to the entrance of the gorge, where a new group of visitors had gathered. Josh showed the local guide their tickets, and then they were outside again, blinking against the sunlight.

"It's boiling out here," Hannah puffed.

"Let's go to Lower Antelope quickly." Josh opened

the car, a wave of heat hitting them in the face. "You want some boiled water?" he asked, tossing her a bottle from the back seat.

"Oh, I don't mind. Anything but boiled soda. Now *that*'s gross!"

"If you were really thirsty, you wouldn't say no," Josh pointed out with a wink.

"Spoke the strict guide," she added, diving away when Josh punched her playfully.

Lower Antelope Canyon was a lot narrower than the upper part, and the bottom was more uneven. They had to scramble over rocks and avoid fissures every now and then. When they reached the end of the canyon, sweat was dripping from Hannah's brow and her feet were aching, though. Her worn-out Converse sneakers weren't the best choice for rock-climbing. Josh was having an easier time with his cowboy boots.

"Do we have to go back the same way we came?" she asked, trying not to sound too desperate or tired.

Josh shook his head. "No, there are stairs leading to the surface further up ahead. We can walk back to the parking lot from there."

Once they'd reached them, Hannah slouched against the staircase railing. "I wouldn't mind sitting down for a minute. Catch my breath." She demonstratively plonked down on the lower steps.

Josh sat down next to her. "Well, okay then. As long as my professional guided tour isn't going to suffer."

"All-righty, Mr. Benally," Hannah drawled. "Whatever *you* say."

"Hmm. Sucking up to the guide?" Josh put an arm around his shoulders, cocking an eyebrow.

"Yeah, of course. It's always good to have friends in high places, they say." Hannah felt her heart skip a beat when he scooted closer and caressed her back.

"Oh, really?" he said in a husky voice. "You're one of those girls? You want me to take you to a special place where no regular tourists are allowed? Just you and me and whatever else pops up?" Josh smiled seductively, waggling his eyebrows, and burst out laughing when Hannah turned beet red.

"You're crazy," she mumbled.

"And I'm crazy about you, *she'at'eed*." He pulled her close and kissed her warmly. Hannah grabbed at the back of his neck as Josh's hands slid up from her waist to her upper body, palming her breasts. His right hand trailed upward past her breasts to her neckline, accidentally touching the medicine pouch underneath her shirt.

His hand stopped, lingering on the spot. Hannah's heart sped up, but this time with apprehension. The last thing she wanted was to explain her medicine bundle to Josh. She had no idea how he would respond. After all, she'd deliberately been keeping things from him, and she'd promised she'd tell him if something was bothering her.

There was only one way to stop him from asking more questions – she had to distract him. Groaning in fake pain, she doubled up and gasped for breath, pulling herself from his arms.

"Hey! What's wrong?" he exclaimed, sounding panicked.

"I have this sudden stab of pain in my stomach," she squeaked.

Josh rubbed her back in consolation and supported her when she got up. "You feeling sick?"

"No, not really. But maybe I should lie down for a while."

"Let's get out of the canyon first. Lean on me, okay?"

"How far it is to the car?" she panted feebly, once they'd reached the top of the stairs.

"Let's find you a place to lie down first." Josh pointed at a shady spot underneath a bush. "Come on. Here's some shade."

Hannah crumpled down with a sigh, rolling onto her back. Her head and upper body were in the shade. Josh sat down next to her, gently stroking her forehead.

Now that she was lying down, Hannah felt how tired she was. She didn't even have to feign feeling nauseous and worn-out anymore. The warmth radiating off the rocks underneath her back made her slip into a slumber. Josh's presence next to her made her feel calm. Everything was so peaceful.

ೲೲೲ

She didn't know how long she'd been asleep, but she jolted awake with a dry mouth and an anxious feeling in the pit of her stomach. Somehow, something had changed. Hannah opened her eyes, shifting them from left to right. She was still lying on her back, her heartbeat hammering in her chest. When she tried to sit up, she noticed her right hand had convulsively balled into a fist against her chest. Propping herself up with the other hand, she stared at her fingers clutching Emily's medicine bundle, sweat pooled up in her palm.

Oh, no. Apparently she'd had a bad dream when she dozed off. She'd pulled the pouch from underneath her shirt, holding it in plain sight.

Now she truly felt nauseous. Josh had probably seen the *jish*. There was no way to avoid questions anymore. Out of habit, she hid the bag under her shirt again and looked around. Where was he, anyway?

Josh had moved to the other side of the bushes,

staring out over the dry, endless landscape, his hand shielding his eyes from the setting sun.

"Josh?" she called out uncertainly. Her breath hitched. Dimly, she felt something in his attitude had changed, and it scared her. He looked lonely, distant and defensive, standing there ramrod straight.

When he turned around and their gazes collided, Hannah felt her heart sink. Something was wrong – horribly wrong.

"Feeling better?" Josh kneeled in front of her and gave her a smile that didn't touch his eyes.

"I'm okay," she said in a small voice. "My stomach feels fine now."

"Good," he said crisply. "Let me take you home then."

Hannah let herself be pulled up and taken to the car. It was a short walk, but the distance seemed to triple in the oppressive silence between them. Sheer panic surged through Hannah's body. Josh's hand in hers felt like it was hewn out of stone. He'd clammed up, and she didn't understand why. If he'd seen the medicine bag, maybe he was angry she had kept things from him, but why didn't he just say so? Or ask for an explanation? His metamorphosis was absolute and unfathomable.

Hannah felt her stomach turn as they sat down in the car, still without uttering a word. Josh started up the engine and turned toward her. "If I drive too fast and you feel sick again, let me know."

Hannah risked glancing up at him. His eyes looked sad and determined at the same time. If only she could reach out and touch him, pull him toward her, but she didn't dare move.

Josh turned his gaze toward the road again, his hands tightly gripping the steering wheel. She couldn't remember what nightmares had plagued her, but the reality to which she'd woken up had to be much, much worse.

When they turned onto Lakeshore Drive and the beach of St. Mary's Port appeared in the distance, Hannah couldn't take it anymore.

"Josh," she started, cringing at her faltering voice. "What's wrong?"

He looked sideways, his eyes distant. "We need to talk," he said, his voice so cool it sent a shiver through her.

Josh kept driving, passing the beach and turning onto the sandy track leading up to the log cabins. He parked the car alongside the road and cut the ignition before turning toward her. The enduring silence between them made Hannah's ears throb.

"I'm sorry," he finally spoke up. "But I need some space. This is all going too fast."

She eyed him uncomprehendingly. "You – you need time?" she croaked.

Silence tick-tocked between them. Josh closed his eyes, slowly shaking his head. "I think I made a mistake."

A mistake?

His words hit her heart like bullets. Tears welled up in her eyes as she stared at Josh, completely lost for words. Her hands started to shake. She wanted to say something, convince him this was nonsense, but a giant hand had locked her throat, preventing her desperate thoughts from spilling out.

"But – why?" she finally whispered plaintively.

"I thought I wanted this, but it's not working for me. I should have thought it over. I'm sorry," he said in a monotone. His eyes didn't betray a single feeling or thought going on in his head.

Hannah swallowed, blinking back her tears. Her

heart slowed down, stuttered, and for a second, she wished she would just disappear. She'd never felt more hurt and betrayed in her entire life. "Oh," she whispered.

He looked grim, his face almost creased with distaste, as if he was about to kick her out of the car.

"Well, I guess I should be going then." Her thoughts were a mindless jumble, spinning wildly. Hannah remembered how Josh had looked at her with such heartbreaking desire when they'd kissed each other for the first time. He'd said how much she meant to him. And now, it was all gone. He didn't want her anymore – just like that.

With teary eyes, she reached for the door handle on her side when suddenly, she felt his hand on her shoulder. Hopeful, she looked up. Was he going to stop her?

"I'll see you around," Josh said softly.

She tried to decipher the look in his eyes, the emotions hiding behind them. No regret. No sadness. No, it was acceptance. And yet, he looked so mournful that she couldn't believe he was only seventeen.

The next moment, his hands were back on the steering wheel, his eyes cold again. He'd shut her out. He had closed the door.

In a daze, Hannah got out of the car. She just stood there, not looking back when Josh turned the car and drove off.

She was still there, motionless, when Ben appeared around the corner, his face a big question mark. "Was that Josh just driving away? Didn't he want to have dinner with us?" He looked more closely at his sister, taking a step toward her. "Hey, Han. You feeling okay? You look like shit."

She shook her head. "No." *No. No.* The only word repeating over and over in her mind. She numbly stared at her brother.

"Okay, you're scaring me. What's up?" he insisted.

"He ... " She felt fresh tears well up in her eyes.

"Who?" Ben put his arms around her and held her close. "Who?" he repeated softly.

"Josh," she sobbed, clinging to Ben.

"Did something happen to him?" Ben gently shook her. "Say something, please."

"He – broke – up – with me," she hiccuped, sounding pathetic. "He's gone. He doesn't want me anymore."

Ben hugged her even tighter, rubbing her back. At the same time, she felt him tense up. He was angry.

"Come on," he whispered in her ear after what seemed like an eternity. "You can't stay here. Let's go back to the cabin."

He carefully led her up the porch steps, dismissing Ivy with a wave of his hand as she approached them. Hannah stumbled into her bedroom, sinking down on the bed.

Ben followed her and sat down on the edge of the bed. "Tell me what happened."

Hannah cleared her throat. "Everything was fine today. And then, he suddenly changed. He was so distant. He – said he'd made a mistake. Said he needed space."

Ben's face grew more puzzled by the second. "Made a mistake?" he echoed. "But that's absurd. I *know* him. I've seen the way he looks at you. It's impossible."

"Please, Ben." Hannah's voice had dried to a whisper. "Emily was right to warn me. Josh pushes people away when they come too close. She said so. I should have listened to her." She turned on her side, staring at the wall.

Ben touched her shoulder. "Okay. I know this must

be horrible for you. I'll leave you alone."

She turned her tear-streaked face toward her brother. "Are you having dinner at the neighbors'?" she sniffed.

Ben smiled. "Yeah, I'll be close. No worries." His voice was sweet. "I guess you want to stay here?"

Hannah nodded wordlessly.

"You still want to tag along to Canyon de Chelly tomorrow?" he went on.

She hesitated for a second. The idea of staying here for two days without Ben to cheer her up when she missed Josh like crazy wasn't exactly appealing. Actually, it was a good idea to leave St. Mary's Port behind for a few days.

"I still want to," she replied. "Tell the Greenes I'll feel better tomorrow."

Ben patted her on the head, then got up and quietly closed her bedroom door. Hannah waited till she heard Ben leave the house before she burst out in another bout of tears. In the end, she slipped away into a restless sleep. The dark taking hold of her felt peaceful and safe.

Fourteen

She didn't feel better.

All morning, Hannah stayed in bed, staring at the ceiling. The weather outside was beautiful, and birds were singing close to her window. It was strange how everything around her just went on like nothing had changed, while she seemed to be frozen in time.

She listlessly threw on some clothes after Emily finally knocked on her door to get her out of there, and walked into the kitchen, waving at Amber and Ivy sitting at the table.

"Tea?" Amber offered, pointing at a pot of green tea in front of her.

Hannah nodded. She poured herself a mug, staring thoughtlessly at the rings in the wood of the table.

"Hey." Emily scooted closer and put her hand on Hannah's. "Are you feeling a bit better?"

"Yeah. I'm okay." The tiniest hint of a smile creased her lips.

"Would you like some breakfast?" Ivy pushed a plate with some pancakes toward her.

Hannah shook her head. "Not hungry," she mumbled.

"When was the last time you ate something?" Emily asked in a mother-hen voice.

Hannah thought back. The last thing she remembered eating was a granola bar she'd had in the car on their way to Lower Antelope Canyon. She shrugged. "Dunno. I don't want anything."

Emily pulled the plate closer and started to cut the pancakes into pieces. "At least have a few bites," she almost begged. "Ben said we should feed you."

Hannah heard the shower turn off in the bathroom, and knew Ben would come back to the kitchen in a minute. Of course she didn't want to worry him, so she reluctantly forced herself to eat some morsels as a poor excuse for a late breakfast.

Pancakes. The last time she'd had pancakes was when Josh had made them.

When Ben was done showering and stepped into the kitchen in clean clothes, she'd managed to eat half a pancake.

"I'm going to pack," she said, giving him a half-smile.

In her bedroom, Hannah haphazardly tossed some clothes into her duffel bag, her gaze lingering on the dreamcatcher above her bed. She wasn't sure she wanted to bring it with her on the trip. Part of her wanted to dream of Josh again, so she wouldn't feel so alone.

Heaving a sigh, she zipped up her bag and left the dreamcatcher hanging above her bed. Then, she slogged to the bathroom to grab her toothbrush, shampoo and a few towels.

Ben was drinking coffee at the counter when she came back into the kitchen. "How are you?" he said.

Hannah quietly leaned against him, settling into his arm around her shoulders.

"Lousy," she mumbled.

"Just take it easy today."

When Hannah got outside and put her bag in the

Chevy, Paul and Sarah eyed her with pity, so they'd obviously heard about what had happened. The Greenes were busy stuffing bags into the trunk of their station wagon.

Josh was probably on his way to Tuba City by now. Maybe that's why he needed space. To hook up with all those nice Navajo girls his own age on campus.

Hannah bit her lip to stop herself from crying again. This was stupid. He wasn't worth agonizing over if he treated her like this.

Ben had offered to drive, so after a few more minutes, they drove off in his car, following the Greenes. The radio blared an eighties tune. Slowly but surely, Hannah relaxed in her seat and managed to un-hunch her shoulders and neck, the sun touching her face.

The medicine pouch rested on the skin between her breasts. She'd put it around her neck again, the memory of the creepy girls at the beach still fresh in her mind.

The landscape scurried past the car in a blur of red, yellow and brown, the blue sky above seeming almost turquoise.

Just like the bead Josh had given to her.

ಊಊಊ

All afternoon, Hannah sat next to Ben with an artificial hint of a smile plastered on her face so she wouldn't worry him too much. The slice of pizza Ben had ordered for her at a drive-thru was on a napkin in her lap, and she was chewing on a bit of crust with a face she hoped looked hungry and lively enough.

"How much further?" she inquired.

Ben looked at the map in his lap. "Uhm – I don't know exactly."

Hannah stuffed the last bite of pizza in her mouth,

crumpled the napkin into a ball and pulled the map toward her. "Let me have a look then."

She calculated it was still a twenty-mile drive to Chinle, and from there, about seven miles into Canyon de Chelly territory to the campsite where they'd spend the night. The place was close to Spider Rock, its slim spire standing tall in the middle of the canyon.

Ben followed the neighbors' station wagon taking the exit to Spider Rock Campground. It didn't take long before they reached the entrance. Paul went into the reception building to announce their arrival and pay for the large hoghan they'd rented.

Hannah smiled as they drove on and the large construction came into sight. It was a beautiful building, made of tree trunks plastered with clay. The location was breathtaking, too. The door, traditionally overlooking the east, offered them a fantastic view of the valley.

She got out of the car and carried her bags to the door. Then, she walked toward the fence near the precipice, her eyes sweeping the canyon.

Ivy settled down next to her. "Isn't this just beautiful?" she said.

Hannah nodded. "It is."

"You want to join us for a walk? My parents are too worn out from driving all the way here, so they're just going to stay here and prepare dinner. Emily and Amber want to take a stroll along the path at the far end of the canyon. We're going to visit the bottom of the canyon with a guide tomorrow."

"Yeah, sure. I'll go ask Ben too."

Her brother had just locked the car when she approached him. "You tired?" Hannah asked.

"Sort of. Why?"

"You want to join us on a walk?"

"Nah." He shook his head. "I promised Paul and Sarah I'd help them cook. You go and take a walk with the girls. By the time you get back here, we'll have a nice meal waiting for all of you."

Hannah hugged Ben, pressing herself against him with a sigh. "Thanks," she simply said. "For everything."

☙☙☙

They drove to the end of the road meandering along Canyon de Chelly. Once she was ambling along the edge of the canyon with Emily, Amber and Ivy, Hannah began to feel a bit better, despite everything that had happened yesterday. It was all so quiet, magical and untouched. There were hardly any tourists on the path, and no sound from the modern world could be heard from here – no car engines, no machines, no loud music. It must have been like this hundreds of years ago. The path took them past scraggly trees, big, red rocks, and patches of sand. Every now and then, their walk took them close to the canyon's edge, and each time it did, the surface dropped away and showed them another magnificent view.

"Come on, let's check out what's up there," Amber called out, pointing at a rock plateau higher up the hill, away from the beaten track. "I bet the view's fantastic."

They came across a fork in the road. To the left, the path disappeared into some woodland, and to the right, a narrower track snaked upwards, leading to an outcropping overlooking the entire canyon.

Hannah gingerly took a step forward, suddenly feeling dizzy. She almost lost her balance and bumped into Ivy. "Sorry," she mumbled, trying to steady herself. She had the sudden urge to run up the hill, even though her wooziness hadn't gone. Instead, it turned into a strange and urgent feeling of *déjà-vu*. Every step Hannah took further upward made her surer – she'd seen this all before. She had walked this road before.

Her heart skipped a beat when she finally reached the rocky edge of the precipice at the end of the track. In her run uphill, she'd entirely forgotten about her three friends behind her. Hannah stood on the plateau at the end of the path and stared at the scene completely dumbfounded.

This was the place in her dreams.

She squatted down, blinking her eyes in disbelief. Her eyes roamed the valley below, the shape of the rocks, the hill sloping down behind her. It was beyond doubt – this was where the skinwalkers had cornered her, their faces morphing into something demonic. This was the wind-swept place where she had almost plunged to her death in order to escape them. This was where she'd broken up with Josh in her dream.

Behind her, Emily, Amber and Ivy had caught up with her, taking in the stunning view in awe.

"Catching a breather?" Emily asked, looking at Hannah still squatting down. "No surprise there. I thought you were trying to set an Olympic record running up this hill."

Hannah nodded absently, still panting. What a discovery. So her dreams really weren't just dreams after all. Amber's theory was correct.

"What's up?" Amber said, sitting down next to her.

Hannah bit her lip. "I know this place."

Amber frowned at her, non-plussed, then caught on. "Wait a minute. You mean – from your dreams?"

Hannah nodded silently, a sudden tear running down her cheek. She didn't understand. If this place was real – if she somehow had visions of a past where Josh and she had shared a life together, why was it all over between them? It wasn't fair. He *belonged* with her. She could feel it in every fiber of her being.

"That is so bizarre," Amber whispered. "So you've really been here before?"

Hannah nodded. Looking around, she tried to search for more clues. Close to the edge of the precipice, there was an old, gnarly tree. In a flash, Hannah remembered a smaller, younger tree being there in her dreams. It was all too remarkable to be a coincidence. She had to talk to Josh about it. Finally tell him about the dreams she'd had.

But by now, it was too late. What was she supposed to say to him? That she had this hinky dream thing going on in which they were lovers in a past life? If all was correct, she had broken up with *him* last time. Maybe he was subconsciously scared to get hurt again. Heck, for all she knew it was a conscious thing. Perhaps he was having the same weird dreams about *her*.

No – Josh wouldn't want to talk about it, because he'd clearly said it was all going too fast for him. Suggesting they had a century-old history together would crank up the pace to lightning speed in no time.

When the girls finally made their way back to the hoghan, Hannah was still mulling things over in her head. She passed Ben frying potato slices in a pan on a gas stove without a word. Sensing her distress, he dropped his spatula and followed her into the hoghan.

It was light inside, thanks to the fire burning in the middle of the building. Someone had put her bag on top of one of the mattresses on the left. Her sleeping bag had been unpacked and unrolled.

"I unpacked some of your stuff." Ben put an arm around her. "I couldn't find your dreamcatcher, though."

"I didn't take it," Hannah replied softly. "I couldn't

stand looking at it anymore."

Ben flopped down on his own mattress with a solemn face, patting the space next to him. Hannah obliged, looking at him with a question in her eyes. "If you want to get out of St. Mary's Port for a while, just holler," he said seriously. "Go visit mom. Take a cheap flight to Alaska and stay with Aunt Beth for a while."

Hannah swallowed her tears back. Damn, Ben was just way too sweet. "No – no, of course not," she stuttered. "I'm not going to abandon you."

"You sure?"

"Yeah."

Ben didn't look convinced. "Well, okay. If you say so."

That night, Hannah sat with the others until the sun set. The few lanterns on the rickety table next to the hoghan lit up the dark, illuminating Em and Amber's happy, smiling faces. Hannah quietly observed the happy couple, and just for a minute, she wished the ground would swallow her up and spit her out again in a place where she could forget Josh and her had ever been that happy.

ೊೊೊ

The following morning, Hannah woke up with a nagging headache. As she stretched her arms, she stared at the fire still burning in the middle of the hoghan. The other mattresses were empty, and one glance at her cell phone told her why – it was almost eleven o'clock.

Stuffing the medicine pouch into the pocket of her PJs, she dragged herself to the campsite shower facilities. As the hot water hit her face and warmed her body, Hannah thought back to her strange meeting at the beach – those three creepy girls, and the way they'd laughed at her. Something had been profoundly wrong about the whole encounter, she could sense it. Clearly, the curse hadn't left her yet and the medicine bundle wasn't powerful enough. She should ask Emily for more help – provided her friend *was* capable of offering more help. Most likely, Sani would have to step in. Trying to lift the curse would help to distract her from the break-up with Josh, moreover.

At twelve o'clock sharp, a Navajo guide showed up at their hoghan, driving an enormous Jeep. As they drove off down the bumpy road toward the valley, Hannah leaned into Emily and whispered, "I had this panic attack the other day, Em. I think I should ask Sani for more advice."

Emily gave her a look of concern. "You get all the bad luck at once, don't you? Well, you should come down to Naabi'aani tomorrow then. Nick's coming too. He asked me if we could both take a critical look at his dissertation. Afterwards, you can go see Sani."

Hannah swallowed the sudden lump in her throat. "But – *he* might be there tomorrow," she objected in a small voice.

Emily looked at her with pity in her eyes. "Honey, I know. But you'll have to face Josh at some point." Grabbing Hannah's hand, she continued: "And I'll support you. I'll be there all the way."

"Thanks, Em."

Hannah leaned back in her seat and stared out the window. The drive into the canyon took them past scraggly trees and bushes, fields of tall grass and red rocks. Their guide parked the Jeep close to a natural hole in the rocks called 'The Window' by the locals. Ivy and Sarah took out their cameras to snap pictures, while the guide gave them some background information about life in the canyon in past and present times.

"When the soldiers of the United States invaded this canyon in 1864, it was a refuge for Diné people fleeing from Mexican oppression in the south. The people believed this canyon would protect them because it had always been a sacred place," he told them.

Hannah's heart skipped a beat. So this canyon had been a safe haven for Navajo people running away from Mexicans. Maybe she'd come to this canyon in her past life to keep safe?

"The Americans ended the peaceful existence of the canyon dwellers when they used the scorched-earth policy to drive them out," the guide continued. "They killed all the livestock, burned the fields and cut down the peach trees growing throughout the valley. There was nothing left for the people but to surrender before winter came to strike them with famine. They were sent to Fort Defiance, and from there, they were forced to march to Fort Sumner, where the Americans had created a reservation for them."

"But – that's more than three hundred miles away," Ivy gasped.

"It is. That's why our history calls it The Long Walk."

"White people have been so cruel in the past," Amber said quietly. She shivered, looking around the valley with sad eyes.

Emily put an arm around her shoulders. "Good thing there are really sweet ones, nowadays," she mumbled, giving Amber a quick kiss on the cheek.

ॐॐॐ

When the Jeep dropped them off at the hoghan, it was already half past two.

"Shall I drive back?" Hannah offered when Ben got

the car keys from his pocket.

"You want to?"

Hannah nodded silently. If she drove, she'd stay focused on the road and her mind wouldn't wander. She'd texted Nick an hour ago to tell him she'd meet up with him in Naabi'aani tomorrow. She'd also told him she and Josh had broken up. His astounded reaction to the news had made her rack her brain once more – if everyone around them thought she and Josh were so good together, then why didn't Josh think so himself?

Ben cleared his throat. "So, if you want to drive, you're going to have to get behind the wheel."

She woke up again. "Yeah. Sure. Sorry."

"You still want to go to the funfair on Saturday?" he asked cautiously, as they left the campsite, following the station wagon. Saturday evening would be the opening night for the funfair in Page, and they'd agreed to meet up there with a bunch of people, Josh included.

"Sure, why not? I haven't done anything wrong, right?" Hannah doggedly kept her eyes on the road in front of them.

"No – *you* haven't," Ben said, his voice taut.

"Well, Josh hasn't, either," Hannah mumbled.

"I don't agree."

"Look." She turned in her seat to look at Ben. "He's just been honest about his feelings. If he doesn't want me, he doesn't want me. Nothing will change that."

Ben frowned. "But, Han... " he tried again.

"No, Ben. No buts." She sighed when she saw the hurt look on his face. "Just – don't. Don't interfere. Don't ask him to explain himself. If he doesn't want me anymore, then it's his loss," she declared, with all the dignity she could manage.

They didn't talk about Josh anymore during the rest of the trip home.

⁂⁂⁂

The next day, Hannah drove to the reservation in her Datsun, Ben sitting next to her. The sky was overcast, and she'd put up the roof of the car just in case. The weather report said it would rain in the afternoon. Hannah clenched her jaw and slowed down a little bit after passing LeChee. They were getting closer. Her stomach churned like she was on her way to the dentist for a horrible root canal treatment.

Em was right. She'd have to face Josh at some point. Of course, Emily had things easy – she was on cloud nine with Amber.

When Emily's hoghan came into view, Hannah honked her horn to announce their arrival, then got out of the car with leaden steps. Emily and Nick emerged from the house a few moments later.

"Hey, you," Nick said warmly, bear-hugging her. "How are you holding up?"

Nick's obvious concern had an adverse effect on her – the tears she'd tried to push away for the past two days suddenly welled up. Quickly, Hannah took a step back. "I'm okay."

"Hey, Han," Emily said, pulling her a bit away from the rest. "Sani can see you later."

"Oh, good," Hannah said with a faint smile.

They all sat down outside around a simple cooking grill where Emily was roasting some yucca. Nick handed Hannah the rough draft of his dissertation.

"Have a look whenever you feel like it," he said with a wink.

Hannah smiled. "I'll try my best."

As she was reading the first couple of pages, Emily passed her a cup of strong coffee. "He's not here," she mumbled under her breath. "I don't know if that's a relief or not, but I thought I'd better tell you straight away."

Hannah gaped at Emily. Mostly, she was surprised. "So where is he?"

"According to Sani, he'll be back on Saturday," Emily replied. "He said Josh was doing something for him that couldn't wait."

And again, it was Sani coming between her and Josh. Of course, Josh hadn't declined when the old *hataalii* needed his help. No, he was running errands for Sani again like a proper lackey. Hannah grumbled inwardly.

"So, he has time to see you this afternoon," Emily went on, a bit taken aback by the look in Hannah's eyes. "Around three o'clock?"

"Fine." Hannah hunched over Nick's draft and didn't look back up until she'd read the whole thing. Just as she was sipping her second cup of coffee, Amber and Ivy were dropped off by their dad.

"So, where is he?" Ivy cut to the chase, sitting down next to Hannah.

"Not here," Hannah replied curtly. "Gone all day."

Ivy pulled a face. "Crap."

"Yeah, that about sums it up."

Hannah abruptly got up and made her way to the toilet building next to the hoghan. Inside, she ran cold water over her wrists and tried to cool down. And calm down, moreover. What was she supposed to tell Sani when she saw him? She wanted him to help her, but she didn't want him to blab about her problems to Josh. Which was inevitable. They were, like, best *hataalii*-buddies.

Hannah turned off the faucet and walked back outside, lost in thought. Nick looked up from the notes she'd scribbled on his draft when she sat down next to him. "So, seriously. How are you feeling?" he asked quietly.

"What do you think?"

"Sad. Confused. Angry."

Hannah winced when he rattled off his analysis. "Pretty much. Oh, well – Josh is busy with lots of things. He probably already forgot about me." Her voice cracked.

Nick's eyebrows traveled north. "Oh, cut it out. That's about as probable as fluorescent hip-hop pants ever coming back into fashion."

Hannah stifled a nervous chuckle. "Geez, Nick. Don't try to cheer me up." She stared at her hands. "There's no reason to."

"See what tomorrow brings. I heard you guys are going to the funfair?"

She nodded. "I'm going to have *such* a good time," she replied sourly.

Nick shrugged. "He'll talk to you about his decision at some point. It's not like him at all to be this nasty."

Wasn't it? No matter how nice Josh might seem, he still kept people at arm's length, plus he was unpredictable. And yet, she hoped Nick was right. At least it would give her some closure if Josh explained to her why he'd decided to shut her out for good.

At three o'clock, Hannah made her way to Sani's hoghan. Emily walked her to the *hataalii's* house, built on a little hill just outside the village.

"Good luck," she said, squeezing Hannah's hand for a second.

"Wait." Hannah suddenly got nervous. "Shouldn't I pay him, or something?"

"No worries. See you later."

Hannah stared at her friend walking down the hill before turning toward the hoghan. The exterior was covered in clay, and the entrance was covered by a hand-woven blanket in bright colors. She walked a few steps, whistling a tune to alert Sani to her arrival.

The blanket was pushed aside, and Sani's face appeared around the corner. "Come in," he said warmly, beckoning her. "*Wóshdéé'*."

"*Ahe'hee*." She stepped inside.

The middle of the building held a fire. A white handprint made with corn pollen showed on the walls of the hoghan in each of the four cardinal directions. A buckskin was on the floor. Sani sat down on it, legs crossed, gesturing for Hannah to do the same.

She inhaled the scent of the incense he was burning. "Juniper berries," he said with a smile, when he saw her trying to place the scent.

Hannah met his gaze, suddenly feeling shy. The way Sani looked at her didn't make her uncomfortable, but it was clear he was seeing right through her. She wouldn't be able to lie to this medicine man. Quite frankly, she didn't want to. Against all odds, she liked him. He seemed sympathetic, warm and caring.

"How can I help you, *shitsói*, my grandchild?" Sani asked softly.

"I am ... " Hannah choked on the words. She didn't know where to start. No doubt this man had heard skinwalker stories before, but not likely coming from the mouth of a *biligaana*.

Then again, she hadn't gone to all the trouble of consulting Sani only to back out now. "I'm cursed," she whispered. "There are monsters after me."

Sani slowly nodded, taking a prayer stick from the *jish* lying on the floor. He waved it in each cardinal direction. "What kind of monsters, *shitsói*?"

Hannah fell silent, her heart rate spiking. "They're *yenaldlooshi*. *Chindi*. Witches. Three of them. They appear to me as shadows without a face, with red, glowing eyes. Like coyotes. Or like common people. They can shapeshift, taking any form they want. They haunt my dreams." She started to stutter in her rush to get things out. "Emily tried to help me, but it's not enough." She started to cry softly.

The *hataalii* eyed her solemnly. "Are you this sad just because of those skinwalkers, grandchild?"

Hannah felt busted. She'd been right about Sani being able to see right through her. "No. I'm not just sad because of this curse. It's just – I've been ... " She hesitated. Would this Navajo elder know the meaning of the English word 'dumped'?

"You feel abandoned," he supplied.

She nodded in silence.

He inched toward her, putting a hand on her shoulder. "You have not been abandoned."

"What – what do you mean?" she stuttered. Of course she had. Josh had callously ditched her and decided to take a Long Walk all by himself.

Sani didn't reply, but stared into the dancing flames in the fireplace as if in a trance. When he finally spoke, his words upset Hannah.

"I cannot help you," he said.

"What? Why not?" she asked, her voice trembling.

"Because your problem is far more complicated than meets the eye." Sani rooted around in a ceramic pot behind him, pulling out a medicine pouch. Handing it over to her, he said: "You can carry this with you to protect yourself. It contains more powerful medicine than the one you're carrying now."

How did he know that? Hannah unwittingly put her hand on the bundle she'd tied around her waist, hidden under the fabric of her loose pants.

"However, it will not be a lasting solution for the

curse," Sani warned. "I can't help you with everything you have in your heart."

"So is there no one who *can* help me?" She bit her lip. This wasn't looking good. Sani was probably going to tell her she had to travel to the other side of the reservation and shell out thousands of dollars for another *hataalii* powerful enough to help her, judging by the weary look on his face.

"Yes," he nodded. "There is."

When he didn't volunteer more information, she urged, "So, who?"

"*Shash.*"

Hannah stared at Sani all bug-eyed. "Josh?!"

"Yes. Your brother's friend."

Oh no. This was *not* happening. Sani couldn't be serious. She'd have to beg for help from a guy who'd dumped her out of nowhere. And Sani dared to claim she hadn't been abandoned? She had never felt more alone and deserted in her entire life.

"That – can't be," she faltered.

"I have told you all I have to say," Sani replied, smiling at her. "*Hágoónee*. Goodbye, *shitsói*."

She scrambled to her feet, the new medicine bundle in her hand. "*Ahe'hee*," she said, trying to sound grateful. She wasn't exactly angry with Sani, even if he was basically throwing her out all 'polite-medicine-man' style. She was just angry with the world for doing this to her.

With an infuriated swipe of her arm, she pushed aside the blanket in front of the entrance and stood there fuming, blinking against the bright sunlight, before stomping off to Emily's hoghan. She'd had it with this stupid curse, this place, these people. Most of all, she'd had it with Josh and his side-kick Sani. All she wanted was to floor her car out of this godforsaken village, drive back home and wallow in self-pity for the rest of the day. Hole up in her bedroom with an irresponsibly big tub of Ben and Jerry's and her iPod blasting death metal at maximum volume.

With a face like thunder, she got back to Em's place, making a beeline for her brother. "I'm going home," she announced. "I have a headache."

Ben looked up at her face and shrugged, apparently deciding there was no use trying to convince her otherwise. "Drive safe, okay?" he only said.

"I will." Hannah bit her lip. Why did she even want to get out of this place so badly? Here they were, all the people who cared about her, who wanted to support her – and she couldn't get out of this 'friends-stick-together' powwow fast enough.

Tears burned in her eyes. Hannah quickly grabbed her bag, turning around and bolting for her car. With screeching tires, she tore off in the direction of St. Mary's Port.

By the time the first houses of the village came into view, she'd somewhat calmed down. After parking the Datsun on the main street, she ducked into Safeway to get herself some chips, ice-cream and pizza. Fortunately, Paul and Sarah were not around when she got back at the log cabin. The last thing she wanted right now was to exchange pleasantries with her neighbors.

As she sat down on the porch steps and spooned up a few chunks of cookie dough from her ice-cream tub, Hannah started to go over the conversation with Sani in her head. What had he made of her visit? Surely he must know why she was sad. After all, Josh told him everything, so he probably hadn't left out an important event like breaking up with her.

Would Sani betray her trust and tell Josh about the curse? Not likely. She sensed he could be trusted, even though he had this mysteriously close link with Josh. Sani couldn't be blamed for that – she had just hopelessly fallen in love with a guy who kept secrets he wasn't willing to share.

Fifteen

"So. Where and when are we meeting up today?" Hannah asked Ben, sitting at the table and flipping through a magazine in feigned nonchalance. It was almost noon, and she'd just rolled out of bed. She'd stayed up late last night to wait for Ben and the others to come back from Naabi'aani. Not least of all because she'd dreaded going to sleep and dreaming about things she'd pushed far away. When she'd crawled into bed at two in the morning, she had been upset and angry, mostly, and she still was. Of course, Josh had the right to break things off, but he could have at least *tried* to be less of an asshole about it. As for today, her mind was set – when Josh showed up, she wasn't going to pay any special attention to him. After all, her life had been just fine before she'd met him. It was not the end of the world.

"Josh called me from his aunt's place." Ben gauged Hannah's reaction. "He said he'd be here at three."

"Uh-huh," Hannah responded blankly, pretending to be engrossed in her magazine. "And Yazzie?"

"He has to finish up some things at the store first. We'll meet him at the fairground. The funfair officially opens at eight."

"Good."

"Maybe we can go out for dinner beforehand?" Ben suggested.

"Sure," Hannah muttered.

"We don't have to," Ben backpedalled.

Suddenly, she felt sorry for her brother. He was trying so hard, but he didn't know how to handle the situation any more than she did. Going all grumpy on Ben wasn't helping anyone. The person responsible for her dark mood wasn't even here yet.

"Sounds like a good idea," she said, smiling up at him. "Where shall we go?"

"Let's have a look around once we get there." He turned back to the stove to stir his scrambled eggs. "You want some?"

Hannah sighed. She hadn't had a decent bite of food after the ice cream last night. She still wasn't really hungry. Okay, Josh had broken her heart, but at least she'd also broken an all-time personal record in losing weight. Eat *that* for breakfast, Dr. Atkins.

"Yeah, sure," she replied flatly.

After breakfast, Hannah took her time in the bathroom, running a hot shower for herself that warmed her entire body. It wouldn't take the chill out of her bones, nor would it wash away all the cold memories she had of her last afternoon with Josh, but it somehow comforted her.

Hannah wiped some tears from her eyes, dried off and padded to her bedroom. She purposefully picked a colorful, flowery summer dress to wear so she'd seem happier.

Just as she was done applying her make-up, she heard a motorcycle outside. Hannah froze, staring at herself in the mirror in full-fledged panic. Her hand flailed toward her bag to dig up her cell phone. Two o'clock. Shoot – he was too early.

Hannah silently cursed herself for taking a shower lasting long enough to irrigate the entire Sahara. She'd wanted to get away to the beach and give Ben the chance to chat with Josh in peace and quiet first, without her sitting by staring daggers at him. That plan just went out the window.

Ben knocked on her door. "Han? He's already here."

Hannah opened her door reluctantly. "I know."

Heart pounding in her chest, she shuffled into the kitchen as Ben stepped out onto the porch.

"Hey, Josh," he called out, his voice artificially bright.

Hannah gingerly stepped back when Josh's gaze drifted to the kitchen door. He must have felt the weight of her stare.

With her last bit of strength she breathed in and out, straightening her back and pasting a fake smile on her face like a façade as she stepped outside. She could do this.

"Hi, Josh," she said in such a composed tone that she baffled herself.

Josh's eyes lingered on her 'you-cannot-hurt-me' mask. "Hey, Hannah," he replied, forcing a smile.

She cringed. He couldn't even genuinely *smile* at her. And the way he said her name – it was so cold and distant she might as well have been on the moon instead of the porch. His eyes betrayed nothing of what was going on inside his head. It was like staring at a blank wall.

Hannah quickly looked away and pointedly sat down at the table. The beach could wait. He was not going to chase her away that easily.

Ben and Josh walked up the steps. "I'm going to grab

a drink," Ben mumbled, inching toward the door.

"Bring me a bottle of water, okay?" Hannah said feebly. She hoped Josh would follow Ben into the kitchen, but he didn't. Feeling sick to her stomach, she watched him as he sank into the chair across from her. Two strangers wearing masks stared at each other over the table.

"So, how are you?" he finally asked.

How did he *think* she was doing? "I'm fine," she replied stiffly.

Josh nodded. "Have you ... " he started out and paused, giving her an insecure look.

"Have I what?" she whispered. The wall suddenly seemed to crumble.

"Have you had any nightmares recently?" Avoiding her eyes, he kept his gaze on the lantern on the table in front of him.

"No, not really," she managed to croak out.

Ben came back from the kitchen with drinks for all of them. "So how was Tuba City?" he asked Josh, clearly trying to ignore the awkwardness between them.

"It was fine. I checked out a couple rooms on campus. Picked up some readers to flip through at home before classes start. And how was Canyon de Chelly?"

"Fine," Ben replied. The word 'fine' was starting to lose all significance due to their combined lacklustreness. "We had nice weather, did one of those shake-and-bake tours through the canyon, stayed in a hoghan. The works."

Josh smiled flatly. "Which campsite?"

"Spider Rock," Hannah piped up, refusing to play wallflower. "Our hoghan looked out over the canyon. We took an evening walk along the ridge, and it took us past this rock plateau with a magnificent view of Canyon de Chelly." She stopped, looking down at the bottle of water in her hands. "It was a place I've seen in my dreams a few times," she then blurted out. "Strange, huh?"

"Yeah," Josh said, sounding so insipid it cut right through her soul. As Ben and Josh were trying to keep up their poor excuse for a light-hearted conversation, she closed her eyes, calling back to memory the rock plateau where she'd stood with Josh in her dreams. Blood rushed in her ears, and Hannah opened her eyes with a start. She had to stop doing this to herself. It was over. They were over.

"You still have my Blackfire CD?" Josh asked Ben.

"Yeah, it's in my car stereo. I'll get it out for you before we leave."

"Just leave it in for a while longer," Hannah said to Ben with a half-hearted smile. "So we can all listen to it while driving to the funfair."

"Oh. So you're still tagging along tonight?" Josh asked her monotonously.

She frantically blinked her eyes. How *could* he? He was the one inviting her to come to the Page funfair in the first place. He couldn't do this to her.

Hannah's breath caught in her throat as she fought to swallow back the tears that she couldn't keep away any longer. She had to get out of here – right now.

Clumsily, she staggered to her feet. "Yes, I'm tagging along. But I won't bother you guys any longer. I'm going to the beach, okay?" Her last word came out like a sob.

As Ben stared at her helplessly, Hannah spun around and fled to her bedroom. Slamming the door shut, she sank down on the bed, her body racking with sobs. Josh was such an asshole. Had he ever really liked her if he was able to be so mean to her now? Tears dripped down her face onto the pillow she buried her face in.

Suddenly, Hannah heard footsteps coming into the kitchen. Gasping for breath, she tried to stop crying. Through the door, she could hear Josh and Ben talk.

"You want another drink?" Ben asked flatly.

"Yeah. Some orange juice if you have it," Josh replied just as flatly.

Hannah heard Ben pull on the fridge door. The bottles inside the door clinked and rattled. He stomped toward the cabinet, taking two glasses out and slamming them down on the kitchen table.

"Listen up." His voice had lost all its flatness. "What the *hell* do you think you're doing to my sister?"

Silence penetrated the kitchen. "We need space," Josh replied at last. "Believe me, it's better that way."

"Yeah, that's my problem, right there," Ben said doggedly. "I *don't* believe you. I've known you for years, and I know you have your moods. Dammit, Josh, we practically grew up together. You're my brother, my best friend. But now you lost me. I don't get you anymore. Why are you being such a jerk?"

Hannah listened, open-mouthed, to her brother rant at Josh. She'd never heard Ben like this. Normally speaking, he was always so easy-going and gentle. But clearly, he wasn't going to let this slide.

"Can't ... " Josh's voice faltered. "Can't Hannah just accept that I don't want to be with her like that anymore?"

"No, she can't, you idiot. Because it doesn't make sense. I see the way you look at her. How you're *still* looking at her."

Her heart started to flutter in the silence that ensued.

"No, don't give me that look," Ben went on. "You're trying really hard to shut her out, but I know you too well. You can't fool me. I don't know what you're up to, but if you keep pushing her away, you're going to hurt both of you."

Josh sighed. "Believe me, the last thing I want to do is hurt her."

"Yeah. But it's still on your list, apparently."

"I can't explain it."

"Try me."

The two guys stopped talking, the silence stretching between them.

"If I told her what's going on," Josh finally said, "she'd agree with me."

"Then tell her. It's time to eat some crow, man. You shouldn't decide about her life. Hannah is perfectly capable of doing that herself."

Hannah bit her lip as tears welled up in her eyes. She still had no clue what was up with Josh's strange behavior, but at least she knew he still had feelings for her.

"Okay," Josh said determinedly.

Hannah sat bolt upright when she heard him make his way to her bedroom door. She tried to wipe the tears from her eyes. Of course, her mascara was completely washed down. She probably looked like a depressed raccoon.

At that moment, the door swung open and Josh stepped inside. Without saying a word, he pulled her up from the bed, cradling her in his arms. Her heart sang in his embrace. As her hand caressed his chest, she felt the quick beat of his heart underneath her fingers. He was so scared. So vulnerable and sad.

"I don't want to lose you," he whispered. "I – I'm in love with you." He kissed her softly.

One of his own tears fell on her wet cheek, making Hannah smile against his lips. "You're making my smeared mascara wash down even more," she half-giggled, half-sobbed. "Now I *really* look like a train wreck."

He chuckled nervously. "Sorry." He pressed his lips to hers once more. "I'm sorry, *shan díín*."

He clung to her like she was a raft on the waves of the wild sea of his emotions. Minutes tick-tocked away as they stood like that.

"Can you forgive me?" Josh mumbled against her lips.

"Yes. But only if you promise me you'll start talking. And I mean *really* talk," she insisted.

He cast down his eyes, heaving a sigh. For a split second, she didn't know what his response would be, and her stomach clenched. But when Josh looked up again, she knew. He no longer wanted to shut her out. The look in his eyes was one of determination.

"I promise," he said simply.

"Thank you," she whispered. "For your trust."

They sat down on the bed together. Hannah snuggled up against him. So many questions were on the tip of her tongue, but the most important question of all had already been answered – he still loved her.

A modest knock on the door made them both sit up straight. "Are we still alive in there?" Ben asked.

"Alive and kicking!" Josh called back. "Come in."

Ben swung the door open with a wide grin, his gaze sweeping over Hannah's happy face. "Love the emo make-up, sis."

Hannah burst out laughing. It felt good, like she was able to breathe again for the first time in days. She got up to give Ben a long, tender hug. When she pulled back, Josh put his hand on Ben's shoulder.

"Thanks, man," he mumbled. They shared a look that told Hannah Josh was indebted to his best friend, and Ben wasn't going to let him hurt her ever again. She'd never seen her brother look so serious.

"Okay, get out," she told the two of them. "I want to re-apply my make-up. For obvious reasons."

Ben and Josh grinned. "We'll be on the porch," Josh said, kissing her lightly on her forehead.

Hannah rubbed the black streaks away from her cheeks. She put on some new make-up and dragged a comb through her hair before grabbing her cell and multi-texting Emily, Nick, Amber and Ivy with the message: 'Believe it or not, but Josh and me are together again :) Happiness!! Xx Han.'

ುುು

Hannah spent the rest of the afternoon together with Josh. They weren't alone, because Ben joined them to the beach, where they bumped into Amber and Ivy. Josh had promised her they'd talk that night, after the funfair. It seemed like a good idea – first, they should relax. Josh needed it. The prospect of having to talk to her about his strange behavior was clearly putting a strain on him.

After meeting up with Yazzie at a burger restaurant, the group of four was ready to explore the fairgrounds. Josh and Hannah walked hand in hand, Ben and Yazzie trailing behind them. Ben had a wide smile on his face, because he loved funfairs. Hannah wasn't a big fan herself – she usually got sick on rollercoasters – but fortunately, there were also bumper cars and a giant Ferris wheel.

"Hey, look, there's a haunted house, too!" She pointed at a fake gray castle, complete with turrets, wooden drawbridge and plastic heads of decapitated people on stakes, eyes bulging and tongues lolling.

"Those things look so fake they make me laugh more than anything else," Josh grinned, looking up at the supposedly gruesome decoration. "You want to go in?"

"Yeah, later. Look at the line!"

The Ferris wheel didn't have as many visitors waiting in line, so Josh and Hannah made their way to the other side of the fairgrounds. Ben pointed at the fast rollercoaster in the corner. "Why don't you guys pick a nice love-seat on the wheel? Me and Yaz are going to try The Deadly Snake. Right?" He poked Josh's cousin in the ribs.

"Knock yourself out," Hannah replied. She watched Ben and Yazzie line up for the rollercoaster she wouldn't go on if they gave her a million dollars, turning around to face Josh when he slid his arm around her waist. "How about some cotton candy before we go on the wheel?" he said.

They both bought cotton candy at the taffy stand to take with them on the Ferris wheel. When they got out again, they spotted Ben and Yazzie at the shooting range, like they'd agreed. "Did you enjoy the Snake?" Hannah asked her brother.

"You bet. Yazzie's going to join me for another round."

"Well, better him than me."

"What about you, Josh?" Ben challenged his best friend with a wink.

Josh grinned. "Come on. I can't abandon my girlfriend, can I? She wants to go to the haunted house."

"Yeah, sure. Let's just pretend I believe that."

Josh grabbed Hannah's hand as they walked up to the booth to buy tickets from a guy in a Frankstein mask. When it was their turn to go inside, they crossed the drawbridge leading up to the castle entrance. Hannah screamed when a zombie with a chainsaw appeared out of nowhere, lashing out at them.

"That – that's a fake saw, right?" she stuttered.

Josh shielded her from the murderous zombie and

grinned at her. "I should hope so. Otherwise, we'll see the owner of this joint in court."

Hannah giggled. They gave the actor a wide berth and continued their way into the haunted castle. The narrow hallway was dark and gloomy. Cobwebs tickled Hannah's face as she pushed ahead. Fluorescent spiders dangled from the ceiling on rubber bands. A ghastly shriek suddenly echoed through the room when a translucent ghost appeared in a mirror on the wall, followed up by a loud boom sounding like a cannon.

Hannah grabbed Josh's hand as the hallway got even narrower. Air cushions protruded from both sides, making it more difficult to go on. According to the sign above their heads, they needed to brave this tunnel to get to the torture chamber.

"Well, we don't want to miss that, right?" Josh chuckled, putting his hand around her upper arm to steady her as they entered the air cushion tunnel.

Hannah stayed close to him, trying her best to squeeze her way through. After about ten steps, the space between the cushions got so narrow she had a hard time moving at all. When her feet hit a dent in the floor, she tripped. Josh's hand slipped away from her right arm. It didn't come back.

"Josh?" she called out in a small voice. "Wait up."

No response. Suddenly, it hit her how quiet the castle was. No screaming visitors, no yammering ghosts, no chainsaw in the background. An abrupt wave of dizziness made her stomach churn. She tried to take a step forward, but a strange pressure beating down on her chest cut off her breath.

And then, she felt a hand on her left arm.

Her back grew rigid, her skin turning cold under the touch of a hand that couldn't possibly belong to Josh. He had to be on the other side of the tunnel if he'd come back for her.

"Who's there?" she yelped, her voice quivering. Desperately, she tried to look behind her, but it was dark – way darker than she remembered. A shiver ran through her entire body, and suddenly, all she wanted was to run. To get away from this creepy place.

Hannah jerked her arm away from the strange hand, forcing her way through the tunnel with all the strength she could muster. Sweating and panting, she pushed at the cushions with her hands and arms. Gradually, she made her way forward, but the ball of fear stuck in her throat wouldn't go away.

All of a sudden, she tumbled forward into a dimly lit room with bare walls that didn't look like a torture chamber. Josh was nowhere to be seen. With a throat dry from sheer panic, Hannah looked from left to right. Where the heck was she? What was going on?

A bone-chilling sound behind her made Hannah look over her shoulder. Her heart stopped. The low, unearthly growl had come from the small opening of the air-cushioned tunnel.

There was a shadow. A familiar one. She could see the outline of the dark creature growing in the few seconds it took her to stumble backward, pressing her shoulders against the far wall of the room in an attempt to get away from the monster.

Her eyes widened as two red, glowing pinpoints of light shaped like eyes took shape in the apparition's head. The shadow shimmered in the air.

"No. No. Go *away*!" she screamed, her voice rising to a high-pitched shriek as the shadow glided through the air toward her, hovering over her in the blink of an eye.

"No!" she howled. "Leave me – alone." Her words dried to a whisper as the skinwalker started to laugh softly. It was a menacing, frightening sound that completely shook her up. Hannah could feel his cold breath on her lips like a kiss of death.

And then she realized – she'd forgotten to bring the medicine pouch. In the rush of the afternoon, Hannah hadn't thought of putting Sani's protection totem around her neck. The medicine bundle was still in her bag – and her bag was in the trunk of the car.

She was all alone, with nothing to protect herself.

"No one can help you," the skinwalker's voice echoed inside her head. A terrified sob escaped her throat. The fear paralyzed her, like a poison slowly spreading through her veins.

"Josh," she whispered. "Ben..." She pressed her clenched fist against her mouth to stop herself from crying out in terror when the shadow came even closer. Her heart was beating so rapidly she was afraid she'd go into cardiac arrest.

The skinwalker came so close his shadow blocked out everything. His outstretched claw scratched her face. She felt a stabbing pain in her cheek, blood dripping down to her jawbone. Still in a panic, she tried to scoot away from her attacker.

And then, she saw something flutter through the air from the corner of her eye. Something blue. Holy crap – was that a *butterfly*?

"Look at your hand." There was a sudden, calm second voice in her head, talking to her out of nowhere. "Count your fingers."

Hannah obligingly raised her hand in front of her face. She had no clue why she should, but the voice sounded trustworthy, and right now, she could use all the help she could get. With a frown and a growing sense of wonder, she stared at her hand. She couldn't count her fingers. The image were fuzzy.

"Six," she finally choked out. "Six fingers?"

This wasn't real. It was a dream.

Emily had said the *yenaldlooshi* broke into people's dreams to drive them insane. Hannah remembered Ben telling her how she could wake herself up from a nightmare.

"This is not real!" she screamed at the top of her lungs. Gasping for breath, she fixed the shadow towering over her, and then her eyes snapped open for real.

Hannah swallowed. She'd never left the cushion tunnel, and Josh was just pulling her into the torture chamber.

"Were you stuck?" he laughed. "You were, like, frozen all of a sudden."

Hannah gaped at him. Apparently, her nightmare had only lasted a few seconds – Josh hadn't even noticed something was wrong. Whimpering, she put her arms around his waist, pressing her face into his chest.

"*Shan díín?*" he whispered, taken aback. "You're shaking! You're really scared?"

"I want to leave," Hannah stuttered, a note of hysteria in her voice. "Please, Josh, let's just go. Right now. *Please.*"

He didn't ask any further. Quickly, he scanned the room, locating an emergency exit in the corner of the torture chamber. They staggered out, down a rickety metal stairway at the back, ending up on a grassy patch behind the haunted house. Hannah tried to steady her breath, holding on to Josh like her arms were covered in suckers. She couldn't stop shaking. Never in her entire life had she been so scared.

"What happened?" Josh asked her quietly, stroking her hair. "I'm sorry I let go of you for a second. I tripped."

She shook her head. Josh couldn't help it. She was the one who'd stupidly forgotten to bring the only thing she had to protect her from a skinwalker attack. Teeth chattering, she couldn't string a coherent sentence together.

"What happened to your cheek?" Josh said with a frown. His thumb touched her skin, and she flinched.

"Why? What do you see?" she whispered.

"A scratch," he replied. "You're bleeding a little bit."

Her stomach turned. But it had been a dream. How the hell could she be injured? That was absurd. Impossible.

"Let's go to the entrance," she proposed feebly. She had no idea how long they'd been away, but she wanted to see Ben and get her ass back to the car as soon as possible.

"Come on," Josh mumbled, draping his arm around her shoulders as they made their way to the front of the mansion. Ben and Yazzie were waiting for them, Ben with an enormous teddy bear under his arm. Smiling, he offered it to Hannah. "Look what I won at the shooting range, sis. That's for you."

Hannah forced a faint, quivering smile. "Thanks."

Ben raised his eyebrows. "What's going on? You look like you've seen a ghost."

"Well spotted, Einstein," Yazzie deadpanned, looking pointedly at the haunted house behind them.

Ben mock-slapped him. "Not like that, you moron."

"Someone was..." Hannah swallowed hard, clutching Ben's bear in her hands. "Somebody was chasing me."

"Wasn't that part of the show?" Yazzie asked, nonplussed. "The whole 'flesh-eating-zombies-are-after-me' angle?"

"No. It was something else." She stared at the ground in front of her feet, feeling like an idiot. What was she supposed to tell them without sounding like a lunatic? Ben would probably cart her off to the nearest mental hospital if she told him the truth.

An inexplicable shiver ran down her spine. When she looked up, her eyes wandered to three people behind Ben and Yazzie. They were observing the four of them in silence.

Her eyes almost popped out. There they were – the three guys who'd harassed her that night at the lake. The skinwalkers as they appeared to her the very first time. She stared at them in utter terror.

Ben followed her gaze and turned around, spotting the trio. "Hannah? Are those guys..."

She nodded, still speechless.

"*Ha'íih*? What's up?" Yazzie shot Josh a questioning look. Josh kept an eye on the three guys behind them, who were still staring at Hannah and him with murderous intent without batting an eyelid.

"They're the assholes who bothered Hannah at the lakeside when she was stranded," Ben exclaimed furiously.

"*Nida'ásh*? Really?" Yazzie turned around as well. "So what are we waiting for? Let's tell them to leave your sister alone." Ben and Yazzie took a step toward the guys, who suddenly snapped out of their apparent trance and dove into the crowd as one, moving like a pack of wolves.

"Hey! Stop right there!" Ben shouted. He and Yazzie shot after the fugitives.

Hannah looked sideways and saw how pale Josh had become.

"Wait!" he called after his two friends. For a moment, she thought he'd join the chase, but he didn't. He stayed put, his arm protectively around her waist and his mouth set in a grim line. When he turned toward her, the desperate look in his eyes made her heart stop.

"*She'at'eed*," he said softly, drawing a deep breath as if buckling up for something.

"Yes?" she replied nervously.

"You got Sani's medicine bundle on you?"

Hannah stared at him dumbfounded. So there – Josh knew about the curse. Sani must have told him, but at this juncture, she was past caring. She was just happy she didn't have to explain anything right now – she was way too shaken up for that.

"In the car," Hannah stuttered, feeling ashamed. "I'm sorry. I put it in my bag and forgot to bring it to the fair."

Without saying another word, Josh pulled a small leather pouch from the pocket of his jeans, pouring its contents on the palm of one hand. She recognized the stuff. It was corn pollen – powerful medicine for protection in Navajo tradition.

Josh rubbed the pollen between his hands and smeared it on Hannah's bare shoulders. She looked up at him, the look in his eyes making her cold inside. He looked outraged and defeated at the same time.

"Are you mad at me?" she mumbled, clasping the teddy bear in her trembling hands. Suddenly, she felt small and stupid. Why hadn't she paid more attention?

He stopped rubbing her shoulders for a moment to put one hand lovingly on her cheek. "No – not at you," he muttered. He leaned into her and gave her a soft, tender kiss on the mouth.

Just then, Yazzie stumbled toward them, panting and looking over his shoulder.

"*Haidzaa?*" Josh asked in a tense voice. "What happened?"

"*Yóó íijéé',*" Yazzie replied. "They ran off."

"Where's Ben?" Hannah exclaimed.

"He kept running after them." Yazzie was still catching his breath. "We chased those guys until they got to the patch of trees near the border of the park. That's when I tripped over a piece of protruding rock." He rubbed his ankle. "I couldn't walk properly, let alone run. Ben told me to wait there until he came back and he ran after them on his own. I stayed put, but it took Ben a while to come back."

"So where is he now?" Hannah persisted.

Yazzie hesitated. "He's still there. He came back and sat down on the ground next to me, but he didn't say anything."

"Is he injured?" Josh asked.

Yazzie shook his head. "No, man. Just - *T'óó náá'áyói*. It was the strangest thing. He was just sitting there, keeping quiet. It freaked me out, 'cause it looked like he was in some kind of shock." He shuddered, grabbing Josh by the shoulder. "Let's go get him together. I didn't want to move him."

On their way to the edge of the park, Hannah felt a cold hand of fear closing its fingers around her heart. What had happened to Ben? She didn't want to consider it, but maybe the *yenaldlooshi* had done something to her brother, cursed him too, because he'd tried to help her.

They found Ben under a cedar pine, hugging his knees and staring into space. Hannah ran toward her brother and kneeled beside him. "Ben?" She gently shook him. "What's wrong? Are you hurt?"

He shook his head. She was happy to see she could at least elicit some kind of response, but it wasn't much. Yazzie was right – Ben looked completely shaken up.

"You want to go home?" she tried.

Ben glanced up at her with a tired look in his eyes. "Yeah. Let's go home."

She pulled him up. Josh supported him as he took a few staggering steps in the general direction of the fair.

"Where did those guys run off to?" Yazzie asked, confused.

"I don't want to talk about it," Ben snapped. Hannah swallowed, mouthing 'sorry' to Yazzie. He shrugged and nodded curtly.

On their way back to the car, Hannah's mind was reeling. So much had happened today – her brain couldn't cope anymore. Ben looked so scared and lost. She wanted to talk to him as soon as possible.

"I'm off," Yazzie said when they got to the Mustang. "My car's further down the road." He put a hand on Ben's shoulder. "Take it easy."

"Yup." Ben didn't look Yazzie in the eye.

Yazzie turned toward Josh. "See you soon, *shitsílí. Hazhó'ó nídeiyínóhkááh.* Get home safe."

"*Hágoónee, shinaaí.*" Josh waved at his cousin before helping Ben into the back seat.

They drove back to St. Mary's Port in silence, all of them lost in thought. Hannah had the teddy bear on her lap, clutching Sani's medicine bundle in her hands. A few lonely tears rolled down her cheeks, landing in the cuddly toy's fur. Even though Josh was back in her life, the shadows chasing her just wouldn't go away.

"Have a good night's sleep," Josh told his friend as Ben stumbled up the porch steps. "See you in the morning."

Hannah bit her lip. She had never seen her brother look more confused. What had happened?

Josh grabbed her hand. "You – want to talk now?" he hesitated.

Hannah shook her head. She was so tired and freaked out at the same time that she couldn't be curious. "I'm too exhausted. Let's do it tomorrow?"

He gently caressed her cheek, pulling her into an embrace. "Okay. Tomorrow morning, then. I'll be here as soon as I can."

Standing in the kitchen, she watched Josh driving away.

"Ben?" she called out, knocking lightly on his door.

"Not now," Ben replied. "Please, Han. I'll – talk to you in the morning."

Hannah's shoulders slumped. This was nothing like him. "Sure," she replied regardless, trying to sound breezy. "I'm going to bed."

Once in her room, she flopped down on the bed still fully dressed and closed her eyes. The medicine bundle was still around her neck, and would stay there for the night, resting on the skin close to her heart.

Her dreamcatcher was swaying in the light breeze coming through the window as she fell asleep, stirring quietly in the whirl of her restless thoughts.

Sixteen

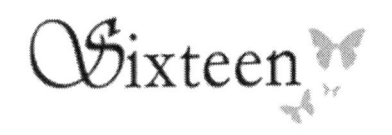

The minute she opened her eyes the morning after the funfair, Hannah immediately felt apprehensive again.

Slogging to the kitchen, she grabbed the keys from the table and unlocked the door, a shiver running through her. It was the first time ever she'd locked the door at night in this place. It was pointless, of course. Deadbolts on the door wouldn't stop skinwalkers – they had the power to break and enter her dreams.

With a frown, Hannah stepped onto the porch, thinking about her terrifying vision in the haunted house last night. She didn't want to consider what would have happened if she hadn't woken up. That strange voice in her head – it had saved her. Did it belong to the blue butterfly she'd seen?

Just as she went back to the kitchen to get some coffee, the bedroom door swung open and Ben entered, his face just as pale as it had been last night.

"Hey!" She hugged him tight. "How did you sleep?"
"Not so well."
"Well, sit down. I'll make you some coffee."

He nodded, still taciturn and remote. What had happened to him? She was starting to get seriously worried. This was not the Ben she knew.

"Okay. Spill," she said curtly after putting a mug of fresh coffee in front of him. "You can't keep this up forever."

Ben sighed deeply, taking a sip of his coffee. He cleared his throat and briefly glanced at her.

"Something..." He hesitated, giving her a desperate look. "Something happened last night."

"Something that scared you."

"Yeah." He let out another frustrated sigh, slamming the mug down on the table. "Sorry for being so weird, but you have *no* idea what I saw last night. I think I'm losing it. What I saw – you can't even begin to imagine."

"Hey, thanks for giving so much credit to my imagination."

Ben smiled feebly. "I'll tell you. But please don't put the shrink on speed-dial straight away. Promise?"

She took his hand. "Scout's honor."

"Those guys weren't human." Ben exhaled forcibly, rubbing his face. "Holy cow, I said the words."

"Go on," she encouraged him.

Ben got a distant look in his eyes. "I kept chasing them. After Yazzie tripped, you know. I wanted to warn them, tell them to leave you alone from now on. We ended up in the woodland – at the edge of the park ..."

In the silence that followed, Hannah could hear the clock tick.

"They turned around and faced me. And then the guy in the middle got a red glow in his eyes." Ben swallowed hard, taking her hand. "He took a step toward me and gave me this uncanny smile. He gave me a look of – of recognition. I swear. Like he'd waited for me. Like I was an old enemy of his. Trust me, I was scared out of my wits."

His statement shocked her, but she tried to keep a straight face. "Keep going."

Ben closed his eyes. "It gets worse. He – he turned into a *coyote*. Suddenly, there was an animal standing in front of me, Han. And then, there were just three shadows. And *then*, they all disappeared in the blink of an eye, and I was all alone." He barked out a laugh. "See? I've gone off the deep end. I'm nuts. I need help."

"I've already asked for help," Hannah blurted out.

Ben looked wounded. "W-what?"

"No. Not for you," she quickly reassured him. "For me. Those creatures are targeting *me*. I'm – cursed."

"What?!" Ben shot her an incredulous look. "So this is not all just in my head?"

"Afraid not."

"So what's their business with you?"

Gingerly, she told her brother about the dreams, her confrontation with the *yenaldlooshi* in their different forms, and the advice Emily had given to her. She explained to Ben everything about the powers the skinwalkers allegedly had, and the ways she'd tried to fight them so far.

"Oh my God," Ben sighed when she stopped talking. "It's a good thing I saw them with my own eyes, or I'd have a hard time believing you. In fact, I'm *still* having a hard time believing it. It's just surreal."

"I hope you understand why I didn't tell you about this straight away. I trust you, but I know you. I didn't want you to think I was insane."

"And now what? How could they suddenly appear like that yesterday?" He held her gaze. "You saw them in the haunted house too, didn't you?"

"I wasn't wearing Sani's medicine bundle," Hannah confessed.

He frowned. "But how do you lift a curse like that for good? And why are they targeting you, anyway?"

"I still don't know. The only thing Sani could tell me

was that Josh could help me with my problem."

"Josh can help you?" Ben stared at the coffee mug in his hands. "You know, the guy never ceases to amaze me. It feels like he's carrying something on his shoulders, something we can't understand. I wouldn't be surprised to learn he broke up with you just to protect you from dangerous stuff he's somehow involved in."

"Like what?" Hannah stared at her brother. She hadn't even considered that possibility yet. The curse – could it be directly related to Josh?

"I don't know, but I bet they're supernatural things. Boys turning into coyotes are paranormal in my book."

"He's coming here to talk." Hannah glanced at the clock. "But I don't know if I can share with you what he's going to tell me. I don't want to betray his trust."

"As long as I know you're safe, I don't really need to know anything else." Ben hugged Hannah, kissing her forehead. "It's a good thing you confided in Emily."

"I wanted to share it with you. I just didn't know how."

"I understand. So, if Josh can really tell you how to stop those, uhm, skinwalkers..." He tried out the sound of the strange word. "You should tell me how I can help."

"I will." She loved her brother so much. Ben supported her without question. He was amazing, and more open to things than she'd expected.

An hour later, she heard a car coming up the road. Ben looked out the window. "Here comes Josh," he announced.

Hannah stepped outside just as Josh parked his car next to her Datsun. A nervous tingle shot up her spine as he walked up the steps, looking solemn.

"Good morning." He softly pressed a kiss to her cheek. "Slept well?"

"Yeah. Ben feels better too. I talked to him."

Josh sighed in relief. "Glad to hear it. I was really worried about him." He looked at Hannah, a haunted expression crossing his face. "Everything will be okay," he slowly said, as if he needed to convince himself most of all.

Hannah noticed his hands were shaking lightly. "Are you nervous?" she asked, rubbing his arm.

His gaze avoided hers, sweeping the mountains in the distance instead. "I don't think there's a word for what I'm feeling right now."

Hannah hugged him. "Don't be scared," she whispered against his neck. "You said so yourself – everything will be okay."

"It will be, for you and Ben. I'll make sure of that."

"For you, too. Really. I don't know what you want to discuss with me, but we'll get through this together."

The look in his eyes made her inexplicably restless. It was like he was saying goodbye to her again, but more deliberately this time. Like he was already somewhere else, even when he was still standing next to her.

"You want to go somewhere to talk?" she asked quietly.

Josh put his arm around her shoulders. "Lone Rock Beach?" he suggested after a few seconds. "Near Wahweap? It's quiet there. And I'd like to be outside."

Hannah nodded. "I'll get my stuff." She went into her bedroom and packed her bag, trying to slow down her heartbeat by taking deep breaths, but it didn't work.

Yesterday, Josh had wanted to open up to her, but now he seemed afraid to have this talk. He'd had a full night to think it over, so maybe the effect of Ben's tirade had worn off a bit.

When she stepped outside, she gingerly walked over to Josh, who stared at her with a slight smile.

"You're so beautiful," he said quietly, pulling her against him to kiss her lips. "So sweet."

She leaned into him and kissed him back. Before she could deepen the kiss, she felt his lips move. He whispered: "*Ayor anosh'ni.*"

"I love you too," she replied. Her own words made all her worries fall away. Whatever Josh would tell her, she had a deeper connection with him than she'd ever felt with anyone else. No one would take that away from her.

During the drive to Lone Rock Beach, Josh didn't turn on the radio, but Hannah didn't mind. She watched the red, lonely landscape glide by, shooting a glance at Josh now and then. He was wearing his sunglasses, so she couldn't see his eyes, but she could sense his restlessness.

He parked some hundred yards away from the main entrance to the beach, and took her hand in his when they got out. "Let's sit down at a sheltered spot somewhere."

Hannah pointed at a giant rock on the beach. Josh nodded and pulled her along toward it. They flopped down, their backs against the rocky surface, their feet in the sand. Hannah could feel the tension in Josh's body spreading to her hand. He still hadn't let go of her.

"I don't really know where to start," he sighed, taking off his sunglasses. He stared out over Lake Powell, where Lone Rock rose up from the water, lit by yellowish light from the early morning sun. The wind tousled his hair and the sunlight touched the planes of his anxious face.

Hannah broke the silence. "Maybe you should start by telling me about those skinwalkers. Sani told me you know more about them. And I talked to Ben this morning – he's seen them in the park as well. In their true form, I mean."

Josh blew out a shaky breath. "Okay. There's a curse – intended for me. I've known this from the moment I came back from my vision quest at age fourteen. The *yenaldlooshi* are only after you because you're with me."

Hannah gasped. So Josh was the reason she was haunted by supernatural beings? Now she understood why he had seemed so desperate and scared when they left this morning. He probably thought she'd break up with him. After all, who wanted to be cursed because of being in love?

Josh kept his gaze on the sand in front of him. "Because I fell in love with you, they could harm you. Because I love you, they *want* to harm you. And they'll keep trying to harm you until you're dead."

Hannah froze. "They – they want to kill me?" she choked out, her heart suddenly beating erratically. Inadvertently, she shook her head, as if to deny or take away the words Josh had spoken.

"You're afraid." His mouth was set in a grim line. "And rightly so. You *should* be afraid. You have no idea what those monsters are capable of."

He suddenly hugged her in a tight embrace. "I shouldn't have allowed myself to fall in love with you, but I couldn't help it," he stammered helplessly.

Tears welled up in her eyes. Josh sounded so guilty, afraid and desperate.

"Hey," she mumbled, crawling into his embrace. "I don't blame you. I'm *happy* you fell in love with me. Despite everything."

He raised his head, locking eyes with her. "You have no idea how careful I've been. How afraid I was things might go wrong. How angry I was – how sad I felt when I discovered those witches were targeting you after all. I discovered the medicine pouch around your neck while you were sleeping at Antelope Canyon."

"So that's why you left me."

"You can still leave me. I'd understand it if you did."

Hannah closed her eyes, suddenly seeing Josh's face in her mind like it had been in her dream about the rock plateau near Canyon de Chelly. Another life – a decision that had caused her so much pain. She shook her head, but Josh didn't seem to notice. He stared into the distance, his mind wandering.

"I was always on my guard against them." The words spilled out like a torrent, now that he'd finally broken his silence. "Ever since I knew what could happen to me and my lover. Actually, I simply didn't allow myself to love anyone, not after everything I'd seen during my vision quest. I vowed never to let myself fall in love." He looked sideways with a slight frown. "And then, something unexpected happened. You visited St. Mary's Port for the first time in years. Ben told me you'd be here for the summer. I was looking forward to seeing you again. In my mind, you were like a long-lost sister."

He smiled at her, and she felt herself blush shyly. "But that's not what fate had in store for me," he continued. "When I saw you sitting there in your car at the gas station, singing along to your radio so enthusiastically, something stirred inside me that I couldn't stop. That evening on the beach only made the feeling stronger. I felt such a strong connection to you. I just wanted to be close to you. Hold you in my arms. Love you without holding back. I wanted to kiss you, make you laugh out loud, make love to you. I felt young – young and reckless in your presence."

Hannah blinked. Josh sounded as if he was so much older than the seventeen years he'd been on this earth, and she couldn't fathom why. She kept quiet, though.

"That Wednesday afternoon in the kitchen..." A small smile played around his lips. "If you hadn't backed away from me, I'd have made my move right there and then. But I thought I'd made a mistake. I guessed you only saw me as a little brother."

"No, I didn't. I just felt shy." She blushed.

"Well, it stopped me right in my tracks, and that's when I came to my senses. I was ready to kick myself. I hadn't considered what could happen. Hadn't considered your safety. I decided to keep a distance and see what would happen." Josh bit his lip. "That Thursday morning, when you were in Page..."

"You saw me standing in front of the music store," she finished for him.

"You saw me look?" he asked, ashamed.

"Yeah. But there was this – *wall* between us. An invisible barrier."

He swallowed visibly. "I was looking at you when all of a sudden, I saw three strange shadows appear behind you. It only lasted for a second – they disappeared so quickly that I could have just made it up, but it was still enough to throw me. I didn't go outside to talk to you. I wanted to make sure I wasn't just hallucinating about things I was scared of."

"Is that why you were so afraid when that coyote howled close to Rainbow Bridge? And I had that vision?"

"Yeah. By that time, I already suspected the *chindi* terrorized your dreams, because Ben told me you had trouble sleeping because you were suffering from nightmares."

Hannah stared at him, feeling guilty. "And a few days later, you found that medicine bundle around my neck. You knew I'd been keeping things from you. And you knew everything you were afraid of was actually happening." She stared at her feet. "I'm so sorry."

"You couldn't help it. I should have told you sooner. I should have warned you. I shouldn't have gotten you involved in the first place."

"Don't say that, Josh. Like *you* had a choice. When you fall for someone, you fall for someone. You can't help it. I couldn't help myself, either."

He smiled despite himself. "Okay, you have a point. I don't regret it."

"Nor me."

"Not even now?"

"No. Not even know."

He grabbed her hand. "After our break-up, I tried to ward off the witches by performing a ritual."

"So you weren't in Tuba City?"

"No. I was in the mountains with a special *jish* Sani lent me. I had to break all ties between us. That's why I ditched you the hard way. It would help the ritual if you weren't in love with *me* anymore. When Sani told me how deeply unhappy you were when you paid him a visit on Friday, I felt horrible, though. He was actually giving me grief about the way I was handling things. He insisted I should confide in you."

Hannah couldn't help smiling. Here she'd been thinking Sani had fobbed her off, but the old *hataalii* had scolded Josh like a stubborn grandson.

"And so you did," she said.

"Yes," he simply said.

So this was it. Josh was carrying an invisible burden, like Ben had said. It was something he hadn't been able to discuss with anyone, except the medicine man of the village. This was his explanation, but it only brought up more questions.

Hannah put an arm around Josh's shoulders. "But – *why* are you cursed? Who are these witches?"

"A vindictive *hataalii* and his twin sons."

"Why are they seeking revenge? What have you ever done to them?"

A bitter smile crept up his face, and he almost squeezed her hand to a pulp. "Something terrible," he replied, so quietly she almost couldn't hear him.

"H-how terrible?" she stuttered. Oh. This story was suddenly taking an unexpected turn.

Hannah's heart hammered in her throat when Josh stayed silent for a very long time. "Be honest with me," she whispered at last.

He pulled his hand free, sitting back against the rock and staring into the distance. "I killed someone. A Spanish woman. She was the *hataalii's* lover, and he turned against me, together with his family." He turned toward her and his gaze didn't leave her eyes. He was really serious.

Hannah swallowed. Oh my God. *Murder?* "But how – *You*? How is that even possible? It can't be. When did you...?" she trailed off.

"During the Pueblo Revolt in Arizona," he replied

Hannah stopped breathing. Her eyes went wide as she stared at Josh in utter bewilderment.

"In the year 1680," he added.

ঌঌঌ

Hannah dug her heels in the sand of Lone Rock Beach, leaning her elbows on her knees. The flip-flops she wore were cutting into the skin between her toes, but she didn't register it. She was only aware of Josh, who'd scooted away from her, grimly staring at the rock rising up from the lake – Lone Rock. The way he was sitting there, he looked like a lone rock himself, unapproachable and untouchable, surrounded by water.

Hannah tried to gather courage to break his silence, gingerly moving closer to put an arm around his shoulders and kiss his cheek.

Finally, Josh turned toward her. "Do you believe in reincarnation?" he asked quietly.

"Yeah. Kind of." Her heart sped up. Where was this going?

"Suppose you had no choice but to believe in it. Because you still remember what happened in your past lives."

She stared at him. Slowly, the truth began to dawn on her. "That must be quite a burden."

Josh let go of her hand, taking his wallet from his jeans pocket. Carefully, he plucked out two photographs from the front compartment and handed them to Hannah. She took the black-and-white pictures between her thumb and index finger, looking at the top one first. It featured a group of soldiers, and it said '1943' in old-fashioned handwriting underneath. The men were all dressed in soldier's uniforms and were clearly of Navajo descent. The man in the upper left corner caught her eye. She rubbed the face with the tip of her finger, as though it would change under her touch.

The eyes staring back at her from the photo were Josh's eyes.

He slowly nodded, like she'd asked him a question. "Yes. That's me. I was one of the codetalkers, the Diné who fought in the Second World War against Japan. I was thirty-three years old in that picture."

Hannah blinked, staring at the soldier with Josh's face, older and wiser, from a different era. She wished she could say something, but she was completely tongue-tied.

Fingers trembling, she put the first picture aside and looked at the next one. It featured an elderly man with a tired, gaunt face. Harsh lines showed around his mouth, but his eyes looked gentle and friendly. The man was dressed in a mixture of traditional Navajo clothes and late nineteenth-century American fashion. Her gaze fell on the date scribbled in the bottom right corner – 1868.

As she squinted her eyes in concentration, she suddenly saw the familiar traits of Josh's face in the old man's expression.

"The Americans called me Barboncito," Josh spoke. "I was one of the Diné leaders. This photo was taken after I signed the treaty with the United States. We were allowed to return to our homeland. I was forty-seven in this picture." He shook his head. "A difficult, unfair life makes you old beyond your years."

Hannah silently handed the photos back to Josh. "Where did it all start?" she stammered. "Who *are* you? And why do you keep coming back as the same person, with the same face and with all your memories?"

Josh put the pictures back in his wallet and hugged his knees, staring at the horizon.

"I was born in the year 1520, according to your calendar. America was untouched and empty. My tribe roamed the southwest, hunting deer and gathering wild plants. We were in balance with nature around us. Asdz Nádleehé, Changing Woman, our goddess, took care of us. The sky and the earth were our parents. We walked the earth in beauty, and we respected the way everything in the universe had its place."

A tiny shiver went through Hannah's body. Josh suddenly sounded so different – so unworldly. She wanted to take his hand and scoot closer, but she didn't dare.

"When I turned fourteen, I went to the desert alone, searching for my animal spirit. It was an intense vision quest. My totem animal, the bear Shash, manifested himself." Josh sounded wistful, the absent look in his eyes evidence that he was re-living the moment he was telling her about. "He told me that the life of our people would radically change during my lifetime. On the third and final day of my vision quest, he showed me how the change would come about. He gave me a terrible vision." Josh shuddered. "I saw people sailing the ocean and landing on our shores. They brought disease. They had hairy, pale faces and they divided the world up into good and evil, thinking everyone should think like them. They walked the earth as if God created it for them alone, believing they didn't need to share any of it with their brothers and sisters. Yet despite all their riches, they were so empty inside. I could see them flooding our continent, changing our culture, destroying our old ways of life. I saw how we'd be torn asunder, how our land would be exploited and abused."

Tears shone in his eyes, and Hannah couldn't help putting her arms around him in a gentle embrace.

"In despair, I turned to Shash. I wanted to know why he'd shown me that vision, and what I could do to stop those things. So he offered me a chance to protect my people, through the centuries. He gave me his life force and his mark, so I'd have a long lifeline."

Hannah swallowed. "And that way, he said you could help your people?"

He nodded. "I return, time and time again. I have the same memories, the same visions, but more wisdom each lifetime. I am Shash, protector of the Diné since the European invasion. My people's medicine men know me. I am a mythical figure that each generation silently waits for, to bring peace and change to our world. Every *hataalii* awaits my arrival and keeps my secret if I appear. In each lifetime, I wake up during the vision quest I take on my fourteenth birthday. It helps me remember who I am and what I'm supposed to do."

"To make peace," Hannah mumbled. "And to find it for yourself." She remembered what he'd told her.

Josh nodded slowly. "I am a man of peace, a peace leader, and I'm thankful for the task that was given to me. I chose it myself. But it gets lonely sometimes. The people around me move, live their lives, touch me and leave me again. And I stay behind – in the shadow of time."

Hannah kept quiet, her mind spinning. Finally, everything was clear. Why Josh seemed so old for his age. Why he knew so much about Diné history. Why he had a birthmark shaped like a bear. And why he always kept his distance from people, not even allowing himself to love her.

"What about those skinwalkers?" she asked feebly. "Are they as old as you?"

Josh shook his head. "That's an entirely different story. The *yenaldlooshi* came to visit me after the Pueblo Revolt in 1680 to confront me. During the attack on a Spanish mission, I killed a woman working at the convent. She turned out to be the *hataalii's* lover. In fact, he'd stopped being a *hataalii* at that point. He practiced black magic – just like his two sons."

"And he was angry."

"Yes. He wanted revenge. He said he wouldn't rest until he'd taken from me what I had taken from him."

"Did you have a wife back then?" Hannah inquired softly.

"No. At the time, I was sixty years old, and quite frankly, I didn't take his threat seriously. I only discovered later that their curse reached far beyond the boundaries of one lifetime."

Hannah's eyes widened. "How? Are they time-travelers or something?"

"They're not really *here*," Josh replied. "They reach out to me from the seventeenth century. Those witches are in a trance. They have entered the veil, the world between worlds, and they are dreaming. They're oneironauts – dream travelers. Using the veil, they can find my long lifeline. They invade my life to seek out my loved one. The only thing they want is revenge. They cursed me, and they will never give up. They don't *have* to. 'Never' doesn't mean anything in this context. Time doesn't touch them."

"They're – dreaming?" Hannah asked doubtfully. "So how can they be here? This is not a dream. This is the real world."

"There are many realities." Josh shook his head. "I can't fully explain it. For some peoples, the dream world is as real as the normal world."

"So they're like ghosts. Mirror images of themselves." Hannah was talking more to herself than to Josh. Only now did she understand why Amber hadn't seen auras around the skinwalkers. They weren't really here. They only appeared as dream images, using the emotional bond between her and Josh to seek them out. And as long as she stayed with him, they would be able to find her. As long as she stayed with him, loving him, they'd keep trying to kill her.

Desolately, Hannah put her face in her hands and started to cry. This was so incredibly unfair. It was like her whole world was turned upside down, leaving her empty-handed. Josh had turned into a stranger with a life she could never really share with him.

"I'm so sorry I'm crying," she sniffed. "I wanted you to open up to me, I wanted to help you. Really be there for you."

"I know." His voice was so understanding and resigned it made her cringe. This was terrible. She couldn't accept that he'd been right all along about leaving her.

When she looked up again, a sudden black cloud veiled her eyes, making her stiffen. Another vision – was she in danger again?

No. Somehow, it didn't feel like that. A bright pinpoint of light shimmered somewhere in the distance, emitting rays of warmth and safety. Holding her breath, Hannah strained her eyes to make out what she was looking at. It was blue, fluttering in the air.

"Follow me," she heard a light voice that sounded feminine, but somehow not human. "Whenever you're lost, follow me."

She tried to focus on the image in front of her, suddenly seeing what it was – a small, blue butterfly dancing above her head. The same butterfly that had helped her in the haunted house.

"I'm not lost," she replied in thought. "I just don't know what to do. I'm scared."

The butterfly darted to the right, and all of a sudden, the sun started to shine. Hannah found herself on the rocky outcropping overlooking Canyon de Chelly.

In front of her were Josh and an unfamiliar Diné woman. A woman with long, plaited hair and a delicate face. Very slowly, the image became clearer, like somebody was adjusting the lens on a camera. The young woman looked up at Josh with so much love and pain in her eyes it took Hannah's breath away.

She was that woman.

Josh looked back at her with a sad expression in his eyes. So sad. It stabbed right through her heart.

Then, she started to talk in Diné Bizaad. The foreign words rolled off her tongue, and she understood them instantly.

"I can't live with the shadow from your past

anymore."

The pain in Josh's eyes was palpable. Her throat constricted in agony.

"I'm sorry," she choked out, turning around.

☙ ☙ ☙

Hannah fell down into the darkness, opening her eyes with a start. She found she was still on the beach with Josh, holding him in her arms. Without thinking, she pressed her lips to his in a gesture of love. The sudden vision had shown her exactly what she needed to see. She didn't know why this butterfly was helping her, but maybe it belonged to her like the bear belonged to Josh.

All pieces of the puzzle had fallen into place. She'd been together with Josh in a past lifetime, until the skinwalkers had started to terrorize her. Josh had told her the truth about his curse, and she'd given up. She had given up their love, and she had always regretted it.

"Josh, I'll stay with you," she said gently.

He gave her a disbelieving look.

"Are you sure?" he whispered.

"Yes."

Josh bit his lip. "Okay. You really want to be at my side and fight the skinwalkers?"

"Fight them? Are you saying we can actually *do* something about the curse?" Hannah stared at him.

"Yes. Although it's not easy."

"Where can I sign up?"

Josh laughed a bit. His laughter sounded relieved, happy and full of love. "I'll tell you all about it later today. But first, I have to talk to Sani."

"As usual," Hannah teased. "I'm sort of jealous of him, you know that?"

He chuckled, pulling her close to his chest. "I'll take

you home now," he said. "But I want you to come to Naabi'aani in the afternoon so we can discuss some things in detail."

As Josh was driving back to St. Mary's Port, Hannah texted Ben she was on her way back. What else she was going to tell him, she had no idea.

Seventeen

Hannah asked Josh to drop her off at the lakeside. She walked back up the hill by following a narrow sandy track leading to the log cabins, wanting to walk off the stress of the past few hours.

It was good to feel her heart beating against her ribs, feel the sweat pouring off her forehead, hear her rapid breathing. She felt alive, and she wanted to live, together with Josh. Fight side by side with him and deal with his ghosts from the past. She wouldn't leave him in the shadow that time had cast upon him.

"Hey there!" Ben called out to Hannah. He was sitting on the porch, reading one of his textbooks while listening to a CD featuring screaming guitars.

"Am I interrupting a study session?" Hannah shot a glance at Ben's scribbly notes in his spiral-bound notebook. He had a pen in his hand, a book about muscle groups cracked open on the table, and a yellow marker behind one ear.

"It's a welcome interruption," Ben grinned, closing his textbook. "So, don't beat around the bush. Where are we standing with this whole curse thing?"

Hannah hesitated. "Well, I'm going to Naabi'aani this afternoon to talk with Josh. About how we can stop it."

"So it can be stopped?" Ben looked overjoyed. "Can

I help?"

"I don't know yet."

"Okay. But did you find out why those skinwalkers are after you?"

"Yeah, I did."

"But you're not going to tell me?" Ben finished when Hannah didn't say anything else.

She sighed. "I don't want to betray Josh's trust. It has to do with him, so that's why he left me. To protect me. *That* I can tell."

Ben frowned. "Okay, fine. But please just tell me you're safe."

No, she was risking her life because she was in love with his best friend. And she'd decided to ignore that risk because she believed in reincarnation, missed opportunities and butterflies showing her visions. Maybe she should skip that part. She'd dumped enough mumbo-jumbo on Ben for now.

"Yes, I am safe," she lied. "Don't worry. Maybe I'll know more tonight."

ॐॐॐ

That afternoon, Hannah anxiously made her way to the reservation. She'd been wondering all morning what Josh needed Sani for. If there was a ritual powerful enough to deal with the skinwalkers, why hadn't he tried that in his previous life? Or *had* he tried, and had it gone wrong?

It wasn't until she got to Naabi'aani's main street that she realized she hadn't even talked to Josh about her own dreams yet. It had completely slipped her mind.

He was waiting for her outside his hoghan. His parents were nowhere in sight, and frankly, Hannah was glad. She was way too nervous to have some casual conversation about the weather with Josh's parents.

"Hey, *shan diin*," he said lovingly, pulling her in for a kiss.

Hannah smirked. "You know I was feeling depressed for days because you called me that? I thought you were addressing me as a sister."

Josh turned red. "Really? I thought you'd notice I had a new name for you." He gave her a shy look. "I was actually hoping you'd ask me about it, so I could use all that gathered-up courage of mine to explain what it meant."

"Well, unfortunately, I *didn't* notice," she chuckled. "Of course, you couldn't have known I was deaf. Or stupid."

"Or both," he laughed playfully.

"Do you love me anyway?" She flung her arms around his neck.

"With all my heart." He kissed her, pulling her closer. "Why don't you come inside?" he gestured.

Hannah's heart leapt up as she crossed the threshold to his house for the second time. No longer a curious intruder, she was invited – and he was truly letting her in this time.

Her gaze drifted to the mirror that had reflected her intense stare back to him the first time she'd been here. Immersed in thought, she stepped forward and touched Edward Hall's autobiography, still lying open on the bookshelf. Josh walked up behind her, sliding his arms around her waist. She let out a sigh of contentment when he planted a kiss in her neck.

"You knew him personally, didn't you?" she asked curiously, pointing at the book and remembering Josh's strange response when she'd asked him about the author.

He sighed. "Yes. Ned was one of my best friends. He worked in Oraibi in the nineteen-thirties, because he was part of a New Deal road-building project in Navajo Nation at the time."

Hannah turned around. "What was it like, meeting him again?"

Josh's gaze dropped to the floor. "Strange. I went up there on stage to talk to him after his lecture. He'd grown old, but I recognized him. I *knew* him. He still had the same laugh lines around his eyes, the same way of looking at the world – and of course, he had no idea who I was. He only saw a high school student with an incredible fascination for his work. It might have crossed his mind for a second that I looked exactly like Sam Yazzie, the name he used to know me by, but that was all. He didn't recognize me. In that moment, I felt so lonely."

"That must have been awful," Hannah whispered.

"It was, but at the same time it was wonderful to see how many good things he'd done in his life. I was proud of him. A fifteen-year-old boy, proud of someone old enough to be his grandfather." He stared at Hannah, a lost look in his eyes. "There are so many things I haven't told you yet."

Hannah bit her lip. "There's something I need to tell you, too."

"Oh?"

She took a step back, sitting down in the chair next to Josh's mattress. He squatted down and put his hands on her knees, looking up at her.

"I can remember being with you before," she started out. "A few days after I got here, I started having dreams about you and me. I saw flashes of a past life, but I didn't realize that until Amber suggested they might be actual memories." She took a deep breath, letting it out in a half-laugh. "I honestly had no idea what to tell you when you asked me what my dreams were about."

Josh was lost for words. "You still remember who you were," he finally spoke.

"Some of it, yeah."

"I recognized you after our first kiss, when I told you I loved you. I could *sense* it was you."

"Is that why you pulled away?" Hannah inquired.

"Yes." He took her hands in his. "I was scared and excited at the same time. Excited because you'd returned to me, but afraid bad things would start happening all over again."

"I'd like to know more about my past life," she said. "I've only seen small parts, you know. What kind of person was I?"

Josh smiled. "Ka'aallanii – that was your Navajo name. You came to live in our village as a refugee, together with your family, in the nineteenth century. I loved you so much. Your belonged to the Clan of the Sun. You were my ray of light."

Hannah blushed a bit. "And what does *Ka'aallanii* mean?"

"Butterfly." His hand reached out and touched her cheek. "You're still the same. A sunbeam lighting up my life in shadows. Somehow, I must have felt it was you when I fell in love with you again. I wanted to give you all the sweet names I'd once given to her – to *you*."

"It's almost like my eyes finally opened this summer," Hannah whispered. "The last time I saw you, you hadn't been through your vision quest yet. You weren't *you* yet."

Josh sat up and put his arms around her. "I've been empty inside since I lost you," he said quietly.

"So, how did it happen?" she asked timidly. "How did you lose me?"

Josh pulled her even closer, and when he looked up at her, tears were in his eyes. "You left me. The skinwalkers had almost driven you insane. I never blamed you."

Hannah didn't say anything, but just watched him with sad eyes.

"You went to that place where you broke up with me," he whispered. "That rock plateau near Canyon de Chelly."

"This time, I won't leave. I'll stay and fight."

"Please realize – they *will* find you as long as you can't shield yourself from their influence. You're seriously putting your life on the line by staying with me."

Hannah felt her heart tapping against her ribs. "Look. I was torn by regret after what happened. In my dreams, it feels like I made the wrong decision. I didn't come back into your life for nothing. I came back for a good reason. I love you too much to walk away again."

"I love you too." His eyes shone with sheer happiness. Softly, he kissed her mouth, and her stomach tingled with butterflies as his other hand slid down her back. Josh pulled her from the chair, drawing her closer as he kept kissing her, slowly and warmly, his hands on her hips. She shot him an almost disappointed look when he let go of her and sat back.

"I'm sorry. You're distracting me from our conversation," he grinned, a bit out of breath. "Let's sit down. I haven't finished explaining everything."

Hannah blushed. She sat down on the mattress next to Josh, feeling the heat radiating from his skin when he took her hand.

"If you want to fight next to me, you have to become one with me by doing a ritual," he explained, sounding a bit uncertain. "That way, you'll receive the power to better prevent the skinwalkers from entering your mind. You'll be connected to my long lifeline, protected by my totem animal. In your previous life, you were scared to death when I suggested it."

"Why was that?"

"You were afraid of spirits and supernatural forces, like most Diné are. Plus, there's the risk of you getting a long lifeline too. You would become just like me."

"I'm not scared now. I'd love to stay with you, even in my next life, if that's possible." She really meant it. There was no fear, only a strong sense of determination.

Josh gently kissed her cheek. "In that case, we have to establish a special bond between you and me as soon as possible. A deep connection."

His eyes were close to hers. Even during a serious conversation like this, Hannah still couldn't help being distracted by his close proximity.

"So that, uhm, deep connection..." She bit her lip. "How are we going to establish that, exactly?" In the silence that ensued, she looked up at Josh shyly, heat suddenly creeping up her face. There were probably a dozen different ways of establishing a deep connection with Josh, but embarrassingly enough, she could only think of one right now.

An amused grin started to spread across his face. "No, not like *that*. Although I like the way you think."

She laughed nervously. "Sorry. So what should we do?"

"I'll ask Sani to assist us. He should lead the ritual. We will both be in a trance when we pass into the veil, so we need someone to stay awake and alert in this world, as a sort of manager."

"What's going to happen once we're together in the veil?"

"I don't know exactly. I've never done this before, obviously."

"But I'll probably find out more about your lives?"

"I think so. You'll experience my memories."

"Wow. That's sort of personal."

He smiled. "Of course it is. I want to share my life with you. My lives, even."

"When are we doing this?"

"Sani has to fast for two days to cleanse his body and soul, or he won't be able to help out as a *hataalii*. Why don't you come back tomorrow night? It's better to stay away from me for the time being, while I take all the necessary precautions. I will have to entertain my guests tomorrow night first. Afterwards, we can talk things through."

"Guests?" Hannah echoed nonplussed. Who else was he planning to invite for their ritual?

"Uhm – it's my birthday tomorrow," Josh said with a teasing grin.

"Oh, crap!" she exclaimed. "I completely forgot."

"Well, fortunately, I didn't," he laughed. "Despite my age, Alzheimer's hasn't yet caught up with me."

She smiled at him in wonder. "That's so weird, actually. You'll be an adult tomorrow, but at the same time, you're hundreds of years old."

"True. It won't be the first time for me to celebrate my eighteenth birthday." He chuckled. "And here you were, thinking you snagged your very own toyboy."

After a quick goodbye, Hannah drove back home. She'd have liked to spend all afternoon with Josh, but it was best to keep a distance for now, as long as she wasn't protected by the ritual. The skinwalkers were keeping an eye on her.

It was a bizarre idea – even though the sun was shining, the radio was blasting out a happy tune, and summer seemed lighter than ever, she was, in fact, in mortal danger.

Eighteen

"So, are you ever going to tell me what kind of show you'll be a part of?" Ben asked her, when they were both sitting on the porch having breakfast the next morning. He sounded breezy, but he was obviously trying too hard. He felt left out.

"I can only tell you once it's over, because truth is, I don't know exactly," Hannah admitted.

"You still don't know? Well, can I be present?"

"I don't know if that's allowed. Sani only needs the two of us, I think."

"I can tag along and see if I can be of any help, right? If Sani tells me to split, I'll be home in no time."

Hannah sighed inaudibly. It was wonderful Josh had told her everything, but now she was faced with having to keep things secret from Ben. Or was she?

She gave her brother a pensive look, suddenly getting an idea. "Why don't you drop by this afternoon and ask Josh yourself? Who knows, he might need an assistant." If Josh was ready to spill the beans to Ben, this would be his chance. Maybe Ben really could help them.

"Yeah, I think I will," Ben nodded. "You have any plans for today?"

"I don't know. Maybe Em wants to meet up. I

haven't checked my phone all morning."

She stepped inside to find her cell. One missed call from her mom, a message from Emily to ask her out to lunch today, and Nick asking her if she wanted to come to a barbecue at his uncle's place.

"Nick is throwing a burger fest tomorrow night," she called out in the direction of the open door.

"I know," Ben shouted back. "We're all going. Maybe you and Josh won't, though."

"Still as chaotic as ever." Hannah stepped in front of Ben, her arms crossed and a grin on her face. "First, you practically fling yourself at me offering help, and now it turns out you don't even have time."

"Well, I can help in the morning. It's not going to take all day, right?"

Hannah stopped short. "No idea." Josh had asked her to keep two days off, but she couldn't imagine they'd need two full days for the ritual. It was probably preparation and aftercare time.

Ben got up. "Well, I'm going to Naabi'aani. I want to do something useful." He gently mussed Hannah's hair. "See you tonight."

"Yeah, see you tonight," she replied absently.

All of a sudden, she felt nervous again.

※ ※ ※

"I really don't need to know all the details of what happened between you and Josh," Emily blurted out that afternoon during lunch. "I just want to know for sure he's not going to hurt you again."

By now, Em knew that the skinwalker curse was related to Josh, but that was all Hannah had told her.

"Trust me, he won't. We talked it over. There are no secrets between us anymore."

"What time are you going to Naabi'aani tonight?" Emily inquired.

"Around dinner time. Ben is with Josh right now. By the way, I don't know if I can come to Nick's barbecue tomorrow night. We might be running late."

Emily raised an eyebrow. "All right, I won't ask any further. I can only hope you're making the right choice and Josh won't change his mind again."

"He won't. I'll see you later. Enjoy work."

They left the restaurant. As Emily walked back to the pharmacy, Hannah looked around a bit desolately. What was she supposed to do all afternoon without letting her nerves get to her? She hadn't heard back from Ben yet, so he might be having a lengthy discussion with Josh. Perhaps he would really be able to help Sani. For all she knew, Ben might be sitting in a sweatlodge right now, decorated with beads and feathers and smoking a peace pipe. Cue mysterious flute music, she thought with a nervous giggle.

Passing Safeway, Hannah suddenly spotted Yazzie leaving the store with two plastic bags. "Hey, Yaz," she called him. "Done some groceries?"

"Hey, *biligaana*!" Yazzie changed course and walked up to her. "I bought some stuff to bake an apple pie for Josh's sweet eighteen. I sure hope it's going to work. My mom's oven is a bit unpredictable."

Hannah laughed. "Why don't you use the oven in our cabin?" she suggested.

Yazzie's face lit up. "Great idea! Let's do that."

Excellent – baking a pie with Yazzie would be the perfect distraction. At least she wouldn't nervously pace back and forth on the porch, waiting for the clock to strike six.

Hannah hitched a ride on Yazzie's motorcycle. While Josh's counsin was busy in the kitchen, Hannah changed into a new outfit for the birthday party. She'd never worn the long, purple dress before. Actually, it was a bit too posh to wear to the reservation, but she wanted to look her best. After putting on the dress and adjusting the spaghetti straps, she put up her hair and fixed it with a hairpin her grandmother had given to her a while ago. It was made of gold filigree and shaped like a butterfly. Very fitting, she mused.

"Wow." Yazzie whistled, doing a double take as she emerged from the room. "You look like a fairytale. Josh will eat you right up, girl."

Hannah laughed. "In that case, let's give him your pie first to distract him from me," she threw back.

At five, Yazzie left to pick up some things from his hardware store in Wahweap, leaving it up to Hannah to transport the apple pie. As promised, Nick showed up in his Jeep at quarter to six to give her a ride.

With a nervous smile, Hannah got into the passenger seat. "Naabi'aani, please," she said to Nick, addressing him like a cabbie. "Please don't leave the meter running. I won't be back anytime soon."

Nick snickered. "I can imagine. On your way to your *legal* boyfriend, huh?"

"Yeah." Hannah bit her lip, clasping her hands primly together and staring down.

Nick patted her hands. "Don't worry. Your secret's safe with me. I won't call the cops on you if you promise to help me with my life's work one more time. Dissertation in need of a critical teacher's eye, yada, yada."

Hannah rolled her eyes. "*What* secret? I haven't done anything wrong, FYI."

"Too bad." Nick winked at her with a cheeky grin. "You should fix that, ASAP."

She turned red, suddenly giggling like a schoolgirl.

What a relief to have her down-to-earth friends around on the eve of stepping into the unknown. After all Josh's supernatural revelations, it felt good to just act silly for a while.

"We'll see," she said with a sly smile, sinking back into the passenger's seat as Nick drove away to the village.

Copper Mine Road was dusty, dry and bumpy. Hannah was tossed back and forth in the Jeep, trying to lean her head against the headrest. She was getting more nervous by the minute. When Nick finally parked next to the Benally hoghans, she couldn't wait to wish Josh a happy birthday and hug him tight. Quite a crowd had gathered in front of the house already. Emily, Amber, and Ivy were there, too.

"Heya, sis!" Ben waved at her. He was busy laying the table next to Josh's hoghan. Five fat candles were sitting in the middle.

Hannah shot her brother an inquisitive glance. He looked happy, so his conversation with Josh must have gone well. She was dying to find out what had been discussed.

More guests had shown up to celebrate Josh's birthday. His cousin Linibah was there, with her husband and kids. Yazzie's parents were grilling yucca plant on the big grill while Yazzie was busy making lemonade for everybody.

"*Shiyáázh!*" Josh's mom yelled in the direction of her son's hoghan. "Your guests are all here!"

Colored balloons were fixed to either side of the traditional blanket covering the hoghan's entrance, a golden garland running around the roof's edge. Because the hoghans didn't have grid-based electricity, Josh's dad had turned on the car stereo – the Mustang's speakers were blaring out Blackfire music.

Hannah's breath caught in her throat when Josh pushed the blanket aside to step out the door. Her gaze skimmed over his new pair of blue jeans, the traditional velvet shirt he was wearing and the big, turquoise pendant he'd worn before during the rodeo. He looked absolutely amazing.

Josh graciously accepted all the food people had brought along, casually pulling Hannah aside when everyone was done congratulating him.

"Let's talk in a minute," he said in a soft voice.

"Okay," she replied nervously.

When he walked back to his hoghan after chatting with his guests for a while, Hannah followed him inside. The light of the setting sun slanted into the room through a small window. Soft light from a few candles sitting on his desk flooded the room.

"So, where's Sani?" she wanted to know.

"In a ceremonial hoghan outside the village, built especially for the occasion. He'll start making a sandpainting tonight – the painting we need to pass into the veil. Tomorrow, at sunrise, we're meeting him there and the ritual will start."

"And what have you told Ben?"

"Almost everything. Except you being in mortal danger because you want to stay with me. I thought it was best not to mention that part."

Hannah gaped at him. "Almost everything?" she parroted.

A smile crossed his face. "Yes. Ben wasn't even that surprised. He always felt I was wise beyond my years, that I was somehow in close contact with my ancestors. It was a small step to embrace the truth that I *am* my own ancestors."

"What the hell?" Hannah blurted out. "He wasn't shocked?"

"No, he took it pretty calmly."

"Hah. Guess he was shocked enough already by the whole skinwalker curse thing," Hannah chuckled. "So does this mean he can help you for real?"

"Not yet," Josh replied cryptically. "But he might be able to later."

"Tomorrow?"

Josh shook his head. "Tomorrow's ceremony is only happening to connect you and me, so we can protect you better. The Evil Way ceremony takes place after that and is supposed to lift the curse. Ben can help us do that. He has strong ties with both you and me, so he's our man."

"But – won't that be dangerous for Ben?"

"It will be dangerous for all three of us," Josh responded in a monotone. "You know that."

Hannah fell silent. "Yeah, I know that," she mumbled, her voice trembling.

She quietly gazed into the smoldering fire in the middle of the hoghan, the coals still simmering with heat. Josh put his arm around her shoulders, and she leaned her head against his chest. "Sometimes I forget I'm in danger, because I feel so safe when I'm with you. So secure. I know it doesn't make sense."

Josh didn't reply. He just gave her a sweet smile. Hannah raised her face up to him, silently asking for a kiss. He pressed his lips to hers, caressing her face with one hand.

A cough at the entrance both made them jump. "I *knew* it. I knew you guys would sneak off to cuddle up again," Ben grumbled. He clomped inside, a teasing grin on his face.

Josh chuckled. "Stop moaning, you party pooper."

"Aren't you getting a little old for feeling up girls in dark rooms?" Ben shot back.

"Oh, I may be a quintuple centenarian, but I'm also

just an eighteen-year-old guy." Josh waggled his eyebrows at Hannah, who couldn't help giggling.

"You still look good for your age, you know," she teased him.

"So do you," he teased back.

"What? You think I'm too old?" she pouted.

"It's called 'ripe', Josh," Ben added helpfully.

Josh bit his lip and stifled a laugh. "Wow. It feels good now that I shared my secret with you guys. I almost feel normal."

Ben patted his back. "You should have done it ages ago. I would have been able to understand you so much better."

☙☙☙

When all the food was ready, everybody sat down for dinner. Josh put on a new CD that Nick had given to him. The upbeat music on the car stereo was the perfect backdrop to an evening full of friends and good food. Josh cut Yazzie's pie, his parents kept pouring everyone drinks, and Ben was busy fishing for compliments asking everyone what they thought of the potato salad he made. Although Josh made sure he mingled with all the guests, he kept close to Hannah all the time, giving her occasional looks so full of love it made her heart melt like butter in the desert.

"Where is your medicine bundle?" he asked as they were both scooping dessert onto their plates and nobody was listening in.

"In my handbag," Hannah answered softly, holding it up.

"Just wear it around your neck. It works better that way. Especially now that we're close to each other, you should wear it at all times."

Slowly, the sun sank below the horizon. When summer rain started to fall, Ben and Josh carried the table back inside the large hoghan and cleaned up. Josh's parents were helping Linibah and her family to pack the car, because they'd be driving them back to Chinle tonight. The others were huddled around the fire burning in the Benally family hoghan.

When Nick, Amber, and Ivy got up to leave, Hannah got nervous again. The birthday party was drawing to an end. She couldn't stop thinking about the ritual tomorrow.

"Will you please be careful?" Emily urged, as Hannah walked her to her own hoghan. "I completely trust Sani, but I don't want you to get hurt."

"We'll be careful," Hannah promised.

She took her overnight bag from the trunk on her way back to Josh's hoghan, taking it inside to put it on the floor next to his bed. She didn't really know where Josh expected her to sleep that night. She could stay in his parents' house too – they'd be staying the night in Chinle after driving Linibah's family back. Perhaps Josh needed solitude on the eve of such an important ritual. That wouldn't surprise her.

"I'm going, Han." Ben entered the house, stepping toward her and pulling her into a warm embrace. "Be safe, okay?" he whispered in her ear. "I want you back alive. So I can help you and Josh with the final reckoning."

Hannah smiled weakly. "Josh will help me. He's got a huge bear to back him up, I've been told."

"In the Big Blue House?" Ben smiled, but his eyes looked serious. After he left her, she heard him talk to Josh outside for a while longer.

Hannah sat by the fire and looked around. She noticed four handprints in white ash on the ceiling in each of the cardinal directions, like the ones Sani had done in his hoghan. She couldn't remember seeing them before, so it was probably an extra precaution. Josh had most likely also made a circle of corn pollen around the house to ward off evil spirits.

Hannah heard the Chevy drive off. Her stomach made a revolution when Josh stepped inside. He stood next to her, caressing her hair. "You nervous about tomorrow?"

"Yeah, a lot, actually." Hannah got up from the floor and sank down into the armchair, staring up at Josh. "I know that what we're about to do isn't even the most dangerous part of the whole operation, but still. I just wonder what's going to happen. All those past lives of yours – am I going to see them all flash by?"

"I don't think so. You'll see the memories directly related to my life with you."

Hannah sighed. "I want to help you so badly. It's not fair those skinwalkers cursed you. You had a task to protect your people so you could bring peace, right?"

"Well, I shouldn't have murdered that woman, then," he replied, his tone grim as he kneeled down next to her. "Times were different, but still.s I shouldn't have done it."

Hannah was quiet. Staring into the fire, Josh got the all-too familiar distant look in his eyes. "I was under so much pressure. You can't imagine how bad the situation was. How everything changed during my lifetimes. How the lands populated by Diné were flooded with gold-seekers from Mexico. How they sent out their soldiers to round up our people as slaves to work in the mines. How my little brother suffered terrible pains, dying of smallpox brought to our continent by the Spaniards." His eyes glazed over, and he impatiently wiped at his tears with the back of his hand. "All those families ripped apart. All those people forced into baptism only to be killed afterwards. They used a select group of converted native Christians as slaves to build their churches in Santa Fe. The oppressors wouldn't leave – nothing would stop them. Something had to be done. My clan members all turned to me, expecting me to do something. Po'pay appeared right on time."

"Who was Po'pay?" Hannah asked quietly, almost afraid to interrupt his story.

"He was the leader of the revolt. A Pueblo headman. I helped him prepare the attack. I couldn't just stand by, watching the Spanish military and priests deliberately destroying our culture." Josh got up and rubbed his face, as if to erase the bad memories. "I participated. I killed people too. Innocent people. Women, children. The Spaniards were resilient. They never would have left if we hadn't been so tough on them."

Hannah sprang to her feet and hugged him. "You couldn't help it," she whispered.

"Yes, I could. I *could* help it. I shouldn't have lost sight of my task. I was swept away on a tide of hate and revenge, and it was wrong." Josh closed his eyes, and a gentle smile spread across his face. "In the life following that one, I roamed the land as a storyteller, so the Diné wouldn't forget their traditions. It was a peaceful existence. The white people had come back, but they usually left me alone. They didn't see any harm in a woman performing as a traditional singer, visiting villages like a troubadour."

Hannah shot him a surprised look.

"Yes, I was a woman in that lifetime," he nodded. "I think my soul chose it like that, after all the bloodbaths and violence in the life before."

"And after that?"

"After that, I was born again as a man, in Tseyi –

Canyon de Chelly. That's where I met you." He caressed her cheek. "That lifetime enabled me to carry out my mission the right way. I saved my people and brought peaceful relations with the white man."

"You said you were Barboncito?"

Josh nodded. Hannah suddenly thought back to all the notes she'd made in the library that one afternoon. She'd seen that name a lot. "But then – you were there during the Long Walk. You were the leader setting the Diné people free from the Fort Sumner reservation. The man who single-handedly put Navajo Nation on the map." She stared at him in utter amazement. This was too bizarre. She was sitting right next to a living legend – who was supposed to have died over a century ago.

"I paid the price for it," Josh said. "I lost you. I lost my two adoptive children."

"I'm sorry you had to suffer so much." She hugged him tighter. "But at least we'll take the first step in destroying the curse tomorrow. Some pain will disappear."

Josh smiled at her and walked toward the table on the other side of the fire to get two incense cones from a wooden box sitting there. "Juniper berry," he explained. "It will give us protection." He lit them both and sat them down on the floor on either side of the fire.

"This is the same incense Sani burned when I visited him." Hannah inhaled the scent, getting up when Josh took her hand to pull her up.

"Why don't we sit here together?" he suggested, leading her to the mattress in the corner.

Hannah sat down next to him, biting her lip when his eyes found hers. In the silence between them, he slowly bent over and brushed his lips against hers. He gave her a simple kiss, cupping her face in his hands. "You're amazing. I still can't believe you're actually doing this."

Hannah smiled. "I'll stick around until you do believe it."

Josh pulled her closer, caressing her back. She pressed her body against his chest, her heart speeding up as his mouth sought hers out again. So slowly, so intensely, and all of a sudden, so clearly wanting more. For the first time since they'd gotten together, there was no reason to pull apart or break off their kiss. The fire in his kiss was the same fire running through her veins. It didn't feel as if he wanted solitude before the ritual.

"So – your parents are staying in Chinle tonight?" she stammered breathlessly, when Josh had to come up for air and stared into her eyes with passion burning in his own.

"Yeah, they are." The husky edge to his voice made her blush.

Hannah laughed uncertainly. "Okay. So, you think we should do something – special before we go to sleep?" The second the words were out of her mouth, she gulped. Okay, this couldn't get more embarrassing. She'd honestly meant to ask about preparations for the ritual, but her question sounded kind of seductive.

Josh chuckled. "No pressure," he mumbled, suddenly sounding very nervous himself.

That's when she realized she had the upper hand here. Josh had never been this intimate with a girl before. Not in this life, anyway.

Hannah smiled up at him, touching his cheek. "I don't feel pressured," she said softly, holding his gaze.

He cast down his eyes. "That's good," he replied hoarsely. "Neither do I."

"So isn't it – dangerous? Us being, uhm, too close maybe? Easy to single out by vindictive witches?"

Josh shook his head. "Sani said we wouldn't be at risk as long as I made sure the the hoghan was protected really well. And I did that. We can't be too careful."

"Hold on. You talked to *Sani* about that?" Hannah stared at Josh all bug-eyed. Oh, this *could* get more embarrassing.

"Well, not exactly." He shrugged, grinning a mischievous grin. "Look, he's not stupid. He knows you're spending the night with me for the first time."

Hannah felt a silly grin spreading across her face. Josh smiled back, his hand landing on her calf, sliding up to her knee in a gentle caress that sent shivers through her entire body. She giggled nervously. His hand slid up a bit higher, making her fall silent all of a sudden.

"I remember you used to enjoy this kind of thing in silence," he mumbled against her lips.

Hannah blushed like a tomato. "That's not fair," she protested. "You know these – *things* about me, but I don't remember anything about you." She shot him a nearly accusatory look.

Josh smiled roguishly. "Which calls for extensive research on your part, I'd say."

"So, you're sure it's – safe?" She bit her lip. This was crazy. It sounded like she was asking him whether he'd had himself tested or bought condoms.

Josh nodded. He rummaged around in her bag, pulling out the gun she'd packed at his request. "Even if those witches manage to slip past the corn pollen circle, handprints and incense in this hoghan, then ignore your medicine pouch and my dreamcatcher, I'll still pump them full of lead," he bit out. "I have bullets dipped in white ash ready to load into your weapon. Plus, I'm going to stay awake anyway." He put the gun next to the mattress.

"What? You're not going to sleep at all? Don't you need to be rested for tomorrow?"

He shook his head. "I have to protect you. Whether

you're asleep here or in my parents' hoghan, you're in danger anyway until the ceremony starts. I'd rather keep you close, in a protected place."

She scooted against him. "How close?" she whispered.

Josh looked at her as if mesmerized. "Close enough to keep me awake," he then replied breathlessly.

ஓஓஓ

She didn't know exactly what had woken her up so early in the morning, but Hannah opened her eyes with a start. A hint of a shiver crawled down her spine. Had she had another nightmare?

She glanced aside to Josh, who'd put his arms around her and was soundly asleep, despite his words. She smiled down at his relaxed face, listening to his slow breathing, pressing a kiss to his forehead. Even when he was asleep, she felt protected in the circle of his arms. It made her forget her fears about the curse. Her anxious feelings dissipated in the light of day playing over his sharp features.

She stretched, carefully wriggling out of Josh's embrace as to not wake him up yet. Quietly, she got up to pour herself a drink from the jug on the table. Then, she padded to the doorway and pushed the hand-woven blanket aside to stare at the first rays of sunlight creeping over the horizon, completely mesmerized. This was the beauty she wanted to walk in.

Behind her, she heard Josh waking up. He got out of bed, walked toward her and covered her bare shoulders with the blanket they'd slept under.

"*Ya'at'eeh abíní.* Good morning." He kissed her shoulder.

"Hey." She turned around. "I was just saying hello to

the sun."

"It's splendid, isn't it?" Josh said, lifting the blanket in the doorway a bit higher to gaze at the sunrise.

Her fingers touched the naked skin of his back. "Aren't you cold?" she whispered. "You've given me the blanket."

Josh pressed his body against her. "I'll survive." He kissed her on the mouth. "I'm sorry I fell asleep."

"Oh well, you deserved a good rest after last night." Hannah blushed as she thought back to him and her. It had been so much more than she'd ever felt before. Sometimes, it had felt like time had stood still, making her wish she really could freeze time and stay in the moment with Josh forever.

He smiled, a sudden cheeky sparkle in his eyes. "Yeah, you think? So I did well?"

"You know that," she mumbled, casting her eyes shyly down to the floor.

She heard him chuckle. "Well, I can never be completely sure. Maybe I'm a little bit out of practice."

Hannah looked back up with a giggle. "Uhm, no. Definitely not. Don't worry."

She kissed him longingly. Actually, she wouldn't mind holing up in this hoghan for the next two days to have some more private time with Josh, but she knew they had to meet up with Sani just after sunrise. With a frustrated moan, she pulled away and grabbed her clothes from her bag. "I'm going to get dressed. Are we having breakfast?"

He shook his head. "Not the best idea. We'll stop by the sweatlodge first in order to sweat out bad influences from our bodies. You have to do that on an empty stomach."

Quickly, she slipped into a flimsy summer dress. The medicine bundle was still around her neck.

Josh put on a sleeveless shirt and loose-fitting pants. He also put on the big, turquoise pendant he'd worn at his birthday party last night.

"That is a really amazing piece of jewelry, you know that?" Hannah took a step toward him, running her finger over the intricately inlaid stones.

"Thank you." He paused a few seconds before he continued. "It's – a sort of heirloom."

"Clan heirloom?"

"No. Mine. I've had it since 1839." He gazed at her with a slight smile before he continued: "You gave it to me."

"Me?" Hannah asked. "You mean, when I was still Ka'aallanii?"

Josh nodded. "It belonged to your mother once. She'd been killed by Mexicans during one of their rampages. You shot two of her killers and grabbed this pendant before the soldiers could get to you. And you gave it to me when you promised to stay with me. It was a wedding gift, actually."

Dazedly, she eyed the pendant. "How did you manage to hold on to it through the years?"

"Every time I awake after my vision quest, there comes a time when I visit the most important places of my previous life, as a kind of pilgrimage. I commemorate the people I buried there, saying goodbye to them for good. I told you about my trip to the four holy mountains to connect with the spirits of my forefathers. Well, that was one part of it. The other part was a journey into my own past." He stared at the medicine wheel hanging on the wall. "As for this pendant – I buried it somewhere safe by the time I knew my nineteenth-century life was nearing its end. The life in which I knew you. When I was born again in 1910, I visited the place I buried it and dug it up so I could wear it again. And during that life, I buried it once more, so I could find it in this lifetime."

"You never forgot about me," Hannah stammered, taken by emotion.

"No," he simply said. "Never."

"I wish I could say the same. I have no long lifeline like you, but I wish I hadn't forgotten you."

He smiled. "You haven't. Because you came back."

☙☙☙

When the sun had risen a bit further in the sky, they left the village hand in hand, following a trail leading into the mountains until they hit a secluded spot in the wilderness with no one in sight. There, Sani had built a temporary hoghan out of tree trunks that somehow reminded Hannah of a large, pyramid-shaped tent.

Next to it, he'd dug a shallow hole in the ground to construct a sweatlodge, covered by blankets and quilts in order to keep the steam inside.

"*Ya'at'eeh*," he welcomed them. "Are you both ready?"

They nodded. Hannah took in Sani's tired but serene appearance. "Thank you for helping us, *shicheii*." She addressed him respectfully as a grandfather.

"*Lá'aa*," Sani replied with a smile. "You're welcome."

Hannah saw Josh stripping off his clothes to enter the sweatlodge. Her eyes darted sideways. Was Sani really planning on standing there and observing her as she was stripping naked? She let out a sigh of relief when he turned around and walked toward the entrance of the ceremonial hoghan.

Inside the sweatlodge, the high temperature rapidly made Hannah nauseous and dizzy. Josh gently supported her as she scooted closer to put her head on his shoulder.

"I can't stand this heat," she puffed.

"Try lasting for a little while longer." Josh handed Hannah the mug of water standing next to the hot pile of coals in the middle, which was actually there to pour onto the coals and create more steam. She took a long drink, still slumped against Josh's shoulder.

After what seemed like an eternity, they heard Sani calling them outside. "Everything is ready."

Hannah waited until she heard the *hataalii* walk away, then staggered out of the sweatlodge. The warm morning air actually made her shiver after the extreme temperatures she'd been exposed to in her first ritual of the day.

Josh followed her, taking two blankets from the top of the lodge. He wrapped one around Hannah's shoulders and used the other to dry off his torso, wrapping it around his hips. Hannah wiped the sweat off her body, glancing sideways at Josh. "Are we supposed to get dressed again?"

He shook his head. "It will work better when we sit down on the *iikaah*, the sandpainting, completely naked." He shot her an apologetic look, and Hannah nodded curtly. She shouldn't be a prude about it. A medicine man was as much a doctor as any other physician she'd ever visited, and she didn't fret about taking off her clothes around them either when she went for check-ups.

Still, it felt strange walking into the hoghan and putting her blanket to the side with Sani in the same room. He was sitting on a buckskin next to the sandpainting they were supposed to sit down on in a moment, busy arranging objects from his *jish* to use during the ceremony. She could make out a rattle, different kinds of colorful natural clay, feathers and dried plants.

In the middle of the hoghan, he'd made a breathtakingly beautiful *iikaah*. Three figures holding prayer stick were in the middle, one of which was clearly a bear. She couldn't identify the other two figures, but she could sense the energy coming off the sandpainting settle into her bones. Sani must have been working on this piece of art all night long.

"Why do we have to sit down on it?" she whispered to Josh. "That's such a shame. We'll ruin his art."

He smiled. "The *iikaah* attracts magic. When we sit down on it, the magic will be absorbed by our bodies."

In silence, they sat down on the floor on the other side of the sandpainting. When Sani finally rose, he started singing and sprinkling corn pollen on Hannah and Josh, walking in circles around them, using the rattle to emphasize his song. Then, he crumbled a few dried plants into a bowl to burn them and fill the room with pungent-smelling smoke.

The hypnotic singing made Hannah dizzy again. She held on to Josh's hand, feeling him squeeze hers in reassurance.

Blinking her eyes, she took a closer look at the wall behind Sani. The air seemed to shiver and whirl around, suddenly forming a looming shadow shaped like a bear.

"Don't be afraid," Josh mumbled, following her stare. "It's Shash, my direction protector from the west. He's here to help us."

Despite his words, Hannah's heart beat in her throat. Lately, she'd seen one too many looming shadows for her own good. She stared at the apparition, trying to let go of her uneasiness. As she did, she felt a powerful, deep and balanced force coming from the totem animal. The bear was benevolent. He was on their side.

"It is time," Sani said at that moment.

As if in a trance, Hannah got up. She was still holding Josh's hand when they sat down on the painting cross-legged, their knees touching.

She looked into his brown eyes, and suddenly, without any clear transition, they were somewhere else. The hoghan had disappeared. All around them was woodland. They were sitting at the border of a small lake, smooth like a mirror. Moonlight illuminated the strange landscape, which looked warm and welcoming despite the cold light.

"Have we entered the veil?" she asked Josh in her mind. Somehow, she knew he would hear her.

He put a hand on her knee. "It's a waiting room." His voice sounded in her head. "We'll be picked up soon."

Silence enveloped them. Hannah took several deep breaths, still feeling the medicine pouch around her neck. Apparently, she still needed its protection in this place.

"My children," a deep, dark voice then addressed them. It could only come from an ancient, animal being. She looked over her shoulder and saw a huge brown bear standing there, observing her and Josh.

"My protector," Josh needlessly explained. "It's time."

A black haze clouded her eyes, making everything around her retreating into the background.

Everything except Josh's hand in hers.

1821 - 1871

1839

It is dark in Tseyi. I am lying on my back, watching the stars above. Somewhere in the distance, I can hear an owl hoot. It makes me smile. Some of my clan members believe the call of an owl is a bad omen, but the sound somehow always makes me feel at ease.

Alas, there is not much reason to feel at ease nowadays. The Spaniards are no longer a part of the motherland across the ocean. Instead, they have proclaimed independence and are calling their country the Republic of Mexico now.

It happened in the year I was born. The lands that used to belong to my people were mercilessly claimed and added to Mexican soil, but my family managed to escape the Mexicans and settled down in the valley we still inhabit today – Tseyi, the canyon which in Spanish they call De Chelly. It is relatively safe here.

Now that the Mexicans are no longer a part of the Spanish empire in Europe, their attacks have only increased. More and more Diné people are abducted to be used as slaves. I never considered the possibility that our people would have to leave the southern part of our sacred land altogether. I wish I could talk sense into the Mexicans, but even my knowledge of their language – learned in previous lives – will not bridge the gap between our two cultures. The only thing they want is to rule us, subdue us or else annihilate us, in order to shape the world around them into their idea of perfection.

With a sigh, I get up when the sky in the east bleeds to yellow at the first crack of dawn, walking back to the village where my clan found refuge so long ago. When I enter the hoghan, Tsosi is already up. "Hey, early bird," I tease my brother. "Awake so soon?"

"Hello, late bird," Tsosi replies with a grin. "Back already?" He knows my habits, including the one where I disappear all night so I can stop my thoughts from spinning and find peace in silence.

"I've got a lot to do still. The headman says we have to perform a Beauty Way ceremony. Yesterday, some new refugees reached the village, and they have seen more than their share of blood and violence. We will restore their balance. Give them *hózhó*."

I am happy I have the chance once more to spread peace among my people, by delivering speeches and by performing rituals. I've learned my lesson during the revolt of 1680 – fighting is not my way of doing things. Now that I am the youngest *hataalii* of the village, I have the fortune of being able to help people restore their balance despite all the hardship they have experienced and the terrible things they have witnessed.

Once I am done preparing the different sorts of colored sand we need for the ceremony, I walk to the village center for the afternoon meeting with the recently arrived refugees. Yas, our headman, has asked them to come out today.

"How are the preparations going?" he inquires when I join him in the village square.

"They are going well. I have fasted since this morning, so the ritual can take place tomorrow night."

"That is wonderful. These people have seen too much war." He nods toward the group of Diné fugitives from the south.

My eyes take in the crowd in front of the village chapter house. Most people look scared and sad. A few of them stare despondently ahead in the distance, their gazes devoid of any hope.

One girl among them draws my attention. She proudly holds her head up high, her eyes filled with determination and courage. There is no fear in her face.

Her eyes find mine, and I quickly look away. I do not want to make her feel uncomfortable. When my gaze drifts back to her after a few moments, she is talking to an elderly man who is probably her father. She is holding his hand, comforting him as he silently starts to cry. I furtively observe her. So much power is evident in her posture and way of talking – it fascinates me. She is not serene. In fact, she is the complete opposite of me, but maybe that is precisely what is drawing me in.

"Who are the two people on the left?" I casually ask Yas, once he has finished his speech and the girl and her father are still in the village square.

"Naalnish and Ka'aallanii of the Sun Clan." His voice grows solemn. "Father and daughter. She has mercilessly killed her mother's two murderers."

I catch myself openly staring at Ka'aallanii now. Who is this girl? She is so different from me, and yet, she reminds me of myself as I was in the past. She confuses me. Do I even *want* to know her?

Quickly saying my goodbyes to Yas, I turn back to the ceremonial hoghan to continue preparing myself further for the coming ritual. Now is not the time to get distracted.

When I come out the next morning to drink a few handfuls of water from the well at the edge of the village, I run into her again. It is still early, and she is sitting next to the water well grinding corn with a pestle.

"*Ya'at'eeh*," I gingerly greet her. Somehow, she makes me nervous. Ka'aallanii looks so unapproachable, the way she is sitting there all by herself.

She looks up. "*Ya'at'eeh*." An unexpected smile breaks the cool surface of her face. It completely baffles me. The smile changes her entire appearance. It is as if the sun suddenly lights up her face, even though the sun has not fully risen yet.

"Would you like some corn porridge too?" She holds out the bowl of crushed corn kernels.

"No, thank you. I am fasting. I will be leading the *hózhójí* ritual tonight, together with the oldest *hataalii*."

"Oh yes, that is true. Yas told me you are a *hataalii* too."

Still a bit hesitant, I sit down next to her. Actually, I have no business here except quenching my thirst, but I would like to talk to Ka'aallanii a bit more. Did Yas tell her about me of his own accord, or did she ask him questions? I hope it is the latter – that would mean she finds me interesting enough to find out more things about me, too. "Where do you and your father come from?" I ask.

"From the south. The situation was getting really bad. Every day, we would be under attack by Mexicans, so Tseyi seemed the safest place to go to." She is staring at her hands.

"I am sorry about your mother," I say quietly.

"Yes. So am I." Her hand touches the turquoise pendant hanging from a chain around her neck. "This belonged to her."

"It must be good to have something to remind you of her." I cannot help myself – I am still staring at her. Ka'aallanii does not look a day over sixteen, and yet, she seems so wise. I feel comfortable around her, but at the same time, I feel nervous.

"So, let me go back to the village. I do not want to tempt you any more than necessary," she suddenly says, standing up.

I look at her, somewhat taken aback. "What do you mean?" I feel caught. Did she see me gape at her indecently?

She chuckles. "With my corn porridge. You are not supposed to eat until tonight, are you? I do not want to make it any more difficult than it already is."

"Oh. Oh, I see," I owlishly mumble back, waving at her when she smiles at me and walks away in the direction of the new section of our village, where we have created newly-built hoghans for the fugitives.

I turn back to my parents' hoghan, where Tsosi is just helping our dad saddle up the horses for a trip to the neighboring village. He follows me inside to wrap up a few pieces of corn bread for the journey, looking at me inquisitively. "Why the beatific smile?"

I raise an eyebrow. "Beatific smile? Me?"

He chuckles. "Well, *yes*. You can tell me all about it later, okay?" Laughing, he steps out of the hoghan.

Feeling confused, I slowly sit down on my mattress to put on some fresh clothes for tonight, mentally going over every small detail of my conversation with Ka'aallanii. I know I should be focusing on more important matters, and suddenly, I wish I did not have to do a ritual or fast all day long. All I want is to work in the orchard and chat with *her* the entire afternoon. Picking peaches and making light conversation would be the perfect opportunity to get to know her a bit better.

But I can't. I cannot want that. I have responsibilities – I know that only too well. All of a sudden, and for the first time in three hundred years, I feel a certain defiance toward Shash, my totem animal and protector. What he expects of me is beginning to feel like too much. But quite frankly, I should not blame him. I do this to *myself* – always putting pressure on everything. The fact I am the protector of the Diné people does not necessarily mean I cannot have a happy life filled with love.

I close my eyes, thinking back to the moment the *yenaldlooshi* appeared to me. The memory of their faces has not faded after all these years. I still remember what they looked like, and the sound of their voices. I just cannot see how they could still haunt me after all these centuries. How could they? They are witches, but they are certainly not immortal. They are dead. They *have* to be.

And then, it hits me. I let out a mocking laugh. What am I thinking? This is all just a daydream. I have hardly spoken two words to that girl, and already, I am plotting my next ten moves. Maybe she is not even interested in me. She probably has a lot of other things besides boys to keep her mind occupied, having only narrowly escaped a bloody war. In all likelihood, she just wants to be left alone.

Still, I feel apprehensive as I make my way to the ceremonial hoghan that night. A number of people are waiting in front of the building. Aditsan, the oldest *hataalii*, greets me warmly. Together, we take the group of six into the hoghan. My heart takes a little leap when Ka'aallanii turns out to be among them. That is no surprise – she is guilty of killing two Mexicans and is undoubtedly in need of spiritually vindicating herself.

The ceremony lasts until well after sundown, and

when we finally emerge from the hoghan again, my face is sticky with sweat and my eyes feel as if they could fall shut at any moment. Despite this, I immediately stand straight and try to look as awake as possible when Ka'aallanii addresses me.

"I feel a lot better now, thanks to you and Aditsan." She smiles her sunny smile, and I can feel my heart skip a beat. She is so gentle and yet so strong.

"You are welcome," I simply reply.

She watches the sky. "I had lost it, you know. The ability to walk in beauty. I found life to be unfair, cold and hard." She steps a bit closer. "But now, I am thankful again. Thankful for everything I *did* get to keep. I am grateful for the safety that Tseyi provides us and all the clans living here."

I glance upward too, taking in the stars that have inspired me so many times. "I am happy to hear you feel at home here."

"That is not so difficult. Just look at this valley. Everything here is still so beautiful and untainted."

I hesitate, my heartbeat quickening. "Have you walked the mountain path yet that takes you beyond the valley to the viewpoint?"

Ka'aallanii shakes her head, looking at me curiously.

"Would you like to join me for a walk tomorrow? Perhaps I could show you around." I smile at her, and the familiar smile that confuses me so much appears on her face again.

"Yes, of course," she accepts enthusiastically. "That is nice of you. When do you want to go?"

"After breakfast?" If possible, I would like to spend all day with her, so I suggest the earliest time possible.

"That sounds good. All right." For a split second, she grabs my hand and her fingers touch mine. "I will see you tomorrow. Thank you for the wonderful ceremony."

"See you tomorrow, *shan díín*," I blurt out without thinking twice. My stomach feels funny when she gapes at me with her eyes wide open. A cute blush creeps up her face, a shy smile trembling around the corners of her mouth as she looks down and intently stares at the earth in front of her feet. Then she turns around and walks away. I stare after her. She nimbly moves away from the square, chancing a look over her shoulder to take in my still beaming face. Then, she almost skips around the corner of the largest hoghan, disappearing from sight. A happily fluttering butterfly.

I exhale. Heavens – I am impressed with myself. I pulled that off quite well, after endless years of dutiful service and detachment.

"Well, that definitely explains the beatific smile this morning," I suddenly hear Tsosi's voice piping up from behind me. Apparently, he has been waiting for me outside after the *hózhójí*. He must have overheard the conversation between me and Ka'aallanii. He meets me with a large grin when I turn around.

"Yes – she is a nice girl," I respond, still lost in thought. "So, how was your trip to the neighboring village?"

Tsosi deflects my question. "Oh no, do not change the topic. We can talk about the neighbors every day. I want to know everything about your new girlfriend."

I start to grin sheepishly. "Well, girlfriend – such big words. I am just going to take her out for a walk, *shik'is*."

Tsosi waggles his eyebrows. "Oh yes. A walk in beauty, I suppose." He shoots me a meaningful look.

I blush. "Right. I am going home. I am worn out, and tomorrow I want to be fit."

"I can imagine," Tsosi chuckles, still in his teasing mood.

As I saunter back home, I catch myself humming a tune. I have not done that for a very long time.

In the days that follow, Ka'aallanii and I cover quite some miles of mountain paths. Sometimes, we sit in silence on the rock plateau overlooking Tseyi, but most of the time, we stroll along the canyon edge. More and more frequently, we are holding hands while we walk or sit together.

Ka'aallanii talks. She tells me about the life she had in the south, the land I know so well from my previous lives. The area has radically changed. According to her, no one can be certain to live through the day, herds of sheep are stolen from Diné farmers to feed the growing population of Mexico, and our people are traded as slaves so the Mexicans can grow richer.

As she talks, I can see how the restlessness gradually fades from her eyes. It had already started after the *hózhójí* ritual, but it goes beyond that now. She seems more relaxed, care-free and happier by the day. She says she is like her mother, who was a strong, brave woman. When she talks about her mother, a light shows up in her eyes that seems more than love alone. Perhaps it is a feeling of loss I see in her gaze, a kind of melancholy and longing for something that will never return.

"Thank you for listening," she says to me one night, as we are sitting next to each other on the plateau near the precipice where I used to watch stars by myself. "I just cannot stop talking. I am like a waterfall."

"I like listening to you." I let out a sigh. If only I could talk to her about the things going through *my* head. I know it is too much for another person to fully comprehend, but still, I wish I could. I would not mind sharing it with *her*.

"Am I boring you?" Ka'aallanii sounds insecure. She

must have heard me sigh.

I throw her an apologetic look. "No, not at all. I was just thinking about my own life, that is all."

"You do not talk much." She looks back pensively.

"No," I say after a short silence.

She smiles. "That is all right. You do not have to talk if you do not wish to."

Without thinking, I put my arm around her shoulders, pulling her closer. "I will talk one day," I say, even though I do not know if I can stick to that promise.

Ka'aallanii relaxes into my embrace. A warm glow radiates off her skin, and it suddenly tips my balance. All week I have spent in her company, but I have only gone as far as holding her hand. She still seems so inaccessible, but at the same time, so fragile. I do know I *could* take this further – the look she gave me when I called her *shan díín* for the first time is etched into my memory. Still, I am hindered by the cautiousness that has become second nature to me through the years, all my conscientious detachment weighing down on me. What will this girl get involved in if she chooses me?

I turn my face toward her. She leans her head against my shoulder, staring into the distance. Very gently, I let my hand touch her hair, stroking the soft strands, and I can feel how she moves even closer. Then, she lifts her face to meet mine, smiling at me innocently and yet seductively.

"Hey," she whispers close to my face.

"Hey." My pulse quickens when I press my lips to hers, the sweet yucca scent of her hair wafting into my nostrils. I hear her moan softly, and I pull her into my arms. She caresses my chest, her hand resting where my heart is beating wildly.

When Ka'aallanii finally pulls away, she stares deep into my eyes. "You saved me," she whispers with a smile full of love. "You saved me from bitterness and the wish to take my revenge inflicting pain on people. You gave me peace."

I am lost for words. "You gave me peace as well. And love. I have never felt like this about anyone before," I finally reply.

We sit on the rocks above the canyon until the sun sets – laughing, talking, kissing, embracing. I almost cannot believe this is happening. Everything is so incredibly beautiful, so good and so pure it brings tears to my eyes.

At the end of that year, I join Ka'aallanii's household, moving into her and her father's hoghan. We organize a small ceremony to celebrate me joining her clan. Normally speaking, I would be joining her mother's household, but of course, Ka'aallanii's mother is no longer alive.

With a solemn gesture, my wife puts the pendant once belonging to her mother around my neck. "I will stay with you," she quietly states, looking at me with eyes full of love and affection, a hint of sadness mingled with those other emotions. During important occasions like these, she misses her mother terribly.

Naalnish puts his hand on my shoulder. "Welcome to the family. I wish you both a long and happy life together."

A longer life than he can imagine, in my case at least. I take Ka'aallanii's hand, pulling her close, kissing her like I have never kissed a woman before. With her, I feel at home.

1841

I have returned from the forest with a bag full of medicinal herbs. Aditsan has put Ka'aallanii inside the hoghan where he often treats his patients with much success, but when I enter, he looks more worried than usual.

"I cannot determine the cause of her fever." I hear how he is trying to suppress the panic in his voice, and that makes me even more scared.

I kneel down next to her. She has been terribly sick since last night. My sweet girl – my sunbeam. Her eyes glitter with fever, her cheeks burning with heat. She is delirious, but she does recognize me. "*Shi'hastiin*. My husband – you have come back."

"Yes, *she'esdzáán* – my wife." I hold up the bag of herbs. "I found you some medicine."

Tears well up in her eyes. "I lost it," she sobs, extending her cramped hands toward me. Puzzled, I look up at Aditsan, who wordlessly shows me a blanket with a large stain of blood on it. It is the blanket Ka'aallanii fell asleep on when I left the village that morning.

"It happened this afternoon," he softly explains.

I am trying to hold back my own tears when I look at all the blood Ka'aallanii lost. She was three months pregnant, but the high fever raging through her body has proven to be fatal to our unborn child. I bite down hard on my lip. There is no time for mourning. I have to keep myself together, or else I will lose my wife too.

"Leg," Ka'aallanii whispers in a hoarse voice, after her tears subside. "Hurt."

"Where does it hurt?" I put my hand on her thigh.

"Not there. My calf. Left."

I bend toward the spot on her leg she is pointing at, drawing my attention to a lump on her calf. It looks like something underneath the skin has caused an infection.

I call Aditsan once Ka'aallanii has dropped off in slumber again. "Can you come look at this? Could this be infected because of a thorn getting under the skin? Or a tick, maybe?" Neither of those two options would cause a high fever like this one, but I do not want to rule out any possibility. Besides, I do not have any other explanation.

Aditsan frowns when he looks at the swelling. "Strange. I suggest we start a ceremony to counter the infection, while also using a knife to cut the skin open. Whatever is hidden underneath, it has to come out, that much is clear."

We work together in silence. My old friend prepares the herbs I have collected, makes a small sandpainting and starts to chant when Ka'aallanii has gulped down the herbal tea with great difficulty. Her fever does not go down – it only seems to be getting worse. I am beginning to feel desperate.

When I finally put the knife to her skin, Ka'aallanii wakes up and sits up straight. She cries out in pain before I have even touched her.

My mouth is set in a grim line as I make a small incision while Aditsan softly chants and shakes his rattle. She seems to calm down a bit, staring at her leg with wide eyes. To my own surprise, I remove a small piece of bone from her skin which is not her own. It is almost like it was implanted by something or someone. A sudden shiver goes through me when I put the bone splinter on the floor next to me. I clean the wound and apply some ointment, feeling slightly relieved when I notice the wild look fading from her eyes. I touch her forehead and notice the fever has gone down, too.

When I look at Aditsan again, he gives me a deeply worried look. He picks up the piece of bone with fingers protected by yucca fiber, and walks outside. After a minute, I can hear him digging a hole in the ground. The smell of smoking fire drifts into the house.

Ka'aallanii has fallen asleep holding my hand, looking completely peaceful now. I wish I could say the same about my own state of mind. Feeling sick to the stomach, I go out, staring into the flames of the fire that Aditsan has lit in the small pit he has dug to burn the bone fragment and yucca fiber together.

"Your wife was cursed," he crisply states. "*Yenaldlooshi.*"

My heart starts to hammer as I choke back tears. This is not fair. This is *impossible*. They cannot have followed me here, to this time, this life – and yet they have.

"I need your help," I finally whisper in total desperation.

Later that night, Aditsan and I are at our usual meditation spot in the mountains. Ka'aallanii is asleep in the hoghan we built together next to her dad's house. After she woke up for a moment and again remembered her miscarriage, she fell asleep crying and holding my hand. I left her with her father so I could complete an important ritual together with Aditsan.

I have explained to the medicine man everything about the curse that was put on me all those years ago, in 1680. Together, we have entered the veil, and we have seen how the *yenaldlooshi* use my lifeline to follow me here – how they use their dreams and dark powers to influence the present from the past.

"Dream travelers," I mumble once we come out of our mutual trance. "That is how they can find me. They will never give up."

My throat constricts when I think of Ka'aallanii, who

was helpless against the poisonous bone fragments my tormentors employed to attack and curse her. They would have taken her away from me if they had succeeded.

"How can I beat them once and for all?" I ask quietly, but resolutely.

"You cannot," the *hataalii* replies.

For a long time, I stay silent. I am almost afraid to snap at Aditsan for telling me the harsh truth I should have known, deep down, anyway.

"Are you sure it is impossible?" I try eventually, even though I already know the answer.

"You know that as well as I do. This kind of *chindi* can only be beaten if you call them by their true name. And their true name cannot be tracked down anymore. They may be able to follow *your* lifeline, but you cannot travel back in time to find out who *they* really are. You would have to know the exact location of their hide-out, and you don't."

I clench my hands into fists. "There must be something I can do to protect Ka'aallanii." I swallow back a sob.

"You could leave her," my old friend finally suggests in a grave voice.

My heart is in my throat, breaking at the thought of leaving the love of my life, of *all* my lives. I would give anything to protect her, but this is a very high price to pay. I close my eyes, taking a deep breath. "Is it not possible to come up with something to keep them away from her, at least?"

"We can, but I do not know for how long. We need to collect juniper wood, white ash, corn pollen..." He sums up a number of powerful medicines, and suggests venturing out that very same night to get all the things we need and make my wife a medicine bundle to protect her from these ghosts from my past.

"Do you not think you should tell her about the danger she is in?" is the last thing Aditsan asks me as I leave the ceremonial hoghan at sunset, holding the medicine pouch in one hand.

I shake my head. "I want to see how this turns out first."

When I walk back home, I am trying to tell myself I do not want Ka'aallanii to be unnecessarily scared. In reality, I am dreading her reaction if she were ever to find out why she lost our first child.

1842

"That was quite a trip!" Ka'aallanii huffs. Hand in hand, we take the last few hundred steps separating us from Nonnezoshe, the rainbow that turned to stone. The sacred place of our ancestors.

For months, my wife and I have mourned the loss of our unborn child, until last week Ka'aallanii had a vision in a dream commanding her to leave the memory of her pregnancy behind at Rainbow Bridge, so the gods could lift up the baby's soul toward heaven. Our sadness should not bind the young spirit to earth any longer.

This is how we ended up making a journey to this place in the middle of winter, and thanks to the days of cold deprivation and physical exercise, Ka'aallanii's mood has taken a turn for the better. I can see the familiar light shining in her eyes when she looks at me, and I can feel the fire flowing through her veins when she stands close to me. I put my arms around her, pressing the cold tip of my nose against hers.

"I am freezing," she starts to complain, giggling a little bit.

"I can help you with that." I softly kiss her with lips

that feel cold and warm at the same time. Under my touch, she melts into my embrace, moving closer to me. For a moment, I forget why we are here, and all I want is to spend hours and hours being close to her. Ka'aallanii has the power to stop time for me, making the sun shine on my face with her love.

When she ends the kiss and steps away, the sun breaks through the clouds. Light reflects off the snow that covers the earth. Her breath is a white puff of smoke in the air. For just a split second, I have the strange feeling I have been here with her before, or I will return to this place with her someday. I blink my eyes.

"I will need some time," she says quietly.

"Of course." I nod, pressing a quick kiss to her cheek. She now has to sit under the sandstone arch and take in the surroundings in order to feel, see and hear what the gods of our land are expecting of her.

I walk away. The snow crunches under my winter boots as I climb the path to a rock overlooking the valley. I hope the magnificent view will help me to stop worrying about my wife.

Until now, my plan to avert the curse has worked out well. For a few months now, Ka'aallanii has been carrying the medicine bundle Aditsan and I made, because she does not want to be sick again. I told her that her disease had something to do with the spirits of people who died by her hand, and that it was imperative that she never take it off. A small part of me feels guilty for lying to her, but a bigger part of me accepts the white lie as a necessity.

While I stare at the sun breaking away the clouds in the sky, I hear Ka'aallanii beneath me singing softly. Her voice is beautiful. She sings a lullaby, and I cannot help but choke up. This is the cradlesong she would have sung for our child, and now she is singing the baby to eternal sleep, so it can play and crawl, gurgle and speak its first words in the hereafter.

Some time goes by, and I am starting to get too cold. Just as I decide to make my way down again and get moving, I suddenly hear an ear-splitting shriek. It is *her* voice.

My heart stops. I break into a run, almost stumbling on my way to her, hurrying toward the sandstone bridge until I end up in front of Ka'aallanii. She is huddled against the rocks, her eyes clamped shut, her open palms in the air, warding off an invisible enemy. Her screams are filled with a fear that flies at my throat as well. Out of nowhere, bloody gashes appear on her face as she kicks and flails at something I cannot perceive.

"*Shan diin!*" I yell, terrified, falling down next to her. In normal circumstances, I would never break off someone's trance like this, but the circumstances clearly call for desperate measures. I put my hands on her shoulders and shake her, pull her up to her feet, slap her in the face a few times.

Finally, her eyes open and the cry of fear dies on her lips when she looks at me. She starts to tremble, teeth chattering, blood dripping from her forehead and face, caused by the mysterious wounds that were inflicted on her.

"Shash," she whispers in a feeble voice. Her sobs are heart-rending as she presses her shivering body against mine. "I – It is – why am I bleeding?" she stammers incoherently.

I try to calm her down and stroke her hair, keeping her in a tender embrace. When I carefully unbutton the winter coat she is wearing, I see the same gashes on the skin of her throat and breasts. My heart turns to ice.

These are coyote claw marks.

I look up, and at that instance, I can hear a terrifying

howl in the distance, followed by something that sounds like a cackling laugh.

With a silent sigh, I close my eyes. I try to determine where the danger is coming from, but I already know the attack is over. The nightmare in my wife's mind has ended, and the influence of those ghostly images in the present time is gone – for now. Ka'aallanii is awake and still alive, but only just. A few more seconds could have proven fatal.

I should have known better than to allow her to enter into a trance at a place like this, so close to the spirits of the past. I should not have left her by herself. I should have told her *months* ago what is going on. Stupid, selfish idiot that I am. Stupid, selfish and in love.

I take a few pieces of dried yucca fruit from the pocket of my cloak and feed her some of it. With trembling hands, she takes the food from me and chews on it listlessly. She will not look at me.

"What have you seen?" I finally ask after a prolonged silence.

Ka'aallanii shivers in my arms. "I cannot explain it."

"Please try." I have a dim hope that I may be wrong – the *yenaldlooshi* may not have found her after all.

But when she starts to tell me what she saw, that hope is shattered. The three ominous shadows, their silhouettes transforming into coyotes, invading the minds of their enemies – I know them only too well. Her voice breaks when she relates to me how their eyes lit up red in the darkness of her dream, how their claws dug into her skin, how afraid and hurt she felt. "I have called upon the wrong spirits," she concludes at last, looking confused. "I must have done something wrong to disturb the balance of this sacred place."

I shake my head. "No. It is my fault. I have done something wrong."

My voice hitches when I tell her about the *chindi*, drying to a whisper when I explain to her why I am cursed. The murder. The many, many long years I have spent as protector of the Diné people, and the deep love I feel for her.

"I love you, *she'esdzáán*." I look at her, afraid to hear her reaction.

Tears shimmer in her eyes. "I love you too. So very much." She gingerly puts her arms around me. "Why did you not tell me about this before?"

"I did not want to scare you unnecessarily. The medicine pouch should have protected you."

"But it did not." She sighs deeply, leaning against my shoulder. I caress her wounded brow. "What can we do?" she asks quietly.

"I do not know. I had no idea those three witches could still find me, until you fell sick. That is when Aditsan and I saw that you were cursed. We made you the medicine bundle for protection, but it will not keep them away forever."

Silence sets in around us. In the distance, dark clouds drift in, and I quickly suggest we pitch our tent before new snow starts to fall. Ka'aallanii and I work in silence, and when we are finally sitting inside, the sun has almost set.

I light a small fire in the middle of the tent so I can treat my wife's injuries with hot water, herbs and bandages. She has not said much since my revelation, and slowly but surely, an all-pervading coldness seeps into my heart. She is scared, and so am I.

"*Shan díín?*" I speak up at last, when she is huddled under blankets in one corner of the tent with a bandage around her head. I sit down next to her and take her hand. "I am sorry. I should never have allowed you to get involved in my problems."

Ka'aallanii smiles feebly. "I know you are sorry," she whispers.

"Do you want to leave me?" I ask, hardly audible.

"Never." She caresses my cheek, wiping away the tears that stream down my face. I feel her arms around me, her body against mine, and allow myself to hope for a miracle.

Months go by. Spring comes to the valley, giving us new lambs in the flock. Ka'aallanii and I are trying to get pregnant again, but so far, it has not happened. To me it is obvious she is not mentally ready for it yet. Sometimes, she wakes up at night, screaming and crying, looking for my calming embrace. I am sure she dreams about the *yenaldlooshi*'s terrifying shadows, but she never divulges what it is that is haunting her. On sunny days, we sit side by side on the rock plateau where we kissed each other for the first time, and it almost feels like she is herself again, as if the shadow of my curse was never cast over her existence. In those moments, I feel perfectly happy, and I hope she feels happy too. However, the night terrors keep tormenting her no matter how sunny our days together are.

One morning I decide to go into the woods to find some willow branches in order to make a dreamcatcher for Ka'aallanii. Maybe that will stop the terrible images from invading her dreams. On my way out of the village, I run into Tsosi, and we decide to venture out together. My brother is hoping to shoot a few rabbits for the stew his wife is preparing tonight.

Laughing and chatting, we climb the steep path toward the plateau above the canyon. We roam around for hours, because we have not hunted together for a very long time, and it makes us feel like youths again. When noon comes, we pause and rest to eat the provisions of dried meat we have brought along.

"What is that?" Tsosi suddenly says, squinting his eyes against the sunlight and pointing at the horizon, where a trail of smoke rises up in the blue sky.

It makes me feel anxious. There are no Diné tribes in the area we are exploring, but to my knowledge, there should not be any Mexicans either. Who has lit a fire causing so much smoke? "I have no idea. Let us go and have a look."

When we sneak closer, I see a regiment of soldiers in unfamiliar uniforms. We crawl up a nearby hill and stay hidden under the shrubs at the top.

"What kind of people are they?" Tsosi hisses next to me. "Surely they are not Mexicans?"

Heart in my throat, I observe the men I once saw in a vision centuries ago. Paler than the Mexicans, but just as belligerent and bearded.

"Let us get out of here," my brother says. "I do not like the look on their faces. It is best they do not see us."

All the way back to the village I keep quiet, and when I hand Ka'aallanii the dreamcatcher I made for her that night, I am apparently still rather quiet, judging by the worried look she is giving me.

"Is something the matter, darling?" She kisses my cheek.

"We saw some strange men up north. They were not Mexicans, but they were other white people. They were a few hours away from Tseyi, exploring the area."

"Do you reckon they are enemies of the Mexicans?"

I shrug. "Who knows. Let us hope so."

As the year progresses, Ka'aallanii turns out to be right. The new palefaces and the Mexicans keep fighting each other. Messages from the north come in from villages where some of our clansmen live. Sometimes, I almost feel happy about someone finally giving the Mexicans a taste of their own medicine, but more often, I feel tense. The 'new white men' may not be any friendlier to us than the Mexicans, if push comes to shove.

A different kind of tension builds in me when I notice Ka'aallanii is a little bit more detached than I am used to. I have not caught her dreaming bad things anymore, but it is evident she feels ill at ease. Maybe she is sad she has not managed to get pregnant again, or maybe she wants to be more actively involved in fighting the *yenaldlooshi* who want to hurt her. That would be just like her, after all.

"Ka'aallanii," I start out one evening, "how about helping me and Aditsan do a ritual to track down the *yenaldlooshi*?"

"Have you found a solution, then?" Ka'aallanii asks in surprise. "I thought you could not beat them."

"Aditsan thinks the union of our two souls could possibly bind my supernatural energy to your energy. That way, you would be protected better."

Ka'aallanii snuggles up to me and keeps quiet for a long time.

"I do not know if I want to do that," she mumbles at last.

"No?" I prompt her, when she is again silent.

She shakes her head. "I am not sure. It scares me. We as Diné people are not supposed to talk about death or ghosts, and now you are suggesting this ritual in which I will experience your powers, the power of death and resurrection, adopting your lifeline and energy somehow – I might even get caught up in it." She looks at me with panic in her eyes. "I do not think I can handle that. You should know I have not felt like myself lately. Ever since I fell sick and we made that journey to Rainbow Bridge,

I feel a dark shadow of constant threat. I feel it everywhere."

"Why have you not told me?" I softly touch her face. "You should not have carried that burden all by yourself."

"What would be the point? I knew you would not be able to stop it anyway." Ka'aallanii starts to cry. She climbs into my embrace as I try to comfort her.

"Can't I just stay with you *without* doing the ritual?" she wants to know, once she has calmed down again.

"Of course you can, my love," I reply, "of course."

I have no idea if it is the truth.

1843

In the middle of that summer, Ka'aallanii visits me one evening wearing a happy face. I am sitting by the fire I have lit outside the village in order to meditate and call up a vision of the new white men, who keep resurfacing in that same area where Tsosi and I encountered them the first time.

"*Ya'at'eeh, Hózhójí Naat'á*," she greets me, using my honorary title of peace leader. She sits down next to me, staring into the dancing flames. "What is the fire telling you?"

"I have not seen much." I sigh. "Very soon, Tsosi and I will have to set out to investigate the white people from the north. I cannot feel their intentions, and Aditsan was not successful in finding out more in his visions last week either." The war that Aditsan did see in his vision is something I refrain from mentioning to Ka'aallanii. She is looking so genuinely happy that I do not want to ruin her good mood.

I turn my face toward her, kissing her softly on the mouth. She scoots closer and smiles broadly when I put an arm around her shoulders.

"Why the broad smile?" I ask her cheerfully.

Ka'aallanii bites her lip. "I am five days late." She nods toward the half-full moon in the sky above our heads.

"Oh?" I say, puzzled, but then I suddenly get what she means. "Oh!" I repeat, my eyes growing wide and eager.

"I am not sure yet, so do not get too excited." She is trying to curb my enthusiasm, but her smile is so infectious that I cannot help smiling broadly too. The possibility that we might be expecting another child pushes all the other things that trouble me into the background. I hold her close and kiss her everywhere, again and again, until the fire in front of us seems to seep into my blood, running through my veins and urging her to pull me away from my meditation spot to take me to bed.

The next morning, I get up early. I push the blanket in front of the doorway aside and stare at the light of the rising sun. Music gently fills my head. That beauty I once walked in still has not disappeared.

Behind me, I can hear Ka'aallanii climb out of bed. She walks toward me, enveloping my naked body with the blanket we have slept under. I turn around, smiling at her and wishing her a good morning.

"Shall we go to the rock plateau?" she suggests, when the sun has risen and we have had our breakfast. "I want to thank Changing Woman."

I put a hand on her underbelly and nod. We do not want to be premature in our happiness, but neither do we want to deny the goddess our thanks for the wonder that happens in every woman's womb, a wonder that may be happening again for us as well.

A warm wind is blowing from the west when we

leave our house. Ka'aallanii lets go of my hand when she walks up the path leading to the viewpoint before she starts to run. She loves the feeling of her heart beating wildly in her chest, exhausting herself by climbing the steep path like this. She always presses her body against my chest in order to let me feel her heartbeat once we are both on the plateau.

"Only you and this cliff can make my heart beat like this," she usually tells me with a playful grin.

I leisurely follow her and watch her while she runs up the hill, her hair dancing in the breeze. I look down at my own feet, when a dried juniper berry on the path catches my eye. What is it doing here?

I squint my eyes and suddenly I can make out a trail of white ash on the dry soil of the path. My stomach turns to stone. I break into a run myself, my eyes volleying between Ka'aallanii in front of me and the path beneath my feet, where I also spot corn pollen now. I want to call out to Ka'aallanii, want her to stop running, but my throat is locked.

The medicine pouch is torn, and all the precious content has leaked out. My wife is stepping onto a rock plateau near a high and dangerous drop to the valley below, and she has no protection whatsoever against the curse targeting her.

"*She'esdzáán*!" I scream, finding my voice again. "Stay there, *shan díín*!"

I stumble onto the plateau, searching Ka'aallanii's eyes. Her back is to the precipice, and she is staring straight ahead, but she does not seem to be aware of my presence. Her eyes are trained on something invisible, her hands trembling with utter terror. I do not know what she will do if I touch her, so I approach her slowly and carefully.

Oh God, no. Not now. Not this.

In horror, I watch her shuffle backward, step by step, edging closer to the abyss. Tears are running down her cheeks as she extends her hands like she is trying to keep away from something in front of her. And then, she shrieks, rubbing her arms, collapsing to her knees while hiding her face in her hands.

My heart falters when she crouches down on her haunches and ends up so close to the precipice it will only take one wrong move for her to plummet to her death.

"Ka'aallanii." I take one step closer to her. "It is me. Do not be afraid."

When I clasp my hand around her upper arm, she starts to scream again, one foot slipping off the edge in her total panic. She loses her balance, but I do not lose the grip on her arm. With sweat gushing down my face, I pull her forcibly toward me and against me. I freeze when her hands slide up and slip around her own throat in a strangling grasp. She stops breathing and turns purple.

"Please don't!" I scream, cry, beg. "Wake up!" I grab her wrists and shake her fragile frame. "Leave her alone!" I howl at the silent sky above me. "Leave her be, you evil witches! You wretched bastards! Don't you dare touch my wife!"

I feel a shiver going through Ka'aallanii's body. And then, she finally comes to her senses. She looks up at me and melts into my arms. Her lips are moving, but I cannot hear her words.

"Come with me." I lift her up in my arms, softly whispering in her ear as I take her back to the village as fast as my legs can carry me. Unannounced, I storm into Aditsan's hoghan. My old friend looks at me in shock when he sees Ka'aallanii's limp body and pale face.

"We need a new medicine bundle," I pant. "I'll tell

you the rest later."

A few days go by in which Ka'aallanii stays with Aditsan to gather strength. I come by every day, but she does not want to discuss what she has seen on the rock plateau. The look in her eyes frightens me. She does see me, but her mind is elsewhere. I have meetings with Yas and Tsosi during which we discuss starting up friendly relations with the newcomers from the north, but my mind is elsewhere, too.

When I enter Aditsan's hoghan on the fourth day after the incident, Ka'aallanii is not there.

"She wants to talk to you alone," the *hataalii* says. "She got up in the early hours, and she told me what I am telling you now. She said you would know where to find her."

With my heart beating restlessly in my throat, I make my way to our usual meeting point. The path uphill suddenly seems too steep for me, and the clouds gathering on the horizon darken my heart. I am so nervous that my mouth is completely dry when I get to the top of the hill. Sweat is pooling in the palms of my hands, but I bravely straighten my back when I approach Ka'aallanii. She is standing at the tree near the precipice, looking at me with eyes full of sadness and love.

When I come closer, I see tears in her eyes. I silently come to a stop next to her, putting a hand on her shoulder. "*Shan díín*," I quietly acknowledge her.

She looks up at me, her lower lip trembling. "How long will this go on?" she asks me in a muffled voice.

"I do not know," I honestly admit.

After that, Ka'aallanii is quiet for a long time. I stare at the hand I put on her shoulder, trying to imprint that image into my memory, combined with the feeling I always get when I touch her.

I cannot fool myself any longer. In the past four days, I have tried to convince myself that all would be well, but I know better.

I know what she is going to tell me.

"I cannot bear this," she finally whispers in a broken voice. "I love you, but I cannot live with the shadow from your past anymore." She is afraid to look at me.

Everything around me stops. The sun darkens. The wind dies down.

"I understand," I mumble from my dark place.

"I am so sorry." She almost stumbles as she walks away, looking over her shoulder one last time and seeing my tears that run freely. And then, I see nothing, and she swims out of view. I am alone.

I do not know how long I sit there after she has left. Time moves slowly, as though slipping away from me. Birds circle above my head, their calls sounding like they are mocking me, making fun of the silly idea I had – that I could live a happy, undisturbed life with Ka'aallanii.

I scramble to my feet when the sun dips below the horizon. Her eyes haunt my thoughts, look at me from every direction and allow me no peace of mind.

"Do you love me?" I whisper against the wind blowing in my face. I stand on the flat rocks, listening to the echo of my own voice in my head. I see an echo of her face in my mind, too, but she no longer has a voice and gives me no answer. I can feel the years stretching out ahead of me, all those years in which I will have to force myself to forget the way she looked at me, the way her hands caressed me, the way her eyes shone when I told her I loved her.

I will only remember how I lost my heart.

That evening, I meet Tsosi in his hoghan. "I am

leaving," I just say. My brother has heard the news about me and Ka'aallanii splitting up. I cannot stand staying here and seeing her every day. My hasty departure will at least serve one goal – I promised Yas I will make contact with the new white men.

"I am coming with you," Tsosi replies, to my utter surprise.

"What about your family?"

"My family needs protection. I can take the easy way out and stay put, but sooner or later, it will catch up with me." He inches closer and continues in a whisper: "This very afternoon, some people from a nearby village came to talk to Yas, telling him the white people from the north keep encroaching on our territory. We have no idea what they will do when they discover us, so maybe it is best if we beat them to it."

I happen to have discussed the very same thing with Yas a few weeks ago. I pat Tsosi on the shoulder with a hint of a smile on my face, grateful he is joining me in this quest. At least I will not have to deal with my sorrow all by myself.

During the following day, we prepare for the journey ahead. By the end of the morning, we have saddled two horses and gathered enough provisions in our saddlebags to last for a while. Our family has come to wave goodbye.

My heart speeds up to a dangerously fast pace when Naalnish and Ka'aallanii make their appearance on the village square too, just as we are about to depart. I turn around in the saddle and cannot help staring at her with pain in my heart. My sunbeam. She is so incredibly precious to me. I am still wearing her pendant underneath my shirt, and I am almost afraid she will want it back now.

She approaches my horse, coming to a hesitant stop

right next to me. Her hand comes to rest on the neck of my horse, inches away from my hand holding the reins.

"*Ya'at'eeh,* Shash," she speaks softly, her voice cracking. "I have come to wish you good luck."

I can feel my veneer of determination beginning to peel. How can I possibly do this? Leave her?

"Thank – thank you," I falter.

Her eyes search mine.

"Come back safely," she mumbles.

"I promise," I whisper.

And then we are on our way, Tsosi and I. For the rest of that day, I can still feel Ka'aallanii's hand almost touching mine.

1846

During the years together with my brother, we stray far away from Tseyi. In our travels, we encounter the Americans – the new white men – and I initially made contact with them by speaking Spanish. By now, I speak a fair amount of English too.

They know me as Barboncito, and my brother as Delgado. I translated our Diné nicknames into Spanish when we first introduced ourselves to the American authorities, and those names stayed with us. They are also mentioned on the treaty that we ended up signing in black ink, writing our names with a white feather as a symbol of peace between Diné and Americans.

I know this is only the first step toward lasting peace, but it has been a satisfactory move. Tsosi and I have set an example, and now it will not be long before other Diné headmen will follow suit and sign their own treaties.

"Will you continue north?" Tsosi wants to know,

while we are roasting some wild roots above a campfire next to our tents that night.

"What you actually want to know is whether I will come home with you at last."

Tsosi sighs, nodding after a moment. "You cannot postpone it forever."

In the three years of our absence, Tsosi has returned to the village a number of times to visit his family. I have never accompanied him on those trips home, because I still did not feel strong enough to meet Ka'aallanii again. I know that she married someone else in the meantime, and I know she has two children. I never dared dwell on the question whether her oldest boy is my son. But finally, the time has come to see my home again. I can feel it.

The next day, we leave for Tseyi. The path leading down to our village has not changed much, and my heart speeds up when the canyon comes into view. Everything is just as beautiful as I remembered, although the atmosphere has changed in this region since we left. Fear pervades the air – fear of Mexicans, fear of the surrounding tribes, who are desperately trying to enslave members of our tribe so as to build a stronger defense line. We do the same thing to them, sometimes. There has been too much war, and with all my heart I hope that the peace treaties with the Americans will contribute to more peaceful years ahead.

The reunion with my parents is emotional. They have missed me terribly. Aditsan and Yas cannot contain their emotions either when they see me again, but above all, they cannot contain their happiness when I tell them our peace mission has been a success.

"You have not wasted your years away from the clans," Yas nods, looking satisfied, as he hauls me and

Tsosi over to his hoghan for a celebratory dinner his wife and daughters are preparing in honor of our homecoming.

And then, I see her standing there, next to Aditsan's hoghan. She looks at me uncertainly, biting her lower lip forlornly. A boy of about two years old is holding her hand, and she carries her baby daughter of a few months old on her other arm.

She is so beautiful. She still has the same radiant eyes, even if they express a certain tiredness I have seen in so many people in the village.

I take a step toward her when I suddenly notice a young man next to her, putting his hand on her shoulder. I gulp down the lump in my throat, then take the final few steps separating me from her.

"*Ya'at'eeh, shilah,*" I greet her as a normal friend, when I stand in front of her.

"*Ya'at'eeh, bislahalani,*" she replies, using the new name the people have given me in my absence – the speaker or orator. "Congratulations with all you have achieved in the years past."

I nod, sighing almost inaudibly. Would I have achieved as much if I had stayed with Ka'aallanii, building a family? Certainly not, but it still stings me to realize at which cost I have established peace. I could have been the one standing next to Ka'aallanii now without the curse that haunts me. I could have been that young man, taking the baby from her arm and greeting me with a friendly smile.

"I will talk to you later," I say to her when I see Yas is beckoning me. Hastily, I turn around and blink away the tears welling up in my eyes. I have no right to be sad. Ka'aallanii is happy. She has a wonderful family, a normal husband and a normal life, and my people have signed a peace treaty with the white people, thanks to me.

Weeks turn into months. In these months, I venture out with Tsosi sometimes to sign more treaties with more parties present in this area. My safe haven is the village in Tseyi, though. This is where I belong.

I had expected the pain of losing Ka'aallanii to wear off, but it does not. I see how her new lover supports her and loves her as a good husband.

My heart will never feel the same, even though I do not blame her for anything. Every now and then she visits me, and we talk like we used to before we parted ways. Occasionally, she puts her head on my shoulder for a few seconds when she is tired and just stares into the fire. I do not risk putting an arm around her shoulders in those moments. I cannot let her come too close. The *yenaldlooshi* never fail to instill fear in me whenever I think of those last few married days with her.

I visit the rock plateau alone. I do not know if Ka'aallanii still goes there too, but I suspect the place holds too many painful memories for her. All the happiness we have shared there passes before my mind's eye when I spend my free hours there. The peace I always felt throughout my body while I was there with her, never returns.

When spring comes, I take off one last time to talk about peace with the Americans. They promise they will build forts on our lands in order to contain the threat of enemy tribes and Mexicans, and we promise to stop plundering their villages, but somehow I am not convinced this is playing out the way we want it to.

Hard times lie ahead.

1850

And then, disaster strikes. After months of insurgent unrest, the Mexicans attack in great numbers.

"Run for your life!" my mother screams, pulling my father along to the escape route leading out of the village toward the caves hidden high up in the rock-face. He has a bad leg, but clenches his teeth and tries to run with us as fast as he can. Behind us, a fire erupts when Mexicans throw their torches on Yas's hoghan.

My hands whip out an arrow and take the bow hanging from my back, but I am too late to shoot the passing Mexican from his horse. As my heart beats a frantic rhythm, I see how my parents manage to slip away unnoticed. Then I run back to the central square of the village, checking up on Tsosi and his family. Deep down, I know I also want to make sure Ka'aallanii is safe, but I doggedly push the thought away.

When I get to the square, I panic when I see she is hiding under the bushes next to her hoghan, looking up at me with mortal fear in her eyes. Behind Ka'aallanii, a handful of soldiers are making their way to her hiding place, and I purposefully look away from her so I will not alert them to the woman hiding right in front of them.

Instead, I take my bow and draw the string to release a deadly arrow. One of the soldiers tumbles down in agony as my arrow pierces his chest. The other two charge into me with a roar, loading the guns they are carrying. I zigzag away from them, disappearing into a hoghan, my hand finding a spear next to the entrance. I grip the weapon, ready to defend myself if need be.

And then, I hear a sound that makes my heart stop.

It is Ka'aallanii, screaming and begging for mercy.

When I step out of the hoghan, I see her lying on the ground, soaking in a red puddle growing alarmingly in size with every beat of my heart. Strangely enough, I did not even hear the shot one of the Mexicans apparently fired at her. I hear nothing. I see black.

I am not aware of my actions in the next few moments, but when I come to my senses again, I am standing next to the Mexican's dead body, a bloody spear in my trembling hand.

My breath is ragged as I kneel down next to her and take her hand. Ka'aallanii is pale and unmoving, as if frozen in time. Her hand is limp in mine. She looks up at me, smiling weakly at me when she recognizes my face.

"Shash," she whispers.

"*Shan díín,*" I softly sob.

"Take care of Bidziil and Doli," she manages to choke out. Her children.

I want to ask her if her husband is dead. I want to ask her if Bidziil is my son. I want to ask her if she still loves me. God, I want to ask her so many things, but it is too late. The sunlight seeps out of her eyes, taking her beautiful soul with her.

"I will," I promise in a quivering voice.

And then, she looks up at a point past my head, the corners of her mouth turning up into a final smile. "That light – so bright," she sighs.

The woman I loved more than life itself dies with her hand in mine that afternoon.

1868

When I close my eyes at night, I see destruction. Houses burned down. Trees chopped down. Horses and sheep shot dead. Scorched earth. Death and despair.

That is what happened in our peaceful valley a few years ago. Large numbers of clans and families were relentlessly hunted down and robbed of everything they needed to stay alive. The only way to survive was to comply with the orders given by the Americans and move to their reservation in the east. Leave our lands behind for good. A part of me did not want to surrender, but I reasoned I would save more people if I did. And so we went.

We have been here for three years. Those years have not been kind to us.

This land has not brought us peace. It is hostile toward us. When we left Dinétah, we left our gods as well. The spirits of the land we were always connected to could not help us here to secure a living. Here, far away from home, spirits of unknown origin wander the earth. Here, I can no longer be a *hataalii* communicating with the forces of nature, for I do not speak the language of this land. Death and disease have followed us like a curse. No matter how hard we work, our labor is to no avail. All harvests have failed.

I sigh and turn around. Now that I desolately stare out over the sad results of our longstanding efforts, I do not know what to say. For it is certain I will have to say *something*. General Sherman is coming to the reservation, and he insisted on talking to the most authoritative headman among the Diné. Everybody agrees that this should be me, but I am afraid of saying or doing the wrong things. The fate of our entire people hangs in the balance, and what I will tell General Sherman will tip that balance one way or the other. The general has heard news that we are having a hard time on the reservation, and he is willing to listen to our side of the story in order to decide whether he will allow us to return home or not.

But how can I tell him our side of the story without reverting to accusations? The Americans have caused us so much pain.

My heart beats in my throat when my brother approaches to call me inside.

"He has just entered the main building." The grooves and wrinkles in Tsosi's face betray the hardship of the past few years. More and more he is starting to resemble our father, who passed away a long time ago already.

"What did he look like?" My mouth turns dry as my slow steps take me to the building where Sherman is waiting for me.

"Like a general." Tsosi shrugs. "They all look the same."

When I enter the main hall, I give the general a scrutinizing look. To my surprise, I see a certain benevolence in the man's eyes. A spark of hope kindles in my heart.

Behind me, throngs of Diné people push through the door opening into the room where he and I will talk.

"Esteemed Mister Barboncito," the general starts, "we have invited you and your brother today to tell us about the situation on the reservation. Reports of an alarming nature have reached me about the health and well-being of your people. Please tell me – why have the Navajos not managed to turn into good farmers and feed themselves with the fruits of their labor in this area designated to them?"

Next to him, an interpreter starts to translate his English question into Spanish, whereupon a second interpreter translates it into Diné Bizaad. For me this is not necessary – I understand both languages well enough – but for the other Diné present it is important that everything is explained and translated to them. I nod appreciatively to both interpreters.

When the elaborate process of translation is over, the room falls silent. The General and the other Americans in attendance look at me expectantly.

To my left, I hear Tsosi cough softly, and to my right, I see the other headmen who have supported me over the past years. They expect me to work a miracle, and the whole situation suddenly lunges at my throat. How can I, the orator, speak about these things after all that has been taken away from me in this life? And all the lives before this one?

When I close my eyes, I recall the endless line of people on their way to Fort Sumner. The Long Walk. A road through hell. I can hear the shots fired at old people and pregnant women, because they did not walk fast enough and were falling behind. I can see the body of Yas, the headman who put his trust in me and was rewarded with a bullet to the head because he fell sick with influenza during the harsh journey east.

I remember us sleeping in ditches dug into the ground at night, tarps covering us so we would not escape in the darkness. I recall attacking groups of Comanches or Mexicans who stole away our children, whom we never saw again. The desperate look in the eyes of Bidzil, my adoptive son, when he was snatched away by a passing group of Mexican slave traders. The morning I discovered that Doli, my daughter, had disappeared without leaving a trace. The deplorable living conditions in the reservation and the despondent look on the faces of my family and friends when it turned out our first harvest had failed. And the one after that. And the one after those two. The humiliating daily trip to the fort to beg the white men for food with our food stamps.

What the hell am I supposed to tell this man? General Sherman has no idea how utterly unfair our lives have been. If I really told him my view on things, I would not help my people at all. I would erupt in anger, pummel the infertile soil beneath me with my fists in powerless rage, cry out how much I have lost. How much we *all* have lost.

Maybe there will come a time when I can express my emotions, but this is not that time. All the Diné standing in this room are counting on me and my oratory skills. Ka'aallanii, who has given me peace, is counting on me, and I will not let her down.

When I start to speak, I speak in our own language. I know General Sherman will get a mangled, translated version of what I tell him, but I want to speak in my own language so my own people will perfectly understand the things I have to say.

"General Sherman, I hope you understand that your leaders have brought us here with force. Bringing us here has caused many of us to die." My voice catches, and I try to take the quiver out of it when I continue. "Our grandfathers have always taught us to live on the land that was intended for us, our sacred land. I do not think it is right for us to do what we were taught not to do."

I look at the general, wondering if he can ever understand how strong the bond is that we have with the land. He does not know our stories, but he might be willing to listen to them. "When the Diné were first made, First Woman – one of our goddesses – pointed out four mountains and four rivers bordering the area that was to be our land. Our grandfathers told us to never move outside those boundaries. Now we have moved, and I think that this is the reason so many of us have died here. This land was never meant for us. It does not nurture us, and it never will. This soil does not sustain our crops. Every time we plant, nothing grows. Our harvests fail. We worked as hard as we could, but for nothing."

Tears come to my eyes. I think of the poverty that

has affected us. The cries of hungry children in the night. When I rub my tears away and fall silent, I suddenly feel Tsosi's hand on my shoulder, and I know I have his support. My brother is backing me up.

"When we lived in our own way, we had plenty of stock," I continue my story after the interpreters have done their work. "We were a proud and happy people. How can we keep our pride when we have to go to the fort store for our food, and be dependent on someone to hand it out to us? I am ashamed to live like this."

The general gives me a disconcerted glance and actually looks shocked when he hears his interpreter's translation. I stare at the soil underneath my feet, a wild hope stirring within me. Is it possible he is really going to help us?

"You are doing a wonderful job," I hear Tsosi mumble at that exact moment. "They have not nicknamed you the orator for nothing, *bislahalani*. I am proud of you, no matter what that general's decision will be."

There is now much ado among the white leaders, and then the general asks me a question in such an unexpectedly mild tone of voice that it slightly confuses me.

"What can we do to help your people?" he asks earnestly.

I blink my eyes. Before the two interpreters have even had a chance to translate his question, I burst out without disguising my bottled-up emotions. "General Sherman, this land does not like us. We cannot be happy here. We have lost so incredibly much. I – I cannot take it anymore."

I can feel the tension thick in the air, and unwittingly my hand closes around Ka'aallanii's pendant beneath my shirt. I have not taken it off in all these years. "I simply want to see the place where I was born before I get sick or older and I die." The place where my wife has died. My voice cracks. "That is all. I realize I am standing before you and pleading like a helpless woman, but that is only because with all my heart I want to be taken back to my land. We will live off it – we do not need your support. And I hope you will do everything, *everything* in your power to help us, for I have spoken nothing but the truth about our situation here. My hope goes in at my feet and out of my mouth. And I hope to your God and my God that you will not ask us to go anywhere except our own country, Dinétah. We do not want to go right or left, but straight back to our own land, where we belong."

On the first day of the American month of June, a treaty is signed by General Sherman, President Johnson and all the headmen of my people, to acknowledge the fact that the Diné are an independent people.

We are free. Our time in Fort Sumner is over for good. I am allowed to return to the place that connects me with Ka'aallanii at last.

1870

No longer is my life ahead of me – it lies behind me. I am not yet old, but my soul feels empty. I have fought the good fight.

Before I accede to my journey to the hereafter, I want to do one last thing.

I walk the familiar road, taking the path to the rock plateau. Climbing up there makes me gasp for breath. When I finally get to the top, I dizzily lean into the tree that has always stood here looking out over the canyon.

"Wait for me," I whisper, when I bury Ka'aallanii's pendant deep under the roots of the tree, protecting the jewel by uttering a simple prayer.

In a way, I hope this will be my last life. I do not know if I want to come back here, carrying all the memories I have now, but if I do come back, at least I will have a token of my wife's love for me in that life. I will find this place again and wear her pendant like I used to. No one will be able to take that away from me.

When I look up, the sun breaks through the clouds. "Hello, my ray of light," I say with a smile. "Have you returned to me?" A lonely tear rolls down my face.

The light caresses my skin, penetrating the layers of my hardened heart. The sunbeams dance across the landscape populated by Diné once more.

Have I brought lasting peace?
Maybe it has been enough.

1910 – 1943

1925

"You just *want* to make me angry, don't you?" my father yells at my mother in an unsteady voice as I walk into the hoghan. He is sitting at the table with a half empty bottle of whisky in front of him and my mother is standing next to him with a pale and expressionless face.

"I have already told you that we have no more money this month," she answers, trying to control her voice. "You will have to wait. That smuggler of yours really is not going to sell you more liquor on the slate."

"Thanks to you we already are deeply in debt," I say in a sharp voice.

My father turns toward me. "Who do you think you are?" He gets up from the table. His face comes close to mine and I can smell alcohol on his breath. "Don't you talk to me like that."

"Leave Samuel alone!" My mother takes a step forward.

All of a sudden my father raises his hand and smacks her in the face. "You shut up. Stay out of this." He rushes out of the hoghan and I can hear him ranting outside.

Wide-eyed, my mother stares at the door, a hand pressed against her cheek.

"*Shima.*" I put an arm around her. She begins to cry without making a sound.

"Why don't you leave him?" I say to her at last.

She looks at me, a weak smile on her lips. "Because he is my husband, Sam."

"Surely you have more self-esteem than this."

"I have," she says, "but he hasn't."

Of course I understand that my father is a victim, just as my mother is. Even before I woke up when I was fourteen and realized who I really was, I had come to understand that my father's work for the railway company had brought him into contact with alcohol, an easy way to forget that things were not going well for his family. In the beginning it seemed like a good idea, spending the evening together with friends from the neighboring villages and drinking a glass of whisky. Before long, however, the drink changed him. It made him unreasonable, almost like a white man. He belched, he yelled and he bossed us around. I was afraid of him when he drank and that happened more and more often. When Prohibition came, nothing changed – he started to buy alcohol illegally and his addiction became even more expensive.

Things went from bad to worse when, five years ago, Nantai, my elder brother, was picked up by the *silao*, the reservation police, and taken to Chinle, where he was forced to go to a white school.

"It is a boarding school and your son will be properly cared for," the policeman had assured my parents. "He will learn to speak English there and come back a real American."

My mother had hidden me in the sweat lodge, under a pile of blankets, and had prayed to Mary that the *silao* men would not find me and take me away as well. After my brother's kidnappers had left, my mother took me from my hiding place with tears in her eyes, and gave me a new Biblical name that day – Samuel, meaning 'God has listened'. We have not seen Nantai since, and my father started to drink even more after the incident.

My mother believes in Jesus, Mary and God, and she goes to church. Fortunately, many people find comfort in the Christian faith, now that our old ways are branded as ridiculous and primitive and there is so much poverty and alcohol addiction. They believe that our own gods have deserted us and that there can only be salvation in an afterlife. And I can see their point.

1928

One cool spring day, Nantai unexpectedly returns.

My mother is folding a few blankets which she recently weaved, when she sees a horse and wagon approaching in the distance. It is driven by a tall young man dressed in *biligaana* clothes.

"Samuel," she cries excitedly. "Come here!"

When I step outside, Nantai is climbing up the path toward our house with hesitant steps. He stares at us, a smile appearing on his face.

"Mother." He puts his arms around her. His hand reaches out for mine. "Little brother," he continues and looks at me with joy.

"What is he saying?" my mother asks in confusion. She cannot stop hugging Nantai.

"He is greeting us in English, *shima*."

My mother starts talking to Nantai in our own tongue and I see a pained expression in his eyes.

"I have come back for good." He stammers and has a strange accent. It is clear that he has not spoken our language for years.

"Where's *shizhé'é*?" he asks when the three of us are sitting outside on the ground eating a simple meal.

"He is working," my mother answers briefly.

"He's gambling," I say, correcting her, "and any winnings will have been spent by tonight."

I can feel how she gives me a wounded look, and I immediately regret my harsh words. "I am sorry," I mutter.

"How have you been all these years?" my mother asks full of interest. "You look nice. You are wearing good clothes." She rubs the material of his jacket.

Nantai remains silent for a long time. "Thank you, Mother. I have mixed feelings about it." He pauses for a while. "On my way home, I met people who accused me of being a traitor because of these clothes. Some people accuse me of being one of the *biligaana* now."

"Around here we call them *bilisáana*," I say softly.

"Apple?" He raises his eyebrows.

"Red on the outside, white on the inside."

Nantai stares at me, a bit hurt. "Is that what you think, too?" he asks anxiously.

I smile at him. "Of course not," I say, but I am not entirely sure that I mean it.

We eat our meal in silence, my mother, Nantai and I. Together we wash the dishes and make coffee. Then my brother starts to talk. In faltering Diné Bizaad he tells us how five years ago he arrived in Chinle with hundreds of other young boys and was taken to a large and uninviting building. The strict men and women who worked at the boarding school cut the hair of all the boys regardless of whether or not they wanted to keep their *tsiyeels*. "It is not civilized for a man to have long hair.

And the girls were treated likewise. No exceptions were made."

That night, all the children in the boarding school were chained to their beds in big dorms. At five o'clock they had to wake up and were given bread and beans for breakfast. They would not have their next meal before the evening arrived.

"There was a deadly silence in the breakfast room as we sat down," my brother tells us. "Nobody dared to speak, because the *biligaana* sometimes became angry unexpectedly, starting to beat children for no good reason." Nantai is staring in front of him. "At some point, I could not take the silence any longer and I started to talk softly with the boy next to me, who, as it turned out, came from near Oraibi. We spoke softly on purpose so that we did not disturb anyone."

"And then?" I ask, because he falls silent.

"Suddenly a fat, gray-haired man appeared behind us. He dragged us from the table, shouting at us in English. We were taken to the washing-room by two sisters. They put soap in our mouths and rinsed them. After that, we were given a beating." Tears come into Nantai's eyes. "Later it turned out that they had heard us talking in our own language. That was not allowed." He looks at my mother, almost imploringly. "*Shima*, for eight years I have not been allowed to speak my own language. I have forgotten things. I do not know anymore who I am."

My mother puts her arm around him. "Do not worry. *We* know who you are."

The weeks pass and very slowly Nantai learns to speak his own language properly again. It is a good thing that, without the others knowing, I understand English, for now I can help him when he does not know how to translate things. I am glad that my big brother is back. He takes care of our mother and tries to calm my father down when he is in one of his drunken fits. He was always better at that than me.

"Let's go to Tseyi," he suggests one morning when the sun has just risen and we are outside enjoying the singing birds. "I have asked the neighbors if we can borrow two horses."

I nod slowly. Of course, Canyon de Chelly is a sacred place for our people, but it is much more than that for me. In my previous life I fought to see that place again – and I also lost there what I had wanted to keep more than anything. We tell my mother that we are going away together for a few days, and when the horses are saddled, we leave in a south-easterly direction.

Before long, the day is pretty hot and I try to lead the horses along a route that will take us past water a number of times. The terrain that we travel is not easy, however, and it is not until the end of the second day that we arrive at Tseyi. The sun is setting behind the walls of the canyon and I hold my breath as I lead my horse into the valley where I lived one century ago. It is so strange to see this place again. There is still a village where my clan used to live.

"Do you mind if we stay the night here?" my brother asks an old man of about seventy, who is sitting beside a fire next to his hoghan.

"Of course not," answers the man with a smile, baring an incomplete set of teeth. "You are welcome to stay."

Although I am tired, I am overcome by a strong urge to walk to the rock plateau. The pendant that the old man is wearing reminds me of the necklace that I buried under the roots of the tree. With all my heart I hope it is still there.

"Shall we take a walk up to the canyon edge?" I ask Nantai after the old man has given the two of us a bowl of soup and some bread. "I saw that there is a path climbing up from the village."

"Okay. I'll put on another shirt first."

On our way to the path we pass a flock of sheep watched over by two young Diné women in long skirts and velvet blouses. They greet us in a friendly fashion and one of them starts to grumble when a few lambs break away from the flock and run toward the brooklet which flows into the valley along the trees.

"Beautiful girls." Nantai gives me a nudge and grins at me. "Do you have a girlfriend, little brother?"

"No." It comes out harsher than I intended. "And I would not know how to pay her family if I wanted to get married, at any rate. We are not particularly rich."

"Oh, well," he says, "love conquers all."

Climbing up the path is easy. In my memory, the path was steeper, but the last time I was here I was over fifty years old and weakened through sickness and years of malnutrition. When I reach the plateau and walk toward the edge to take in the view, I fall completely silent. Nantai, who is standing next to me, somehow understands how I feel. He does not speak and stares out over the valley.

"It is beautiful here," he says softly after some time. "So untouched."

My eyes blink and I try not to think of our village burning to the ground and our livestock being killed.

When my brother sits down on the rock to meditate for a while, his legs tucked up under him, I turn around. My heart beating fast, I walk up to the old tree, which is now much bigger than the last time I was here.

"I have come back," I whisper softly as I lay my hand on its bark. "Have you looked after my pendant well?"

In my pocket there is a small spade that I have brought with me. I take it out and scrape away the hard soil around the tree roots. Slowly but surely I make a hole in the ground that becomes deeper and deeper. The sun is now so low that there is a red glow over the horizon and I hope that I will manage to find what I am looking for before it is too dark to see anything.

Then I strike against a fragment of an old pot and my mouth turns dry. I had hidden the pendant in a handmade pot to bury it, but now I only find these broken pieces. Has someone found my treasure?

I dig hurriedly on, when I suddenly see a fine turquoise stone half buried in the earth. I manage to get my fingers under it, dig away some more soil and then hold Ka'aallanii's pendant in my hands.

Everything around me stops and I feel the weight of the pendant in the palm of my hand, feel the weight of years gone by on my shoulders. I am squatting on my haunches, wiping the soil from the pendant. My fingers are trembling and my eyes suddenly fill with tears. I am now as old as I was when I met Ka'aallanii in my former life. So many things have happened – I am now another person living another life with a different background, but yet I still miss her. I miss her so much.

I sit down on the ground sobbing softly, wiping away my tears. I do not want to cry any more. There is nothing to be done. The shadow of time keeps me in its grip, but time will also heal my wounds. I am intensely grateful that I have been able to at least preserve one thing given to me by the love of my life.

"Is something wrong?" I suddenly hear Nantai's voice next to me. I look up and my brother sits down beside me. "What happened, *shik'is*? Why are you crying?"

Speechless, I stare at my hands and I see how his hand glides over mine, partly removing the pendant from my cramped fingers. "Have you found something?"

"This is my pendant," I answer almost inaudibly.

"Then how did it end up here?"

The wind blows softly over the rocks, rustling the leaves in the trees and blowing through my long hair. Slowly, the sun dips below the horizon.

Suddenly I can hear myself starting to talk.

I tell Nantai about my former life as Barboncito, about my lives before that, about my life's mission and about the curse that has come upon me. I do not pause for a moment and I do not look my brother in the eye. In all these years, I have never confided in anyone apart from the *hataalii* men and women who accompanied me and even then, I did not tell them all the things that had happened to me. My story is like an unstoppable flow of pent-up emotion and I no longer have the power to stop it. I want to have someone with me. I no longer want to carry my burden on my own, to decide everything all by myself. I want to be an ordinary human being again, not a mythical figure whose coming is expected and praised by *hataalii* in all of Dinétah.

When I finally stop talking, my brother puts his arm around my shoulders. He talks to me in English. "My God, Samuel. You are carrying one hell of a burden. I will help you, I swear."

I answer back in English. "I don't know if you can. You don't really need to. Just listen to my ranting every now and then."

"I'll think of something. You have my support," Nantai says in our own language again with a smile.

"And here I was, always wondering where you had picked up all those English words."

I chuckle. It feels good to laugh and to be able to share a part of my burden with someone from my own family.

1933

I wipe the sweat from my forehead after climbing the last hill that separates me from Keams. The day is hot and my drinking bottle is practically empty. I only hope that the trader in Keams has work for me, for I have been on the road for almost a week hoping to take part in the CCC program that is now being set up in the reservation.

Some weeks ago, Nantai returned from the trading post in Kayenta near our house, all excited. "John Wetherill has told me that they are going to build roads in the area south of Black Mesa," he told us full of enthusiasm. "President Roosevelt has extended the New Deal to include our land. He also wants the people here to be trained as carpenters, car mechanics, builders, you name it."

I had only once seen an automobile in my entire life. A year ago, an important *biligaana* had come to Kayenta driving an automobile. In spite of the fact that the Civilian Conservation Corps was an invention of the white man, I could not stop myself from sharing Nantai's enthusiasm. I was rather curious to know more.

"Join the corps," Nantai had impressed upon me that night. "For centuries you have had a mission in our tribe and you can play an important role in the development of the reservation. Try to learn as much from the *biligaana* as you can. They are here, and they are not going to leave again, so we might as well learn how we can be a part of their world."

"Won't you join me?" For a moment I felt abandoned.

"I am staying here." Nantai's gaze swerved to the weaving loom outside, where my mother had started on a new blanket, and at the empty whisky bottles near the tree on the left side of the hoghan. I understood his decision perfectly well, and not just because he had recently started to train as a *hataalii* in the village.

"We will keep in touch," I had said softly.

Now I am walking slowly down the hill into Keams in search of the trading post. After I write a short letter to my family, the man from the post office offers to drive me to a camp just outside Keams that afternoon. It seems that there are Diné working there, supervised by a white inspector, to make gravel for the roads that are to be built. "The work pays well," he says, as I sit beside him in his car. The speed at which we drive away makes me momentarily dizzy, but after that I start to enjoy the velocity at which the car is traveling. The prospect of a good wage also makes me happy. I will make sure that the money goes directly to my brother and mother without my father being able to squander it.

There is a pleasant atmosphere in the camp. There are local Diné working there, but other men and boys come from further afield. The white man who organizes the work and teaches us to blow up rocks with dynamite is really no more than a boy. He is about my age.

When I walk to my tent that evening, I see that the young inspector is sitting by his car with a thing that I have never seen before. He is making music on a wooden sound box with six strings attached to it. It sounds wonderful and I am curious enough to stop and listen discreetly to the song that he is playing for a while.

After a few minutes, the white boy looks up. "Hi, there! Would you like to sit with me and sing along?" He gestures at me, probably because he cannot be sure that I understand his English.

I start to smile and walk towards him. "Sure. I like your music. It's beautiful."

"*Hózhó?*" he says, laughing, using a word from my own language. I sit down next to him. This white man is clearly interested in our culture.

He introduces himself in the typically American way. "My name is Edward, Edward Hall, but all my friends call me Ned." He puts out his hand and shakes mine. "And what's your name?"

I hesitate slightly. "Sam Yazzie. In my culture we do not usually call ourselves by our real name."

Ned raises his eyebrows and looks somewhat ashamed. "Oh, sorry. So, what do you call each other?"

"It depends. Relatives we call 'brother', 'sister', or 'father', and people that we know well we call 'friend'. We usually have nicknames for people that we are close to, so that we do not diminish the power of their real name by using it all the time."

He nods slowly and begins to smile. "What a beautiful thought."

"I do not mind you calling me Sam, since it is not my real name," I grin.

Ned chuckles. "I do not mind you calling me Ned, since that is a nickname, too."

We go on talking. I actually really like Ned, the first *biligaana* I have ever liked in my whole life. He tells me about his studies and his work for the CCC program. He shows me how to play his guitar and even teaches me how to play a simple song. I tell him about my family up north, my brother, who has been to boarding school, and the traditions we still cherish. Only when we are very tired do we decide to turn in.

"I liked talking to you a lot," Ned says cheerfully. "Will you come and play the guitar again tomorrow night?"

"Yes, I'd like that. I also liked talking to you."

In the course of the following weeks we get to know each other better and better, and I learn a lot of English by talking to Ned. Although I already had a reasonable command of the English language, my new friend teaches me a great many words and expressions that did not exist fifty years ago and I also come to appreciate different, more positive aspects of the *biligaana* civilization. We discover that we have more in common than we thought.

At the end of the year there is a long letter from Kayenta. I read the letter in total shock, tears running down my cheeks.

"Sam!" Ned sees me sitting against a tree. "What's wrong? Why are you so sad?"

Sullenly, I throw the two sheets of paper on the ground and look away from him when he sits down beside me. "It's my mother's animals. The Indian agents have slaughtered all her sheep. Without asking or explaining anything."

Nantai's English words staring at me from the page cannot adequately express what my brother must feel at this moment. He is writing that my mother does not know what to do with herself, that my father has sunk into a perpetual state of drunkenness and how the whole village is coping with the same problems.

"There is an enormous drought in your reservation," Ned begins to explain hesitantly. "There is a good deal of overgrazing. That is why the animals have to go, or else the grass will never return."

"Nonsense. The agents do not understand that we have had this drought since the turn of the century. That has nothing to do with our sheep. Further up north, there are farmers completely ruining the land – American farmers who have no idea how to preserve and respect the land so that you can live in harmony with it for centuries on end. We have had sand storms in Dinétah for years. We can hear that the wind from the north is different. We can feel that the rain is different. The birds tell us that the grasses have gone." How can I explain to Ned what a Diné can feel, see and hear when he lives in complete harmony with nature? These things do not exist in his world.

"Sometimes I wish I could see with your eyes," I hear him say. He sounds almost melancholic, as if he has lost something in the confusing and busy world he has grown up in.

"Believe me, you do not wish to see through my eyes," I am about to reply bitterly, but I stop myself. After all, Ned knows nothing of my centuries-long history and the things that I have witnessed. I get up, fold the letter and put it in my pocket. "I am going home."

"What, right away? If you go now, you will not get your wages."

"I don't care. My family is more important."

"Then come to Oraibi after the spring," Ned tells me. "There are a few new projects planned. We are going to build roads and dams. Ask for my team."

"I will do so." Then I embrace him briefly and give him a warm smile before I walk to my tent and get my things.

After a week I arrive at Kayenta. The trip has tired me. I am not used any more to walking such distances. If I wanted to go to Keams, I usually went with Ned in his car or I went on horseback with a few other Diné.

The land near our hoghan looks shockingly empty without animals, and again my eyes fill with tears when I think of all the slaughtered sheep.

I slowly approach the hoghan singing a soft song so as to alert the people inside, and when my mother comes out, she rushes into my arms sobbing. "*Shiyáázh*! Oh, I am so glad to see you again."

I give her a firm embrace. Behind her, Nantai walks up to us and grabs my hand. "It is good that you have come home, *shik'is*."

We sit down and my mother goes inside to make coffee. I sit with Nantai saying nothing and gulp down the coffee that my mother pours us when she comes outside again. My gaze drifts over the things outside the hoghan – the weaving loom with a blanket on it, half finished, the pots and pans, and the tree to the left of the house. Only now do I notice that there are no empty whisky bottles there.

I turn toward Nantai. "Has Dad stopped drinking?" I ask almost incredulously. I do not want to confront my mother with that question, so I ask him in English.

My brother stares out over the empty field in front of our house. "Yes, he has stopped drinking." His voice sounds strangled.

All of a sudden my heartbeat increases and I start feeling dizzy. Nantai sighs. "He stopped drinking forever, Sam. He passed away."

I swallow something. "When?" I ask hoarsely.

"Four days ago. My letter to you was already on its way when he died."

Later, when I am standing by the graveside all by myself, I do not know what to say. I do not know with what final words or thoughts I have to leave *shizhé'é* behind. Should I tell him how insecure we felt? How afraid we all were when he was drunk?

It does not matter anymore. It is over. He has gone away. He had lost his roots by following the path of outsiders, but now he may find his roots back again. He is cradled by the earth. And the earth embraces everyone, regardless of someone's background or the life they have lived.

1937

For a number of years, Ned, Nantai and I work together on several road-building projects. The three of us get on very well. At the end of 1937, we finally go back to Kayenta where my mother still lives in our family hoghan together with her younger sister. Ned has left Oraibi to continue his studies. Nantai builds a new hoghan close to our old house and he gets engaged to Tahnazbah, a girl from the village. He has now completed studying with the old *hataalii* in Kayenta.

"Are you sure you don't want to meet Tahnazbah's cousin?" Nantai asks one afternoon when the wind outside is howling and we are sitting inside by the fire. My brother is prodding the fire with tongs and the flames light up his slightly worried-looking face.

"No," I wave his suggestion away. "I should not do that."

Nantai sighs. "Do you really think it is still dangerous, *shik'is*?"

"I cannot be sure, of course, but I don't think I want to find out, and I don't reckon Tahnazbah's cousin wants to find out either. I have no wish to drag anyone along in my misery. What happened to Ka'aallanii must never again happen to anyone, whoever it is."

"Think of yourself. Surely you are entitled to your share of love and happiness?"

I do not speak and shiver in spite of the fire. When I sleep very deeply, I sometimes dream of the Spanish woman whom I killed in cold blood. She was not a soldier and did not hold a position of power. She was just an ordinary colonist who only acted according to what her culture had taught her.

I do not answer my brother's question, but after a moment's silence he continues: "I will find out how we can tackle those *yenaldlooshi*, believe me. Even if it takes me years, I will help you."

He looks at me and I smile at him. "Thank you."

1942

The world has changed. I can smell it in the air. I can read it between the lines in the letters that Ned sends us. There are more and more roads. Noisy cars that spew out smoke frequently drive through Kayenta and the first coal mine has opened in Black Mesa. The *biligaana* are digging into Mother Earth and claim that they can harness and capture Her energy. They need a lot of energy, for on the other side of the ocean a dangerous leader has arisen who is a threat to America. In his last letter, Ned wrote that he is going to command a regiment in Europe. I have no idea how long he will be gone and if he will be able to write any letters when he is there, but he asked me if Nantai and I could pray for him.

So we did. My brother organized a Protection Way ceremony to ask the gods to help Ned in the war. We went to the highest mountain top in our area and made a smoke offering to the gods. As the sun was setting, we stood next to each other, both singing and lost in thought. Shash, the bear, and Né'éshaa, the owl who is Nantai's totem animal, are our companions on the other side of the veil, the spirit world which is never far away as long as you open up to it.

We have given up trying to find the *yenaldlooshi* in the past. During one of his vision quests, Nantai heard from Né'eshaa, his totem animal, that my spirit tormentors can only be defeated in the place where they are physically hiding in the past. We have no idea how we could possibly find out, and I am now resigned to the fact that in this life I will not know love. My memories of Ka'aallanii are still with me and do not fade. It has been more than a hundred years now since I held her in my arms, but I can still see her face. I am keeping her pendant in a beautiful little box in my hoghan. Every now and then I take the jewel out and stare at the turquoise colors of the inlaid stones. A blue butterfly – that is how I will recognize her if her spirit ever decides to visit me again.

The unrest in America increases. The war that is raging in Europe is coming our way. Every so often Nantai and I get to see a newspaper through the trading post. The papers write about the Japanese enemy at the other side of the Pacific Ocean, who want to attack our country. With a growing sense of indignation we read about this. I have never before felt the urge to fight for something together with the white men, but now that I have read such horrible things about our mutual enemy, things are different.

"We have to do something," I say one evening, before throwing down the newspaper in disgust. My brother is sitting outside his hoghan, cutting a groaning stick for next week's ceremony.

He looks up. "About what?"

"The war."

Nantai sighs and nods. "That is how I feel, too. The war throws a shadow over everything we do here. Tahnazbah even asked me if it wouldn't be a good idea if a number of men from the village joined the army."

"Well, I am quite prepared to enlist, but we are not even allowed to vote in elections. The *biligaana* do not see us as full-fledged members of society. Why would they ever allow us to fight for our country and our freedom?"

One week later, out of the blue, there is a chance for Nantai and me. A certain Sergeant Johnston visits Kayenta. He is accompanied by a man from the Diné people, John Benally, who serves in the American army. I am quite excited when Sergeant Johnston explains during a meeting how, having grown up on the reservation, he got the idea of using the Navajo tongue as a code language. He and Corporal Benally are looking for people who want to join the Navajo Communication School and fight in the war.

Thirty minutes later, five men from Kayenta, including Nantai and I, have put their names forward to go to the Marine Boot Camp. The idea is that we will be trained first to fight in the army and then go to Camp Eliot to be trained to use our language as a code language. There are no words in Diné Bizaad for most of the army terms, so for us, too, it will be a kind of secret language that we have to learn.

"At last we can make ourselves useful," Nantai says happily while we are arranging a few formalities at the provisional recruiting office. "We are recognized by the palefaces. We are no longer outsiders."

I nod, and hope that my brother is right. It would seem that the Americans finally see us as respectable citizens. Here is a chance to show our strength and prove our worth. They will know who the Diné are, even though we will be called Navajos.

1943

Boot camp is tough. From early morning to late in the evening we are trained. For me it is particularly difficult, since I have been in a war before and have only bad memories of it. Yet I am proud that we can defend our country, even though we are being led by white commanders. In the spring of 1943 we are taken to Camp Eliot, where we will be trained in the Communication School. Although we are not physically put to the test, the mental strain is just as great, if not greater. Every night I dream of the code words we had to learn during the day.

After the summer we finally get started. We are drafted into the Second Marine Division and are transported across the Pacific to Betio, a small island that will bring us a good deal of strategic advantage once it is our hands.

The night before we arrive in the waters around the Tawara Atoll, my dreams are not about war. In the ship's hold where we sleep, Ka'aallanii comes to me in my dreams. She smiles at me and stretches her hand out toward me, telling me that everything is going to be all right. When I wake up in the morning, I can feel tears on my face. I would have loved to hold the pendant in my hands for a while, but I have chosen to bury it by the lake behind my house. If I were to die here on this little island in the Pacific, I would never be able to find the pendant again should I be reborn once more.

"I do hope that everything is going to be all right, *shan díín*," I say softly to her dream image, the only thing of her I have in this place.

The next day, our ships fire their guns for hours on end and bombers throw their deadly cargo on the little island, destroying most of Betio. Most of the Japs' defenses have been wiped out. Then we are taken to the island in landing craft. The white soldiers are fully convinced that there will be practically no Japanese left alive after the deadly bombing.
"Hell," shouts the soldier steering our craft. "We are running aground." With a scraping sound the boat stops. The other craft are doing no better.
"It is low tide," another soldier calls out. "We are too deep in the water."
After some confusion it is decided the soldiers have to wade through the water to get to the island. I peer at the coastline. There is an eerie silence there and the island presents some kind of threat that I cannot explain.
"Here we go," says Nantai with a nervous tone in his voice, grabbing my shoulder. *"Ayor anosh'ni, shik'is."*
"I love you, too, my brother." I smile at him encouragingly before we lower ourselves in the water. I can sense that Nantai is more afraid than he wants to let on.
With difficulty, thousands of soldiers wade toward the beach. It is a long, painful procession, as occasionally our feet meet with coral reefs rising up from the seabed. Then all of a sudden, hell breaks loose. We can hear the rattle of machine guns and next to me a young, white soldier disappears under the water, without making a sound, a bullet hole in his head.
"Watch out," I cry, dragging Nantai with me under the water. Without seeing much, we struggle on to try

and get to the beach. When we finally come up again to draw some breath, we dare not raise our heads above the water further than our chins.

Speechless, I look around me. As far as the eye can see, bodies of soldiers who have been shot float on the water. Blood is turning the ocean red. Some soldiers have managed to reach the beach and are crouching against the wall that separates the beach from the land to stay out of enemy range.

Miraculously, we reach the wall unharmed and Nantai collapses in a trembling heap. I lean against the wall beside him and look out over the beach. The sea is calmly washing ashore the bodies of Marines. More and still more. I gasp for breath when an Amtrac tank, which has just plowed across a coral reef, suddenly explodes and bursts into flames.

The shooting continues for hours. The few soldiers who were able to reach the shore are sitting still with petrified faces, shivering with cold. They offer a sorry spectacle. One of the Amtrac tanks has managed to get to the beach, the corporal who was in it now cautiously creeping toward us.

"Start transmitting," he shouts, and rapidly spews out tactical data and coordinates. Nantai and I switch on the radio equipment, which has remained undamaged in the watertight D-packs we are wearing.

Slowly the sky turns dark. The Japs have stopped firing. The only remaining tank is used as a shield when, in turns, we get to have a few hours of sleep. I cannot catch any sleep, nor can Nantai.

"This is barbaric," he says, when he finally speaks again. We have been sitting next to each other for hours without speaking. He stares at the remains of the second tank that reached the beach, then drove over a mine. "How many people are dead already?"

I close my eyes. "I do not know. Too many."

At the end of the next day, we have achieved our mission: the western part of Betio is in American hands. But at what cost? Death is hanging in the air like a disgusting, odorous stench. Tears come into my eyes when I think of all the dead people on the beach, who will never be properly buried. The battered and bombed hills of the island remind me of the coal mines in Black Mesa. Wounded Earth.

I sleep back to back with Nantai. I am very, very happy that he is here and that I do not have to go through this alone.

When a watery morning sun wakes up the soldiers, I pass on our plans to the troops further on, and a little later there is a message ordering us to push ahead to the location where the second regiment is hiding.

The sun is already low on the horizon when, suddenly and unexpectedly, we come under fire again. I crawl away and hide behind an uprooted tree.

"*Shik'is!*" I shout at Nantai. Twenty yards from where I am, he has crawled into a shallow hole in the ground. He sticks his head out over the edge of the hole and then cautiously crawls towards me, occasionally pausing. I can see how he is only a few yards away from my hiding place, when all of a sudden, there is a deafening explosion. With eyes wide open, I see Nantai disappearing in a cloud of smoke that makes me cough vehemently. I narrow my eyes into slits and try to see where he has gone.

Then the smoke lifts and I understand what has happened. Nantai has stepped on a mine and is mortally wounded. Risking my own life, I crawl out from behind the tree trunk, grab Nantai by his arms and pull him away from the place of the explosion. I do not want to look at the bloody stump where his left leg used to be. I do not want to look, for I know what it means.

"*Shik'is*," he mutters weakly. "What happened?"

"You fell," I lie. "Just keep calm."

He smiles and grabs my hand. "My leg is tingling all over." He wants to lift himself to look at the leg that is no longer there.

I push him back. "I'll dress it in a minute." I squeeze his hand, reassuringly, while holding back my tears.

Then, in the midst of grenade and gun fire, in a soft voice, I sing a traditional song for my brother, whose face gradually draws pale. The light in his eyes is fading and when finally reinforcements arrive from behind, he has practically lost consciousness. His spirit is already somewhere else, in a more beautiful and peaceful place.

When he finally breathes his last breath, the sky has turned dark. Above my head, the stars twinkle, every now and then hidden by the smoke of grenade fire. I do not listen any more. I do not hear anything. I do not feel much when a thumping explosion shakes the earth close by. A pang of pain goes through my body.

I look beside me. It is as if I am dreaming. I can see Nantai. My brother looks at me, whole and radiant. He still has his leg and he embraces me, smiling. "I will look after you, *shik'is*," he says, with confidence. "I will not leave you alone. I will help you to get rid of your curse, I promise."

Then there is an owl looking at me with curious, wise eyes. It spreads its wings and flies up to the full moon, which lights up the night in my dream.

I awake and look up at the night sky over Betio, where the moon is absent. It has not risen yet. Dear God,

I feel tired. A tiredness that I can no longer hold back takes possession of me.

I do not think that I will see the moon tonight.

Nineteen

With a shudder, Hannah jolted awake. Her eyes fluttered open, but she couldn't see clearly. "Where are we?" Her voice cracked, her throat feeling like it was made of sandpaper.

Just then, she noticed someone behind her who put a towel around her shoulders, lifting a cup of water to her lips.

"Drink," Sani said close to her ear. She did, gulping the water down eagerly. Her entire body felt like she'd been wandering in the desert for weeks.

Slowly, her eyes adjusted to the sparse light in the hoghan. Across from her, Josh was still sitting in a trance,, his eyes closed and his hand holding hers.

"Is he okay?" she croaked, tilting her head to Josh.

"He is almost awake," the *hataalii* replied. "I think he is still conversing with his animal spirit."

Hannah furiously blinked her eyes, sudden tears welling up. All the emotions she'd felt, all *his* emotions, the memories she'd seen through his eyes, the experiences she'd lived through with him – it was too much. The things Josh had done for her in his previous life spoke of an infallible, never-ending love. The way he had stood by his people and guided them through the years, leading them on a mission of peace, spoke of his unwavering perseverance, of an almost impossibly strong faith in God's hand in everything.

Hannah couldn't stop crying, completely overwhelmed by all she had seen. Despite her tears, she wanted to comfort Josh, and she grabbed his hand tighter to do just that, wherever he might be in spirit. Her entire body felt cramped up, goosebumps spreading across her skin when a gust of wind blew into the hoghan.

She turned around to face the doorway, looking past the partially pulled-back blanket into the starry night sky.

"What time is it?" she asked in confusion.

"Almost midnight," Sani replied.

Hannah shot him an incredulous look. "We sat here all day?"

"Two days," he calmly said. "It is Friday evening."

That was incredible. No wonder her entire body was aching and she'd been thirsty like hell when she'd woken up.

Oh no. Where was Ben? He was probably worried sick – after all, he had no way to contact her. "My brother – I have to – is he..."

"He knows where you are." Sani smiled reassuringly. "Last night, Emily came up here to check up on us without interfering. She told me she'd talk to your brother."

Hannah silently thanked her friend as she watched the *hataalii* exit the hoghan. Maybe he was going to get Ben.

At that moment, Josh drew in a deep breath. He opened his eyes, fastening his grip on Hannah's hand. "You're crying," he whispered, rubbing the tears from her cheek with his other hand.

"I'm crying for you," she explained, sliding toward him, hugging him gently. He felt cold, and she decided to share her blanket with him so her body could warm him up.

"Why?" His hand gingerly trailed down her arm.

"For all the things you did. For all those people you gave your love to, while you were in pain yourself," she replied in a wavering voice.

"I'm proud of the lives I've led," he mumbled into her hair. "It has always served a purpose that there was sadness, and the hurdles I had to take made me grow as a person."

Hannah looked up, holding his gaze. "From now on, it won't be a lonely fight anymore."

"Not in this lifetime."

"No, not in *any* lifetime. I don't know what fate has in store for me, but I'm sure of one thing. I won't leave you alone anymore." She took the pendant around his neck in her hand and pressed it against her chest, close to her heart. For a moment, she could feel the weight of centuries pressing down upon her, just like Josh had felt it in the course of many lifetimes. And she hadn't even seen all of his lives – only the last two before this one. Suddenly, she wondered why she'd seen memories of a life she hadn't been a part of. Maybe it had to do with Josh still longing for her in that lifetime.

A sudden shiver ran through her. The skinwalkers' hate, directed at her from a dark place behind the veil, was almost palpable. It was an unsettling sensation – very different from the panic and sense of haunting she'd had before, when the curse made her believe she was crazy.

"I can feel them watching us," she whispered, without mentioning them by name. "They're angry because we are now connected. I'm stronger, and so are you. Together, we stand a better chance of fighting them, and they know it."

"Are you more terrified, now that you can feel them so clearly?" Josh asked.

"No. They are no longer shrouded in shadows. I can look them in the eye, and it makes me stronger than before."

After that, they sat in silence, limbs entangled under the blanket. The fire had almost gone out, but Hannah didn't feel like stirring it up again. In that moment, she felt completely at peace. Josh's breath tickled her neck. His hands rested on her lower back.

He was so beautiful. He was such an amazing person, and she loved him more than ever after this experience. The burden of a world at war had borne down on his shoulders for centuries, and yet she had managed to make him incredibly happy by giving him her love. It gave her silent hope that everything would work out in the end.

"Are you guys finished?" Ben's voice suddenly came from outside. Her brother hesitantly stuck his head round the door. When he saw his sister and his best friend, a relieved smile appeared on his face. "Oh, good. You're still alive."

"Yes, we are." Josh grinned. "And have been for centuries."

Hannah blinked up at her brother, her heart suddenly beating wildly in her chest. She saw Ben looking at Josh, a warm, gentle light in his eyes. And she recognized him – not as her brother, but as someone else. So that's why she'd seen more than one of Josh's lives. Shash had given her access to more information for a good reason.

When Ben had still been a little boy, he'd been plagued by horrible nightmares for months. Sometimes, she'd go to him if she heard him crying in his sleep and their mom didn't wake up. Ben had been too young to properly explain everything about his nightmares, but time and time again, he'd told her that he saw planes, smoke, and angry people shooting guns. And he always woke up screaming the moment his one leg was blown off by a big bomb in the ground, as he'd called it.

After a few months, the dreams had vanished. As he grew older, Ben couldn't remember his dreams about war anymore, but Hannah had never forgotten it, always wondering why her little brother had seen such terrible things in his sleep. And now, she finally knew.

Ben was Nantai. He'd been Josh's brother in his previous life – which meant Nantai had returned as well, keeping his promise. He would help Josh in this life to lift the skinwalker curse.

Hannah smiled. The universe wasn't as unfair and senseless as it sometimes seemed. Everything was connected. Ties between people never really disappeared. She was a part of something bigger that she'd never be able to fully comprehend, and didn't necessarily need to comprehend in order to trust in it.

"Sorry I was MIA for so long," she mumbled to Ben. "I had no idea it would take two whole days."

"I didn't know either," Josh hastily added. "Shash clearly took his time with us."

"Did he choose the memories I was allowed to see?" Hannah asked.

"Yes. Everything that was important to you and me was shown to you." He caressed her face, and Hannah remembered how her own eyes had lovingly stared into his, one hundred and fifty years ago, the day she blew out her final breath.

"I never stopped loving you," she whispered. "I know that now. I felt it in my dreams, too. I regretted leaving you." She pressed her lips to his mouth, making him sigh almost inaudibly. Now Josh finally had the answer to one of the many questions that had plagued him, even though it was more than a century later.

Ben plonked down next to them, stirring the fire. "So, aren't you guys starving by now?" he inquired, bringing them back to earth. "Or did that bear cook up a meal for you in the other dimension?"

Hannah and Josh both burst out laughing. "Nutjob." Josh playfully pushed Ben.

"No, we never even got snacks," Hannah deadpanned. "Shash was such a bad host. Unbelievable."

Ben grinned. "Well, fortunately for you, I'm a good host. I convinced Yazzie and Nick to prepare a big feast for you here. Lots of food. What do you guys say?"

"Sounds great! Let's go." Josh started to get up, but Hannah pulled him back down, holding on to the blanket covering them both.

"Uh, wait. My summer dress is still outside, next to the sweatlodge." She gave Ben an imploring look. "Could you get it for me?"

Ben tentatively raised an eyebrow, but decided to keep his mouth shut. A few moments later, he returned with Hannah's dress. She wriggled into it while still under the blanket.

"Soooo – how did you like the 'ritual', sis?" Ben asked her with a hardly suppressed laugh in his voice.

Hannah shot him a sullen look. It wasn't hard to make out the air quotes in his remark. "It was sublime," she quipped.

Josh caught her eye, a teasing smile playing at the corner of his mouth. "Sublime?" he quietly repeated, pulling her closer. "Wow. Thanks for sharing that with me." The heat creeping up her face made him chuckle.

Ben cleared his throat. "O-kayyy. Hands above the blanket now, people, or we'll be sitting here till the trumpets sound. Please follow me to the banquet."

Josh grabbed the blanket to sling it around his hips. Outside, he picked up his clothes and disappeared behind the sweatlodge to change.

"So. Sublime, huh?" Ben winked at her once Josh was out of earshot.

Hannah smirked. "Of course. He's got *centuries* of experience."

They both erupted in laughter. When Josh reappeared, Hannah and Ben were still snickering queitly.

"What's so funny?" he wanted to know.

Hannah put her arm around Josh and kissed his cheek. "I love you," she just said.

ಹಿಹಿಹಿ

"Han, *please* tell me what kind of ritual you've been involved in," Emily almost exploded when the whole gang was quietly enjoying a midnight dinner next to the Benally hoghan. She scooted closer to her friend, giving her an inquisitive look.

Hannah sighed. "I can't without breaking Josh's trust, but it means we have a better chance of lifting the skinwalker curse now."

"And when will that happen?"

"When we're ready. Ben is going to help us."

"*Ben?*" Emily echoed, her voice traveling up two octaves.

Ben turned around to face the two girls. "Yes? You want more potatoes?" He held the bowl out to Emily.

"Sure, thanks," Emily mumbled, turning red.

"Ben has a strong bond with both me and Josh. That's why he's our man," Hannah softly explained when Ben turned away again.

And not just because of that – she knew that now. Hannah silently observed Ben, Josh's friend and brother. Not just in this life, but also in the life before this one. Once again, she couldn't help but marvel at the interconnectedness of it all.

"Let's go to sleep," Josh suggested when Hannah let out a loud yawn after dinner. "I think we need to rest."

Ben stifled a yawn next to him. "Yeah, same here. And I still have to drive home."

"Why don't you sleep over?" Hannah said. "There's plenty of space in Josh's hoghan."

Ben's face took on a playful smirk. "Nah, I shouldn't. I don't want to interfere with another one of your *sublime* nights."

Josh chuckled. "Forget it. After two sleepless nights, I doubt I'd be able to turn it into a sublime experience anyway."

"Are you two going to use that word in front of me all the time now?" Hannah asked miserably.

"Yes," Ben and Josh replied simultaneously. Then, all three of them snickered.

"I'm going," Ben repeated. "I'll see you tomorrow." He hugged his sister goodbye and shook his friend's hand before driving off into the night with Nick and the neighbor girls in the back seat.

"Shouldn't we thank Sani?" Hannah inquired, yawning again as she crawled under the Navajo blanket on Josh's mattress.

"We'll do it tomorrow," Josh replied. "He's probably fast asleep by now."

As Josh slid under the covers next to her, Hannah suddenly realized she hadn't even discussed her discovery about Ben with Josh yet.

"Do you have any idea who Ben is?" she said, a note of excitement in her voice.

He laughed, nonplussed. "Uhm, yeah, he's your brother. Why?"

"He's *your* brother too. Ben is Nantai."

Josh blinked. "What?" he choked out.

"It's true! I recognize the look in his eyes whenever he looks at you, now that I've seen your memories. Ben even had dreams about his death on the Betio battlefield when he was a kid. He remembered his leg being blown off by a landmine."

Josh shook his head, his eyes wide. "So he forgot those dreams later on? He never mentioned them to me."

"The nightmares stopped after a few months. He quickly forgot about them after that."

"How old was Ben when he had those dreams?"

She thought for a second. "Three years old. I think."

Josh nodded pensively. "Did they start happening around my birthday?"

Now it was Hannah's turn to give Josh a bug-eyed stare. "Now that you mention it – his dreams started the day *you* were born."

"His soul must have sensed I'd entered this world again," Josh mumbled, a broad smile spreading across his face. "And here I was, feeling so lonely – thinking everyone had left me. You know, I've always felt so comfortable around Ben, even after my vision quest when my life changed so radically."

Hannah smiled. "Well, you found the two most important people from your previous lives again. And this time, we can finally help you!"

Josh winced. "I hope so. The fact we're all here doesn't mean we will win no matter what."

"Well, I have a good feeling about it. Sani can help us again, right? What kind of ceremony do we need to get rid of the skinwalkers, anyway?"

"An Evil Way ceremony."

"Will it take as long as this one?"

"I'm not sure. I've never done an Evil Way ceremony in order to beat creatures that aren't even really here. We'll have to reach back into the past again."

"Maybe Ben has all this knowledge from his previous life stored away somewhere, waiting to be unlocked," Hannah philosophized.

"I don't know." Josh sighed, looking anxious. "I just don't want anything bad to happen to you both. I know what those witches are capable of."

"I get you." Hannah grabbed his hand. "I feel it too, now. Constantly." She snuggled into his embrace, closing her eyes when Josh kissed her forehead.

"Let's talk about this with him when we go to St. Mary's Port tomorrow," he said. "Try to get some sleep, okay?"

"I'll try," she mumbled.

☙☙☙

Thankfully, Hannah had a peaceful night without nightmares. She even felt slightly embarrassed when she finally woke up at half past one. As she opened her eyes, she dug around in her bag to find her phone and look at the time.

"I'm such a sleepyhead!" she called out to Josh, who just came in carrying two plates of frybread.

He squatted down next to the mattress and kissed her forehead. "That's all right. I just woke up myself. Don't feel ashamed."

After a quick breakfast that was actually lunch, they both went to visit Sani before going to St. Mary's Port.

"I can't wait to get back to the cabin." Hannah slipped her hand into Josh's. "Don't get me wrong, I love Naabi'aani, but I have the feeling so many things have happened here. I'd almost say I need a vacation."

He couldn't suppress a laugh. "Well, you still have a few weeks left."

"When will you go to Tuba City, anyway?"

"In a month."

Hannah fell silent. All of a sudden, a month didn't seem that long. At the end of summer, she'd have to go back to her everyday life and leave Josh behind in Navajo Nation. The thought quietly stabbed at her heart.

"I have one week off in the fall," he said, as though he'd been reading her thoughts.

She smiled, squeezing his hand. "Me too."

When they arrived at Sani's hoghan, the old *hataalii* was sitting outside, reading a newspaper and sipping some coffee. He looked so blissfully mundane it made Hannah giggle a bit. Who'd ever guess this man had hosted a spiritual ceremony to miraculously bring them back to the past?

"*Ya'at'eeh*," he greeted them, putting down his paper. "Would you like some coffee?"

"I would really like to thank you for everything you have done for us, *shicheii*. Without your help, I'd never have been able to stay with Josh," Hannah spoke quietly once they were both seated with a cup of hot coffee.

The *hataalii* smiled, laugh lines appearing around his eyes. "I'm happy to have been of help to you. Josh's animal spirit has helped you, but the biggest help here was your love for each other."

Sani got up and went inside his hoghan, to emerge again with a small leather pouch which he handed to Hannah. "Here. I saved some of the colored sand I used for the *ikaah* during the ritual. Mix this with the content of your medicine bundle. It will make its protection extra strong."

They quietly conversed about all kinds of things, time passing by slowly. Hannah noticed how comfortable Josh felt around Sani. Of course, the medicine man had been an important refuge to him after his vision quest. How had she ever been able to feel jealous of this old man? He was a wonderful person who'd always been there for Josh. When they got up to leave for St. Mary's Port, Hannah felt almost sorry to say goodbye to Sani.

"So, your parents – they really don't know anything about your task as Shash?" she asked, once they were driving down Copper Mine Road in Josh's Mustang. "Surely they must suspect something is going on with you."

Josh looked sideways. "They know Sani and I share secrets I cannot discuss with anyone else, but they're too discreet to ask me about it, though. My parents know I'm trying to do really important work for our country – they just don't know why exactly."

"How much longer?" she asked, almost inaudibly. She wasn't sure Josh had heard her, but when he replied, it turned out he'd understood the underlying question as well.

"Only Shash knows. How many more lives will follow this one depends on how things will develop. What my world will look like."

"It is my world now, too." Hannah put her hand on his, feeling once more how much her life had changed in a matter of weeks.

When Josh parked the car next to the cabin, Ben was sprawled out on the lawn with a pile of books and a can of beer. He looked up, taking off his sunglasses as Hannah and Josh sat down next to him.

"Hey lovebirds," he grinned. "How did you sleep?"

"Like ten tons of logs," Josh replied dryly.

"And how's your study session going?" Hannah asked, looking down at the books piled up in the grass. She raised an eyebrow when she saw they all came from Page Library, and none of them had anything to do with physiotherapy. They were all history books about early American history.

"Yeah, I thought it'd make sense to read up on stuff," Ben excitedly explained his book selection. "I mean, we have to know what we're up against, right? What kind of time period those witches are from. I sure know a lot more about the Pueblo Revolt now than I did this morning."

Hannah smiled. "You rock, bro."

"Thanks," Josh added softly.

"I'll go grab some more drinks," Ben said, scrambling to his feet. When he returned from the kitchen with three cans of soda, Hannah had one of the library books cracked open in the middle of a chapter about Pearl Harbor.

"Hey, Ben," she started, her voice traveling up into a question. "You don't remember having those war dreams when you were a toddler anymore, right?"

Ben put down the cans. "Actually, I do," he answered just as hesitantly. "I never told you about me – visiting that hypnotist, did I?"

"Uhm, no."

Her brother stared at his hands. "It started during the summer vacation when I moved to Dallas to go to college. Katie and me got that room on campus together. Then, I started having nightmares. I'd wake up in the middle of the night screaming bloody murder, and Katie was worried sick. Sometimes I'd sleep peacefully, but most of the time she'd wake up during the night because I was crying or yelling. After about three weeks, I was fed up with the whole thing. Katie's best friend knew this reliable hypnotherapist, so I asked him to help me remember what I dreamed about. That was the strange thing – I always forgot what I dreamed about once I woke up."

"Then what happened?" Josh asked curiously.

"I went to see this hypno-dude. He helped me remember my dreams about a gruesome battle field where I got mortally wounded." He looked at Josh. "And the last thing I always saw was *your* face, but older. You were sitting next to me, tears in your eyes, and after that, I blacked out. I just heard someone singing."

"Holy smoke," Hannah blurted out. "And you never told me? Why not?"

Ben shrugged. "I wanted to keep it to myself, I guess. It felt too personal. Katie doesn't know what I saw either. She just knows the nightmares stopped after I visited the therapist and talked about the images I saw. That's when I also remembered having those same dreams as a kid."

Silence ensued, in which Ben calmly lit a cigarette. "I'm guessing it wasn't just a dream, then," he slowly spoke. "In the light of recent developments."

"You died next to me," Josh said, his voice strangled. "I sang for you."

"Who was I?"

"My older brother."

Ben smiled faintly. "Nothing much changed, huh?" Shaking his head in disbelief, he took a drag of his cigarette. "This is quite the yarn. It won't be long before people start calling me Born-Again Ben."

"I understand why your dreams returned during that summer," Josh said. "It was when I took my vision quest, and all *my* memories returned."

"So what kind of person was I in my previous life?" Ben inquired. He had stopped being surprised at anything. "Were we both soldiers?"

"No. We did fight in the war, but originally, you were a *hataalii*, and you'd given yourself the task to lift my curse."

"Really? But that's amazing! While we're doing that ritual, I might remember more, so I can really help you. That's why I came back into your life, I suppose." He stared at Josh. "Hey, now I understand why those skinwalkers seemed so familiar to me when I saw them in the park. And why they looked at *me* like they knew me." He resolutely slammed his hand down on his knee. "Time to come up with a strategic plan."

"Where do we even start?" Hannah turned to Josh.

"Nantai discovered the skinwalkers could only be beaten at the location they're hiding for real. They are hiding somewhere, in a place protected by black magic, in the past," he said.

"And once we find that place, we can fight them there?" Hannah asked.

"Yes. Which won't mean the outcome is set. We might not win."

"But I never found out where they are hiding?" Ben said.

"Well, I remember you having a vision once, in which you saw them sitting in a large cave. Not much detail there, I'm afraid. The black magician and his sons were sitting around a fire in triangle formation, wearing coyote furs on their backs, like they were continuously preparing themselves for a transformation."

"It has to be a cave where nobody would bother them," Hannah concluded. "Okay, not much risk of that in the past, I guess. No curious tourists visiting caves to look at petroglyphs."

"I wouldn't be surprised if the cave they're hiding in is still avoided in our time," Josh said. "The Diné have a certain aversion to places simmering with evil energy. We can sense it, and we will never enter them because *chindi* haunt those places."

"Where can you find large caves in Navajo Nation?" Hannah mused.

"Uhm, practically everywhere. We have lots of mountains, so plenty of caves to go around."

"Where did you live when those three warlocks first visited you?"

"In the vicinity of Santa Fe, where the revolt played out. But that doesn't mean they're hiding somewhere around there. They were probably willing to go to great lengths to protect themselves. They could have picked a spot far away from their original dwellings, so I'd have a harder time finding them."

"In other words, they could be anywhere?"

Josh's shoulders sagged as he nodded despondently.

In the silence that ensued, Hannah noticed Ben was observing the two of them with an almost excited look in his eyes. He hadn't said anything for a while. "What's up?" she mumbled.

Ben cleared his throat. "You know – this might sound crazy, or too obvious, but..." He turned to Josh. "You once told me what the name of your village means. Naabi'aani means 'cave of the enemy', right?"

Josh slowly nodded. "Yeah. That's right."

"Where is this cave? And what enemy does the name refer to?"

"It's a cave just outside the village. People who set foot in it about a century ago all came back reporting an evil presence. Ever since, my people have believed the place was home to a hostile tribe that must have left some sort of malevolent energy."

Hannah shivered. "But then, isn't it possible..." she started out.

"Wait a minute – just hold on. Isn't that too much of a coincidence?" Josh objected. "Why would the cave hosting my mortal enemies only be a stone's throw away from my native village?"

"Because *you* live here," Ben threw back, looking excited. "Think about it. This whole scenario, us showing up in each other's lives, becoming friends and family and all, seems too much of a coincidence too. Except it isn't. It was all pre-ordained somehow. I came back in your life as your best friend to help you fight the skinwalkers. Hannah came back to you because she was your lover, and now she can be with you again if we manage to lift the curse. Nothing is accidental, so you were born in this village for a good reason. We were *supposed* to find that cave. Call it help from above, if you must."

"I think you're making a lot of sense, Ben," Hannah said quietly, staring at her brother in awe. He'd changed so much in just a few days. It was almost like his previous personality was shining through.

"You could be right." Josh bit his lip, seeming indecisive. "Which means we have to check out that cave. Once we have, I'll ask Sani to start preparing the Evil Way ceremony. It will take him at least a day. That way, we can do a protective ritual before really stepping into the cave together." He shot Hannah and Ben a fearful glance. It was obvious the idea scared him to death.

Ben nodded. "Yeah, let's do this. You've waited long enough, Josh. Of course there's risk involved, but I believe in a happy ending."

"So do I." Hannah snuggled up to Josh. "We'll make this work."

"Are we going back to Naabi'aani?" Ben got up. "I want to take a look at that cave. Maybe I'll sense something."

"I'll join you," Hannah chimed in.

"No, you shouldn't," Josh almost snapped. "You – you just stay here. Okay? Let me and Ben take Sani there to investigate. Please, *shan díín*. We really have to be careful. The closer you are to these witches, the better they'll be able to feel you and do something to you."

"Okay, whatever." Hannah blew out a breath and kissed Josh on the cheek. Of course, he didn't want Ben to know she was running the highest risk of the three of them. "You guys go. I'll stay here and hang out on the beach. I'll call Emily and ask where they're camping out."

They all got up, Hannah hugging Ben and Josh both. "Be careful," she mumbled to Ben. "Just a scouting mission, okay? You don't need to storm the barricades on your own."

"Got you, sis." Ben ruffled her hair, then followed Josh to the Mustang.

Hannah watched them drive away before walking inside with leaden steps to make some food and call Emily. Her friend turned out to be on the beach near The Winking Shrimp, together with the entire Greene family.

"So, feeling better?" Ivy asked, as Hannah spread out her towel and gratefully took a bottle of water Sarah handed her from the cooler.

"I guess."

"You still look exhausted." Ivy narrowed her eyes. "Is everything all right between you and Josh?"

Hannah smiled. "Yes, of course. That's not the problem. The ceremony just took a lot of my energy."

"So are you – done now?" Amber inquired curiously.

"No." Hannah shook her head. "Next stop is an Evil Way ceremony. Sani is going to be hosting that one, too."

Emily raised an eyebrow. "What the heck are you guys up to?" she wondered out loud, shooting Hannah a worried look. "Ben said he was going to assist. What with, exactly?"

"I'm not entirely sure," Hannah lied. "You'd better ask him personally. Or Josh."

Emily snorted. "Yeah, like *he's* going to blab."

"Josh promised to tell us what's been going on when everything is over," Amber came to his defense. "He told me so yesterday."

"Okay." Emily bit her lip. "Sorry I'm being a bitch about it."

"Don't worry," Hannah replied. "I understand. You feel left out."

"Tell me about it," Ivy grumbled. "I was left out of the loop entirely. Nobody even bothered to tell me you'd be meditating in some hut all weekend long. Or why."

Everyone giggled. "All will be revealed," Hannah promised. She took in her friends' faces, a sudden shiver running through her. If the ritual didn't work, would she live to tell her friends what was the matter with her?

For the first time since the ritual with Josh, it hit her – she could die. This was the most perilous thing she'd ever done. Somehow, it didn't seem quite real, but it was the truth. Josh's concern about her, him trying to keep her away from the cave this afternoon, was completely justified.

Staring off into the distance, Hannah put her arms around her knees, absent-mindedly sipping from her water bottle. The medicine pouch with the added sand from the *ikaah* rested against her anxiously-beating heart.

Twenty

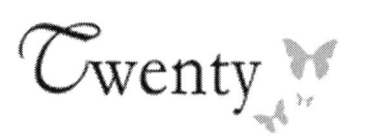

That evening, Hannah decided to invite everybody to a barbecue at their place. It was a bit morbid, but she wanted to see her friends one more time before she, Ben, and Josh set the Evil Way ceremony in motion. She was getting more nervous by the minute. Nick and Yazzie, who were both busy grilling sausages on the barbecue, were chatting to her about their day in Page, but she couldn't focus.

Her heart skipped a beat when she saw Ben's Chevy trundle up the sandy path to the cabin in clouds of dust. So Josh and Ben were back – with news.

"Can you help me in the kitchen?" she quickly asked her brother as he stepped out of the car.

"Sure." He followed her inside. It was obvious what she wanted to know.

Josh followed them both, pulling Hannah in his arms when she leaned back against the kitchen counter, her face a mask of warring emotions. "So?" she asked, her voice taut.

"Ben was right," Josh mumbled, his face pale.

"I suddenly had a sort of vision when I neared the cave," Ben said breathlessly. "And I felt that same fear I felt when the skinwalkers confronted me in the park."

Josh pulled Hannah closer. "I spoke to Sani. It's really going to happen. On Monday morning, just before sunrise."

"So we'll spend tomorrow night with you in Naabi'aani?"

"Yes. So we can do some preparatory work."

Hannah pressed a soft kiss to his mouth. His trepidation was almost palpable.

"I've had some really interesting discussions about my past life with Josh today," Ben babbled on. "I finally understand why I hate studying so much. In my past life, I was beaten and abused at boarding school. Quite a revelation, huh?"

Hannah smiled feebly. "Sounds more like a petty excuse to me."

"Say what you want," Ben said smugly, a smirk on his face. "You can't erase the past."

He piled some glasses onto a tray, balancing it in his hands as he stepped onto the porch. Hannah stared at him with a frown, because Ben sounded annoyingly breezy. Not at all like he was taking the situation seriously. Suddenly, it grated on her that Ben seemed so chipper about everything, while Josh only seemed to tense up more by the minute.

"Why are you so scared?" she whispered, caressing his cheek. "Remember, you told me yourself – together, we're a lot stronger, now that we're spiritually connected. And don't forget Ben will be there, too."

Josh clenched his jaw. "That's just it," he muttered. "I know you'll both be there, and it frightens me. If either of you is hurt again because of me, because of this curse – I'll never forgive myself."

"What do you mean, because of you? I was murdered by Mexicans, and Ben died on the battlefield in the Second World War. I hardly think there's reason to blame yourself for that."

"But people keep dying around me. As soon as I let them in, they're taken away from me."

"It's a coincidence, okay? Please, don't make yourself responsible for our lives and accountable for our deaths. That's just nonsense." She looked at him, staring him down until he trained his eyes to the floor and suddenly shrugged like a small child.

"Let's just go outside." Josh grabbed the bottle of ketchup from the table and stepped out the door. Hannah wanted to follow suit, but changed her mind when Ben came in again to grab the garlic butter from the fridge.

"Look, Ben. You really need to talk so light-heartedly about what happened today?" she addressed him, keeping her voice low so Josh wouldn't hear. "It's almost like you're not taking things seriously."

Ben impatiently whacked the fridge door shut, giving her a reproachful glare. "Give me a break here. How the hell do you think I should act? This very afternoon, we found the cave where his mortal enemies have been holding a stake-out for the past few centuries. Josh has been this big bundle of nerves for hours now, and I'm trying to be positive here and take his mind off things. If you want me to wallow in gloom too, we might as well start digging our own graves in front of that damn cave." His mouth contorted in a nervous half-smile. "You think *I'm* not scared?"

Hannah bit her lip. She should have kept her big mouth shut. Of course Ben was scared shitless. Moreover, he had no idea just how dangerous the whole thing would be for her, because Josh had never clued him in. "I'm sorry," she mumbled shamefully. "I could hit myself right now."

"Not gonna happen." Ben said decidedly. "There's a time and place for self-flagellation, and this is clearly not it. Come outside now – we're going to have a good time with our friends."

They both chuckled clumsily, Ben putting his arm around her shoulders. "Come on, lighten up. There's three of us, and don't forget Sani. He'll be there too, so we outnumber them."

They went outside. Hannah grabbed a veggie burger and picked a spot on the grass next to Josh, who was eating a hotdog himself. Yazzie had grabbed the guitar from the living room, trying out a couple of complicated basslines. Amber and Ivy were sharing a fish skewer, and Nick was playing a game of badminton with Emily. Everyone looked so care-free and normal, and it was so beautiful in all its simplicity.

Hannah swallowed hard. Her stomach felt weird, as if she was some kind of homesick. It was a deep feeling of longing for the uncomplicated, simple summers of the past.

But then, she looked sideways at Josh. Those carefree summers were gone, but the summers ahead would be beautiful. She loved Josh, no matter how complicated their life together was at the moment. There was no turning back now, and she was okay with that.

જીજીજી

"Monday night in the park! Be there or be square!" Nick yelled from his car window later that evening, as he drove off in his Jeep giving Yazzie a ride to Wahweap. The entire group would go to Movies in the Park on Monday.

"I'm happy we have something to look forward to on Monday night," Ben mumbled as he was clearing away the barbecue together with Hannah. "It makes me feel like life goes on. As long as we're expected somewhere later that day, all will be well."

"True, but I'm really starting to get the jitters now," Hannah quietly replied, staring after the Jeep as it rounded the corner.

"We're going to hit the sack," Emily announced, sauntering toward them hand in hand with Amber.

"Uh-huh, I bet you are," Ben grinned.

Amber turned red. "See you tomorrow," she quickly said, dragging Emily to her parents' log cabin before Ben could crack more jokes.

"Stop teasing my little sister like that!" Ivy smacked Ben on the head.

"Hey, cut me some slack. I can't tease my own sister. She'll beat the crap out of me."

Hannah chuckled. "You got that right." Putting a hand on Ben's shoulder, she continued, "Are you going to tag along to the beach tomorrow morning?"

Ben shook his head. "I'm staying here." His eyes darted to Josh, who just stepped out of the kitchen, and Hannah left it at that. Her brother probably wanted to have a one-on-one with Josh tomorrow – about her, or about what exactly would be waiting for them on Monday morning.

Together, they carried the cleaned barbecue back to the shed. Ben gave her a quick hug. "Sleep tight, sis. Can you wake me up before you go to the beach? I'm afraid I'll sleep right through my alarm clock – I'm that tired."

"Maybe you need a good rest."

"No. I want to use the opportunity to talk to Josh tomorrow," Ben said decidedly. He stepped inside and disappeared into his room.

After Hannah had blown out the candles still burning on the porch, she went into the kitchen, where Josh was just drying off the last plate on the dish rack. He leaned into her and put his arms around her. "Where do you think we should sleep?" he said.

"I guess we could take my mom's room. That's easier than cramming ourselves into my single bed."

"Sounds good." He kissed her forehead and let go of her. "I'm going to take a shower first."

While Josh was in the bathroom, Hannah changed into her pajamas and crawled under the covers. Absently, she grabbed an old magazine from the bedside table to leaf through and distract herself a bit.

Every time she closed her eyes, she could see coyote eyes in her mind. Even though she was wearing the medicine bundle, she was still afraid she'd have nightmares tonight. Her entire body felt restless. When Josh finally emerged from the bathroom, his hair still dripping and a wet towel around his shoulders, she was nervously staring at the ceiling. He walked to her side of the bed and sat down on the edge, softly touching the skin of her face.

"You can feel them, can't you?" he asked.

"Yes. I see – their eyes. They're watching me."

"Are you absolutely sure you want to do this thing?"

"Yes." Hannah sat up and pulled Josh closer. Her hands pushed away the towel to caress his back, which was still clammy from the shower. He cradled her in his arms and captured her mouth with his.

Despite her nervousness, a shiver of pleasure ran through her body. This was probably the best way to stop herself from analyzing things too much. Josh's nearness never left her cold. His hands roamed her body, and Hannah slowly eased herself on her back again, pulling him on top of her. "So, are you going to take off your jeans too?" she whispered seductively.

Josh started laughing. "Impatient," he grumbled a rebuke.

It didn't take long before the old magazine was lying forgotten on the floor. For the moment, all anxious thoughts had completely disappeared into the background.

☙☙☙

The next morning, Hannah was woken up by birdsong outside. It had to be early, then. She'd better stay in bed for a while longer. Putting her head on Josh's chest, she scooted closer under the arm he'd slung around her in his sleep. Smiling, she listened to his soft breathing as she took in his relaxed face, so peaceful and innocent in his sleep.

All the summers she'd spent here passed through her mind's eye. She'd seen this boy grow up, watched him get older every year, and now he was suddenly beside her as an equal, bound to her in supernatural ways. It felt good, having known him for so many years before getting to know him again like this. Everything about them together felt like it was meant to last.

As she lay there musing on their history together, Josh slowly woke up. He yawned loudly, stretching his arms and opening his eyes. "Hey, honey," he mumbled, rubbing his nose against hers. "You been awake for long?"

"Not that long." She kissed him.

"What were you doing?"

"Watching you," she smiled.

Josh smiled back. "So? Your conclusions?"

"You're beautiful when you sleep."

"Praise indeed. Only when I sleep?" He pulled her closer.

"You shouldn't push your luck," she giggled, burying her face in his neck.

Josh chuckled when her stomach suddenly grumbled loudly. "I guess that means it's breakfast time. Shall we get up?"

Hannah shook her head. "No, I'll make us breakfast. You have to stay in bed. It's breakfast in bed."

"Okay, I'll stay put," he promised with a twinkle in his eyes. "That's sweet of you."

Hannah walked into the kitchen with a wide smile on her face. This was what life would be like, once they'd dealt with those skinwalkers. No more scary situations. No more fear. A normal, ordinary life for Josh.

Whistling a tune, she put on the oven to bake croissants. When she stepped into the bedroom again after fifteen minutes, Josh was staring at the ceiling, enjoying the sunlight streaming in from the window.

"This is good," he mumbled, his chin covered in croissant crumbles as they both tore into their breakfast. "We should do this more often."

"Yeah, we should. Well, tomorrow is a no-no, I guess. I bet we'll have to do that ritual on an empty stomach again."

Josh was silent for a moment. "That won't be necessary this time. We only need to be in a state of light trance when we enter the cave. There won't be any sandpainting to sit on this time, either. I suspect Sani will start the first part of the ritual tonight, after sunset."

"Can you split up a ceremony into two parts?"

"In this case, yes. The first part will weaken the evil magic, and the second part will help us to reach the creatures in the cave."

"By the way, Ben wanted to ask you a few things today. You should explain this to him, too."

"I think Ben's priority is to find out how to protect you as well as he can."

"Ben doesn't even know how dangerous this is for

me."

Josh quirked an eyebrow. "Of course he does. He sees how I behave around you. He'd have to be really stupid *not* to know, and Ben just so happens to be a smart guy."

Hannah held her breath for a second. "Well, he can't talk me out of this anymore, so he'd better just accept the situation," she said stubbornly.

Josh let out a deep sigh, cupping her face in his hands and looking her in the eye. "Just keep in mind how much everybody loves you," he said softly, yet passionately. "Don't be reckless. Don't put your life on the line just because you feel like you have to stay at my side no matter what."

Hannah stared back at him, tears welling up in her eyes. Of course, Josh was right. And he loved her so much he'd be willing to give her up, even now, to protect her. But she wouldn't change her mind. Her life was connected to his for good.

"No, I won't be reckless," she promised in a hoarse whisper, laced with emotion. "I really won't. It may seem as though I'm blindly stepping into the unknown just so I can be with you, but I'll keep my eyes open, trust me."

She crawled into his arms, her breakfast plate forgotten on her lap. In the silence, they both felt just how much closer they could grow together, if only the shadow of time wouldn't catch up with them and pull them apart.

☙☙☙

After breakfast, Josh took off with Ben to go back to Naabi'aani, and Hannah went to the beach with Ivy in a last-ditch effort to unwind. When Ivy and Hannah came back home by the end of the afternoon, Emily and Amber were playing a game of badminton on the lawn while Paul and Sarah were enjoying a glass of wine on the porch.

"We've decided to work out," Amber said with a large grin as she hit the shuttlecock with a loud thwack and made it land on Emily's head.

"I can't believe I'm wasting my free afternoon on this bullshit," Emily moaned, rubbing her scalp.

"That's because you love me," Amber laughed, skipping to her girlfriend and planting a kiss on her mouth. Emily's arms snaked around her waist and she kissed Amber back.

"Yeah, the two of you strike me as very ambitious," Ivy taunted them. "I've never seen such driven people in my entire life."

Hannah listened to her friends' banter with half attention. Her gaze drifted to her own cabin. Where could Ben and Josh be? The Mustang was still gone. She'd hoped the guys would be back from Naabi'aani by now. Digging around in her bag, she found her cell, which started ringing the second she wanted to punch in Ben's number.

It was her brother. "Heya, sis. You back from the lakeside yet?"

"Yeah, we just got back. Where are you?"

"Still with Josh. Can you come here tonight? Around ten?"

"Yep." She swallowed down the sudden lump in her throat. "You need anything?"

"Cigarettes," he replied dryly. "I already smoked my entire pack. I'm kind of edgy."

"I'll bring some. See you tonight." She quickly clicked off to stop herself from asking more questions about the preparations Ben and Josh were undoubtedly making right now.

When she got into her car at half past nine after a nice dinner with the neighbors, darkness had fallen. Venus was visible as a twinkling star above the horizon. The sound of the engine drowned out the chirping crickets in the bushes on the roadside, but for some reason, the silence in the red-brown desert still felt oppressive.

After parking the Datsun and cutting the ignition, Hannah indecisively stared at Josh's hoghan in the distance. A log fire was burning inside. Smoke rose from the smoke hole in the roof.

She grabbed her bag, switched on her phone and called her mother.

"Hey, Mom," she said, hoping she sounded cheerful enough. "How are things over there?"

"Fine! Did you get my last e-mail with all the photos?"

"Yeah, they were amazing."

"Aunt Beth wants to talk you and Ben into visiting her for Christmas, but I told her you'd probably want to go to St. Mary's Port to celebrate Christmas with Josh. Am I right?"

Hannah listened to her mom's light-hearted chatter, putting in a 'really?' or 'uh-huh' every now and then.

"Is everything all right with you?" her mom suddenly asked. "You sound a bit down."

"Oh, no, we're fine." Hannah lied. "I'm just tired. I haven't slept much in the past few days."

"I see," her mom drew out, and Hannah could visualize the cheeky grin spreading on her face. Suddenly, she choked with emotion, wishing there was a reason to grin like that about her sleepless nights with Josh. She wished she could see her mother's face one more time before launching into this precarious adventure with Ben and Josh. She missed her.

"Mom, it was good hearing your voice," she ended the conversation, her voice quivering a little. "I'll e-mail you some pics soon, okay?"

"Looking forward to that, pumpkin. Say hi to Ben from me. I love you guys!"

"I love you too." Hannah quickly switched off her phone and stared at it for a few seconds before dragging herself to the hoghan, hoping her eyes weren't red-rimmed from the tears she was trying to hold back.

Ben and Josh were inside. In the meantime, Ben was wearing his own medicine bundle. It was dangling from a leather strap around his neck. Her brother looked worn out.

"Is everything ready?" she asked softly, sitting down between the two of them.

Josh nodded. "We're heading out to the cave in a few minutes. Sani is waiting for us there. I told Ben the whole story about the curse, about my life in the seventeenth century and the situation in Navajo Nation. He knows the whole background now."

Josh's arm slipped around her shoulders, and Hannah leaned into him, sighing slightly. "I just spoke to Mom on the phone," she told Ben. "She said hi, and she loves you."

Ben blinked away a few tears. "Thanks," he rasped, taking her hand. "I'll protect you, okay? Everything will work out just fine."

"I brought you smokes," Hannah blurted out quickly. She didn't want to show Josh how emotional she was. It was hard enough for him as it was, guilt slowly eating at him ever since they'd agreed to help him with the ritual. If only her boyfriend could let go of things that were in the past. Maybe his burden would be lighter if he stopped believing he'd made the wrong decisions in the lives before this one.

Ben eagerly took the three packs, lighting a cigarette immediately. "A smoke offering," he declared.

Hannah laughed nervously. "When are we going?"

"Let's just go now," Josh suggested. "There's no point sitting around any longer."

Her heart beating wildly, she got up, slipping her right hand around Josh's fingers as Ben took her left hand. Linked together, they walked out of the village, into the mountains, under the light of the half moon. No one spoke, the silence only emphasized by their quiet footsteps on the dusty path, which gradually dissolved to make way for flat rocks.

As they rounded a rocky outcropping, Hannah caught sight of Sani. He was sitting in front of the cave entrance, tending a fire with a small sandpainting next to it. The *hataalii* had put his *jish* in front of him. He silently stared into the flames.

"It's time to start the *hóchxóó'ji* ceremony," he spoke softly, gesturing for them to sit down. Hannah shot an anxious look at the dark entrance to the cursed cave. A feeling of almost indescribable dread settled in the pit of her stomach, now that she was so close to the place where the witches were hiding.

Sani gave her a friendly nod and smiled at her briefly before taking some yucca fiber from the *jish* and touching all three of them from head to toe with the plant. Josh handed him a few incense cones, which Sani lit and blew on to start the smoke. After that, the medicine man got up and walked to the cave. He dipped his hand in the bowl of corn pollen he'd brought along, carefully putting a handprint on the floor in front of the entrance in each of the cardinal directions. Now Josh handed his old friend a bundle of oak twigs from the *jish*, and Sani put one twig on each of the four handprints.

When the *hataalii* sat back down again, he picked up an object Hannah recognized as a groaning stick – a primitive musical instrument attached to a string of buckskin that people whirled around in the air to chase away spirits with the roaring sound it made. Sani put the groaning stick in another bowl full of *piñon* needles, flipping the instrument several times to make sure it had been touched by the needles all over.

"Lightning medicine," Josh explained in a whisper. "The needles of a pine tree hit by lightning. Sani uses it to invoke the power of the black lightning now."

Sani got up and started whirling the groaning stick, faster and faster, until the whine it made grew to a deafeningly high pitch. Hannah felt her spine tingle. Glancing sideways, she saw Ben felt dizzy too. It was like all the energy around the cave entrance was being sucked into the groaning stick.

Abruptly, the *hataalii* stopped whirling the instrument and took it in his right hand, stepping into the cave. Hannah sucked in a breath. "What's he going to do?" she hissed at Josh, her eyes wide with fear.

"He will use the *tseen di'ni* – the groaning stick – to touch the walls of the cave. That should extract the evil influence from the inside out. Don't worry."

Despite Josh's reassuring words, Hannah couldn't help sighing with relief when Sani came out again in one piece. Again, he started to whirl the *tseen di'ni* around, casting the evil energy away into the air. Part of the black shadow hovering over the place had gone.

Ben sagged against her shoulder, wiping the sweat from his face. "I feel sick," he whispered. "For some reason, there's too much energy flowing through the air. I can't explain it."

"Sani partly eradicated the evil magic," Josh softly

replied.

The three of them watched Sani as he sat down on his own sandpainting, chanting softly. Josh joined in the chant. Finally, the ceremony was ended by Sani throwing the sand of the *ikaah* away in all four cardinal directions, letting the wind blow away the demonic influences he'd sucked out. The cave had been cleaned up.

"So what's next?" Ben asked in a low voice, when Sani once again sat down at the entrance, getting his *jish* out for yet another ceremony that looked just as mysterious as the previous one.

"We're not supposed to actively do anything," Josh replied. "We'll stay here and we'll try to contact the *yenaldlooshi* by meditation or dreams. I know that sounds scary, but the only way to beat them is to enter their world. So don't panic when you sense them, or hear them, or even see them. You are both protected by the medicine pouches you're wearing, and the small Evil Way ceremony that we've just witnessed. We will only enter the cave when Sani has finished doing the second part of his ritual. He is going to establish a pathway into the veil, allowing the three of us to step inside without losing track of each other." He turned to Hannah. "It's a little bit like what we did, but much more complicated. We're not going to look at memories from the past, but we'll be stepping into a small fragment of the past *itself*. What's more, we have to stay conscious."

"Why?" Ben wanted to know.

"If we really got into a trance, the risk of them influencing our thoughts would be too great," Josh said curtly.

Hannah shivered when she thought back to the haunted house at the funfair. Those horrifying images would be forever impressed in her memory.

"Are we just going to sit here?" she whispered nervously.

"You can sleep if you want," Josh reassured her. "I'll hold you."

She smiled, nodding her head. "I'll do that." She lay down, her head in his lap, as he looked down on her with a gentle look in his eyes.

Hannah drifted off into a light sleep. Every once in a while, she heard Ben and Josh talking. Fortunately, they were an anchor to reality for her, because the images she saw scared her senseless. She heard coyotes howl in her sleep. Her dreams were populated by black shadows with red eyes glowing up in the dark, claws with nails of pitch black steel wanting to grab her. Using all her willpower, she tried to stay as focused on the *chindi* as she could, knowing it would be harder for them to use their powers on her once she set foot in their domain for real, a few hours from now.

When Josh gently touched her head, she jolted awake from a confused slumber. "It's time," he simply said, his mouth set in a firm line.

Hannah scrambled to her feet, embracing Josh for a few seconds. Ben was next to her, and she embraced him too when Josh took a few steps toward the cave.

"We'll be fine," she whispered to her brother. "You were a kick-ass *hataalii* in your previous life, and you'll be kick-ass now. I trust in you."

Ben just let out a sigh, throwing away the butt of his cigarette.

"Here we go," he mumbled.

Twenty-One

At the cave entrance, Sani was waiting for them, dark rings under his eyes. "Inside, it is dark," he said solemnly. "Do not lose each other. Whatever you do, don't let go of each other."

Josh nodded. He and Ben each took one of Hannah's hands. It seemed easy enough, stepping into a cave, but they were about to enter the place that was most dangerous to Hannah in the world.

The *hataalii* handed Josh a torch. "Keep the fire burning," he said intently, like the torch wasn't just there to give them light, but also had a symbolic meaning.

And then, it was really happening. Josh stepped forward, pulling Hannah and Ben along. "*Hózhó nahastlin*," he whispered. "All will end in harmony."

Hannah gulped down the lump in her throat as she crossed the imaginary threshold separating the cave from the outside world. A gust of cold air touched her skin. She could hear Ben behind her, breathing heavily. They turned the corner and then entered a large cave, illuminated by the dancing light of Josh's torch. Hannah felt her knees buckle, and straight after that, a strange sensation in her abdomen. She blinked her eyes, trying to push away the dizziness slowly creeping up on her.

All of a sudden, it was pitch-dark.

"What happened?" Ben's voice piped up anxiously behind her.

"The torch is out," Josh answered in a tense voice. "There must be a draft. You have a lighter?"

"Obviously," Ben said, too nervous to make it sound dry. Hannah heard him fumbling in his jeans pocket, and she desperately tried to suppress the panic building up inside of her. She couldn't see a thing.

"It's in my other pocket." Ben turned toward Hannah. "Just let go of me for a second, Han."

Gingerly, Hannah let Ben's hand slip out of hers. "We were supposed to hold on to each other at all times, right?" she said in a small voice as his left hand pulled out the lighter they needed. He took it in his right hand and a tiny flame illuminated the darkness.

"I got you," he said soothingly, grabbing her hand again. "Don't worry."

Josh walked up to Ben and held the torch close to the flame. It lit up immediately – Sani had to have dipped the tip in inflammable oil for it to catch fire so easily. Hannah didn't understand how the slight draft could have extinguished the torch, but maybe it wasn't just that. There was a certain oppressive quality to the atmosphere in the cave, like there was less oxygen in here than outside.

"Now what?" Ben asked, now that they could make out their surroundings again.

"Over there," Josh pointed forward. They rounded another corner, stepping into a second, larger cave with a blackened spot right in the middle.

"The fire," Ben whispered. "The fire they were sitting around. Or *are* sitting around."

"Why don't we see what's happening in the past?" Hannah asked with a worried frown. "I thought Sani had made a passageway?"

"Maybe they're hiding." Josh looked around furtively, taking a few tenuous steps forward.

Hannah hadn't expected him to be this insecure, and it made fear take a sudden hold of her. Clearly, Josh had no idea what was going to happen, or what was waiting for them here. He was scared out of his wits.

At that moment, a horrible, unearthly sound emerged from the far corner of the cave. A corner shrouded in darkness. It was a cackling, eerie whine, sending goosebumps all over her body. Terrified, she squeezed Josh's hand, half-tempted to desperately start yammering herself.

"What – what the hell is *that*?" Mortified, Ben stared at the dark corner the sound had come from. His mouth fell open.

Hannah followed his gaze. The corner wasn't shrouded in shadows at all – no, a shadow had been *hiding* in that corner. It took a step forward, suddenly standing erect, towering over them in all its horrible, dark splendor.

"Oh my God." Josh pulled Hannah closer. The skinwalker almost touched the ceiling of the cave. He opened his eyes, a terrifying glow emerging from the narrowed slits in his face. Not red, but a ghastly, cold blue. The panting sound of raspy breath filled their ears. It was laughter – mocking, cruel laughter, coming from the mouth of the apparition.

"What do you want?" the creature thundered, booming with a volume high enough to make the floor shake. Out of nowhere, two other shadows popped up on either side of the skinwalker, growing to the same proportions in mere seconds.

The shadow on the left growled softly, which sounded even more threatening. Hannah backed away and bumped into Josh, who didn't say a word. The torch was shaking in his trembling hand.

"We have come to beat you," Ben faltered.

That caused the skinwalker on the right to start laughing, spitting out an insane cackle before taking a few steps closer to Ben. His mouth opened into a muzzle full of sharp teeth.

"Don't be ridiculous," the middle and tallest shadow then spoke haughtily. "In this place, we are invincible." His gaze drifted to Josh. "How on earth did you convince these poor mortals to join your cause?" he softly asked. It almost sounded like a reprimand.

Hannah cowered when she saw a lonely tear sliding down Josh's cheek. Had he given up hope? Were these dark, vindictive creatures right?

"This was our choice," she managed to whisper, not casting down her gaze when the skinwalker directly fixed her with his stare. "We won't abandon him."

The skinwalker smiled cruelly. "You should have run when you had the chance," he replied, cold and without mercy.

Suddenly, the shadow with the muzzle full of pointy teeth stood next to Ben. The monster was twice as tall as her brother. Lashing out with one giant paw, the skinwalker sunk his nails into Ben's chest. Hannah's heart skipped a beat when Ben slumped to the floor, blood oozing from the wound on his chest, soaking the light fabric of his shirt. Struck down by a predator from a realm of shadows.

"Ben!" Hannah and Josh simultaneously screamed. Hannah kneeled down next to him, staring at him as if frozen in time.

"Help me," her brother whispered, his eyes wide open in terror.

Before they could do anything, the shadow creature

grabbed his ankle, lifting Ben up and flinging him against the far wall with a sickening thud. He hit the floor like a rag doll, and the witch cackled in cruel pleasure. The tallest skinwalker walked over to pick Ben up and slam him against the rock wall once more.

Hannah's body refused to move. The skinwalker wasn't more than a hazy, motion-blurred shadow in front of her, hacking away at Ben with his claws, slamming him against the wall over and over again, not showing the slightest pity for the boy softly begging for mercy. His cries sent shivers down Hannah's spine, but it was even worse when the cries subsided altogether. No sound came from his lips when he was finally left alone, his skin bruised and bloodied, slamming down on the soot-stained floor in the middle of the cave.

"No," Hannah whimpered. "God, no, please. Let it stop. They're *killing* him!"

Josh rushed forward, trying to use his torch to drive the threatening shadow away from Ben, but he was quickly swatted aside by one of the other skinwalkers. "Josh," Hannah cried out as he landed on the floor too, his head hitting the stones with a smack. He slumped down next to Ben's lifeless body, temporarily distracting the skinwalker from his first prey. Tripping over her own feet, Hannah ran to her brother and her boyfriend. The torch was still burning on the floor next to Josh's limp hand. She picked it up to try and keep the shadows at bay, even though she knew it would be to no avail. She bent over Josh, putting a hand to his face.

"*Shan díín,*" he rasped, clutching her hand as she sank to the floor between him and Ben, still sobbing. "You have to – get away."

Through her tears, she focused on his face. It felt like something had punched a hole in her soul. She didn't dare look at Ben's face, but she knew he was in a bad shape.

He was dying.

Her little brother had gotten involved because he wanted to help her and Josh, but most of all, her. He'd believed in a happy ending, and now, he'd never see the light of day again.

She couldn't lie to herself. She knew how this would end. The look in Josh's eyes didn't leave her any illusions. They would die here, all three of them, and it was her fault. Her love for Josh wouldn't just prove fatal to herself, but to Ben and Josh as well.

"I can't – leave," she heaved. "I can't leave you here. Where's Sani?"

Behind her, she felt the skinwalker coldly breathing down her neck. The draft extinguishing the torch had actually been their evil influence all along, lurking in the darkness.

Josh grabbed her hand more tightly. "He's – on the other side. The real world – he didn't pass through the veil. Didn't use the passageway." His eyes rolled back in his sockets.

"Don't leave me alone," Hannah shivered. "Josh, please, don't leave me. We have to help Ben. We must …"

In a flash, she felt the heat of burning fire on her skin. One of the skinwalkers had pulled the torch from her hand and thrown it on the floor, where a mighty ring of fire sprang to life, imprisoning her, Ben and Josh. There was no way out anymore. She was trapped.

Faintly, she heard a high-pitched scream shrieking in her ears with an edge of hysteria, and realized that it was her own voice. The searing pain of the flames on her skin was unspeakable. Trying to beat the licking fire away, she lifted Josh and Ben to drag them away from the blaze, but it was like her knees were locked and her feet were glued to the floor. She couldn't get up. Smoke filled her lungs, causing her to start coughing and retching with tears in her eyes. The hairs on her arms were singed as the smell of burning skin filled her nostrils. Gagging, she tried to crawl away from the fire, her back against the wall, her knees pressed to her chest.

Floating. She was floating. The pain she felt was so bad she was beginning to drift in and out of consciousness, and in a sick way, it made her almost relieved and happy. She welcomed the silence. The darkness. She couldn't take any more. With tears still streaming from her eyes, Hannah looked up at the heavens she couldn't see from the bottom of this dark cave.

Her breath faltered as her gaze caught on something unexpected. Amidst the red glow of relentless fire torturing her body, she saw a bright-blue, dancing light.

"Whenever you're lost, follow me," she heard a light and friendly voice in her head. It was the same blue butterfly that had shown her the way in that vision she saw before saying yes to the first ritual. The butterfly from the haunted house.

"What the …?" she mumbled, dumbfounded, trying to reach out to the butterfly. She lifted up her hand, hoping the butterfly would come nearer, somehow comfort her in her death throes, when she took a closer look at it. Her hand. The outline was fuzzy. She couldn't see her fingers.

A dream. This had to be a dream.

"This is not real," she stammered. "This is not happening!"

Gasping for breath, she fell down a deep, dark hole. And then, she opened her eyes for real.

༄༄༄

Hannah stared into Josh's brown eyes. They were filled with a fear bordering on insanity. She was on the floor of the cave, Ben and Josh hunched over her. Ben had tears running down his cheeks. Josh was holding the torch in a death grip, his other hand caressing her forehead.

She coughed, sitting up straight to draw a deep breath. Her arms still hurt like hell. When she looked down at her forearms, she saw huge burn marks on both of them. Real burns, caused by the visions planted in her brain by the skinwalkers. Lost for words, she gaped at the red wounds on her skin.

"Honey," Josh whispered in a broken voice. "I thought we'd lost you." He put the torch away, balancing it against the wall, and scooped her up in his arms, almost knocking the air from her lungs.

Ben embraced them both in his turn, shaking his head as if in a daze. "You're back, sis," he mumbled, staring at her vacantly.

"I thought I'd lost both of *you*," Hannah cried in relief, clutching the two of them. She wished she could stay in this embrace with her brother and her boyfriend forever. The burn marks made her nauseous with pain, but it was bearable now that she knew Josh and Ben weren't dead. They were unharmed.

"What – what happened?" she stuttered. "Where did I go?"

"We don't know," Josh replied, his voice still shaky. "We stepped into the cave, and then I noticed you fell back, like you were hesitating. Ben said you let go of his hand. Seconds after that, you fainted."

"At first, you were there, completely still, but then you started wailing," Ben whispered, wiping away his tears. "Like you were being murdered. And then we saw those – those burn marks appear on your skin, out of nowhere."

"You were burning alive, right in front of our eyes," Josh said quietly, "and there was nothing we could do. We couldn't wake you up."

Hannah swallowed. "The torch went out," she whispered.

"The torch was burning all this time," Josh said.

"So that wasn't real." Hannah turned to Ben. "I let go of your hand because you wanted to let go of mine."

"No, I didn't. Not for a second. I would never do that. Sani told us to hold on to each other."

Hannah gave her brother a baffled look. "How on earth is that possible?"

"When we entered the cave, the *yenaldlooshi* must have invaded your unconsciousness at once," Josh muttered monotonously. "They're stronger than I thought. They led you to believe you had to let go of Ben's hand, and once you did, the bond between the three of us was severed, and they pounced on it. Sani wasn't joking when he warned us."

For a moment, they were all completely silent.

"How did you manage to wake up?" Ben asked, puzzlement in his voice. "We tried everything, and I mean *everything* to make you come back." He balled a fist.

"That butterfly," Hannah breathed. "I saw the same butterfly I'd seen before, in a dream. It showed me the way."

Josh smiled in surprise. "Your animal spirit," he simply said.

"You think?" she said, her face in awe.

"It used to be, in your previous life."

"Let's not dawdle." Ben determinedly picked up the torch, reaching out for Hannah's hand. "I came here to lift the curse for Josh, and that's what I'm going to do." His voice sounded grim. "Besides, no one burns my sister to a crisp without paying the price."

His words brought a small smile to her face. Josh grabbed her other hand, and once more, they made their way through the tunnel. Hannah slowed down as Ben turned the corner. She half expected to see the same large cave as before, with the same soot mark on the floor, but that didn't happen. Instead, they were in a ceremonial cave with masks on the wall and a burning fire in the middle. Around it were three men in a deep trance, coyote furs around their shoulders.

"We have come," Josh spoke.

Hannah looked sideways, suddenly spotting Shash, the bear, near the furthest wall of the cave. An echo from the world beyond the veil. An owl was perched on his shoulder, and a butterfly fluttered the bear's head. Apparently, they had a back-up team.

The oldest of the three warlocks opened his eyes, inhaling sharply when he saw Josh standing in front of him.

"Murderer," he hissed, hatred burning in his eyes. "You will never find peace."

His sons awoke from slumber as well, turning around to face the trio. Hannah blinked when she saw their faces. She recognized the man and the twins from that bizarre encounter at the Safeway parking lot. So this was what they really looked like.

Heart hammering in her chest, she didn't hesitate as she stepped forward to face the *yenaldlooshi*. She addressed the oldest skinwalker imploringly. "I understand the pain you must feel. The idea that anybody would ever take Josh away from me tears me up inside. That's what you must have felt too, when your lover was taken away from you."

The black magician looked at her, unperturbed. "My soul died that day," he spoke quietly, but clearly. His voice cut right through her.

Hannah held her breath. When the skinwalker didn't say anything else, she apprehensively continued. "Your soul is immortal – it cannot die. Just take a look at Josh and me. We've found each other too, and who's to say that won't happen to you and her as well, once you leave this life and this world behind? That's what *she* believed too, right?"

The old man blinked. "What would you know about that?"

"I know what message she wanted to carry out," Hannah replied. "She was a missionary woman with faith in life after death. And the message she wanted to convey as a Christian woman can't have changed much since then. 'Love thy enemy.' So why don't you? Hate will only fuel the pain you feel." Her voice had dried to a whisper. "Honor her memory that way. The only way she would have wanted."

Silence pervaded the room. The father closed his eyes for a second, a wistful smile on his lips. When he opened his eyes again, tears were spilling out.

"She was so loving and peaceful," he whispered. "So gentle. She didn't deserve to die." He turned to Josh, a new fire alight in his eyes. "Why did you do it? Why did she have to die by your hand?"

Josh turned pale. "I never wanted to kill innocent people. I would have preferred to see the Spaniards go without bloodshed, but it simply wasn't possible. What else could we have done to save our country?"

The skinwalker nodded. "I know your reasons. But war is a case of man against man, soldier against soldier – and it didn't happen like that during the Pueblo Revolt. These were women. Innocent women. My beloved."

Hannah bit back her tears when Josh hung his head in defeat. He wasn't getting through to them, and neither was she. The skinwalkers' pain was still too recent. To them, this hadn't been a battle waged for centuries. They were forever stuck in their own time, as their curse had weighed Josh down during all these years.

"We won't forget what you have done," the father spoke in a cold tone.

"Our curse will not know an end," one of his sons added. "Remember that."

"Yes, it will," Ben suddenly piped up. "It *will* stop. Right here, right now."

In utter amazement, Josh and Hannah turned around to face him. He sounded so confident and cock-sure that even the three *yenaldlooshi* eyed the boy suspiciously.

"Ah, the *hataalii*," one of the sons said affably. "Nantai, am I correct? You have fervently sought us out in your dreams and visions to help your brother. Well, at last. Here we are. How will you defeat us?" Despite his challenging words, a hint of insecurity gleamed in his eyes.

"You don't know our real names," their father said. "You can't touch us."

"I don't need to," Ben replied, a grim smile on his face. "For all I care, you can practice your black hocus-pocus until the day you die, but you will not bother us anymore."

The three skinwalkers all got to their feet now, looking at Hannah's brother completely baffled, undeniable fear in their eyes.

"What do you mean?" one of the twins spoke up uncertainly.

"I now understand how to get rid of you. But in my previous life, I was blind to the solution." Ben took a step forward, holding up his hands. "Josh has always had the power to lift this curse." Turning toward his friend, he continued: "Trust me. Last night, I saw it in a vision when we were holding vigil in front of the cave."

"So what is it, Ben?" Hannah urged him on.

Ben stared down the skinwalkers without blinking even once. "Guilt," he spat out. "A guilty conscience. *That's* what this curse draws its power from. That's how these three bastards keep him in their clutches. The only reason Josh could be cursed and *stay* cursed was because he never forgave himself for murdering that Spanish woman. Of course, it's normal he regrets doing it. But to him, it wasn't just regret. It became a terrible burden. One he couldn't let go of."

Everyone in the room was stupefied, including the warlocks.

"You can only be cursed when you believe in it. When you're open to the suggestion," Ben continued, driving his point home. He locked eyes with Josh, using all his oratory talents to convince him. "Apparently, you feel as if you made an unforgivable mistake when you killed that woman. That's why you inadvertently allowed these witches to target you. As long as you allow yourself to be a victim, they'll be able to touch you. Let go of that thought. Refuse to feel guilty, and don't let them blame you. That's the key."

Hannah gasped for breath. Could it really be that simple?

"*He's* not the victim here, *we* are," the old skinwalker shouted at Ben. "You fool." He sounded angry, but also slightly unsettled.

Ben shook his head. "The biggest fools in this room are the three of you, because you won't allow time to heal your wounds. And foolishly, you insist on visiting your misfortune on someone for centuries on end, making the past seem like today. But let's face it, the past isn't really relevant to Josh's mission anymore. There's enough stuff to fix in the present as it is. Navajo Nation needs him. Poverty, uranium pollution, unemployment, drug abuse – these things reach far further than one death in a long-forgotten war. A war that prevented your culture from being completely obliterated, by the way. No Pueblo Revolt, no Navajos. It's that simple. Josh was doing what was necessary. It's regrettable that there were innocent victims, but it isn't his fault." He turned to Josh. "It isn't your fault," he repeated, putting emphasis on every word.

Josh slowly grabbed Ben's hand, giving him a look of wonder. The silence between them stretched for several minutes. And in those minutes, a halo of light seemed to grow around Josh, pushing back the shadows in the cave. His power was coming from inside, but it was fuelled by Ben's presence next to him. When he finally let go of his friend's hand, Josh had dispersed the chilly air from the room with his newly-found aura of confidence, driving the cold from Hannah's bones, setting her soul on fire. With her heart thudding in her chest, she saw how Josh turned around to face his tormentors again.

The skinwalkers' silent power seemed to drain away as Josh took a step forward. "I am letting this go," he spoke clearly. "Ben is right. I have to be here, now. You have no power over me. Not anymore. What has happened isn't just my fault." The fire slowly began to die down. "It's not my fault," he repeated more quietly to himself, sounding staggered and elated at the same time.

In the darkness slowly crawling out of the cave, Hannah heard a voice bouncing off the walls like a rustle of wind.

"You are free," it whispered.

Ben, Josh and Hannah watched in incredulous wonder as the skinwalkers took off their coyote furs, casting them into the fire. Their figures melted into the shadows dancing on the wall of the cave, the flickering flames devouring their disguises along with their magic. The masks on the wall crumbled to dust. The coldness disappeared from the air around them, the atmosphere trembling as if shivering with pleasure. And then, the room fell silent. The skinwalkers were gone. Their threat had vanished.

At last, Ben broke the silence. "Freaking hell. I was *right*," he stammered.

"But you sounded so..." Hannah blinked. "You weren't sure?"

Ben shook his head, his face still pale.

"But I knew you were," Josh said solemnly. "You were right, Ben. No curse will hold on an unbeliever. Deep down, I always felt I deserved it. And it was wrong to think that. But it's over now. Really over."

He let go of their hands, walking over to the fire in the middle of the cave. It was still burning faintly. "Give me your medicine pouches, please," he whispered, holding out his hand.

The leather pouches were tossed into the flames.

"Naalíl sahanéinla. Seetsádze tahee'ndeenla. Neezágo nastlín," Josh quietly recited. "Your curse has been taken away from me. You have taken it away. Far away it has gone." And with those words, he finally relinquished the curse he'd been carrying for hundreds of years.

Hannah's gaze swept over Josh, taking in his appearance. He looked young, alive, almost ordinary. An ordinary guy in an ordinary world that still wasn't perfect, but would now offer him a home full of people who could love him without endangering themselves.

She put her arms around his waist from behind, pressing her cheek against his shoulder. "I'll stay with you," she whispered. Her eyes sought out the bear's gaze. Shash was still observing them all from the sidelines. In her eyes, there was a question only he could read.

"He'll come back one more time," she heard him speak inside her mind. "There is still one important task awaiting him."

"And you can follow him, if you want," the blue butterfly added, dancing and fluttering in the air, flying toward Hannah and landing on her hand.

Yes, she did. Hannah smiled. For some reason, it almost felt like the two totem animals were marrying them. The butterfly flew back to the bear and the owl now circling Shash's head.

Ben tapped Josh on the shoulder. "Who's the owl?" he asked curiously, pointing at the colorful group of spirit guides.

"He's yours," Josh replied, and Ben understood immediately. Staring at his own totem animal, he shook his head. "Bizarre," he mumbled.

"Let's leave this place." Suddenly, Hannah couldn't stand being in the cave for one more second. "We're finished here, right?"

Josh turned around in the circle of her arms, kissing her softly. "Yes, we are."

Together, they made their way to the exit. The cave was once again shrouded in darkness when Josh picked up the torch and left the place where they'd lifted his curse. By now, the fire had simmered out, the ghosts of the past dissolving into nothingness as the light cast by the torch disappeared from the cavernous room.

Time no longer cast its shadow on the three friends who had stuck together throughout the centuries.

༺༺༺

When they stepped outside, Hannah couldn't believe her eyes when she saw it was late afternoon.

"How long have we been inside?" she asked, looking at Sani incredulously. The *hataalii* sat cross-legged next to the last *ikaah* he had made before they entered the cave.

He looked up and smiled at them. "Time runs differently here." His eyes drifted to the burn marks on her arms. "You need herbs and ointment. Let's go back to the village quickly." He didn't ask how the ceremony had turned out. It wasn't necessary – their happy, glowing faces were telling enough.

Back at Josh's place, the medicine man carefully bandaged Hannah's arms. Josh's parents rushed out to ask what happened, and their son quietly put them at ease. The joy radiating from his eyes as he talked to his parents made Hannah feel all fuzzy inside. Now Josh would finally be able to explain to them what had bothered him all this time. He'd never have to be afraid again. Sometimes, she loved him so much her heart couldn't keep up with her emotions.

"Care for a beer, *shik'is*?" Josh asked, once they were all sitting in front of Josh's hoghan enjoying a pumpkin stew his mom had made for them.

Ben looked up in surprise. "Is that a trick question? I thought you guys didn't have alcohol on the rez?"

Josh chuckled. "Well, I happen to know my aunt always keeps a few cans of beer in the fridge for Yazzie. Of course, my rebellious cousin tries to dodge the law of the rez. He says he can hold his liquor, and no one dares to argue."

Ben grinned. "Oh, I think he just found the person to argue with him. That beer has got my name written all over it!" He killed his cigarette and got up to pay Yazzie's parents a visit.

After Ben left, Josh put his arm around Hannah's shoulders. "I still can't believe everything is over now," he said in awe. "It's incredible I can just sit here with you and hold you without being scared."

Hannah sighed. "Yeah, I know. It still has to sink in with me, too. But that's okay. We still have a full month to get used to the idea." She kissed him. Would Josh know himself he was coming back one more time, to complete one more task? She was dying to tell him she would stay with him – after all, the totem menagerie had approved of their future-life union – but maybe she'd overstep a boundary of secrecy by blabbing about it. She wasn't sure.

"We still have two full *lives* to get used to the idea," Josh whispered just then, caressing her face.

She smiled. "So, Shash told you?"

"Yeah." He let out a sigh of relief, kissing her again. "I'm happy you'll stay with me, *shan diín*."

By the time Ben came back with two cans of beer, Emily had texted Hannah with the plans for that evening. "Em just suggested getting take-out pizzas and having a picnic in the park before the movie starts," she announced.

"Let's go soon." Josh got up, tilting his head toward his parents' hoghan. "But first, I want to talk to them for a while before we leave."

Hannah smiled at him as he walked away. She turned around to steal one cigarette from Ben's packet. As she looked into his eyes, tears suddenly welled up. "Ben, I'm so happy you're still alive," she mumbled.

"What did you see in that cave?" Ben asked quietly, gently rubbing her back.

Hannah hesitated, then shook her head. "Actually, I

don't want to discuss it anymore. It was a terrible nightmare, and I've had too many this summer. Let's forget it. We're still alive, and that's what matters."

ಌಌಌ

That evening, in the park, Josh finally opened up to all of them. Movie fans poured onto the grassy fields of the park, the sun sank below the horizon, and the pizzas turned cold in their cardboard boxes, as the circle of friends from St. Mary's Port, Page and Naabi'aani listened breathlessly to Josh's life story.

At first, he had trouble talking, but gradually, he opened up to them, telling his friends who he was and what his task had meant to him. His monologue turned into a conversation as everybody started to ask him questions.

"I don't think I even need to see a movie anymore," Nick exhaled when Josh had finally finished talking. "This was excitement enough for one evening!"

Emily was still watching her clansman with a gleam of amazement and admiration in her eyes. "Say, Josh – Can I be your mentor when – when Sani won't be there for you anymore?" she quietly spoke up.

Hannah turned to her friend in surprise. Of course – Emily had had a partially traditional education to become a healer. She probably knew about the Shash legend already.

"I know I'm not really the kind of *hataalii* you're used to, but..." Emily backpedalled when Josh remained silent for some time.

"Of course you can," Josh interrupted her. "I couldn't ask for a better one." He smiled at her warmly.

"You know what? You're a total trickster, *shitsílí*," Yazzie grumbled, chomping on a slice of cold pepperoni pizza. "I knew there was something fishy about you joining a band, picking up a guitar and playing like Slash in no time. And you feeding me that line that you couldn't help 'being so musically gifted'. Ha."

"Yup, you've seen through my ruse," Josh joked. "In my previous life, I used to crank out Guns 'n Roses tunes together with Edward Hall. Hence the insane talent."

"You get my drift," Yazzie persisted with a wide grin.

"So, could you have another look at my thesis?" Nick winked at Josh. "I don't think I'll ever find a more suitable editor again."

"Leech." Ivy shoulder-bumped Nick with a smile.

"Oh, I think the movie's starting," Amber said, glancing over at the big screen. She snagged the last slice of pizza before Ben had a chance, giving half of it to Emily.

Hannah let out a satisfied sigh, cozying up with Josh as they turned to face the movie screen. The ordinariness of things around her felt amazing, and the easy way Josh was now able to talk to everyone was a wonderful thing to behold.

Of course, *nothing* in her life from now on would truly be ordinary. She was part of something bigger, together with Josh. Gratitude swept through her as she watched all the everyday things happening around her. She heard Ben laughing out loud at the opening sequence of Austin Powers. She saw Amber and Emily cuddling up in front of her. She felt the heat of Josh's skin on her own where his arms circled her waist.

The rest of summer would be fantastic like never before.

Twenty-Two

"We're *off*!" Ben hollered, his voice rising a few notches on the last syllable. He waved across the lawn at the people on the porch of the neighboring house, while slamming the trunk of his Chevy closed.

Amber, Ivy, and their parents made their way to Ben and Hannah to say goodbye. Emily had already hugged them goodbye a million times yesterday evening. Hannah and Ben would drive back to Las Cruces today. September was just a few days away, and their vacation was over.

"We'll miss you guys so much," Amber quivered once she was facing Ben and Hannah. She hugged Hannah. "I'll see you in the fall, though. I'll be here with Emily."

Ivy hugged Hannah and Ben tightly, Paul and Sarah shook hands with everyone, and then the Greenes got into their station wagon to make a final day trip before they left, too. They'd waited until Ben and Hannah were ready to say goodbye.

Ben stared after the station wagon as it trundled down the sandy track. "I'm really going to miss them all. We were so lucky getting such friendly neighbors. Makes me all warm and fuzzy inside. Not to mention all the love in the air all summer long ..." A smile broke out on his face. "Wow. I'm gonna see Katie tomorrow."

Hannah patted Ben on the back, her gaze drifting to their own porch. Josh was just stepping out of the kitchen. He'd been helping them pack their stuff and tidy the cabin so they'd leave it in a clean state. Hannah wouldn't be back here until her fall break, when her mother would join her for a trip to St. Mary's.

A pang went through her heart. This was the moment she'd been dreading for a week. She would have to say goodbye to Josh and leave him behind for two months. It almost hurt physically.

"Hey, sweetie," he mumbled into her dark-blonde hair, after she ran up the steps to fling her scarred arms around him. The burn marks had faded to light scars, thanks to Sani's treatment and Emily's aftercare, but they would always remind her of the dangers she'd overcome in order to stay with Josh. Two months should be no biggie after all she'd been through, but her tear-ducts didn't agree with her. "I'm going to miss you so much. Excuse my blubbering," she sniffed.

"You are excused," he softly replied, with a few tears rolling down his cheeks. "Ditto with the blubbering here. I'm going to miss you like crazy."

They stood on the porch, glued to each other until Ben had retrieved the very last box from the kitchen. He put it in Hannah's Datsun, looking up at the inseparable couple. "We really need to go, sis! It's a long drive back."

When Hannah disentangled herself from Josh's embrace, he slid his hand in the pocket of his jeans and pulled out a beermat, handing it over to her.

Hannah looked at it, nonplussed. "What's this?"

"A beermat."

"I can see that," she giggled, still confused.

"Why don't you turn it over."

Hannah obliged. On the white backside of the cardboard coaster, she saw a cellphone number. She bit her lip.

"Call me," Josh said, a playful smile on his lips.

"You have a cellphone?" she yelped.

"Since yesterday." His hand stroked her hair. "I don't have a private line on campus in Tuba City. So that's going to be a problem if I want to call my girlfriend every day and be able to coo down the receiver without being interrupted or ridiculed by my fellow freshmen."

"O-oh," she said eloquently.

"Or maybe I'll text her. Once I've figured out how to actually do that, of course." He grinned.

Hannah blinked, beaming at him breathlessly. Her heart sped up with love, once more having a hard time keeping up with all the emotions tumbling through her body.

"Get real," she suddenly heard Ben snickering out loud. "A *beermat* with your phone number on it? Finally succumbing to the ways of the white man?"

Hannah and Josh both burst out laughing. "Only because palefaces are too stupid to remember a phone number by heart," Josh challenged Ben. "Or would you rather listen to your sister's yammering for two months because she forgot my number and can't call me?"

Ben bounded up the steps and slapped Josh on the shoulder. "I'm going to miss your bad jokes, man. I'll take Katie here for Christmas. Will you be all right without me until then?"

After another ten minutes, Ben and Hannah were finally behind the wheel and ready to leave. Hannah waved at Josh, dried-up tears on her cheeks and a loving smile on her face as she drove away. All the memories of her summer vacation would stay with her and help her to survive the next two months. Keeping her eyes on Ben's Chevy in front of her, she pulled onto the main road and dreamily reviewed the past eight weeks. Sunshine, new friendships, mortal enemies and eternal love. She had a lot to share with her mom.

She got fuel at the same gas station where she'd bumped into Josh for the first time this summer. Ben waited by the side of the road while she filled up her Datsun. Whistling, she trotted to the counter, remembering Josh had said hello to her here at this very spot, giving her that playful smile she'd come to love so much. Who would ever have guessed she'd become his girlfriend, entering this very same building carrying a beermat with his phone number on it in her bag?

Hannah got back into the car and dug up the beermat and her cellphone from her handbag to save Josh's number to her contacts.

"I <3 u!! :)" she texted him.

She chuckled when it took twenty minutes for a reply to come in, and read his text with a broad and amorous smile.

"i love you too"

Want to be notified of new book releases by Jen Minkman?

Sign up here: > http://eepurl.com/x1X9P

Want to know more about Jen Minkman's books and other riveting novels in English by Dutch YA authors? Visit http://doors2dreams.blogspot.nl/

More books by Jen Minkman

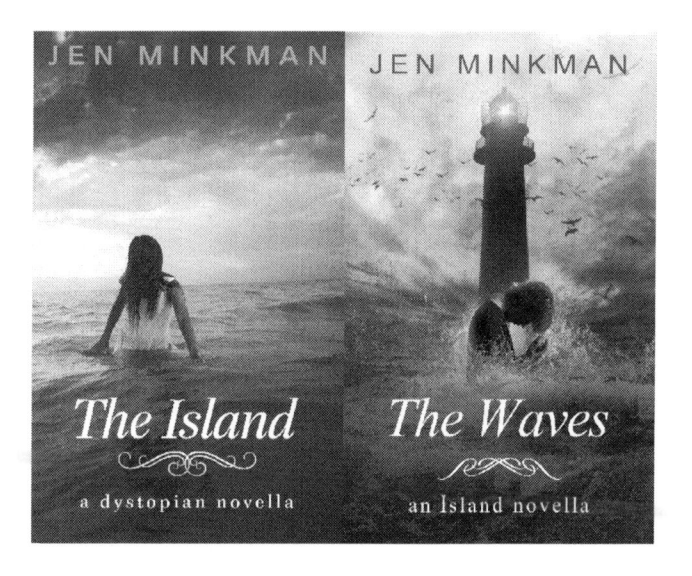

The Island Series – YA dystopian novellas

The Boy From The Woods:

A YA Romance, mixing the best of contemporary and paranormal

Publication date: December 2013

Acknowledgements

A big thank you to my proofreaders Marije Minkman and Maaike Plugge, without whose valuable advice I couldn't have turned this book into the story it is today. Another big thank you to my Dutch publisher, Larry Iburg of Ellessy Publishing, who took a chance on me and offered me a contract to put the very first Dutch-authored, traditionally-published paranormal romance novel 'Schaduw van de Tijd' on the market in the Netherlands and Belgium. And a big thank you to all the family and friends around me who had to put up with my incessant 'Native American' anecdotes, quotes and tidbits while I was writing and researching stuff for this novel. I can get quite OCD when writing novels – or actually, in general. My sincere apologies!

It doesn't stop there. I have to thank all the bloggers who agreed to review, promote and cover-reveal my book. Without you, no one would even know this book existed. Translating my own book from Dutch into English and self-pubbing it through Amazon meant a lot of promotion and marketing, and you have all gratuitously given me your time to help me out. I can't thank you enough.

Secondly, my editor Alexis Arendt deserves a big round of applause. I hired her to make the manuscript U.S.-proof (as I mainly speak British English), checking spelling and grammar along the way.

Last but not least, my parents Berry and Sia Minkman

helped me out, translating bits of the historical part of this novel. This way, I made sure the chapters from Josh's perspective really had a different feel to it. Thank you for all the hard work!

I tried my very best to describe the Navajo culture and reservation as well as I could. Since I'd never been to the U.S. (let alone Navajo Nation) before writing this book, I had to do all my research from a distance, using literature, movies, Internet databases, YouTube (thank you, DaybreakWarrior!) and dictionaries to really get to know the rich Diné culture and background.

And of course, my utmost gratitude to you, the reader. I hoped you enjoyed this book, and if you did, don't hesitate to drop me a line. Check out my website, where you can listen to the songs Hannah and Josh are singing in this book (I write soundtracks for all my books) too!

http://www.jenminkman.nl

Twitter: @JenMinkman

Facebook: http://www.facebook.com/jenminkman

e-mail: jenminkman@hotmail.com

Printed in Great Britain
by Amazon.co.uk, Ltd.,
Marston Gate.